BIG BOOK OF BOYS' ADVENTURE STORIES

A Hamlyn Double-volume

Mystery and Adventure Stories for Boys

Open-Air Adventure Stories for Boys

Edited by Eric Duthie

Hamlyn
London · New York · Sydney · Toronto

First published in this double-volume edition 1977
Second impression 1979 by
The Hamlyn Publishing Group Limited
London · New York · Sydney · Toronto
Astronaut House, Feltham, Middlesex, England
© Copyright 1962, 1965, 1977 The Hamlyn Publishing Group Limited

ISBN 0 600 32932 1
Printed in Great Britain by
Butler & Tanner Ltd, Frome and London

BIG BOOK OF BOYS' ADVENTURE STORIES

Volume One

Mystery and Adventure Stories for Boys

Contents

The Visitor

HENRY TREECE

I WAS standing at the farmhouse door, hands deep in my brown corduroys and chest like a pigeon, pretending that I, and not my father, was the owner of the ivy-fronted Georgian house, the snug stockyard and the quiet, grassy orchard. My boy's proud eye ran down the neat gravel path, across the cropped front lawn to the white gates, and then on and on across the heathland, westward to where the great hills of Wales crouched, half asleep, hatching some new devilry in the late afternoon sun.

When the whole family left for the market after an early breakfast, taking labourers and stockmen, I had felt rather neglected, almost affronted, at being left alone. Then, as the morning drew on and I wandered round the farm, noting the state of a gate here or a tractor there, I suddenly saw that my father had left me in charge because he thought I was the most capable of looking after the farm until he returned, and not because he preferred the company of my brother on the important expedition to market.

The black kitten nuzzled my leg. I bent, and lifted her

possessively by the silken scruff of her neck on to my shoulder. Then, feeling like a god, I groped in the secret lining of my jacket and found my little tin box of cigarettes.

"Caught you! Caught you smokin'! You young devil. I'll tell 'em all, I'll split on ye! I'll tell everybody!" suddenly shouted a thick, cracked voice from behind the box hedge near the road. I did not know that voice, and so I instinctively threw the offending stub on to the gravel path and screwed it out with my heel. My heart beat like an engine with surprise and guilt.

"That won't help you, treading on it, because I *saw* you doing it, and I'll tell everybody," the voice almost screamed.

My surprise suddenly turned to red anger. I stooped behind the water butt at the side of the porch, and threw a handful of sharp gravel, with all my strength, in the direction of the voice.

A yell and a volley of oaths came from the other side in the same thick voice, and then the strangest little old man I ever saw, burst out from behind the box hedge and scrabbled wildly up the path towards me. He was as small as a jockey, slight almost to emaciation point, with pale eyes, rimmed red as a ferret's, a thin cruel beak of a nose that seemed to reach nearly to his chin, ponderous bluish lips that sagged as he ran, revealing an empty blackness where there should have been teeth, and a flapping grey jowl covered with rough reddish hair. His great head was roughly wound with a filthy piece of old red flannel, which completely covered his ears, giving him a gnomish look. His jacket was a disused potato sack, inverted, with holes carelessly torn in it for neck and shirt-sleeved arms, and tied round the waist with a length of binder twine.

His movements were unco-ordinated, and savagely abrupt, like those of a dog with partial paralysis of the brain, or a badly jointed wooden doll on a string, and as he shambled towards me, screaming abuse, I automatically stepped back into the porch and made to shut the heavy oak door against

8

him. But I was a second too late. A dirty grey foot was jammed into the doorway and a hand clutched round the door. It was a long hand, powerful though thin, and as prehensile as an ape's. The attenuated fingers fascinated me as they gripped the edge of the door, sinewy, with bulging knuckle joints. The finger nails were long and broken and yellow, as though they had but recently come from the earth. It was a hand that I could associate with no known human trade, a forgotten, neglected hand. My fascination was turning to horror.

"Let me in, you young brat," growled the thick panting voice. "Let me in, or I'll do for you!"

My face went ice cold with fear, and I pushed as hard as I could against the door. I saw the grey foot creep slowly through the aperture it had made, and then I saw that the old man had thrust in his leg also, regardless of the pain it must have caused him.

"Be off," I yelled at him. "If you don't clear out now, this minute, I'll ring for the police."

His reply was a chesty laugh, and a harder push from the other side of the door. "Why, you little fool," he said, "you've got no 'phone wires, so you can't have no 'phone! What do you take me for!"

I was madly angry that he had so quickly and easily countered my ruse, and before I could help myself I hacked wildly at the blue trouser leg. But the leg remained jammed in the door, firm and unfeeling as a tree.

"Blast you," I shouted, "go away. Get out of here!" I could almost have wept for sheer rage. His only reply was a growl, then, with a sudden and remarkable effort, he pushed the door half open, and almost fell into the room, gasping painfully for breath.

I jumped back to the fireplace and stood against the fender, sweating, a heavy brass poker in my hand. The muscles at the back of my knees and thighs were trembling so violently that I thought I should fall down.

We stood and stared at each other for a minute or more.

9

My mouth was dry and my throat shrivelled and tight, as I said, "Well, what do you want? What game are you up to?"

The old man breathed hard and leaned against a table: "Ah, now you're talking, my cock sparrow," he wheezed. "Now you're talking!"

His blue lips writhed, trying to shape themselves to a smile. The result was a sneer. Then, with a quick but deliberate and practised movement, the old man thrust his grey hand under the short skirt of his sacking and pulled out a long thin knife.

"Do you see what this is, cocky?" he sniggered.

I could see that it was a crudely vicious weapon. A foot length of old barrel iron, hammered out and honed down to a stiletto thinness, with a haft of wound cord.

I nodded my head.

"Yes," said the visitor, "you can see it is a real nicker! It took me nearly a month, day and night, to make this, I can tell you, grinding and filing in the dark. . . . Grinding and filing, come sun, come moon, and pushing it down my trousers when they came to see me! Hiding it from them, who thought they knew everything about me! Hiding it, so that they wouldn't take it away from me, so that I could lie on my plank at night and feel its teeth. . . . And you ask me what I want? . . . Now, you can see sense when it's grinning you in the face, I know, and I'm going to tell you just what I want. . . . I want a meal first of all, a real meal, with ham and eggs, and real white bread, and a cup of tea, and a great big piece of cake with cherries in it, and a slice of ham, and eggs, and a cup of tea. . . ."

He licked his lips as they named and renamed the food. Then the old man suddenly tottered against the table, and seemed on the point of falling. I stepped half a pace forward, the poker still in my hand but forgotten in my automatic impulse to help. The nightmarish figure tautened into awareness again.

"Get back, boy, get back. I'm not done yet, not by a long chalk I'm not," he shouted, and the roped veins at

The old man ate like an animal, his ferret eyes hypnotic.

the side of his neck quickened and tensed. I stood back, and
then understood that this creature was weak with hunger,
almost fainting with it.

He stared at me again, without speaking. Then he steadied
himself against the table, struggled for breath, and said, "Go
before me into the kitchen, and get food for me, for behold
I have come among you and all things must be made ready
for me."

The ferret eyes were hypnotic and certain. I put down my
poker and walked to the kitchen. After a second or two the
grey canvas shoes shuffled along the flags after me.

The old man ate like an animal, gnawing his bread held
in both hands, and drinking his tea with a loud sucking
sound, his knife stuck upright in the table boards, within
easy reach, just before him.

The grandfather clock tramped on through time, steadily
and safely, my only link with the reality of one short hour
ago. I stood facing the old man, by the clock, almost counting its ticks, and thinking, "It's nearly six. . . . In three hours

11

someone of the family is sure to be back. My father will have supper with his farmer friend at The George, but my mother will be home from her shopping in the evening, and Jim will be with her, perhaps some of the men even . . ."

And, as my mind walked back and forth in its cage, I even wondered for a moment whether I had mistaken the day, and whether the traveller from the Grocery Stores in Church Stretton might not be coming, hooting up in his van for our week's orders at any minute. . . . Or the policeman pedalling up the road to see about our tickets for the Police Ball. . . . Or the curate to see when Jim was thinking of being confirmed. . . . And I found that I was inventing helpers and fantastic situations of relief, when suddenly the old man banged his cup down so hard on the table that it broke, leaving only the handle dangling on his forefinger. His face was contorted with passion:

"Don't stand there staring at me," he shrieked, his mouth full of bread. "I'm not a baboon in a cage! Are you moonstruck? Are you daft? I want respect from you. I want obedience. I want love. Get on your knees and kiss my foot. Go on, do as I say, get down now!"

I stood, dumbfounded by the old devil's order. He looked angrier than ever and began to froth at the mouth, his red eyes twitching in a paroxysm of unutterable fury. His shaking hand reached for the knife.

"Get down! Get down! Get down!" he screamed at me, beating a tattoo of frenzy on the floor with his hanging feet.

The hair at the nape of my neck prickled, and I almost flung myself down on to the cold tiles, the muscles of my arms and back quivering.

"Lick my boots, lick them, go on! I have ordered you," he shouted.

I went forward on all fours hoping to get within reach of his chair that I might grab the legs and tip him over, but he thrust out his leg which kept me at a distance. Then, as I was bending my head to obey him, he kicked out at me maliciously and I just saved myself by springing back.

"Go on! I have ordered you," he shouted.

The fiendish old man shrieked with laughter, bobbing up and down in his chair and slapping his thin thighs with his cruel hands.

Then his laughter stopped just as suddenly, and he bent quickly and rolled back his ragged trouser leg. I saw that the starved skin, knotted with veins and hairy as a monkey's, had bled in several places. My steel tip had caught him, though he had not murmured.

He rocked himself and smoothed the wounds gently. Then he looked up at me and said grimly, "You shall pay even more dearly for this. Yes, money, good money. I want money, even as much as ye hath shall ye give unto me. Get it, now!"

His hand twitched out like a snake. I rose to my feet and backed out of his reach. His eyes were restless then and shifted back and forward, up and down, taking in the whole room. At last they were still, and he pointed to my mother's ball of wool, and length of knitting that lay on a side table.

"Whose is that? Whose is it? Who did it?"

My voice was scarcely more than a painful whisper: "It is my mother's," I said.

The old scarecrow spat at it and laughed: "Your

mother's, eh? She likes doing that sort of tomfoolery, does she, while the poor starve, and prophets go without honour? She likes it? Well—burn it! Throw it in the fire and burn it! Now, straightaway!"

His eyes were two embers of pale fire burning into my own. I reached forward, without coming nearer to him, and flung my mother's half finished jumper into the fire. The coloured wool crackled and writhed in the flames, while he roared with laughter.

I watched him, standing stock still, in disgust. Then he looked down at the floor, and seemed to be trying to recall something that had been said earlier.

Suddenly he stood up and pulled off the tablecloth with one wrench of his hand. Food and crockery fell to the floor. My mother's willow pattern cream jug lay intact by his chair. He bent and picked it up, and with a snarl flung it with all his force into the open fireplace. Pieces of china flew about the room and pattered on the walls.

"Get me money, I say, money, money, money!" the old man shouted, banging on the table till it cracked again.

His sudden fiendish energy stupefied me, and I backed towards my mother's bureau in the corner of the room, and slipping a key from my chain, I unlocked it and opened the top drawer. Normally this drawer would have been empty, for my mother would have banked the money while at market; but today, by unlucky chance, there were at least thirty pounds, lying in neat banded bundles—the accumulated takings of weeks of poultry keeping, waiting there until such time as the local contracting builder should call to be paid for certain repairs to a fireplace and an orchard wall.

The old man was close behind me, breathing quickly in his sudden excitement. I handed him bundles of notes with both hands, playing for time and safety.

He passed his thin hand across a quivering face. Then he looked at me as though I had found some means of insulting him. His voice was broken with contempt and anger. "Money? This is not *money*. Gold money, not papers, is what I want. Real money, not papers. Are you trying to trick me again? Are you? Are you? Tell me. . . ."

He came towards me, making threatening motions.

I was unable to speak, for my throat had contracted again, and I could only hold out the bundles of notes, dumbly and terrified. I stood with the small of my back against the bureau while perspiration trickled down between my shoulder blades and my legs trembled violently. I wanted to wriggle my woollen vest free where it stuck. My mind became as blank and featureless as snow. I still held out the bundles of banknotes.

Then, as though his fury had reached the extreme at which it overwhelmed its reason for being, he flung down his knife, clutched wildly at the two handfuls of money, and began tearing the notes to shreds, throwing the pieces high above his head like a madman, so that they cascaded about him and down to the kitchen floor in a continuous stream, until he had torn up everything I had given him.

His breath was quick and laboured now. "More," he groaned, "more papers." He held out both hands, almost imploring. And then my head cleared and my throat loosened. My legs felt firm and strong again, and I had lost fear. I turned once more to the drawer, while he watched anxiously, and again I offered him two thick bundles of notes. Then, as he stretched out his hands, I kicked hard sideways at his legs, just above the ankles. He fell to the floor, his hands still stretched out and his eyes wide open in surprise.

I did not see him strike the floor, for my eyes became misty and I felt faint, but when I was able to see again, he was lying still, on his side, with arms out and eyes closed.

I kicked his knife across the room, and then went carefully up to him. He did not move and was scarcely breathing. Through the thin cage of his chest, through the painful skin, I could feel his old heart beating tiredly, as though it might stop without warning after the next throb.

I forgot my fear and my anger. Now all I wanted was that this pathetic bundle of bones and rags should not die in our

. . Tearing the notes and throwing them high overhead like a madman.

peaceful kitchen—with myself as the murderer. I was terrified once more, but this time at the thought of having killed an old man. I almost ran into the scullery for water, telling myself that this poor old creature had come to the door, asking only food and a little money in his eccentric way, and that I had lost my head, had knocked him down and killed him. . . .

My hands at last found a milk can, and I stumbled to the tap. I was shaking so violently that I overturned the can when I first tried to fill it. I tried again, and ran back along the passage without remembering to turn off the tap.

I pushed open the kitchen door with my foot, and half bent to pour water on the old man. . . . But there was no old man there. I looked across the room; the knife had gone too. I put the can down on the floor and stared about me, hardly believing anything I saw—the floor littered with food and crockery, the remains of the willow pattern cream jug in the hearth, the handle of the cup, still under the table where it had dropped from the visitor's finger, and the banknote confetti that seemed to be everywhere.

As soon as my eyes had taken all this in again, I ran to the front door. It was open, and the front gate creaked in the evening wind.

I could see no one on the road, or out on the moor. I ran down the path and shouted, but no one answered. I walked back into the house then, suddenly afraid of staying in it alone. I put out the lights, locked the doors, and ran out along the main road, with the hope of meeting my people as they returned.

As I got on to the road, the moon came up from behind a cloud, showing me a world of silver and black, in clear sharp outline. The white road ran curling between heavy dark hedges, crossed here and there in front of me by the shadows. I started at each black shape, and walked in the middle of the road so as to be ready for any sudden rush from either of the hedges. From time to time a cloud would hide the moon, then the white road would suddenly become grey,

As I ran, a pair of headlights came up to meet me.

or even black, and I would stop in my tracks, standing dead still and listening for the sound of canvas shoes scuffling behind me along the road. I even visualized the little old man suddenly appearing before me on the road, as the moon broke through again, gibbering and cackling in the silver light. . . .

Then, with the road clear in front of me, I walked on, in a sweating spurt of fear, going faster and faster, until at last my legs were unable to keep pace with my heart and I had to run.

And so, at last, I stumbled over the top of the rise, and saw the road leading down to the town. . . . I started off down the hill towards the lights and the sounds of traffic, and as I ran a pair of headlights came up the road to meet me, friendly orange things. . . . The church clock rang the hour, and I realized that the headlamps must belong to the village bus. . . . There would be folk in it whom I knew, unambitious, kindly folk, perhaps even some members of my own family.

I waited on the kerb, hoping to see who was on the bus as

it struggled up the hill. But as it drew up to me it stopped. The driver had recognized me and, knowing my mother and brother were on board, thought that we must surely want to travel back together. I pushed my way past the farmhands who were standing, smoking their old briar pipes and smelling of market day bitter beer, and stumbled over shopping bags to where my mother and Jim were sharing a seat. Heavens, how safe I felt!

"Hello!" my brother said, "look what the tide's washed up! I suppose you didn't expect to see us on this bus?"

My mother said: "What *are* you doing here? I thought we left you to mind the house."

Later that night my story had been heard by them all, as we sat in the still littered room. No one really seemed to believe me, and least of all my brother. My father, who had had a very good day, merely looked at me searchingly, but said nothing. My mother was at first angry, and later she said that I could go down to the bank on my cycle in the morning, to see the manager and find out the possibilities of replacing the torn banknotes.

On the way up to bed my brother simply said: "Well, would you believe it! A nasty little old man with a huge big knife!"

I tried once more to explain to him, but he slammed his door, and I could hear him laughing as he got into bed.

I did not sleep much that night—and I did not cycle to the bank next day, either. Instead I went with my father in the car to the police station to tell my story to the Inspector there.

He heard me in silence. Then he opened a drawer in his desk and took out an object wrapped up in brown paper.

"Is this the thing with which you were threatened last night?" he asked.

I stared at the old man's home-made knife and nodded —and stared again at the dull red smear on it.

"Then it's a good thing you're alive," he said solemnly. "Another was not so lucky."

There was no more jeering at home.

19

He Talked in the End

LT.-COL. ORESTE PINTO

I T is always dangerous for a Counter-Intelligence officer to
trust to his impressions of suspects. The expert spy will
be trained to create a good impression; part of his stock in
trade may be his open, honest-seeming countenance and his
air of frankness. He is out to establish the idea that he is a
genuine and decent citizen and, if he is anything of an actor,
his ability will be diverted to that end. A really honest and
innocent man, on the other hand, will not be practised at
creating good impressions, unless he happens to be a sales-
man or commercial traveller in private life where the ability
to express a pleasant personality is important. Further, the
innocent man has not the same pressing need to establish his
integrity under a cross-examination. He *knows* that he is
innocent and expects his interrogators to realize the fact
without assistance from him.

It is, therefore, unwise to jump to conclusions at first sight
in Counter-Intelligence work. Nevertheless, the man with

great experience can often make an immediate summing-up which may appear intuitive but which is in fact based on certain signs that appear to him at once although they would probably be missed by the untrained observer. It is unwise to follow hunches blindly, but all the same hunches often lead one to the demonstrable truths.

I cannot now recall which sense or combination of senses warned me that Emile Boulanger may have been a German spy. The break-through had begun and the Allied spearheads were driving into Belgium. The tanks and motorized infantry were thrusting ahead and the restless thunder of the guns was just beyond the skyline. Near a road and lane junction we had set up a temporary intelligence headquarters, a thing of slit-trenches and dug-outs with their walls shored up by sandbags. The neighbouring farm buildings and out-houses had been taken over by divisional headquarters. As comparative interlopers, my small unit had to fend for itself.

This man, Emile Boulanger, was brought to my command-post by two field security officers from the divisional staff. They had found him wandering about in a dazed condition near an evacuated Belgian village where blackened stumps of walls and mounds of stone rubble were the mute results of concentrated shelling. I looked at Boulanger for a long time without speaking. He was dressed as a typical farmer and the few words I had heard him utter were spoken in the Belgian-French and with the true accent of the Walloon countryman. But something in his bearing and in the bright glitter of his blue eyes made me suspicious. He was bull-necked and his muscular control differed from the shambling posture of the ordinary peasant in that part of the country.

"You are a farmer?" I asked.

"I was a farmer," he replied. He gestured with limp hands. "Now I have no farm. The Boche took my animals—even my little ducks. My fields are covered with shell-holes, my cottage is in bits. My wife lies there dead—under the smashed roof. The others have gone—vanished."

Suddenly he held out his hands. He bent his fingers like

claws. I could see that the finger-nails were cracked and seamed with dirt. The finger-tips were scratched and raw. Dried blood was caked in the crevices of the nails.

"I dug for her—my wife," he muttered in a half-whisper. "She was under the ruins in the darkness and she was always afraid of the dark. I scratched like a hen—but she was dead." He lapsed into a brooding silence.

"Can you count?" I asked, breaking into his reverie.

"Count?" He blinked at the odd question.

There happened to be a dish of dried beans at hand, "liberated" by our troops from some thrifty peasant. I pushed the dish towards him. "Count these," I said, "—aloud."

He picked up each bean slowly and in a wondering voice began in French, "Un—deux—trois——" When he reached seventy-two I stopped him. He had passed one test successfully. If he had been a clever German linguist masquerading as a Walloon Belgian, he would probably be expected to say the orthodox French for seventy-two, "soixante-douze", and would not have known that Walloon farmers always say "septante-deux" for seventy-two. So far, so good. But I was still not satisfied that Boulanger was really what he purported to be—an honest Belgian farmer, dazed with grief at the loss of his house and his wife. Fortunately there was something of a lull in my activities at that time and I was able to devote more attention to him than I would normally have been able to. If he were proved innocent, no one would lose anything by it. If he were found guilty, we should have done a good job in maintaining the security behind the advancing forward troops.

I ordered him to be put in a small room by himself. It was part of a disused cowshed. The door was barred on the outside and there was a crack between two beams which acted as a natural spy-hole. Through this crack he was kept under constant watch. Before going to bed that night, Boulanger knelt down to say his prayers. He could not have known that keen eyes were watching his every movement, yet he said his prayers in Belgian in the simple, homely phrases that a

Walloon village priest might have taught him as a child. A rat scurried across the bare floor. Startled, he said, *"Dieu!"* a typical Walloon ejaculation. He stretched out on his mattress and seemed to drop asleep. A little while later I arranged for some straw to be placed against the outside of his door and lit. As the acrid smoke curled under the door, several

He could not have known that keen eyes were watching.

soldiers ran clattering down the flagged corridor, shouting, *"Feuer, feuer!"* the German for "fire!" Boulanger stirred, appeared to wake up momentarily and then rolled over on his side again. A few moments later the soldiers ran down the corridor once more, shouting, *"Au feu, au feu!"* the French for "fire!" Boulanger sprang at once from his mattress and, screaming in fear, pounded on the heavily barred door. When I opened it, he was sobbing prayers in Belgian-French.

He had passed yet another test but I was still not satisfied.

Was he genuine or was he a German spy with an excellent nerve and much acting ability? It was still not possible to say, although admittedly I seemed to have fewer grounds for doubting him.

Next morning I decided to try another way of testing him. I arranged for him to be brought to my field headquarters and a short while before he was due to arrive, told my plan to one of my junior officers who was to be present at the interview.

After I had asked Boulanger several questions, I would mutter, *"Armer Kerl"*, which means "Poor chap" in German. The officer was to reply, *"Warum?"* (Why?) and then he was to let me go on speaking in German.

Boulanger was escorted in. On the folding camp table behind which I sat were spread the few possessions we found on him at the time of his arrest. They were ordinary enough. There was the stub of a pencil, a bit of string, a sodden lump of partly chewed tobacco, a clumsy, home-made crucifix and a few francs. There seemed to be nothing very sinister in this pathetic collection of odds and ends.

Boulanger stood there, patient and sullen like an animal in its stall. I turned over his few belongings and then picked up the pencil. "Why did you carry this on you?" I asked, in French.

"It is only a pencil," he said, shrugging his strong, heavy shoulders.

"Did you carry it so that you could write messages to the enemy?" He smiled vaguely and looked at me almost with contempt, as though the question were too foolish to require answering.

I turned to the security officer and said in German as arranged, "Poor chap."

He took up the cue promptly. "Why?" he asked in the same language.

Still speaking German, I went on, "Because he does not realize that he will be hanged within an hour from now. It is after eleven o'clock," I glanced at my watch, "and I have ordered his execution for noon. He is obviously a spy and cannot expect a better fate."

All the time I was speaking I watched Boulanger keenly, especially his eyes and his Adam's apple. However brave and self-controlled a man may be, he usually has little control over what are technically called the vasomotor nerves which react automatically. Just as a man will blink unconsciously if an object suddenly approaches his eyes, so also will a man who hears of his impending death be liable to go pale, or blink in astonishment or swallow as his mouth grows unbearably dry. But Boulanger did none of these things. Although he must have known himself to be under suspicion as a spy, he stood there stolidly without moving or showing the least signs of alarm. The obvious deduction was that he had not understood the language I had used and could not, therefore, be a German spy.

By this stage I had to admit to myself that my original swift summing-up, based as it was on intangible evidence, appeared to be very wide of the mark. Perhaps it was stubbornness on my part or the dislike of seeing my vanity wounded by admitting that I had made a mistake or even the prompting of my subconscious instincts. Whatever the reason, I decided to test Boulanger again.

Next day I arranged for a loyal Belgian countryman to meet my suspect. I was present at their meeting. When at my prompting the countryman began to talk of farming, Boulanger for the first time became animated and broke eagerly into the discussion. Even to my non-expert eye he seemed to know a great deal about local farming and the countryman told me afterwards that he had not made a single mistake over crops or local conditions and methods.

Once again I had to admit reaching a dead end in my tests. The suspicion was growing with each rebuff that I had made a big mistake in suspecting him in the first place. After advising all the beginners who had ever learned Counter-Intelligence methods from me that one should never allow first impressions to sway one's judgment, here had I fallen

*I looked up and said sharply in German: "All right, I am satisfied.
You can go. You are free."*

into that very same trap with all the clumsy haste of the rank amateur. I sat long in the night trying to analyse the feelings that had made me suspicious of Boulanger at first sight. Then I mentally ran through his actions and words from that moment to this, trying to find some hint or clue that would endorse my earlier judgment. Wrack my memory as I might, I could not find the elusive point that would have reinforced my suspicions. Finally, before turning in for the night, I decided to try one last test on him in the morning. If it failed, I was prepared to admit freely that I had unjustly suspected him of being a spy and would have him released on the spot. I was even prepared to make him a handsome apology for having doubted him.

He came into my office next morning and stood there, just as stolid and patient as ever. My head was lowered as I read a typed document on my desk. Reaching the end, I took up a pen and signed at the foot of the page. Laying down the pen, I looked up and said sharply, *"So, jetzt bin ich zufrieden. Sie können gehen. Sie sind frei."* ("All right, I am now satisfied. You can go. You are free.")

He breathed a deep sigh of relief, shook his shoulders as though a heavy weight had fallen from them and lifted his face happily to gulp in the air of freedom. When he heard my chuckle, he stiffened and tried to relapse into his previous resigned posture but it was too late. At a quick signal the hands of his escorts were already gripping his shoulders.

"Mein lieber freund," I said and stood up. From then until his execution a few days later we spoke nothing but his native German.

Murder Fish

JOHN KRUSE

I GUESS really that I should never have got up that morning.
If I had stayed in bed and kept in bed maybe nothing
would have happened. One glance out of my shack window
at the leaden-looking dawn should have been enough. There
had been lightning in the night, and the dawn atmosphere
on that part of the Ceylon west coast was as hot and moist
as a butcher's armpit.

But, as it was, I dragged myself down to the sea and flopped
in, let the tide stir me round for a minute while I put on my
fins and mask, then, trailing my spear-gun, struck out lazily
for the reef.

I should have known it would be a rotten day for spearing.
But no—I had to find it out the hard way. I had swum half-
way to the reef, through water that was a little clearer than
milk, and dodged about a thousand jellyfish, before it finally
got through to me. There were whitefins farther out, and a

28

man can go crazy in cloudy water worrying about shark.

I came back. I was sitting in the undertow, slinging my fins up on to the sand, before I saw the crowd.

When I had left half an hour before, the hotel beach, farther along, had been empty. Now, upwards of a hundred people were standing about the small rocky bay. They seemed to be intent on a fishing-outrigger, crewed by two natives, which was paddling around the inlet. One of the natives was peering down into the water through a sponging-glass.

The crowd had that hushed, shocked look I had seen once round a mine pithead back home, and I knew right away something bad had happened. I went along and asked a group of Sinhalese fishermen what was up.

"A mem-sahib from the hotel," one of them said.

"Drowned?"

"Not drowned. Taken."

"Taken!" I asked him by what.

The fisherman shrugged. "She was swimming and she vanished. That's all I know."

I looked along to where Billy Beechum, the hotel proprietor, was fussing round a grey-haired woman in a sundress. She was probably a relative of the girl who had disappeared, I thought. She had just that kind of expression —very white about the mouth. Billy was fidgeting the ring on his plump hand, but she was acting as if he didn't exist.

I knew what was worrying Billy Beechum. This sort of thing could kill a hotel stone-dead. People came here for the swimming. The word had only to get round that this was a dangerous beach and his clientele would drift away in less time than it takes to medium-boil an egg. This was the second death here in two months. Hit-and-run stuff, probably —shark, coming right in, made bold by the murky water. Nothing one could do anything about, short of fixing a net. It was tough, I thought, looking at the woman. She was holding herself together pretty well. Tough on fat Billy. Tough on everyone.

I watched a bit longer. Presently the outrigger put into shore. In ones and twos the hotel people began to move away. Whatever had got the girl had got all of her. I turned, with a nasty taste in my mouth, and sweated it back through the steamy heat to my hut.

I had been in there less than ten minutes when a voice behind me said, "Master?" It was a barefoot waiter from the hotel. "Master, please. Mr. Beechum want to speak with you."

Here we go—panic, I thought. It was too hot to get mixed up in one of Billy's panics. I thought of refusing; but Billy was a friend of mine.

I sighed. "O.K."

Slipping on a pair of pants and a shirt, I went with the waiter along the beach to the Grand Hotel.

Billy's office was large and bare. Overhead a pair of big fans whisked the dead air about hopelessly.

Billy Beechum stopped in mid stride and came towards me. He had his glasses in his good hand like a captive butter-fly. He came right up to me, blinking short-sightedly. "Mike! Something terrible has happened."

"Yes," I said, "I know."

"That poor woman—I didn't know what to say to her. It was her niece, you know. Devilish business. I asked you to come up, Mike. We've got to do something."

"I told you what to do before."

"I know, but—heavens, do you know how much a net would cost? I've had the place only six months. Three-quarters of everything I make goes to the Building Society. Until I get established I'm on my uppers, Mike."

Billy had bought the Grand Hotel with the last cent he possessed. This was the sink-or-swim period for him. I guessed that was why he was in such a panic now. If he lost custom at this juncture all his hard-earned cash would go down the drain. Down there on the beach I hadn't realized just how important this affair of the girl could turn out to be. Now it came home to me and it worried me. Billy had been a good friend to me. A year ago he had used his influence and paid all my legal expenses to squash an attempt to have me deported for vagrancy. I owed him a lot.

"Tell me exactly what happened," I said.

"Thought you knew. This lady, Mrs. Mowat, says she was sitting reading outside the changing-rooms. Her niece— pretty girl, awfully pretty girl—was swimming in the bay. Suddenly Mrs. Mowat looked up and she was gone—gone without a trace. What could have done it, Mike?"

"Was she near the rocks?"

"I don't think so. In the middle, I understood."

"Might have been cramp."

"Oh, come now. Without a sound, just like that?"

"Maybe not." I scratched my head. "If she wasn't near the rocks it couldn't have been octopus. Shark is my guess. Shark or a jewfish."

Billy's eyes popped open. "What's that?"

"Big, ugly fish. They swallow things by suction. The green ones will attack anything. A really big one coming up under a person could suck them straight down."

Billy shuddered. He pushed his face close to mine. "Well, I think there's one in the bay!"

I told him I didn't think a jewfish would come into a busy bay like that. Billy ducked his face down. He came up wearing his glasses.

"I do. Exactly the same thing happened to that child the other month. Identical. I think there's something big in that bay. And I want you to get it out."

I said, "Hmm. I'll take a look in there for you, Billy, if it'll make you happy. Tomorrow, if the water clears."

"Not tomorrow. Today. Now! You don't understand— I've got to have something to show the clients. 'Here it is— we've killed it—now you can go in there and bathe to your hearts' content.' Don't you see, tomorrow will be too late. They'll have started to leave."

"Then you'd better tot up their bills for them. I'm not going in there today. Holding my spear-gun at arm's length

31

"I'm just a guy who spears fish for a living."

under water this morning, I could just about see the tip.
What you're asking is a tall enough order in clear water.
I'm not Superman, you know. I'm just a guy who spears fish
for a living. You've seen the fish I shoot. They mostly run
about ten pounds. Every once in a while I shoot one weighing
sixty or seventy and they give me plenty of trouble."

"Nonsense! How about that twelve-foot shark you———"

"That, Billy, was a matter of life and death."

He was right up against me, his breath making fat, desperate sounds in his nostrils. "So is this."

I stared at him. I saw his point.

"I'll give you fifty quid."

"I don't want your money, Billy. I tell you———"

"A hundred."

I hauled back and straightened my eyes out. That was
folding money.

"You're kidding," I said.

Billy pressed his lips together. He went over to the desk,
took his cheque-book, and wrote out a cheque. He showed
it to me.

I took it and looked at it. Sure was pretty. I tore it up.

32

"O.K.," I sighed. "If you're that worried, I'll go."

Billy watched the little bits flutter to the ground stupidly; jerked his eyes up to mine. "Mike!" he cried, his face wrinkling delightedly. He grabbed my hand and pumped it. "You're a gentleman!"

"Gentlemen must be suckers," I said.

Twenty minutes later I was standing thigh-deep in the waters of the bay. I had my steel hand-spear and a coil of shark line. One end of the cord was fixed to the head of the harpoon; the other to a palm tree on the beach. I was still a bit dazed about the whole thing.

Billy was leaning over the rail outside the changing-rooms. His face was suitably grim. He raised one thumb.

I made a wry face and pulled on the mask. I thumbed the schnorkel under my lips and launched myself. I beat slowly out into the bay, paying out the line as I went.

The white sand beneath me became rocks, dead-looking in the bad light. A few small-fry flaked away in front of me. The rocks heaved up and down for about twenty feet, then suddenly dropped away.

I hung there in the grey fog, looking down into the darkness. Something seemed to open up inside me and let the draught in. I was pretty sure there was nothing down there, but it gave me a bad feeling just the same.

I couldn't see anything.

I checked where I was with the shore. Right in the centre of the bay. Well here goes I thought. I took in a load of air and dived.

I went down vertically for about thirty feet. It was fog all the way. The pressure squeezed the mask in against my face. Something began to sort itself out ahead of me. It was the bottom—rock laced with tongues of sand. I levelled off and worked over it cautiously, trying to look in all directions at once.

It was gloomy down there. There weren't many fish. A few cat-fish were browsing along the bottom, trailing their whiskers in the sand. They ignored me stolidly.

Suddenly, looming above me, I saw the shelf. Under the overhang there was a big black hole. I tried to see into it, but there wasn't enough light. It was just the sort of place where a big fish might lie up. I couldn't pass it over—and live with myself afterwards.

I surfaced uneasily and rested for a few moments. Then I took in another load of air and went back down.

The hole was about the size of a big doorway. I pushed the spear out ahead of me and, scooping the water upward with my hand to keep me down, edged in.

At first nothing happened. The hole was a lot deeper than the spear was long. I had to go right in.

Suddenly something seemed to explode in my face. I fought with it, twisted round, lost a lot of air, threshed back to the entrance, the thought filling my mind: octopus!

A fat black body panicked past me and away into the fog like a bat out of hell. A grouper. The relief nearly choked me. I got out and surfaced quickly, my heart doing crazy things inside me.

When I got up I hadn't enough air left to blow out the schnorkel. I took in a lot of water and started coughing. I lay in the water coughing and cursing.

After a while I went down again. I worked along under the shelf. Then I worked down one side of the bay; then the other side. It was a slow, nerve-racking job in the murk.

With every shape that loomed up in front of me there was a moment of tension before it resolved itself. I could hear fish that I couldn't see. I kept hearing the rustling flight of what must have been a big shoal of salpas; but I never caught one golden glint of them.

Presently I started lacing backwards and forwards across the bottom of the bay. There were long patches of weed down there. The first one I hit I thought was a shark. But there was nothing.

At last I waded up on to the beach, coiling in the line. Half a dozen people from the hotel were watching from the sand by this time. Billy Beechum came hurrying down to meet me.

"Nary a thing!" I called out.

"But you didn't go over anything like all of it, did you?" he said loudly.

"I most certainly——"

"No, you didn't," he cried out. "There were a number of places you missed. I was watching."

"Look——"

"You'll do them later, won't you? I expect you're tired now." He was talking very loudly and oddly. "You'll come back after lunch, won't you? We'll all come back after lunch and do it properly."

He put his arm round my shoulder as I came up out of the water. "I've got to kid them," he said under his breath. "You'll do it this afternoon?" he shouted. "Splendid!"

I untied the line from round the tree without saying anything and started back for my hut. Billy trotted beside me.

"Don't be angry," he said. "I had to do it. Don't you see— we can't tell them there's nothing down there. It wouldn't make any difference. We've got to *show* them something. You're sure there was nothing?"

"Sure as one can be."

"Oh my lord. What are we to do? Listen, Mike——"

"No."

"What?"

"I said no. Too much is enough. I've done what you asked. Now I'm going home to have a long drink and cool off."

Billy looked at me. "This isn't like you, Mike."

"No," I admitted. "It's not. But there's something about today I don't like. Maybe it's the weather. Maybe I'm just getting old."

"Don't let me down, Mike," Billy said. "I wouldn't ask you if there was any other way out. I'd do it myself if I could swim."

I sighed. "What was it you were going to say?"

"I was going to say, if there's nothing in the bay, couldn't we catch something somewhere else and drag it to the bay—something big enough to have killed the girl—anchor it somehow on the bottom, and then—fish it up?"

I stared at him and then laughed. "Brother! You really are desperate, aren't you? Of all the cock-eyed notions! Where in the name of heaven do you think I'm going to find that kind of fish?"

"I don't know. You must know somewhere. You're supposed to be the fisherman. Couldn't you find a—what was it —jewfish?"

I stared at him. As a matter of fact I did know where I could find a jewfish. I knew where there was a jewfish as big as an ox. They don't move around much and this one lived in the hull of a sunken dhow about a mile up-coast. But working as I do without a boat, you don't shoot that kind of fish, not unless you want to be towed straight down to the bottom or swallowed alive.

"We could stage it properly," Billy said. "Get everybody down to the beach, and you could go in with your harpoon stick it in the thing, and we could haul it up. Everyone would be happy and you'd be a hero."

"What would happen when they cut it open and found there were no human remains inside?"

Billy looked blank for a moment. "We would have to rush it away quick. It could be worked."

We had reached my hut. He followed me in, pleading. He used every argument he knew. I did a few jobs around the shack while he was talking. I could have the hotel motor boat, if I wanted it, and any of his staff.

While I was working, I was thinking about the jewfish. I had wanted to get him for months. He was about six feet long. Not much under four hundred pounds. If I'd been able to afford a boat I'd have had a stab at him long ago. This offer of a motor launch seemed too good to miss.

I let Billy talk me into it. I put up a feeble resistance for half an hour. Then I gave in.

.   .   .   .   .

36

It was midday when we sighted the wreck. She lay about two hundred yards offshore, with her mast just breaking the waves. The whole scene looked kind of ominous. The sea had the texture of molten metal, and the noon sun lit up the atmosphere like a white-hot blanket.

I had three natives with me—the changing-room attendant, who was an old man, very frail-looking in his white singlet and sarong, and two boatmen. The boatmen were boys. They looked as if they could just about whip cream with an outboard motor. It was a great little set-up.

I checked the harpoon head to make sure it came off the shaft easily; tied the two-hundred-foot line to the metal frame of one of the seats. I told the boys to cut the motor and drift in. Big fish get kind of drowsy around midday and I thought maybe if we were quiet enough I might catch him taking a nap outside his lair.

I got a cushion off one of the seats and told the boys they were to keep it under the line all the time to stop it from chafing on the gunwale. I arranged about signals. Their eyes were big and scared-looking. The old man kept taking snuff and sneezing nervously. It could have been funny, but it wasn't.

Fifty feet from the wreck I went over the side. I ducked my head under. The water seemed to have cleared a little, but I still couldn't see bottom. I knew the country pretty well, though. It was no deeper than the bay—all big boulders. Real grouper country. I headed towards the mast with my heels well down, so they wouldn't splash.

When I got to the mast I stopped. The wreck was below me, but I still couldn't see it, not the faintest shadow of it. I had left the schnorkel behind so I shouldn't make a noise blowing through it. I lay in the water holding my breath and looking down and listening. Not a sound.

I gulped in some air and went down, careful not to touch the mast or set up the least vibration. The stoved-in deck of the dhow loomed slowly up towards me. I hooked one finger under the coral-encrusted gunwale and hung there, looking in every direction. There was a greenish tinge to the water—a sort of jungle twilight.

The timbers of the boat were half rotted, and pen coral was forming like clusters of undeveloped grapes along their broken edges. A host of tiny red-striped chætodons glided about my head, stiff as chips of painted wood.

I was strung up tight to resist the shock of seeing the gigantic proportions, the deep belly, and yard-wide mouth of the fish I was after. With the magnification, he would look not much smaller than an elephant.

I peered carefully at every half-discerned shape; then I eased myself gently away from the side of the boat and looked down at the hole in her bows. This was his lair.

There was no sign of him.

I surfaced slowly, took in some more air, and went down again. Very carefully I circled the wreck. I did it in about six breathing stages, covering only a few yards each time. I knew that a green jewfish the size of this one would probably come straight at me in a headlong rush, with no warning but the water gurgling in the back of its cavernous throat.

I worked my way round to the bows again. Nothing. Either the creature was inside its den or it was away foraging in deep water. There was only one way to find out which.

Taking in as much air as I could cram into my lungs, my throat, and my cheeks, I sounded bottom and picked up a small rock. Then, with the rock holding me down, I half walked, half floated to the hole in the bows. I stood square in front of it with the harpoon couched to withstand a rush.

I waited a few moments. Nothing happened.

I shifted the harpoon and thumped the wood hull with it; quickly levelled it again. The sound beat through the water like gunfire.

I edged a bit nearer, trying to pierce the darkness. I could see nothing. I listened to the water with every inch of my skin in an effort to discern the presence of a great body.

I felt something. There was suddenly a terrible sense of nearness. It was like a shadow moving up over me. The water

Sucked towards it like a bit of fluff into a vacuum cleaner.

stirred, whispered against me. The skin crawled on the nape of my neck. My chest filled with almost uncontrollable panic. I dropped the rock and twisted round.

I thought at first it was the hull of a boat. It was so close it seemed to fill the entire sea. I didn't know what it was. Even as I turned, the whole thing seemed to open up, become a yawning chasm. I felt myself drawn towards it like a bit of fluff into a vacuum cleaner. I struggled to get the spear round. I could never have done it, but the suction twisted me. The harpoon cut round, straight into the gaping mouth, tore on in and in, lodged with a jerk that brought me up short, jammed against the bony bottom jaw, my hand actually inside the mouth.

Before I could recover, a regurgitating blast hit me full in the face, knocking me backwards half a dozen feet. The water around me seemed to shake. I scrambled upwards blindly towards the surface, burst up above the sea, gesticulating to the boatmen.

They started to haul on the line. I splash-crawled back to the motor boat, expecting the most tremendous convulsions; scrambled aboard. I seized the line and threw my weight back on it; fell over. There was hardly any resistance. The harpoon must have come out.

I got up, cursing. The brute must have spat the spear out as a river fish spits out bait. I threw my mask off; beat my fists on the gunwale.

The boys took in the rest of the line. Suddenly there was a shout. I started up. A great shape had heaved up alongside. It was the jewfish. And it was dead.

It was over on its side, the spear still protruding from its gaping mouth. When we had stopped rocking the motor boat and shouting up at the sky, I got the boat-hook and turned the brute over. I saw then what had happened. The tip of the harpoon had gone through the throat and out of the top of its back, pushing the scaly skin up like a tent at the base of the dorsal. It had virtually stabbed itself to death with its own suction. The spear had severed its spine.

Even seen without magnification, it was a monster. Between six and seven feet. Over three hundred pounds, I judged—thick-lipped and hunchbacked and gross.

We ran a rope through its gills and secured it alongside where I could protect it with the boat-hook in case of shark. We chugged slowly back to the hotel. On the way we each took some of the old man's snuff. There was laughing and sneezing and I told them how it had happened. I just had to blab to someone. My pulse was doing about ninety-eight.

Round the point from the hotel we stopped and I went over the side with the rope tied to my belt. The boys took the boat back to the boat-house, while I towed the big fish round to the bay. It was heavy going and it gave me a funny feeling each time I looked back into that great open mouth. It was like towing a railway tunnel.

When I reached the bay I got astride the thing, gripping its scaly barrel with my knees to keep it out of sight under the water. But it was lunch-time in the hotel and there was no one on the beach, which was just as well as it took me three dives to get the clumsy thing down to the bottom and wedge the knotted end of the rope under a rock.

I waded ashore guiltily. For the first time I began to realize what an underhand trick we were trying to bring off. If it hadn't been for the girl getting killed that morning it might have been quite a good stunt; but that took the kick out of it somehow.

I went back to my shack and changed. Then I trudged up to the hotel and asked at the desk for Billy Beechum. The page-boy went off to fetch him. In less than a minute Billy came hurrying along, dabbing his mouth with a napkin and swallowing down a mouthful of food.

He chivvied me away from the desk and along a passage. "Well, did you get it?" he whispered, breathing curry all over me.

"Yep."

"Good man! I knew you would. Splendid. Come and have something to eat."

"Not in this ritzy joint."

"You could eat in my office. Was it a big one?"

"Big enough."

"Well, have a drink."

"I don't drink."

"Nor you do." He looked at me. "What's the matter?"

"Nothing." I hesitated. "You're perfectly happy about all this?"

Billy pinched his nose and regarded me over the top of his glasses. "Yes. Why?"

"Nothing," I said. Billy was a good chap. I supposed I must be getting fussy.

"I'll lay everything on for three o'clock then," he said.

"I suppose you must."

I left him staring after me thoughtfully. It was my fault, I

41

thought, pushing a hole through the heat of the garden. I just should never have got up that morning in the first place.

At three o'clock I rolled up out of a cat-nap and collected my equipment. I stepped out of the hut; stopped in astonishment.

The hotel beach was packed with people. They were sitting on the rocks and along the rail outside the changing-rooms. The diving-tower looked like a small grandstand.

This was taking things a bit too far, I thought. Stepping out on to the sand, I felt like a first-night ballerina leaving her dressing-room. The nearer I got to the crowd the worse the feeling got. Group by group, every eye turned in my direction. I went hot and cold all over. My walk seemed to go haywire. How was I going to make a fight with a dead fish look convincing before so many people?

Billy came hurrying to meet me.

"You idiot!" I said when he got close enough.

He showed his teeth. "Make it good!" he muttered.

Then, taking my arm, Billy led me along in front of the onlookers, and fussed around me trying to help me on with my fins and mask.

I tried not to look at all the people, but I couldn't help it. They were everywhere I turned my eyes. They had on serious expressions, most of them, but one or two of the kids looked as if they were looking forward to seeing me get eaten.

I walked with the shark line towards the palm tree; but Billy stopped me. He had brought three natives down with him to take care of that. I guessed they were all part of the act. Maybe he had briefed them, I don't know; but they were big, muscular fellows and they looked better than the palm tree.

When I was ready I started to go in, but the crowd hadn't done with me yet. They clapped. I pulled the mask down over my face and plunged into the sea quickly, before someone started throwing me flowers.

I beat out into the bay, as if looking for something. When

I had got over the shelf I made half a dozen token dives. I filled my lungs to capacity each time, went down about ten feet, and hooked my fingers under the rock. This way I managed to make each dive last about three minutes. That should impress them, I thought.

The water was murky, and I kept an all-round look-out just in case. There wasn't much to see, though—a few grunts, a pair of cuttlefish frilling along like tiny, padded bedroom stools. I worked along to where I judged I had moored the jewfish and went down all the way to the bottom.

Once again the oppressive gloom. I finned along just above the rock, bracing myself again to take the shock of seeing the huge shape loom up through the water. First time I missed it. I tried again. I worked backwards and forwards. I still couldn't see it.

A nasty little seed of panic split open inside me then, and began to grow. Maybe I hadn't moored it securely enough. I began quickening my beat. I was certain this was the spot. Yes, there was the rock. With the last of my air I swam to it. The jewfish had gone!

. . . . .

I felt down under the rock. The rope was still there. It lay snaked along the bottom. I found the end of it. All that remained of the jewfish was one big gill-plate and half a jawbone.

I kicked to the surface. What on earth was I going to do now? Either the creature had come alive and torn itself free, wrenching half its head off to do it, or something had come along and chewed it up. How was I going to explain that to Billy? To all those people? Desperately I went down again. Maybe the thing had come adrift somehow and was just floating around.

I went about two yards and stopped. There was something in the murk ahead of me that looked like the flange of a huge anchor. I looked all round; couldn't see anything. Edged forward. Something inside me was screaming *stop*, but I was too upset to listen. I had drifted right up against the "anchor" before I realized what it was. Everything inside me seemed to seize up. The back of my neck contracted like a slug with salt on it.

Very, very gently I let the air in me take me to the surface. I lay there gasping. I wanted to yell out; tell everyone what I had seen. It had been a huge tail-fin.

I looked round at the people. Every eye was on me. They were like a fight crowd, hungry for something to happen.

I shook out the line in the water, checked the harpoon. Then I dived. The creature was lying along the bottom. It stretched away into the gloom like a torpedo. If I had been swimming in nitro-glycerine I wouldn't have moved more delicately. Along and above the grey back I finned, above the big triangular dorsal, which leaned over to one side a little, lazily. Just behind the head I stopped.

It was a hammerhead shark.

The grotesque skull, shaped like a mallet, was three feet across. The tiny eyes, set in what would have been the striking ends of the mallet, were invisible to me. It was sleeping, which was hardly surprising if it had eaten the jewfish.

Its skull was virtually impenetrable. There was only one place where I stood even a chance of killing it. I scooped myself down silently till I was directly behind its head, raised the harpoon, and plunged it with all my strength into the back of its neck.

The whole water seemed to explode. I let everything go and beat away to the surface. Spitting out the schnorkel, I yelled to the natives to pull on the line. I started to race for the beach.

The three natives had begun hauling in the slack, but almost instantly the line sprang up white and taut out of the water. The next moment the Sinhalese were flat on their faces, being dragged down the sand. They splashed about in the surf, trying to brace themselves, but it was no good. First one let go; then all three.

The line whipped along past me. I grabbed at it. For an instant my hands seemed to be on fire; then I was moving

A moment afterwards the whole water seemed to explode.

through the bay at a great rate. My mask was dragged off The water punched into my eyes, my mouth, blinding and choking me. I craned my neck and managed to snatch a look.

There was no sign of the shark, but the line was dragging me straight out to sea. The creature must have turned then, because I found myself slewing sideways through the water. The diving-tower loomed up over me. I thought I was going to hit it, but somehow I swung round inshore of its wooden piles.

With sudden, desperate inspiration I kicked right on round the nearest pile and braced my feet against it, hauling on the rope.

The line tautened. Suddenly there was a crash. The pile broke. The rope leapt from my hands. People started dropping into the sea around me, screaming. Timber was falling. A great jagged flame leapt up behind my eyes and I went out cold.

· · · · ·

I came to with the idea at the back of my mind that I was in hell. The whole of my body felt as if it was on fire. Then I opened my eyes and saw that I was lying stretched out on hot paving-stones, and someone seemed to be kneeling on my back.

Whoever it was was wringing me out like a wet dish-rag. When he had finished I was helped up and people started congratulating me and shaking me by the hand. Then somehow Billy was there. He clapped me on the back and kept saying, "Marvellous! Wonderful!" But his eyes were mystified. He couldn't make out what had happened.

"Sorry I couldn't hold him," I croaked.

For a moment he looked more mystified than ever. Then he grinned. He raised his finger. "Hear that?" he said.

Above the noise of the crowd came the sound of, "Jumbari-wallah!" In Ceylon, whenever natives haul on a rope, you hear their song, "Jumbari-wallah!" I pushed my way to the rail. It was coming from the beach. Incredulously, I saw

He clapped me on the back and kept saying: "Wonderful!"

twenty or thirty natives throwing themselves back on a rope in unison. "Jumbari-wallah!" Slowly the great body of the hammerhead was coming up through the surf. "Jumbari-wallah!"

"That last jerk did it," Billy said. "It must have levered your harpoon up into its brain."

That night I put on my suit. There was a big celebration up in the hotel and I was guest of honour. I sat at Billy's table and we had twenty-seven different dishes of *hors d'œuvre*, oysters, followed by *kingfish au gratin* and duck.

There was just one thing, though. Towards the end of the evening the girl who had caused all the trouble turned up. She was accompanied by a guy whom nobody in general and her aunt in particular didn't much like. He had a car and they had been up to Kandy in it. She had ducked out of the bay and gone off with him when her aunt wasn't looking.

Things broke up a little after that. The aunt had the screaming jeebies in the foyer. There was a grimly silent slugging match outside between the young man and another young man.

Me, I had a headache. As quietly as possible I left. I was half-way across the lawn when Billy caught me up. He fell into step beside me. We walked back towards my place in silence.

"Well," Billy said at last, "even if it didn't work out quite right, you put up a darn good show. I won't forget in a hurry what you did for me today."

I didn't say anything. Instead, I took a deep breath. The monsoons were coming. Their salty foretaste feathered the air. Maybe after all I would hitch across to Trincomalee. It was summer there now and the reefs would be ablaze with fish. It made me feel better just thinking about it.

"I know what's been keeping you here," he said. "You owed me a bit, but now our debt's settled. You can go ahead and drift. . . ."

He grinned at me, and I grinned back.

"Wish I could come along," he said, "you old fish killer!"

The Remarkable Case of Davidson's Eyes

H. G. WELLS

THE transitory mental aberration of Sidney Davidson, remarkable enough in itself, is still more remarkable if Wade's explanation is to be credited. It sets one dreaming of the oddest possibilities of intercommunication in the future, of spending an intercalary five minutes on the other side of the world, or being watched in our most secret operations by unsuspected eyes. It happened that I was the immediate witness of Davidson's seizure, and so it falls naturally to me to put the story upon paper.

When I say that I was the immediate witness of his seizure, I mean that I was the first on the scene. The thing happened at the Harlow Technical College, just beyond the Highgate Archway. He was alone in the larger laboratory when the thing happened. I was in a smaller room, where the balances are, writing up some notes. The thunderstorm had completely upset my work, of course. It was just after one of the louder peals that I thought I heard some glass smash in the other room. I stopped writing, and turned round to listen. For a moment I heard nothing; the hail was playing the

49

"What in heaven's name has come over me?"

devil's tattoo on the corrugated zinc of the roof. Then came another sound, a smash—no doubt of it this time. Something heavy had been knocked off the bench. I jumped up at once and went and opened the door leading into the big laboratory.

I was surprised to hear a queer sort of laugh, and saw Davidson standing unsteadily in the middle of the room, with a dazzled look on his face. My first impression was that he was drunk. He did not notice me. He was clawing out at something invisible a yard in front of his face. He put out his hand slowly, rather hesitatingly, and then clutched nothing. "What's come to it?" he said. He held up his hands to his face, fingers spread out. "Great Scott!" he said. The thing happened three or four years ago, when everyone swore by that personage. Then he began raising his feet clumsily, as though he had expected to find them glued to the floor.

"Davidson!" cried I. "What's the matter with you?" He turned round in my direction and looked about for me. He looked over me and at me and on either side of me, without the slightest sign of seeing me. "Waves," he said; "and a remarkably neat schooner. I'd swear that was Bellow's voice. *Hullo!*" He shouted suddenly at the top of his voice.

I thought he was up to some foolery. Then I saw littered about his feet the shattered remains of the best of our electrometers. "What's up, man?" said I. "You've smashed the electrometer!"

"Bellows again!" said he. "Friends left, if my hands are gone. Something about electrometers. Which way *are* you, Bellows?" He suddenly came staggering towards me. "The damned stuff cuts like butter," he said. He walked straight into the bench and recoiled. "None so buttery that!" he said, and stood swaying.

I felt scared. "Davidson," said I, "what on earth's come over you?"

He looked round him in every direction. "I could swear that was Bellows. Why don't you show yourself like a man, Bellows?"

51

It occurred to me that he must be suddenly struck blind. I walked round the table and laid my hand upon his arm. I never saw a man more startled in my life. He jumped away from me, and came round into an attitude of self-defence, his face fairly distorted with terror. "Good God!" he cried. "What was that?"

"It's I—Bellows. Confound it, Davidson!"

He jumped when I answered him and stared—how can I express it?—right through me. He began talking, not to me, but to himself. "Here in broad daylight on a clear beach. Not a place to hide in." He looked about him wildly. "Here! I'm *off*." He suddenly turned and ran headlong into the big electromagnet—so violently that, as we found afterwards, he bruised his shoulder and jawbone cruelly. At that he stepped back a pace, and cried out with almost a whimper, "What, in Heaven's name, has come over me?" He stood, blanched with terror and trembling violently, with his right arm clutching his left, where that had collided with the magnet.

By that time I was excited and fairly scared. "Davidson," said I, "don't be afraid."

He was startled at my voice, but not so excessively as before. I repeated my words in as clear and as firm a tone as I could assume. "Bellows," he said, "is that you?"

"Can't you see it's me?"

He laughed. "I can't even see it's myself. Where the devil are we?"

"Here," said I, "in the laboratory."

"The laboratory!" he answered in a puzzled tone, and put his hand to his forehead. "I *was* in the laboratory—till that flash came, but I'm hanged if I'm there now. What ship is that?"

"There's no ship," said I. "Do be sensible, old chap."

"No ship!" he repeated, and seemed to forget my denial forthwith. "I suppose," said he slowly, "we're both dead. But the rummy part is I feel just as though I still had a body. Don't get used to it all at once, I suppose. The old ship was struck by lightning, I suppose. Jolly quick thing, Bellows —eh?"

"Don't talk nonsense. You're very much alive. You are in the laboratory, blundering about. You've just smashed a new electrometer. I don't envy you when Boyce arrives."

He stared away from me towards the diagrams of cryohydrates. "I must be deaf," said he. "They've fired a gun, for there goes the puff of smoke, and I never heard a sound."

I put my hand on his arm again, and this time he was less alarmed. "We seem to have a sort of invisible bodies," said he. "By Jove! There's a boat coming round the headland. It's very much like the old life after all—in a different climate."

I shook his arm. "Davidson," I cried, "wake up!"

It was just then that Boyce came in. So soon as he spoke Davidson exclaimed, "Old Boyce! Dead too! What a lark!" I hastened to explain that Davidson was in a kind of somnambulistic trance. Boyce was interested at once. We both did all we could to rouse the fellow out of his extraordinary state. He answered our questions, and asked us some of his own, but his attention seemed distracted by his hallucination about a beach and a ship. He kept interpolating observations concerning some boat and the davits, and sails filling with the wind. It made one feel queer, in the dusky laboratory, to hear him saying such things.

He was blind and helpless. We had to walk him down the passage, one at each elbow, to Boyce's private room, and while Boyce talked to him there, and humoured him about this ship idea, I went along the corridor and asked old Wade to come and look at him. The voice of our Dean sobered him a little, but not very much. He asked where his hands were, and why he had to walk about up to his waist in the ground. Wade thought over him a long time—you know how he knits his brows—and then made him feel the couch, guiding his hands to it. "That's a couch," said Wade. "The couch in the private room of Prof. Boyce. Horsehair stuffing."

Davidson felt about, and puzzled over it, and answered

53

"I know you're close beside me on the couch—and there is the sun just

presently that he could feel it all right, but he couldn't see it.

"What *do* you see?" asked Wade. Davidson said he could see nothing but a lot of sand and broken-up shells. Wade gave him some other things to feel, telling him what they were, and watching him keenly.

"The ship is almost hull down," said Davidson presently, apropos of nothing.

"Never mind the ship," said Wade. "Listen to me Davidson. Do you know what hallucination means?"

"Rather," said Davidson.

"Well, everything you see is hallucinatory."

"Bishop Berkeley," said Davidson.

"Don't mistake me," said Wade. "You are alive and in this room of Boyce's. But something has happened to your eyes. You cannot see; you can feel and hear, but not see. Do you follow me?"

rising and the ship and a tumbled sea and penguins and birds flying. . . ."

"It seems to me that I see too much." Davidson rubbed his knuckles into his eyes. "Well?" he said.

"That's all. Don't let it perplex you. Bellows here and I will take you home in a cab."

"Wait a bit." Davidson thought. "Help me to sit down," said he presently; "and now—I'm sorry to trouble you—but will you tell me all that over again?"

Wade repeated it very patiently. Davidson shut his eyes, and pressed his hands upon his forehead. "Yes," said he. "It's quite right. Now my eyes are shut I know you're right. That's you, Bellows, sitting by me on the couch. I'm in England again. And we're in the dark."

Then he opened his eyes. "And there," said he, "is the sun just rising, and the yards of the ship, and a tumbled sea, and a couple of birds flying. I never saw anything so real. And I'm sitting up to my neck in a bank of sand."

He bent forward and covered his face with his hands. Then

he opened his eyes again. "Dark sea and sunrise! And yet I'm sitting on a sofa in old Boyce's room! . . . God help me!"

That was the beginning. For three weeks this strange affection of Davidson's eyes continued unabated. It was far worse than being blind. He was absolutely helpless, and had to be fed like a newly hatched bird, and led about and undressed. If he attempted to move, he fell over things or struck himself against walls or doors. After a day or so he got used to hearing our voices without seeing us, and willingly admitted he was at home, and that Wade was right in what he told him. My sister, to whom he was engaged, insisted on coming to see him, and would sit for hours every day while he talked about this beach of his. Holding her hand seemed to comfort him immensely. He explained that when we left the College and drove home—he lived in Hampstead village —it appeared to him as if we drove right through a sand-hill—it was perfectly black until he emerged again—and through rocks and trees and solid obstacles, and when he was taken to his own room it made him giddy and almost frantic with the fear of falling, because going upstairs seemed to lift him thirty or forty feet above the rocks of his imaginary island. He kept saying he should smash all the eggs. The end was that he had to be taken down into his father's consulting-room and laid upon a couch that stood there.

He described the island as being a bleak kind of place on the whole, with very little vegetation, except some peaty stuff, and a lot of bare rock. There were multitudes of penguins, and they made the rocks white and disagreeable to see. The sea was often rough, and once there was a thunderstorm, and he lay and shouted at the silent flashes. Once or twice seals pulled up on the beach, but only on the first two or three days. He said it was very funny the way in which the penguins used to waddle right through him, and how he seemed to lie among them without disturbing them.

I remember one odd thing, and that was when he wanted very badly to smoke. We put a pipe in his hands—he almost poked his eye out with it—and lit it. But he couldn't taste anything. I've since found it's the same with me—I don't know if it's the usual case—that I cannot enjoy tobacco at all unless I can see the smoke.

But the queerest part of his vision came when Wade sent him out in a Bath-chair to get fresh air. The Davidsons hired a chair, and got that deaf and obstinate dependant of theirs, Widgery, to attend to it. Widgery's ideas of healthy expeditions were peculiar. My sister, who had been to the Dogs' Home, met them in Camden Town, towards King's Cross, Widgery trotting along complacently, and Davidson, evidently most distressed, trying in his feeble, blind way to attract Widgery's attention.

He positively wept when my sister spoke to him. "Oh, get me out of this horrible darkness!" he said, feeling for her hand. "I must get out of it, or I shall die." He was quite incapable of explaining what was the matter, but my sister decided he must go home, and presently, as they went uphill towards Hampstead, the horror seemed to drop from him. He said it was good to see the stars again, though it was then about noon and a blazing day.

"It seemed," he told me afterwards, "as if I was being carried irresistibly towards the water. I was not very much alarmed at first. Of course it was night there—a lovely night."

"Of course?" I asked, for that struck me as odd.

"Of course," said he. "It's always night there when it is day here. . . . Well, we went right into the water, which was calm and shining under the moonlight—just a broad swell that seemed to grow broader and flatter as I came down into it. The surface glistened just like a skin—it might have been empty space underneath for all I could tell to the contrary. Very slowly, for I rode slanting into it, the water crept up to my eyes. Then I went under and the skin seemed to break and heal again about my eyes. The moon gave a jump up in the sky and grew green and dim, and fish, faintly glowing, came darting round me—and things that seemed made of luminous glass; I passed through a tangle of seaweeds that shone with an oily lustre. And so I drove down into the sea, and the stars went out one by one, and the moon grew greener and darker, and the seaweed became a luminous purple-red. It was all very faint and mysterious, and everything seemed to quiver. And all the while I could hear the wheels of the Bath-chair creaking, and the footsteps of people going by, and a man in the distance selling the special *Pall Mall*.

"I kept sinking down deeper and deeper into the water. It became inky black about me, not a ray from above came down into that darkness, and the phosphorescent things grew brighter and brighter. The snaky branches of the deeper weeds flickered like the flames of spirit-lamps; but, after a time, there were no more weeds. The fishes came staring and gaping towards me, and into me and through me. I never imagined such fishes before. They had lines of fire along the sides of them as though they had been outlined with a luminous pencil. And there was a ghastly thing swimming backward with a lot of twining arms. And then I saw, coming very slowly towards me through the gloom, a hazy mass of light that resolved itself as it drew nearer into multitudes of fishes, struggling and darting round something that drifted. I drove on straight towards it, and presently I saw in the midst of the tumult, and by the light of the fish, a bit of splintered spar looming over me, and a dark hull tilting over, and some glowing phosphorescent forms that were shaken and writhed as the fish bit at them. Then it was I began to try to attract Widgery's attention. A horror came upon me. Ugh! I should have driven right into those half-eaten —— things. If your sister had not come! They had great holes in them, Bellows, and. . . . Never mind. But it was ghastly!"

For three weeks Davidson remained in this singular state, seeing what at the time we imagined was an altogether phantasmal world, and stone blind to the world around him. Then, one Tuesday, when I called I met old Davidson in the passage. "He can see his thumb!" the old gentleman said, in a perfect transport. He was struggling into his overcoat. "He can see his thumb, Bellows!" he said, with the tears in his eyes. "The lad will be all right yet."

I rushed in to Davidson. He was holding up a little book before his face, and looking at it and laughing in a weak kind of way.

"It's amazing," said he. "There's a kind of patch come there." He pointed with his finger. "I'm on the rocks as usual, and the penguins are staggering and flapping about as usual, and there's been a whale showing every now and then, but it's got too dark now to make him out. But put something *there*, and I see it—I do see it. It's very dim and broken in places, but I see it all the same, like a faint spectre of itself. I found it out this morning while they were dressing me. It's like a hole in this infernal phantom world. Just put your hand by mine. No—not there. Ah! Yes! I see it. The base of your thumb and a bit of cuff! It looks like the ghost of a bit of your hand sticking out of the darkling sky. Just by it there's a group of stars like a cross coming out."

From that time Davidson began to mend. His account of the change, like his account of the vision, was oddly convincing. Over patches of his field of vision, the phantom world grew fainter, grew transparent, as it were, and through these translucent gaps he began to see dimly the real world about him. The patches grew in size and number, ran together and spread until only here and there were blind spots left upon his eyes. He was able to get up and steer himself about, feed himself once more, read, smoke, and behave like an ordinary citizen again. At first it was very confusing to him to have these two pictures overlapping each other like the changing views of a lantern, but in a little while he began to distinguish the real from the illusory.

At first he was unfeignedly glad, and seemed only too anxious to complete his cure by taking exercise and tonics. But as that odd island of his began to fade away from him, he became queerly interested in it. He wanted particularly to go down into the deep sea again, and would spend half his time wandering about the low-lying parts of London, trying to find the water-logged wreck he had seen drifting. The glare of real daylight very soon impressed him so vividly as to blot out everything of his shadowy world, but of a night time, in a darkened room, he could still see the white-splashed rocks of the island, and the clumsy penguins staggering to and fro. But even these grew fainter and fainter, and, at last, soon after he married my sister, he saw them for the last time.

And now to tell of the queerest thing of all. About two years after his cure I dined with the Davidsons, and after dinner a man named Atkins called in. He is a lieutenant in the Royal Navy, and a pleasant, talkative man. He was on friendly terms with my brother-in-law, and was soon on friendly terms with me. It came out that he was engaged to Davidson's cousin, and incidentally he took out a kind of pocket photograph case to show us a new rendering of his *fiancée*. "And, by the bye," said he, "here's the old *Fulmar*."

Davidson looked at it casually. Then suddenly his face lit up. "Good heavens!" said he. "I could almost swear——"

"What?" said Atkins.

"That I had seen that ship before."

"Don't see how you can have. She hasn't been out of the South Seas for six years, and before then——"

"But," began Davidson, and then: "Yes—that's the ship I dreamt of; I'm sure that's the ship I dreamt of. She was standing off an island that swarmed with penguins, and she fired a gun."

"Good Lord!" said Atkins, who had now heard the particulars of the seizure. "How the deuce could you dream that?"

And then, bit by bit, it came out that on the very day Davidson was seized, H.M.S. *Fulmar* had actually been off a little rock to the south of Antipodes Island. A boat had landed overnight to get penguins' eggs, had been delayed, and a thunderstorm drifting up, the boat's crew had waited until the morning before rejoining the ship. Atkins had been one of them, and he corroborated, word for word, the descriptions Davidson had given of the island and the boat. There is not the slightest doubt in any of our minds that Davidson has really seen the place. In some unaccountable way, while

"By the bye," said he, "here's the old Fulmar."

he moved hither and thither in London, his sight moved hither and thither in a manner that corresponded, about this distant island. *How* is absolutely a mystery.

That completes the remarkable story of Davidson's eyes. It's perhaps the best authenticated case in existence of real vision at a distance. Explanation there is none forthcoming, except what Prof. Wade has thrown out. But his explanation involves the Fourth Dimension, and a dissertation on theoretical kinds of space. To talk of there being "a kink in space" seems mere nonsense to me; it may be because I am no mathematician. When I said that nothing would alter the fact that the place is eight thousand miles away, he answered that two points might be a yard away on a sheet of paper, and yet be brought together by bending the paper round. The reader may grasp his argument, but I certainly do not. His idea seems to be that Davidson, stooping between the poles of the big electromagnet, had some extraordinary twist given to his retinal elements through the sudden change in the field of force due to the lightning.

He thinks, as a consequence of this, that it may be possible to live visually in one part of the world, while one lives bodily in another. He has even made some experiments in support of his views; but, so far, he has simply succeeded in blinding a few dogs. I believe that is the net result of his work, though I have not seen him for some weeks. Latterly I have been so busy with my work in connection with the Saint Pancras installation that I have had little opportunity of calling to see him. But the whole of his theory seems fantastic to me. The facts concerning Davidson stand on an altogether different footing, and I can testify personally to the accuracy of every detail I have given.

The Wild Sky

A. TYSON

RODDY skied down the slope, took off from the snowy hump, leaned forward to balance himself in flight, skimmed the snow thirty yards away and sped down the rest of the slope, stopping on the flat plain which spread before the blue lake.

"It's a little faster than it was yesterday," he shouted to the top of the slope.

His voice carried well. This was sunny Quebec where the crisp air was so clear it was possible to see distant mountains with the same clarity as those so near. This was the land of the caribou, of reindeer herds and fresh water lakes. This was a vast territory where a handful of people were still pioneers. This was also the land of the grizzly bear and the long winter. Only last year a Canadian airman came down by parachute into the Hudson Bay a few miles away. Though he was spotted and picked up within two minutes, he was dead, frozen stiff. However, the northern Canadians knew how to handle the cold. This land was their home. They loved the Christmas card scenery and the sunlit summer

63

nights. It wasn't always cold. In the sun, in the sheltered valley, it was quite warm. The boys were skiing in their brightly coloured sweaters.

Frank, Roddy's younger brother, pushed himself away and skimmed down parallel to his older brother's tracks. On the hump he jumped as high as he could. He flew thirty-five yards before touching down to skim to the bottom.

Both were expert skiers. Roddy was fifteen and had learned to ski before he could walk. Frank had walked first but only because he had reached walking age in the summer when there had been no snow.

Mrs. Lomax came after her sons. She avoided the hump, but she was quite fast and graceful.

"I can't compete with you boys any longer," she smiled. Her accent was English. "Now let's go to the control hut to find out when your father will be back."

"Can I radio Father?" asked Frank.

"If the controller doesn't mind."

Mr. Lomax was a geologist who was looking for mineral deposits in the islands of the Hudson Bay. He was an ex-naval airman and travelled by air to these remote islands, using as his base the lake towards which the boys and their mother had sped. Near the shore stood the trading post from which Mr. Lomax got his stores, and beside it was the control hut for the trapping company's Beaver seaplanes.

The air traffic controller was at his microphone.

"Roger, Alpha, you are clear to come in. There's a slight cross wind but it's not dangerous if you watch it."

"I'll be with you in two minutes."

"Roger, out." He turned away from the set. His expression was not happy. "Hallo, Mrs. Lomax."

"I know I'm a little early, but I wonder if my husband has given his time of arrival."

The controller frowned. "He did call about an hour ago but we lost him again. To tell you the truth I'm worried. He should have been here ten minutes ago."

"Oh, that's impossible," said Mrs. Lomax. "He's not due

until eleven o'clock and that's at least an hour away."

"I'm afraid there aren't sufficient aircraft in this territory to cause any mix-ups. I'll call him again. What's his call-sign, Pierre? Lima Bravo?"

"*Un moment. Qui!* Lima Bravo," nodded the French-Canadian controller.

"Lima Bravo, Lima Bravo, how do you read?"

The radio crackled but there was no reply. The controller tried again.

"I'm sorry Mrs. Lomax, I can't raise him yet. Say, why don't you go back to the trading post and have a coffee. I'll keep calling and fire a yellow Very light as soon as I have contact."

"Thank you, I think we will," said Mrs. Lomax calmly.

"You can read morse, can't you?" the controller asked Roddy.

"Sure!"

"Good, I'll flash your father's estimated time of arrival on the green Aldis lamp."

"Can I come back and talk to Father?" asked Frank.

"As soon as we contact him."

Roddy and his mother walked back along the side of the lake to the trading post. The news had not been encouraging. The grace had gone out of Mrs. Lomax's walk. Frank had stopped outside the control hut to put on his skis. He wanted to try that slope again, but he, too, had lost his enthusiasm. He fiddled with his ski-straps.

"*Pauvre madame.* Was it good to tell her so soon?"

Frank could clearly overhear the French-Canadian.

"I'm glad to get it off my chest. It will be easier to break the sad news."

"Do you think we should call out ze Mounties or Air Sea Rescue?"

"We've already alerted Air Sea Rescue, but they can't start a major search while there's still a possibility he's airborne. If he's come down in the Hudson I don't give much for his chances."

"*Qui!* I think that you are right. I think he must be—what is the word for *mort*?"

Mort! Frank stiffened outside the control hut. *Mort*—that was French for "dead". Frank could hardly believe what he heard.

As quietly as he could he walked after his mother, hoping he would not be seen by the controllers. His father could not be dead. He was so full of life. He had taught his sons to ski, ice-skate, to fish, canoe and even to fly. How can a man who talked, laughed and played with them suddenly cease to exist?

A Beaver circled the lake and touched down on the blue water, breaking it into white spray. Frank was certain this was his father, even though he had heard the company pilot's voice over the radio. He ran to meet the seaplane at the pier, but kept out of sight behind the open doors of the hangar.

"Sorry I'm late, chief," said the pilot to the ground mechanic. "I was diverted to look for Lomax."

"Any luck?"

"No, couldn't see a thing, nor did I expect to. Lomax was a brave man. It's dangerous enough keeping to the sparse air routes. It's worse flying into the wild north alone."

Frank turned away, too empty to cry. In the trading post, his mother looked pale and Roddy looked bored.

"Where have you been, Frank? Hurry up, your coffee is nearly cold."

Frank sat down at the little wooden table, not knowing how to break the news.

"I am going outside to see the Beaver unload," said Roddy.

"I'll come," said Frank.

As soon as they were outside, Frank pulled his brother's sleeve.

"Rod, when I was outside the control hut I overheard the controllers talk about Father. They think he's dead."

"Dead?"

"Yes. They say he must have come down in the Bay and you know what that means."

"Rod, I overheard the controllers. They think Father is dead."

"Why haven't they called a search?"

"They've alerted Air Sea Rescue, and they are diverting their own aircraft to search the area."

Roddy looked grim. They waited and watched the empty sky. All this time men were unloading skins from the Beaver, then they refuelled it. This activity was usual yet strange. Life to the boys had stopped, and they could not understand why men should work so casually.

The Beaver was left moored to the pier. There was still no message from the tower.

"I'm going to look for Father," said Roddy.

"How?"

"In this aircraft."

"But you can't fly."

"Dad has shown me often enough. I'm not leaving him in danger without trying to help. You can come if you wish

His younger brother stood in doubt. "Are you coming, or not?"

but if you don't, don't dare to tell anyone before I've gone."

No one was watching so Roddy stepped on the float and climbed inside the aircraft. Frank saw him slide into the pilot's seat.

Little red ribbons fluttered from the aircraft wings. These were part of the aircraft locks which held the control surfaces steady to prevent them being damaged in the wind. Aircraft locks must always be removed before flight otherwise the control surfaces could not respond to movements of the joystick.

"Rod!" called Frank in a low voice. "You've left in the aircraft locks."

Roddy climbed out of the aircraft, the perspiration standing out on his young face. He glanced around to make sure that he was not being watched, then he slowly removed the

aircraft locks from the rudder, and from the control surfaces
on the wings and tailplanes.

"Are you coming or not?"

Frank followed his brother into the aircraft. They sat side
by side in the cockpit. Rod switched on the electric and
the instruments flicked into life on the control panel. The
fuel tanks were full and the artificial horizon stabilized itself
to show that they were quite level.

Roddy switched on the ignition, generators and fuel cocks.
He checked the rest of the panel. He could still change his
mind. There was now only the red starter button to press.
After that he must go on. He bit his lip and pressed. The
engine, after its recent flight, was warm enough to start first
time. The noise inside the cabin was deafening. He opened
the throttle and the aircraft turned into the pier. Opposite
rudder could not correct the fault. Roddy shouted into
Frank's ear, but because of the noise of the engine, his words
could not be heard. Frank shouted back, "I can't hear you,"
but his words, too, were deadened by the engine noise.

Roddy jumped out of his seat and through the little door
on to the float. He had forgotten to untie the aircraft!

With a jerk the aircraft swung itself away from the pier,
and Frank found himself in full control. He counteracted all
the aircraft's movements. He didn't want to do anything with
the aircraft, but he didn't want it to run away with him.

Roddy returned to the cabin in a rush. He slammed open
the throttle, a dangerous procedure even when the engine
was thoroughly warm. The aircraft jumped away and Roddy
was flung back into the cabin against the rear bulkhead.

Once again Frank was left in complete control. The seaplane was racing across the blue lake. He steadied her as
best he could but his tendency to overcorrect caused the
aircraft to buck like an unbroken stallion. As the aircraft
approached flying speed it tended to hop and drift sideways.
Frank then remembered the cross wind. It could flick him
on his back before he could be aware of it. He applied rudder
to turn into the wind. The aircraft banked like a speedboat,

then hopped, then was airborne. They were dangerously low, very unstable and had only sufficient airspeed to keep them above the surface.

Now they were cutting across the lake which was too narrow for safety. The spruce trees ahead were dangerously close. It seemed inevitable that they would hit them.

Frank violently jerked back the joystick. The aircraft swooped up on its tail. The dense forest dropped away to be replaced by an empty view of blue sky. Frank slammed the stick forward and they were diving into the forest. Then they were up, down and up again. There was an immediate danger of Roddy, in the back, being thrown through the skin, where without a parachute, he would have a second or two of smooth flight before striking the uppermost branches of the spruce trees.

In any other aircraft Frank would have crashed on take-off. The Beaver, with its heavy floats and fuselage slung below the high wing, was inherently stable. Left alone, it would fly straight and level. Frank handled the joystick as a railway signalman would handle a signal lever. However, the corrections became less violent and Roddy, badly bruised, managed to get to his seat, level the aircraft and slap Frank's hands clear of the co-pilot's controls.

The engine vibrated and the noise was deafening. They were still flying on maximum revolutions per minute! Frank stretched out his hand to ease back the throttle but was again slapped hard. Roddy controlled the aircraft with one hand and strapped himself in with the other. Every time Frank moved his hands they were slapped hard.

Somehow Roddy found his earphones and put them on shutting out some of the terrible engine noise. He signalled Frank to do likewise but was ready to prevent him from interfering with any of the aircraft's controls.

"The engine's running on maximum revs," said Frank into his microphone.

Roddy's eyes flashed to the panel. Slowly he eased back the throttle. The engine sighed like a tired horse. However,

The lake was too narrow—the spruce trees rushed at them.

all was smoother now. Frank's father had often said that an aircraft should be steered with two fingers. Roddy gripped the joystick with a hand like a vice, so that his knuckles showed white. Nevertheless they were airborne, more or less level, a good two hundred feet clear of the ground, and in no immediate danger of crashing. As if he was struggling with a gigantic monster, Roddy eased the aircraft over the Hudson Bay in the direction from which they expected their father to come.

"Can't you relax your grip?" asked Frank.

"What do you know about flying? You nearly killed us."

"I did take-off, didn't I?"

"And nearly broke the aircraft's back. Listen, this world is divided into two, one half earth, the other half sky. You got into the right half by sheer luck. You must have been trying to keep on the water."

Roddy was almost foaming at the mouth, but Frank was only trying to be helpful.

"Father said you can fly an aircraft with two fingers."

"Shut up about flying. You keep a sharp lookout from your window. I'm flying directly to the Belcher Islands. The visibility is clear and we can see for miles so I'll fly as high as I can. Keep your eyes open and tell me of anything you see."

There was nothing ahead but the broad expanse of sea.

"Do you think we'll do any good by coming?"

"We haven't started yet, but if Air Sea Rescue come after us we will have achieved something."

In spite of the great visibility they flew out of sight of all land. The Bay is a sea in itself and over this lonely vastness, they may just as well have been over the Atlantic Ocean.

Frank's mind drifted as he watched the seascapes below. He still could not believe his father was dead. Nor could he see the wisdom of coming on this flight. He could see nothing but sea below and its empty vastness took away any hope of ever finding anything. Had there been a sound reason for a search, the Air Sea Rescue teams would have been out by now.

It seemed that they were trying to be too clever. They had no experience of flying. Taking-off and straight and level flying is comparatively easy, yet in these operations they had first of all forgotten to take out the locks, untie the painter which moored them to the pier, take-off into wind and cruise at normal revolutions per minute. Besides any other dangers which may arise out of their ignorance, they had still to touch down which was the most dangerous part of flying.

Roddy still gripped the joystick with a hand of iron.

If their father had come down in the Bay, he would have perished in the icy waters. If he had not come down he would probably be at the trading post now, safe and sound. There was a faint possibility that his engine had failed, that he had glided down to the waters and was adrift now. In this case he would be picked up in due course by Air Sea Rescue.

Even if the boys found their father adrift there was nothing they could do. Their father would never abandon an aircraft because of a faulty engine. Frank could not see what Roddy hoped to achieve by coming.

If the boys themselves survived they would certainly have to face the wrath of the officials who owned the aircraft they had stolen, besides the wrath of their mother. Poor mother! They had caused her endless anxiety. She had met their father when he was serving in the Fleet Air Arm in England. After they were married, he served in the Mediterranean while she was left alone. Even after the war, when they returned to Canada, he was often away in the north looking for mineral deposits. Now the boys were at boarding school, she was often left alone, following her husband to see him for brief periods at far-flung trading posts. She had never complained of her pioneering life but it was only on occasions like this that Frank realized how much she meant to them. Frank felt particularly mean because he had forgotten his mother's last birthday. He hadn't meant to forget, of course, but away from home at the boarding school he had mixed up the dates. If ever he saw his mother again, he would buy her the biggest box of chocolates he could afford.

His father had often said that once he had discovered minerals, they would open up a mining town. He used to smile and say perhaps they would even call it Lomax City, and there they would all settle down. They would have a big house in the forest by the banks of a blue lake. They would go riding, fishing, shooting and canoeing in summer, and in winter they would ice-skate, ski and swim in their own heated indoor swimming pool.

Frank brushed a tear from his eye. Now these castles in the air could never come true. Frank regretted coming on this flight for many reasons, but mainly because their foolishness might cause their mother to be childless as well as a widow.

On the other hand Roddy was now in complete control of himself. His grip on the joystick was much more relaxed, his eyes systematically scanned the sea, switched to the instrument panel, then back to the sea again.

They flew for an hour. Then Frank saw a hull in the water.

"Look there, Rod. See it? It looks like an upturned boat."

Roddy banked the aircraft towards the object. Now Frank was enthusiastic. At last there was purpose in their mission.

"There's a man lying across it in yellow oilskins," said Frank.

They flew lower. The upturned vessel was a heavy fishing-smack. They flew close enough to make out the fisherman's bearded face, but the sea, apparently calm from above, was rough. There was a strong wind which flung spray over the floating wreck.

"We can't land in that," said Frank.

"You're right."

Roddy circled and switched over to the distress channel on his radio set.

"Mayday! Mayday! Mayday!"

This was the distress call which originated from the French translation of "Aid Me". There was no reply. Rod called again and again. There was still no reply.

"We've done the best we can," said Roddy. "I hope our call has been picked up and our position plotted."

They continued their search for their father. A lump came up into Frank's throat. They were deserting a dying man.

"Do you think we should leave him, Rod?"

"What else can we do?" replied Roddy dejectedly. "We can't land in that sea. It will be suicide to try. The best we can do is keep calling base."

"But we should stay with him."

"Circling in silence won't do any good. If we keep trans-mitting we may break through."

This reasoning seemed sound, but in the cosy cabin, with the heat playing around Frank's legs, he still felt the lump in his throat.

"This will worry me for the rest of my life," Frank said.

"I know, I know."

The Belcher Islands first came into sight. They flew over the base where their father had kept his aircraft. There was no sign of his camp. They had searched the whole route.

They turned back for the trading post, still transmitting on the distress frequency. On route they passed the upturned boat with the motionless figure astride.

"I'm going down to get him," said Roddy.

He peeled off the aircraft. Frank felt relieved. It is easier to face death than to live with a guilty conscience.

They touched down in a trough and with the engine ticking over, taxied the heaving swell to the wreck.

"Hop on the float, Frank, and help him in."

Regardless of danger, Frank faced the icy wind and spray. The body was motionless and Frank could not see how he could handle such dead weight. But it was to be easier than he thought. He stretched out his hand as they converged. The wind drove the hull straight at the seaplane, splintering the side of the float. The impact flung the unconscious fisherman between the struts and over the float, and Frank caught hold of his belt to steady him before the sea could wash him away.

Roddy sensed the danger of being battered to pieces and was committed to get out of the way quickly. The aircraft, on half power, was threatened to be cartwheeled by the wind. Roddy opened the throttles and took-off, praying that Frank would have the sense to hang on. It was the only thing he could do.

Once airborne, the slipstream behind the racing propeller froze Frank's wet garments. Now the spray was broken up into fine droplets which froze on impact to cover him in thick ice. He was fixed with his arms through the fisherman's belt and around the aircraft's struts. He was practically immobile, and it was an effort to blink away the scales of ice on his eyelids.

The Beaver flew slowly. The weight of the ice on the wings and floats made it difficult for Roddy to climb clear of the spray. The extra weight on the float tended to roll the aircraft

Frank grabbed at the fisherman as float and boat collided.

and Roddy had to use all his strength to keep it level. Frank could not move without disturbing the fisherman and remained where he was, frozen to the struts. Slowly Roddy descended to settle on the water. The tops of the swell rose almost clipping the floats.

With an effort, Frank gestured with his hand. "Keep up! Keep up!"

He knew the impact with the waves would throw him into the water, then he would be lost. The collision with the boat had splintered their float and this would cause the seaplane to capsize and sink.

Roddy frowned at Frank's gestures, unaware of the hole in the side of the float, yet anxious to get the others inside. Again he attempted to touch down, but Frank's signals, though slow, were persistent. Frank pointed up to the sky then to the south-east. That was the way home. Slowly Roddy climbed away and set a course for the lake. To Roddy, the aircraft moved agonizingly slowly. To Frank, the wind was a howling gale. Both he and the survivor were caked in ice from the spray. But this ice protected them from the sub-normal temperatures in the wild sky.

Now Roddy's arms were tiring with the continual strain of holding the joystick hard to one side. He was forced to relax, and the aircraft banked into a graceful turn. Roddy knew he could not afford the fuel for such manoeuvres over these empty wastes. The aircraft's endurance was already stretched to the limit.

With considerable effort he levelled the aircraft and put his foot against the co-pilot's joystick. This cramped position was more painful than a torture rack, but Roddy had to stick it out to save his brother. The sun shone on him through the cabin windows making him uncomfortably hot.

Shortly the Beaver was sighted by a Neptune reconnaissance aircraft of the Royal Canadian Air Force which formated on them. The sight of this stirred the brothers' blood. Roddy smiled. Frank gritted his teeth. They were determined to stick it out.

77

The sight of the approaching Neptune *stirred the brothers' blood*

The fisherman moved slightly. Frank was immediately afraid the man would slip off the float, for he could only steady the body. It was impossible for him to hold it. But at least the fisherman was alive and, with renewed hope, Frank hung on.

A launch was waiting to pick them up as they approached the lake. Roddy sat up and using all his strength brought the Beaver straight in. The slight cross wind seemed to cancel the turning tendency of the seaplane, and just before touchdown, Roddy banked the aircraft so that the good float touched first. The Beaver slowed considerably before the damaged float struck water, and Frank and the fisherman were thrown off into the lake. Within seconds they were picked up by the launch, and the listing seaplane was towed to the slipway. Roddy, with the others, was hauled off to a warm bed.

The fisherman, a French-Canadian, had lived long enough

—*Roddy smiled and pointed; Frank, half-frozen, gritted his teeth.*

in the north to know its dangers, and had taken the precaution of wearing rubbers under his oilskins. He got away with a mild, though painful, touch of frostbite.

As for Mr. Lomax, he had discovered rich deposits of copper, lead and iron ore in these northern islands and had set out early with the good news for home. On route he had seen the shipwrecked fisherman but was unable to contact base because the substantial mineral deposits extending under the bay distorted his transmissions. He suspected radio failure and did not try to transmit from a greater height which would have produced better results. In fact he tried to rescue the fisherman as did Roddy. He landed into wind and the drifting hull smashed his propeller, leaving him unable to help the fisherman or himself. The fishing smack was deep in the water and was affected by the tide. The light seaplane, on top of the waves, was affected by the wind. They drifted far apart.

Another R.C.A.F. Neptune, searching downwind of the abandoned hull, soon discovered Mr. Lomax's smoke signals coming from an island and brought him to the trading post.

Frank was the big hero at the camp, his efforts outshining even those of his brother. The family was re-united. Everyone was proud of the young air venturers. Even Mr. Lomax refrained from remarking on their foolhardiness.

"What are you going to do now you've thawed out?" one of the company pilots asked Frank. "Hi-jack another Beaver?"

"I'm going with my father and mother and Rod to our new home."

"Where is that?"

"It's a little place you'll soon be hearing plenty of," said Frank. "It's going to be called Lomax City."

The Extraordinarily
Horrible Dummy

GERALD KERSH

A<small>N</small> uneasy conviction tells me that this story is true, but
I hate to believe it. It was told to me by Ecco, the
ventriloquist, who occupied a room next to mine in Busto's
apartment-house. I hope he lied. Or perhaps he was mad?
The world is so full of liars and lunatics, that one never
knows what is true and what is false.

All the same, if ever a man had a haunted look, that man
was Ecco. He was small and furtive. He had unnerving
habits: five minutes of his company would have set your
nerves on edge. For example, he would stop in the middle
of a sentence, say *Ssh!* in a compelling whisper, look timor-
ously over his shoulder, and listen to something. The slightest
noise made him jump. Like all Busto's tenants, he had come
down in the world. There had been a time when he topped
bills and drew fifty pounds a week. Now, he lived by perform-
ing to theatre-queues.

And yet he was the best ventriloquist I have ever heard.
His talent was uncanny. Repartee cracked back and forth
without pause, and in two distinct voices. There were even

people who swore that his dummy was no dummy, but a dwarf or small boy with painted cheeks, trained in ventriloquial back-chat. But this was not true. No dummy was ever more palpably stuffed with sawdust. Ecco called it Micky; and his act, *Micky and Ecco*.

All ventriloquists' dummies are ugly, but I have yet to see one uglier than Micky. It had a home-made look. There was something disgustingly avid in the stare of its bulging blue eyes, the lids of which clicked as it winked; and an extraordinarily horrible ghoulishness in the smacking of its great, grinning, red wooden lips. Ecco carried Micky with him wherever he went, and even slept with it. You would have felt cold at the sight of Ecco, walking upstairs, holding Micky at arm's length. The dummy was large and robust; the man was small and wraith-like; and in a bad light you would have thought: *The dummy is leading the man!*

I said he lived in the next room to mine. But in London, you may live and die in a room, and the man next door may never know. I should never have spoken to Ecco, but for his habit of practising ventriloquism by night. It was nerveracking. At the best of times it was hard to find rest under Busto's roof; but Ecco made night hideous, really hideous. You know the shrill, false voice of the ventriloquist's dummy? Micky's voice was not like that. It was shrill, but querulous, thin, but real—not Ecco's voice distorted, but a *different* voice. You would have sworn that there were two people quarrelling. *This man is good*, I thought. Then: *But this man is perfect!* And at last, there crept into my mind this sickening idea: *There are two men!*

In the dead of night, voices would break out:

"Come on, try again!"—"I can't!"—"You must."—"I want to go to sleep."—"Not yet; try again!"—"I'm tired, I tell you; I can't!"—"And I say try again." Then there would be peculiar singing noises, and at length Ecco's voice would cry, "You devil! You devil! Let me alone, in the name of God!"

One night, when this had gone on for three hours, I went

"In a bad light you would have thought: The dummy is leading the man!"

to Ecco's door, and knocked. There was no answer. I opened the door. Ecco was sitting there, grey in the face, with Micky on his knee. "Yes?" he said. He did not look at me, but the great, painted eyes of the dummy stared straight into mine.

I said, "I don't want to seem unreasonable, but this noise. . . ."

Ecco turned to the dummy, and said, "We're annoying the gentleman. Shall we stop?"

Micky's dead red lips snapped as he replied, "Yes. Put me to bed."

Ecco lifted him. The stuffed legs of the dummy flapped lifelessly as the man laid him on the divan, and covered him with a blanket. He pressed a spring. *Snap!*—the eyes closed. Ecco drew a deep breath and wiped sweat from his forehead.

"Curious bedfellow," I said.

"Yes," said Ecco. "But . . . please——" And he looked at Micky, frowned at me, and laid a finger to his lips. "*Ssh!*" he whispered.

"How about some coffee?" I suggested.

He nodded. "Yes: my throat is very dry," he said. I beckoned. That disgusting stuffed dummy seemed to charge the atmosphere with tension. He followed me on tip-toe, and closed his door silently. As I boiled water on my gas-ring, I watched him. From time to time he hunched his shoulders, raised his eyebrows, and listened. Then, after a few minutes of silence, he said, suddenly, "You think I'm mad."

"No," I said, "not at all; only you seem remarkably devoted to that dummy of yours."

"I hate him," said Ecco, and listened again.

"Then why don't you burn the thing?"

"For God's sake!" cried Ecco, and clasped a hand over my mouth. I was uneasy—it was the presence of this terribly nervous little man that made me so. We drank our coffee, while I tried to make conversation.

"You must be an extraordinarily fine ventriloquist," I said.

"Me? No, not very, My father, yes. He was great. You've heard of Professor Vox? Yes, well he was my father."

"Was he, indeed?"

"He taught me all I know; and even now . . . I mean . . . without him, you understand—nothing! He was a genius. Me, I could never control the nerves of my face and throat. So you see, I was a great disappointment to him. He . . . well, you know; he could eat a beefsteak, while Micky, sitting at the same table, sang *Je crois entendre encore*. That was genius. He used to make me practise, day in and day out—*Bee, Eff, Em, En, Pee, Vee, Doubleyou*, without moving the lips. But I was no good. I couldn't do it. I simply couldn't. He used to give me hell. When I was a child, yes, my mother used to protect me a little. But afterwards! Bruises—I was black with them. He was a terrible man. Everybody was afraid of him. You're too young to remember: he looked like —well, look."

Ecco took a wallet out and extracted a photograph. It was brown and faded, but the features of the face were still vivid. Vox had a bad face; strong but evil—fat, swarthy, bearded and forbidding. His huge lips were pressed firmly together under a heavy black moustache, which grew right up to the sides of a massive flat nose. He had immense eyebrows, which ran together in the middle; and great, round, glittering eyes.

"You can't get the impression," said Ecco, "but when he came on to the stage in a black coat lined with red silk, he looked just like the devil. He took Micky with him wherever he went—they used to talk in public. But he was a great ventriloquist—the greatest ever. He used to say, 'I'll make a ventriloquist of you if it's the last thing I ever do.' I had to go with him wherever he went, all over the world; and stand in the wings, and watch him; and go home with him at night and practise again—*Bee, Eff, Em, En, Pee, Vee, Doubleyou*—over and over again, sometimes till dawn. You'll think I'm crazy."

"Why should I?"

"One night I . . . there was an accident."

"Well. . . . This went on and on, until—*ssh*—did you hear something?"

"No, there was nothing. Go on."

"One night I . . . I mean, there was an accident. I—he fell down the lift-shaft in the Hotel Dordogne, in Marseilles. Somebody left the gate open. He was killed." Ecco wiped sweat from his face. "And that night I slept well, for the first time in my life. I was twenty years old then. I went to sleep, and slept well. And then I had a horrible dream. He was back again, see? Only not he, in the flesh, but only his voice. And he was saying, 'Get up, get up, get up and try again . . . get up I say—I'll make a ventriloquist of you if it's the last thing I ever do. Wake up.'

"I woke up. You will think I'm mad.

"I swear. I still heard the voice, and it was coming from. . . ."

Ecco paused and gulped. I said, "Micky?" He nodded. There was a pause; then I said, "Well?"

"That's about all," he said. "It was coming from Micky. It has been going on ever since, day and night. He won't let me alone. It isn't I who makes Micky talk. Micky makes me talk. He makes me practise still . . . day and night I daren't leave him. He might tell the . . . he might . . . oh, God; anyway, I can't leave him . . . I can't."

I thought: *This poor man is undoubtedly mad. He has got the habit of talking to himself, and he thinks——*

At that moment I heard a voice; a little, thin, querulous, mocking voice, which seemed to come from Ecco's room. It said:

"Ecco!"

Ecco leapt up, gibbering with fright. "There!" he said. "There he is again. I must go. I'm not mad; not really mad. I must——"

He ran out. I heard his door open and close. Then there came again the sound of conversation, and once I thought I heard Ecco's voice, shaking with sobs, saying, *"Bee, Eff, Em, En, Pee, Vee, Doubleyou. . . ."*

He is crazy, I thought; *yes, the man must be crazy. . . . And before he was throwing his voice . . . calling himself. . . .*

But it took me two hours to convince myself of that; and I left the light burning all that night, and I swear to you that I have never been more glad to see the dawn.

Old Warrior

DAVID WALKER

NEIL'S father sat in one armchair, his mother in another, Neil in the third with his legs under him. The log fire was burning big, and the wet hill air blew in through open windows. The tree frogs were loud outside. Everything was near and sharp and loud. Going away to school tomorrow.

Then the door creaked. Toby ambled straight over to the fireplace, flopped as usual like a ton of bricks, let the bone roll on to the rug, and lay, nose against it. He grunted with satisfaction and drooled a bit at the ripe smell of his prize. It was a high old bone all right.

Mrs. Mackenzie had been reading, lost deep in her book. But she sniffed; then erupted with volcanic indignation, "On my best Bokhara rug! Oh, that stinking animal!"

"He's not stinking! You're st——"

"That'll do," said Father. "Remove the offending object."

Neil removed it between finger and thumb. It was true about Toby being smelly nowadays, but this time it was the bone and not him—both reasons for being angry at Mum.

He took the thing out to the edge of the lawn, got a firmer

grip, threw it as far as he could, wiped his hand on the grass, and felt a bit better.

Inside, Major Mackenzie was saying, "It's a sensitive subject, Celia. Don't you realize the dog means more to him at this moment than you or I or——"

She sighed. "I know, darling. Have you spoken to him?"

"I will."

Toby was asleep when Neil came back. Toby was eleven. Toby's father had been a bulldog, his mother a bull terrier. The result was seventy pounds of muscled ugliness. When he walked through Darjeeling with Neil, ignoring grown-ups but wishing to greet children, he caused alarm among strangers. "He only wants to say hullo," Neil often had to explain.

Toby was a famous dog, and a famous fighter when provoked. There was the mastiff which attacked every smaller dog it met. It made a mistake about Toby. Neither beating, nor pepper, nor water, nor anything else would make him let go of that mastiff's throat. Fortunately, there were dozens of witnesses to say he hadn't started it. Now he was old, dim-sighted, deaf, smelly, and stiff from battle. Age arrives early in India.

Neil thought of everything as he came in and saw his dog asleep. Toby was making dream yelps, which was a funny thing about him because in real life he hunted mute.

"I'm sorry, Neil," said his mother. "I didn't mean to say that. He's the best dog in the Himalayas. . . . Aren't you, Toby?" But Toby did not hear.

Neil grunted.

"What are you going to do this afternoon?" asked his father.

"I thought I might go for a walk." Toby was deaf to everything except walks. He woke up.

"Come to the office for a minute, boy."

Neil followed his father, wondering what it would be this time, and Toby followed Neil. Father shut the door. He went to the window and stared out. "Going to be more rain," he

muttered. "This blasted monsoon will never end." Silence.
He turned round. "Neil, I want to talk to you about Toby."

Neil looked at the tiger skins and at the snow leopard
which was his father's rarest trophy. He knew what was
coming. It was what Mr. Chatterjee had said last week at the
animal hospital. He looked at the Gurkha kukris on the wall.
He looked up.

"Yes, Father?"

". . . It's your decision, Neil. Think about it and tell me
before you leave tomorrow."

"Why can't they just be like old people?"

Jim Mackenzie turned again to the window. "I remember
asking my father that once—your grandfather—and he said,
because they can't tell us about their aches and pains. One
reason, Neil, and a good one. Let me know what you decide."

"Yes, Father." Neil did not look at Toby.

"Do you want to take the .256 this afternoon in case you
see a karkar?"

"Oh gosh, yes!" Neil's own .22 was too small for deer.

"Here you are." His father gave him the Mannlicher
carbine from the gun rack, and half a dozen soft-nosed shells.
"No firing at dangerous game; not that you'll see any."

"O.K. Thanks awfully." He slung the rifle. It felt good.

Neil put on his jungle boots, slung the old fieldglasses
round his neck, strapped the rolled ground-sheet round his
middle, and shouted good-bye to Mum.

She came to the door. "Well," she said, being silly, "if it
isn't Jim Corbett himself. What are you hunting today,
colonel?"

"I'm going after a barking deer," Neil said, ignoring that
crack about Jim Corbett, the tiger hunter. But his mother's
face changed. It never stayed the same for long, and now he
saw it change to wanting to come with him. He might have
offered to take her, because she was what Father called "a
good jungle woman", but he didn't. "See you later," he said.

"Be back by six, darling. And please stick to the paths. I
heard that panther twice last night." She made a harsh

"Do you want to take the ·256—you might see a karkar?"

pantherish rasp exactly right, and laughed, and looked rather sad again. "The house is going to be so quiet after tomorrow."

He escaped. Toby gave one deep woof, and gambolled about like his old bouncing self, or his young self, as he always did for a minute at the beginning of a walk. Then he sobered down to a double limp from the mastiff wound on his right shoulder and a panther swipe on his left quarter.

I wonder if Sher Bahadur could come? Neil thought. So he went by the weighing shed. Sher Bahadur had been his father's orderly in the Gurkhas. He was a square, short man, just about as broad as he was long. He sprang to his feet and quivered into a superb salute. "General Sahib!" It was an ancient joke and still funny.

"Oh, great brave tiger Sher Bahadur, and chopper of many heads by night," said Neil in Nepalese, "can you come hunting?"

"Not this baby, Nee-ul," said Sher Bahadur. He had picked up that one in the Italian campaign and was proud of it, almost his entire spoken English vocabulary, although he could understand a bit. "There is a dangerous Major Mackenzie in these hills who orders that I weigh tea this afternoon."

Toby had come over to say hullo. He ignored non-family adults, but Sher Bahadur was a friend of many walks. He patted Toby once on the head. "Old Warrior."

Neil told him what his father had said. He couldn't have talked about it to anybody else. "I have to decide."

"You are a man, Nee-ul, and you will decide."

"Come on, Toby." He wasn't a man, and he didn't want to decide.

They left the buildings and followed a path through trees. The hillside was bursting green with growth. You could hear a seeping trickle of water everywhere under the cicadas trilling "rain" more loudly now than ever. Three months' rain, a hundred inches, and more to come before the monsoon rolled back in October. The mist had thinned to wisps of cloud climbing out of the valleys. Far away south and six thousand feet down, there was sunshine on the plains, a different, sticky world.

Neil and Toby came to terraced slopes where tea bushes were dark green and the hillwomen were picking green tips and chattering nineteen to the dozen while their fingers flew at the work. He quickened pace because lately they seemed to stare and giggle and make remarks.

Somebody did now. "Aaaiii!" she called. "See the beautiful boy sahib!" Which was quite embarrassing, and meant for his ears. They knew he understood the hill tongue as well as they did. Cackles of laughter.

"So many fat, lazy old cows mooing!" he said loudly. It was a great success.

He reached the end of the tea garden. The country beyond was too steep for cultivation. The path swung into a gully where the stream gathered, and out round the next shoulder.

"School in England,"
thought Neil, "will be a
change from all this."

Neil stopped to look back at the red-roofed house and
buildings. You never thought much about home until there
was only a week to go. Then it was the last day suddenly.
And after Christmas you were going to school in England.

"Good boy, Toby," he said. "We'll have a rest in a
minute." Toby wagged his tail. He was wheezing. There were
no level walks, but this was the easiest one. They crossed
the shoulder.

Neil unrolled the ground-sheet. It was Father's, from the

93

war, too noisy a thing for stalking, but waterproof and very good for wearing when you sat still because of the blotched brown and green camouflage.

He did not wear it now, but sat on one half and put Toby on the other. The hillside dropped off almost vertically for a few hundred feet; farther down there were trees again, and ferns among the rocks, and lush green grass. Somewhere out beyond all that, two hillmen were having an across-the-valley conversation, voices pitched high; they might be five miles from here. But the sounds of home, which was only just round the corner, were cut off completely.

Neil watched. There were many tints of green, brown, grey; some of the wet rocks were black. Nothing was the colour he wanted—the russet red of a karkar, the barking deer that lurked so daintily in shaded places. He would have had a much better chance lower down, but this was Toby's walk, and Toby was not able. Toby snoozed.

Neil spied through the glasses for a while, searching clump by clump methodically, but nothing doing. "Monkeys," he said, putting his hand on the dog's square head. Toby did not have the cramped, shallow skull of a modern bull terrier. He had a head on him, ugly though it was. At the word "monkeys" he opened his right eye in the centre of its black patch, and rumbled. Toby had it in for monkeys, particularly the big grey langur males, who had it in for him. These now were langurs, too far away for the dog to see. They swung through trees and over the ridge. After that, a party of minivets flashed across, the males bright scarlet, the females yellow. Neil had a good feeling of birds and beasts and him and Toby. It was time to go on.

They came to a sandy ravine. There were pug marks and the tracks of lesser game.

"Toby!" he said loudly. "Want to go on? You old fool, Toby." Calling him an old fool was the way to make Toby smile. He did now; a hideous, disreputable leer before he rolled on ahead. The path swung into the next cascading stream. wound out to the next spur or shoulder: the teeth of a giant lumberman's saw—it was that kind of hill country.

Toby led. He could decide for himself how far he wanted to walk. That, anyway, could be Toby's decision. They went through loud water, and now were following the shoulder. The air was damp and thin and cool. Clouds were piling in, grey again. The distant plains were not visible.

Toby's head had been low, but suddenly it came up; the skin wrinkled on his shoulders; he sniffed. Then he gave a whimper, quite an insignificant noise. He made it only when he caught a hateful scent—monkey or panther or bear or pig.

"Steady, boy," said Neil, putting him on the leash. Nowadays he ran into things and hurt himself.

The dog pulled hard. He was still tremendously strong. I wonder if I should turn back? thought Neil. Then he thought, perhaps this is our last time, and it'll only be some old monkey scent; he'll quieten down in a minute. But he unslung the carbine and held it in his right hand.

Toby did not quieten down. The hackles bristled dark all along his back, and he took charge, blundering along the path. It narrowed from three feet to two feet to one foot, and there was the point of the shoulder now.

"Stop, Toby!" Toby heard, and eased a little.

Neil knew this place. You crossed the shoulder, and then for twenty yards or so, as you swung in again, you were not on a path, but on a ledge below a vertical cliff, above steep scree. They would stop there to have a last spy for karkar and then turn home. Toby whimpered again, but was well in hand as they reached the apex of the spur. They turned.

It was not old monkey scent. At the far end of the ledge stood a panther.

A great many things flashed across Neil's mind in that second. Too narrow for the brute to turn. Too steep for it to climb. Could come on. Might break down the scree. Himself with leash in one hand, carbine in the other. Had to hold Toby. Horrible, slender, wicked panther. . . .

He was hauling his hardest on Toby when the panther crouched, tail switching, coiled to——

95

The hill panther had hunted and killed many dogs, but never a dog like this.

Toby attacked, tearing the leash from Neil's fingers. As Neil stumbled forward, he watched his dog hurl himself along the ledge, bunched bone and muscle, silent but for scrabbling claws.

The hill panther had hunted and killed many dogs for its favourite meat. But it had never seen a dog like this, a dingy-white monstrosity with one black eye, a braver fighter than it was itself. The panther charged also—a hundred and forty pounds against seventy. The cat snarling, the dog mute. They met in a thudding fury of fangs and claws; then the two twisting, contrasted bodies rolled over the edge and down the scree.

Neil watched them go—writhing, tangled, the dog at the panther's throat—heads over tails in a showering rattle of loose stones. He dared not fire. But a moment later he realized that he should have risked the shot, because there could be only one end to this. However brave Toby was, however firm his throat-hold, the panther would break him.

But Neil was too late. He saw it happen before they reached the bottom of the scree. The pale body swung out and away from the tawny body, and the cat had the space it needed. Forepaw smacked hindquarters. It was a vicious stroke, nearly too fast to see. Toby's jaw-grip was loosening already as they tumbled out of sight into green undergrowth.

Silence. Only the drip-drip of water and the eternal tree frogs. No movement at all below. Neil ran down the moving scree, stumbled, recovered, slithered to the bottom. He shouted. It was a cracked imitation of a shout to scare the panther. Then he was into bushes, ferns, grass, thorns, carbine at his waist, forcing a passage down. Now a rustling clump of bamboo, but no white Toby, no deadly panther.

My fault, he thought. All my fault. His coat was torn, his face scratched, his body soaked. He went on. Was that——?

No, it was not the crouching leopard. It was a dappled rock. And that flicker of white was not old Toby. It was a paradise flycatcher, flitting away with streamer tails.

Then he saw Toby. His dog lay at the edge of the stream. Toby was alive with a broken back and many wounds. He was only just alive, but he knew Neil's hand. He opened both eyes.

"Oh, Toby." It could not be long.

Toby growled. "I smell you, enemy," he growled. There was another noise above the tiny splashing of the stream. It came from higher up. It was the panther swaying long grass, a bold hill panther with a sore throat, wanting its kill.

Neil held the rifle in his shoulder. He was not afraid, although his heart thumped fast. Father had said, "Never take on a panther in closed country. Never!" And this was an angry panther.

There was movement in the grass again from right to left. It might come straight or it might cross that open patch of rock to complete the circle. They generally circled first, didn't they? Neil had not shot a panther, but he had read every big-game book he could find.

The panther did not come straight. It crossed the ten yards of rock in two galloping strides.

Neil fired, saw the hindquarters slew slightly, heard it grunt. Then it was out of sight behind that clump of bamboo. He had hit it, he thought, but he knew the shot was too far back, probably a flesh wound. The brute had not even stumbled.

He looked down.

"Poor Toby," he said. "Poor boy. I'm sorry, Toby."

Neil did not have time to think about Toby's death, for the panther growled from the bamboos. And it was not thinking but feeling that said, You're not going to eat my dog. You killed him and I'm going to kill you.

But then Neil did think; he thought fast. Could he put Toby's body on his back and climb the other side of the gully where it was open ground for a shot? No, too heavy and too steep. A tree? Yes, there was a tree beside him, gnarled and small, but with a fork low down. Climb it and leave Toby where he was? But if you missed, the panther would take the dog and be gone in a flash.

Neil had made his plan. He began to carry out the plan now without ever taking his eyes off those bamboos where the panther growled again. He loosed the belt which held his ground-sheet, undid the cords, unrolled it on the steep ground, spread it wide, hauled the body, still limp, on to the centre. Then his heart jumped because the bamboo fronds were moving. But it was only the monsoon deluge beginning again, pattering on his ground-sheet, on leaves overhead, drowning lesser noises.

All this Neil had done with one hand. Now he laid down the .256, gathered the corners of the ground-sheet, tied them

98

with the cord, making a sack for old Toby. Would it come now? If it has any sense it'll come now, he thought in a standing-outside-himself sort of way.

But the panther did not come. Now Neil had the belt fixed, too, and buckled round his neck. He picked up the rifle, staggered to his feet, and tried to clamber into that fork. He tried desperately in the loud rain, but he was not strong enough.

Down again, belt over his head. What a clever idea about the ground-sheet sack, and what a waste of time. He took seventy pounds dead weight in his arms and managed to raise it to the fork. Then he climbed above, wedged himself, heaved, steadied it again.

Bit by bit, Neil dragged his own body and Toby's body higher. It was an easy tree to climb, the kind of tree you pretty well ran up when you heard game moving and wanted to spy. But it was not easy now.

He rested. Legs, arms, stomach, lungs all ached, and the lights of exhaustion flashed. His hand, grasping at a green, slimy bough, trembled like some old man's. The rain fell in a drenching, solid wall of noise. But gradually his breathing slowed, the shakes and aches lessened, heat dwindled into the middle of his body. No panther.

He was ten or twelve feet up the tree. The camouflaged sack that was Toby, or had been Toby, hung from a branch stump just below him. It was secure. Neil was secure enough himself—that is, he was wedged so as not to fall out. But he knew that he could be pulled out. The panther could get at him with a jump or it could get at him by climbing. I should just have slipped away, he thought. What difference would it make, when Toby was dead already? Slipped away? No, sneaked away after letting him be killed for me. I never even did anything. I just let it happen.

Neil watched the clump of bamboo. It was about on a level with his own head. No movement at all. Was the panther still there? Had it moved down left to take him from behind? Had it gone altogether? Behind! Yes, that was what the shivers in his spine said. He whipped his head round. No panther.

And now the light was fading, and every dancing leaf or blade could be dancing from rain or from a long slinking body. That sound! But there was no sound anywhere except rain.

Neil began to shiver again—this time from cold, and because he was afraid. As he shifted position, the panther growled. It was in the same place still. It was waiting for the dusk that was not far off.

Not knowing had been the bad thing. He stopped being afraid. He had the sights aligned just this side and below, finger on the trigger. If only it would show itself. If he could just get a glimpse of where the head was.

But the panther did not move. He knew that when the time came for it to move, it would not stroll in a lord-of-the-jungle way as a tiger would stroll. It was a panther, and it had been touched up by a bull terrier at the throat and by a bullet somewhere far back. That growl had said, "I'm going to get you." It would kill for its dog meat.

Neil should have been feeling sad about Toby, but suddenly he was rather happy in a calm, murderous kind of way. He had never felt like that before. You're wrong, you stinking panther. I'm the one who's going to get you.

It was much darker. He looked at his watch. Six-twenty. "Be back by six, darling," she had said, and it was a grey, wet, early night, and she would be in an awful stew already, particularly if they'd heard the shot. They might not have.

"Don't imagine horrors, my love," Father would be telling her. He treated her as a joke when she got fussed, which was quite clever of him, although she was much cleverer than he was. What's Father going to say when I get home? If I get . . .

Neil watched. He took his left hand off for a moment to wipe the rain out of his eyes. He heard an owl scream along the hill, and jackals howling far down in the deep valley. Otherwise, rain. He was very cold. He wondered what would happen if the panther did not come? Was that voices?

Just then lights appeared. They came round the shoulder where he and Toby had met the panther, and men were shouting. They were quite close.

"Neil!" in Father's loud bellow, and "Nee-ul!" from Sher Bahadur.

Neil did not answer. He was watching the bamboos. They were indistinct. He could not make out one slim shoot from another, but something was happening there.

"Neil!"

"Nee-ul!"

"Shut up," he said under his breath as the panther launched itself, a dark, long shadow of speed and hate. His bullet flame stabbed. Reload. Hit? Panther below, not dead, very much alive. Neil swung round, straining himself to get the barrel down. He saw it crouched there, head back, snarling.

Then it climbed, paws on either side of the trunk, clawing. Like a house cat climbing from a dog, he thought in the galloping moment. But this was climbing to, not from. He fired. It came on. Eyes vertical slits. Reloaded. Stink of breath was hitting him as he fired yet again into the panther's face. It did not climb the last two feet. It stayed where it was. Then the devilish energy slackened. Neil saw that happen. He saw his panther slide down, claws rasping, strike the first fork, and roll back dead.

"Neil!"

He could hear them on the scree. He should answer now, but coldness and weakness were everywhere, and deep.

Father with his big rifle, Sher Bahadur with the five-celled torch. Men carrying lanterns. The light shone on the dead panther, then up to the ground-sheet sack, then blinded Neil.

"What the hell's all this?" Father did not sound pleased or relieved. He sounded red-hot angry, and when Father was angry, which hardly ever happened, then the whole shooting match exploded. "Didn't I tell you——"

"Major Sahib!" Sher Bahadur said. "See!" The beam was on Toby's shroud dangling from its branch.

"What happened?"

Neil told it. He could not say much. He was just realizing what he had done to Toby. "The panther broke his back, and it was all my fault, and I——"

"Well, I'll be darned," Jim Mackenzie muttered at the end. "Help the boy down, Sher Bahadur."

Neil got down all right, but as soon as he reached the ground something went wrong. He couldn't help it. He just couldn't.

"Steady now, old fellow," Father said after a while. Tears made him feel awkward.

"A man who is a man may weep," said Sher Bahadur.

But Neil stopped crying.

"Drink this, Neil." He drank the burning stuff from a flask, and choked. The heat went through him. The coolies cut a pole to carry the panther.

"Take the rifles, Sher Bahadur. I'll carry old Toby."

Which his father did, and they climbed past bamboos sounding in the rain and up sliding scree, and here was the ledge where Toby had killed himself for you, and on towards home.

Father stopped in the darkness. "Are you all right, Neil?"

"Yes." Neil was warmer again, but he was not all right.

Jim Mackenzie did not always understand his moody, hot-headed son; he understood now. "Sher Bahadur," he said in Nepalese. "Oh, brother! Did Toby die well?"

"As one brave soldier for another," said Sher Bahadur. "And few old warriors may die thus."

Moonrise

ELLESTON TREVOR

I

THE attack lasted two days more; the rain three. The
bridge had gone down before the rearguard armour
was across; but the infantry was already fighting its way
into the bridgehead on the east bank of the river, and held
its positions. The second night had been the worst; men had
died in it as yet uncountably.

Of "C" Squadron, ten tanks were still on their tracks,
but only four were fit to fight on. Three were missing. No
one had seen them.

One British fighting-tank, still on the missing list, was
ploughing slowly through the rain, driving almost blind
with its wireless broken down. It had been moving for an
hour, turning laboriously at tangents to the main direction,
finding its way again and then losing it, bogging in the mud
and struggling clear, with its commander and crew fighting
nothing more deadly than exhaustion. Minute by minute it
was beating them down, implacable and overwhelming. This
tank was Top Dog.

The co-driver, Soaper, was asleep in the forward compartment, lolling with a doll's inertia against the headplates.

The driver, Luff, had stopped talking to him, seeing he was asleep, but felt no loss of companionship or support. Soaper was no help to anyone, awake or asleep; he was a dead weight in the tank, a bit of ballast. Luff stared through the driving-slit at the rain, at the lift and fall of the ground and the ghosts of trees that swayed past him, coming out of the silence and losing their way, wandering back as the tank turned again, trying to find the river. Then the engine stopped. Luff tried to re-start it.

"'Ave a look," said Pike briefly. Luff had a look at the engine.

"Timing-gear stripped."

Corporal Pike said after a moment, "That's our lot, then."

"Well, we can't move. It's a replacement job."

Pike nodded. Top Dog stood within fifty yards of a wood, facing east.

There was good cover there, but they couldn't reach it. Behind him a crack of the sky was lightening, even as late as this.

Under the turret Lance-Corporal Munro was crouched on the occasional seat, head going down, jerking up, nodding again, lifting. His eyes came open as Pike said:

"Well, we got trouble, an' that's that."

The gunner, Weston, leaned against the breech, one fond arm draped over it. The metal was cold. The gun had not fired for three hours; the drops of rain fell without sound, without their *tiss—tiss—tiss* on the warm metal. He did not like a cold gun. He said to the corporal:

"Is that all we got? Trouble?"

"We're lost," said Pike.

"No, honest?"

Pike sank down on to his little platform, dangling his legs, looking at Munro in the gloom. "Can't you get that wireless working, Gutsy?"

"Valves are duff." Munro's head had jerked up again; his answer was automatic; he had known the question would come, as soon as they stopped.

104

"Ain't we got no spares?"

"I've used three. Others're bust."

"Well this is a turn-up, this is. We don't know where we are, we got no engine, an' no wireless."

Munro said : "Then for cripes' sake let's have a fag."

Weston gave him one. "You want a fag, Luffy?"

"Nope. Fresh air's what I want."

"Go an' get it then, boy."

Luff looked at the pale blur that was the corporal's face. "Okay, Corp?"

"Okay. Go careful, though."

They heard their driver drop to the grass. There was no mud here, for they were on a gentle slope that ran down to the east bank of the river, and nothing had passed this way to churn up the ground. Feeling the soft grass springy under his feet, Luff pulled his boots off, and his socks, and walked slowly round the tank, watching the trees, the gun-fire, the widening crack of light in the west sky. He wanted to call out to the others, about how good his feet felt, cool on the soft wet grass. It was marvellous, he thought, how easy it was to find ecstasy in the midst of its opposite. You take your boots off, and suddenly feel like this, floating about with your heart free, just because of a bit of wet grass; it was marvellous.

A close salvo from two mortars punched the wind and the bombs burst short, blossoming in the gloom. He turned his head. They had fired from the east; the bombs had burst in the west; he stood half-way along their trajectory, some quarter-mile from its path.

The answer came from a tank-gun, west to east. He waited, worried, turning to catch the location of small-arms fire as a patrol opened up and was engaged. The smell was in the breeze, driving away the last hope of pretending that the war had passed beyond. . . .

He swung round as a big gun banged, firing west from a tree-belt a mile down the slope. Firing west, from west of where he stood. He exclaimed at that.

"Stop shoutin' the odds. . . . We're on enemy territory. I don't 'ave to tell you more than that, do I?"

Someone was moving about, near him.

"Luffy? See that, did you?" It was Weston.

When he came up, Luff said, "I told you, we're not safe here."

"We're right among the Jerries, eh?"

"Right there, mate. Does Alf know?"

"He'll have heard that gun. We better get back."

"Pssst!"

They looked up. Corporal Pike was between them and the tank. "Stop shoutin' the ruddy odds! We're up be'ind Jerry!"

They went towards him in the grey light. Above them the cap of cloud that had covered the sky for three days was drawing east, and the twilight was sharpening. Pike said softly, "Keep near the tank, ready to 'op in. You know where we are, eh?"

"Up a creek," said Luff.

Pike creased his face up. "Now listen. You 'ear anything,

you report to me, see? Don't matter what it is—guns or shoutin' or transport, you come an' tell me. We got to get our bearin's, quick."

Munro was leaning with his back to the tank, smoking. He said, "We'll have to get out of here, Alf."

"Where to? It's better to stop 'ere with Top Dog than go walkin' straight into Jerry."

"Well, I'm willin' to take a chance."

Luff said, "Don't talk daft, Gutsy. At least we've got three guns an' some armour plate here. Corp's right."

"I'm not only right," said Pike reasonably, "I'm the geezer that gives the orders, too." He looked at Weston. "George, how's the ammo?"

"Five rounds in the gun, an' two Besa belts. An' a few grenades."

"They won't get us far."

"They'll have to get us as far as we've got to go."

Pike turned as Soaper came over the side and pitched on to the grass. "What's on, then, Corp?"

"We're on enemy territory. I don't 'ave to tell you more'n that, do I?"

Soaper got up slowly, staring at the corporal. *"Enemy territ'ry?"*

"That's it."

"Oh God. Oh God." He said it softly.

"'E won't 'elp, neither. 'E's got quite enough on 'is 'ands. . . . See what you can find in the way of camouflage nettin', kid, back on the racks. An' then start 'angin' it out. All right?"

"But we can't stay here. We can't stay, Corp." It was embarrassing to hear the thin tone of fright in his voice.

"You just get the scrim, an' put it up." He turned away before Soaper could say anything. "Munro, you an' Luff start diggin', under the rear, good and deep. And watch out you don't hit any metal with the spades. It's goner be a nice peaceful night, see?"

They moved, and Soaper moved with them, calmed by

their easy obedience. Standing very close to Weston, the corporal said:

"Listen, George. I don't think much of our chances 'ere, but we got to stay. If Jerry comes, we fight it out. There's not much ammo, but it'll 'ave to do."

"What's going to happen in the morning, Alf?"

"For one thing, we shall 'ave 'ad some sleep. We need it bad. And if we get a bit o' luck we can look after Top Dog till our lot take this area. I'm not 'andin' a good tank to ruddy Jerry for the sake of a crocked engine. Not Top Dog, any'ow. Now go an' check the guns, mate. We may want 'em."

Weston left him, climbing into the turret, careful with his boots. He didn't have to check the guns. They were ready. Outside, Soaper was dragging some scrim over the gun barrel; he sounded like a mouse trying to get in through the wainscoting. And there was the soft thud of spades behind the tank, reminding him of the burial parties on the way from the coast to here. This could be another by the morning.

II

The moon grew bright as it rose to clear atmosphere. Its light was sharp on the ground; it shone against the leaves here and washed over the grass. In its milky glow the wink of gunfire on the dark earth was feeble and red-eyed.

The corporal no longer felt tired. His wits were far from alert, but the fatigue had lifted, soothed away by the knowledge that his tank was in good harbour and the crew sleeping.

Leaves moved below him. He looked down. For a moment he resented the invasion of his solitude.

"Alf?"

"Up 'ere."

It was Luff. His face was pink in the moonlight, above the stubble of his chin.

"What you doin' up 'ere?"

"Relievin' guard."

"I don't want no relievin'."

"You been up 'ere a good two hours, y'know."

Pike turned Luff's wrist and looked at his watch.

"So I 'ave. Why the 'ell can't you sleep then?"

"Well, *you* needn't talk!"

Luff dropped to the grass, and took a step, and heard the engine. He stopped, listening. It was a tank engine. The low murmur of it rose and died on the wind, but each time it rose it had loudened.

"Alf!"

"Don't worry. I'll watch it."

In the rhythm of the engine there were throttle variations, so that Pike knew it was a tank on the move.

"Alf, what nationality's that ruddy thing?"

"It's comin' from the west, ain't it?"

"But it could be one of ours. Lost, or something."

"Yeh. Or it might be a bus for Balham."

Pike thought he saw the tops of saplings move at the edge of the wood; but it might be the wind or his nerves. Through the gap in the leaves he could see the hill brow. It would come over the horizon, over the brow there. He said:

"Go and wake the boys."

Luff went down. "Listen, George. Jerry's here. Wake up. Gutsy, get up quick!"

Weston leaned on Luff, arms slack. Luff gave him a light punch in the chest.

"Jerry's here. Jerry. German."

"Where?" He swung about, one arm flying. His hand hit the gun and he yelped.

"Gutsy. The Germans are here."

Weston said clearly, "Where, then? Where?"

"Listen. That's a tank. Panzer."

"Where's Alf?"

"Up top. Gutsy—*get up!*"

He stooped again, put his arms round Munro's waist, and heaved. Munro swung a fist. "Ger off!"

"It's a self-propelled gun—havin' a look this side of

"Jerry's here. Jerry."

The leaves rustled as Corporal Pike came down, crouching into the armour. Munro was up now, swaying, holding his face. They were all on their feet and awake.

Pike said, "George, up at the gun. Luffy, forward Besa." Munro swayed towards him.

"Where's Jerry?"

"Comin'. Get up there, quick. An' keep it quiet."

For a few seconds no one moved. Pike and Luff were listening, wanting to know if the tank were nearer. Weston wanted to get his bearings on its sound. Munro, for the first time, heard it. Then they all moved. The throb of the engine was heavier by the time they were inside Top Dog, but there was nothing in sight as Pike stood on the top armour with the moon behind him.

the hill. Don't make a noise . . . we're a Christmas tree!"

He called down : "Gutsy, we got smoke bombs?"

"I got 'em," Munro said.

He heard Munro shifting about in the darkness below. His eyes were watering as he stared at the thin line of the hill brow. He wanted badly to see the tank. Once he could see it he'd be all right. The noise alone was a mounting strain.

"Alf, can you see it?"

"No."

"Where the 'ell's it got to, then?"

"Shuddup."

The throb was so loud now that Pike cursed it and moved round on the armour plate, pulling at the leaves and making new gaps. Through one of them he saw the tank come over the brow, well to the left. He was startled by its dark shape.

111

In the same moment the throb died away to a murmur as the engine idled. He said, "It's a self-propelled gun."

Munro came up beside him.

"Stopped, has 'e?"

"Havin' a look this side of the hill." He could see moonlight flashing across a pair of field-glasses and the shape of the commander, a dark stump above the gun.

He spoke a little more loudly so that Luff could also hear. "Listen. 'E's two 'undred yards, ten o'clock. We can't move, an' we can't swing the turret."

"How can we fire, then?"

"We can't, that's what I'm telling you. Not till we can move, an' that'll be when they've seen us. We jus' got to sit 'ere, see? An' if anyone drops anythin' on metal, they'll hear, an' we're goners. Don't forget that."

He straightened up slowly, turning his body to face the ten o'clock direction before he stood upright. The self-propelled gun had not moved. Munro murmured, "He's takin' a ruddy good look."

"Don't make a noise. We're a Christmas tree."

Beyond the S.P. gun the sky flickered to a distant barrage, silhouetting it. Pike was quivering with frustration. If Top Dog were standing head-on to that Jerry, they could have blown it apart with one six-pounder before he knew they were there. He was a perfect target, high on the hill, silhouetted against the light sky, motionless. But they could not move the turret. They were a Christmas tree.

Munro said, "Better if we swing the gun on 'em before they can do anythin'."

"Don't be daft. Once we move, they shoot, an' that's an eighty-eight. We got to keep our 'air on."

Munro touched his arm as the S.P. began to move. It lumbered down from the brow of the hill, and stopped again. Now there was silence.

"He's switched off, Alf."

"Yeh."

They could hear the voice of the commander speaking into his wireless. Pike crouched, and put his head over the dark hole of the turret, speaking in a forced whisper. "George, 'e's got 'is engine off. We got to keep dead quiet. Tell Luffy."

Munro said, "The commander's got out. Havin' a walk round." Another man dropped. "An' there's the gunner or the wireless-op."

"Driver to come."

The German crew were out. There were four. They were lighting cigarettes. The commander was lifting field-glasses again, looking this way, straight at Top Dog. Very quietly Munro said into Pike's ear: "If we could get 'em while they're all out. . . ."

"It's no go, boy."

They did not move. Their faces must not catch the moonlight. The commander was studying them. The moonlight was on his glasses, glinting. He held them steadily. Pike began to sweat.

One of the Germans laughed, walking a few paces on the soft grass, enjoying himself; his cigarette-end traced a winking pattern as it moved about. The commander had not lowered his glasses. They were trained on Top Dog. There was something he did not like about this isolated clump of brush. Pike wondered vaguely what it could be: a bit of shine on the left track where the metal had polished on a stone, or a badly-placed bush, or his own face among the leaves. It was no good moving now. He listened to Munro's breathing.

The German laughed again, and then walked towards his commander, who turned, as if answering a question. The two of them stood facing this way across the slope, and the commander gave the other man his field-glasses, and he raised them, and Pike waited again.

Below him a sound came, Weston or Luff moving about. Pike couldn't even turn his head. Facing the men with the field-glasses he spoke, using the left corner of his mouth.

*The commander did not lower his glasses—there was something
he did not like about that isolated clump of brush.*

"They're watching us. They're watching us."

The commander took his field-glasses back and raised
them again. Under his breath Munro said something to
himself in rich English.

Pike said in his throat: "Gutsy, there's goin' to be some
action, mate."

"I'm ready."

"Goo' boy."

When the German commander lowered his glasses, he
started to walk in this direction, the other man with him.
"Inside, quick."

Munro went first, sweating with the effort of moving
with no noise in the dark confines. Pike felt for his Bren
gun and brought it up slowly inside the turret rim, clearing
it with the barrel. He was whispering.

"Stand by on the co-axial. George, stand by on the gun."

He raised himself on his platform, finding a gap in the

114

leaves. Using it as a sight, he moved his head until he could see the two Germans. They were walking steadily towards Top Dog. He could hear them talking. He ducked again, whispering.

"Stand by. They're comin'."

He straightened himself again, and had trouble remembering which gap in the leaves he had been looking through.

"Any minute now."

"We're ready, Corp."

He was calmer, at once. They were ready. He wasn't alone. His left eye, closed for sighting, watered. The heat from his body touched his face. His scalp was a cap of needles. They were still walking. Then they stopped and the commander put his glasses up. The range was less than a hundred yards. Through the gap he could see the tops of their bodies and their heads.

The commander jerked the field-glasses down and hit the other man's arm and they turned to run back.

Pike fired. He fired a second burst.

"Gunner traverse left!"

The turret swung with it and the camouflage broke up as the gun came round, shedding the stacked bushes and tearing the leaves aside, exposing him. He crouched, his eyes an inch above the rim. The two Germans lay where they had dropped. Then Pike heard the S.P.'s engine start up.

"Steady...."

The turret slowed.

"On!"

He waited for his gunner to find the target. The turret shifted another degree. He heard Weston's shout: *"On!"*

"Fire!"

The self-propelled gun was moving, turning quickly to face its enemy. The recoil of Top Dog's six-pounder shook more of the camouflage away. The shell hit low and ploughed into the earth so that for a moment the German was hidden by the dark flying wave of it. Munro, loading for his gunner, slammed another shell home.

115

Pike called to Weston. Weston fired.

The first shell from the German's eighty-eight cracked across Top Dog's back with the percussion of a thunderclap and sent Pike dropping for cover. He heard the big shell burst somewhere in the wood.

Weston was shouting.

"It's a smacker!"

Pike took a look. Weston's shell had caught the S.P. square below the barrel at two hundred yards' range, buckling plate and leaving an eddy of smoke. He heard Munro putting another shell in.

Pike waited. It looked like a knock-out.

Weston said: "Finish him, Alf?"

"I think 'e's finished already, boy."

Weston caressed the hot breech, itching to send another one. Pike breathed in the fumes that were rising, relishing them. He said: "Keep on the target." He raised himself a few more inches, using his field-glasses. The S.P. looked derelict. He lowered the glasses. A popple of flame ripped in the moonlight and he dropped, grazing his arm as the machine-gun bullets fluted across the turret. He squeezed his arm, sick with the agony. When he could speak he said: "All right, Weston. *Fire*."

The ears blocked. The fumes rose. The breech came back. The shell-case hit the scoop and dropped. Munro said:

"Alf, you hit?"

"No, Funny-bone." He pressed his feet down, sliding his shoulders against the rim to raise himself. It was the second direct hit. Luff shouted:

"It's a brew-up!"

Flame was fanning out of the S.P. They watched as the petrol went up first, and then the ammunition. The flames settled down to a flicker. The rose light died away across the grass, and the chill of the moon came back.

None of them felt triumphant. It was a big gun, an eighty-eight with a crew of four. Top Dog had knocked it out, and not even been able to move her tracks. That was very good; but they did not feel triumphant. There were two men on the grass, and two human clinkers in the burnt-out shell. That was the way things had gone. . . . In a little while Pike said quietly:

"George."

"M'm?"

"We've got two rounds left, eh?"

"Two, yes."

"An' a bit of ammo for the Besas, and grenades. . . ."

A ripple of ack-ack came from the sky. There was the drone of planes up somewhere. It was a remote and strangely peaceful sound.

III

Pike had worked alone for an hour replacing the ragged camouflage. If he had lain down, he would not have slept; so he had worked. The gun was still traversed left, so that the shape under the massed leaves was a little different; but it still looked more like a crop of bush than a fighting tank.

Once he had sat down, and had said to himself: "Alf, your number's comin' up tonight. You're goin' to die." But he had no deep feelings about this. Once a man was this deep in his war, his sense of drama was blunted. But he hoped that Top Dog would do well tonight. Then he could die happy.

"Alf!"

He looked up. "What?"

"There's a lot of stuff movin'. Tanks, by the sound of it."

"All right, mate. The others still asleep, are they?"

"Yes," Munro said. "I'll go an' get 'em up."

Munro left him. Now he could hear the sound from over the hill. It was tanks, all right.

When Luff came, the corporal told him: "On the forward Besa, mate."

"Okay."

Weston came down with Munro. Pike said to them: "George, you're on the gun. Gutsy, unbolt that smoke-mortar and get it outside. It'll give me a bit o' room in the turret."

Munro got a spanner. "When shall I get the smoke out, then?"

"Soon's I give you the tip. You know where the wind is. But don't let 'em off too early. We want them to come in close." He slapped the breech of the gun. "Two knock-outs is top score. We ring the bell, we get the cigar."

Weston said: "We get the ruddy cigar, all right. Over you go, Gutsy."

The sound of tanks grew enormous, filling the night . . . impossible to do anything but die here.

Munro's boot scraped on the metal rung. He went over the turret rim with the two-inch mortar. Pike dropped a bag of smoke-shells after him. The noise of the tanks was rising. Munro stood outside the leaves, his body facing the direction in which he must send the smoke, his head turned to listen for the tanks and for Pike's order. He was the one who had to put out the smoke-screen. If he did it right, there might be a better chance for all of them. If he made a mistake, it might kill one of them or all of them. The best thing to do, before his knees gave way, was to concentrate on that.

He had never thought he was a coward. It was just this waiting.

The sound grew enormous, filling the night. There was half a squadron coming. He wanted to shin up to the turret and tell the corporal it wasn't going to be possible to do anything but die here, with so many of them coming. He was aware, as the noise rose, that he was saying the corporal's name, "Alf". Every few seconds, saying it aloud. To try to tell him it was no good. But he knew Alf couldn't hear.

"You all know what to do." The corporal stood in the turret, watching the moonlit grass through a hole in the leaves. The Bren gun was in his hands, its barrel resting on the turret rim. His stomach was filling with a slow delight. They would come and pass the crop of bush and saplings, and then hear Top Dog's gun, and feel its shell. It would be a big shock for them, as good as the water-bucket on top of the schoolroom door, as funny as the snatched-away chair.

He shouted again: "We're goin' to knock 'em in the Old Kent Road!"

Below him Weston sat with his gun. Alf had gone mad. Only a madman could have that joy in his voice at a time like this. He envied him.

Forward, away from the others, Luff sat at the Besa machine-gun. His thoughts were technical. In the moon-

light it would be possible to make out the driver's slit if a
tank came within fifty yards. A commander's head would
be an easy target.

Very faintly a voice rose through the din of the tanks.

"Here they come!"

It would be Alf's voice. He looked along the sights of
the Besa, his impatience at explosion-point.

Pike had seen the first three tanks cross the line of the
hill in arrowhead formation and at a fast pace. They would
have heard the exchange of shots between Top Dog and
the self-propelled gun, and would have seen the light of its
fire. That they came at all after this warning was a sign of
their numbers. Three more came over the skyline, clearing
at full throttle and spreading out over the slope, no longer
silhouetted.

The leaders were Mark Fives, carrying long seventy-five-
mm. tank-killing guns. They were already below Top Dog,
running on past the ambush without giving it attention.
The second wave was nearer, with the flank man a few
score yards distant, but again there was no sign that the
ambush was suspected. The leading tank of the second wave
was opened up, its commander visible above the turret rim,
swaying easily to the motion of its passage across the ridges
and mole-hills towards the base of the slope. He saw the
ambush and looked away deceived.

Corporal Pike was bewildered. The camouflage was too
good. They were going past in a bunch, certain of their
ground. The whole of the Wehrmacht could go past here
and Top Dog would be missed.

The third wave rose on the hill brow and came over,
running into the mud that the leaders' tracks had left, bruis-
ing the wet turf and churning it up, streaking the moonlit
slope with dark earth stripes. Half a squadron over, and
more coming. Top Dog was watching a parade.

Pike became afraid that the whole unit would go past
with no time for engagement.

"George. The next wave. The nearest one."

Weston's face turned pale in the gloom. He nodded and moved his head down, sighting. Pike straightened, looked through the leaves, saw the next three top the hill and crouched again.

"Swing 'er, George!"

Straightening again he rocked to the movement as Weston put the turret in traverse, swinging the six-pounder to fix on the nearest tank. Then he traversed back, keeping on his target while the range came down from a hundred yards to fifty as the enemy Mark Five swung heavily down the slope with its turret open and commander mounted. Its flank was fully exposed.

Pike hit Weston's shoulder.

"*Fire!*"

Weston delayed two seconds to make certain he was aimed at the turret. Then he fired.

Pike had stood upright to watch. The German commander was turned in this direction, perhaps attracted by the movement of Top Dog's camouflage as the gun had traversed, disturbing it. The commander was raising his field-glasses. Then Pike could not see him because the shell hit the turret at the rim, obliterating the commander and bursting against the raised armoured hatch. It smothered the tank under a shock of light. Below Pike, Weston was re-loading with his last shell, taking his time. The fumes rose from the breech. Leaves fell away in front of the corporal as the recoil displaced the camouflage. He watched, absorbed. The tank had stopped. The turret didn't swing. The commander was dead and the crew shocked, dazed, perhaps the gunner and wireless operator dead too from shell-splinters. The driver would be without orders.

Beyond the crippled tank, two others were turning to face the ambush and their turrets came round.

Pike leaned over and shouted to Munro:

"*Smoke, Gutsy! Smoke!*"

He saw Munro move, then dropped inside the turret, to find Weston sighting. "'Old it! Wait!" He slammed the

*Beyond the crippled tank two others were turning. To Munro
Pike shouted: "Smoke, Gutsy! Smoke!"*

hatch down. Weston saw his sights blank out as the smoke came past, enveloping Top Dog and drifting towards the enemy. Into the air Pike said: "Save that last one, mate. Save it."

Weston sat with his shoulders hunched, watching the moonlight go out as the smoke billowed and brought total night. It muffled the sound of the enemy's engines; they had the remoteness of a noise outside a closed window.

Top Dog had become isolated. She was as alone as a submarine moving through the dark of enemy waters, as imperilled as an underwater target that is known to be there, that must be searched out and killed.

A shell came with a whip-crack sharpness, flighting through the smoke and bursting low, its blast hitting the tank like the flat of a spade. Others came, and when they came, Weston bobbed his shoulders and sucked in another breath. It would be the next one . . . the next one . . . this one, now—*wheep*—and beyond, not that one but the next . . . going into the breech now and the lever closing . . . the German voice and then the slam of the air shock—*this one* —wheep!—and still alive. . . . I can't stand this—*make* it come! The smoke and the dark and the engines, Pike in here, blast his eyes for keeping us here to die—*wheep!*— oh, make it be the next one . . . the next one . . . this one, now. . . .

He sat with his mouth open, his back to the dark that was the armour-plate, staring at the dark that was the floor, his body alive with the last-minute terror of the bird over the gun, the rabbit under the snake, his body a thin-skinned vessel of frail veins and singing nerves, the heart itself trapped in it and quivering for escape. He was spread-eagled for the kill. It wouldn't come.

Wheep!

Pike was laughing, shouting something about Jerry and bad shots, and his gunner sat hating him for this.

A machine-gun began rattling, and the bullets came picking at the dark with the sound of their soft flight suddenly nearing until the gun's aim crossed Top Dog and they struck, hammering on the iron. The enemy was locating his target. Now the turrets would swing, and the long barrels fix on the line that the little gun had drawn for them.

Pike shouted again: *"Traverse right!"*

Weston moved by habit, finding the lever with a blind man's certainty in his familiar room. The turret swung. Pike hit his shoulder. He had watched the tracer coming and took his aim from it. *"You're on. Fire!"*

Weston dragged his hand. Their heads exploded with the gun's sound. The recoil came. Pike eased past him and shouted:

"Luff! Luff!"

There was a faint answer. He shouted again:

"Bale out! We're gettin' out!"

Weston tried to stand but crumpled, gashing his cheek on metal. Pike knocked into him, grabbing at his arm: *"Come on!"*

The fumes thickened, creeping from the breech and the spent case in the bag. Luff came aft, calling something that was cut off by the crash of a shell that hit Top Dog in the left track. Weston began sobbing. Pike dragged at his shoulders. He could smell the wind. His hands clawed at Pike. They went over the turret rim.

A shell hit Top Dog's flank and ripped the armour. The tank heaved on its springs. Pike, on the lee side, threw Weston against the leaves of the camouflage and climbed to the turret. The white of flame dazzled him and its heat struck his face. He could see Luff, a moving thing with one arm up. He reached him, blinded now by the flame and feeling his way through nightmare, shouting to Luff. They were together when the third shell came. It burst in the heart of the fire.

Munro had fired two more smoke-shells. He clawed his way back through the leaves, stupid with terror, and brought his hands up as the heat struck him across the face. Something tugged at his leg and he kicked out, but the hand still

clung to his ankle and he fell, and saw a face in the red light
It was Weston's face.

"Don't leave me!"

"Get up, then! Get up!"

Weston lurched to his feet, sobbing. Munro pulled him
through the smoke, his feet tripping on the rough ground.
They came to the source of the smoke, and went forward
beyond it into the clear moonlight.

Ammunition went up in Top Dog. The Besa belts had
caught.

Weston cried out.

"Shuddup," Munro said. He was over his terror now and
ashamed of it. He stopped and looked back at the drift of
smoke. The blaze was in its midst. He said between heaving
breaths: "Alf's gone. Alf an' Luffy. They've gone!"

Weston swayed on his feet. He said:

"Serves him right!" His voice was pitched to a childish
temper. "He asked for it!"

Munro grabbed him again. "Who?"

"Pike."

Munro hit him and he fell, crying out. Bullets rattled
inside the tank, and sparks flew up. Munro turned his back
on it and began walking to the wood. He could hear Weston
still crying out, the voice growing fainter behind him. At last
it was lost in the drum of engines as the Panzers rolled
down the hill.

He reached the edge of the trees and fell forward among
them. He had blood in his mouth. There was no wound that
he could feel in his body, but he could taste the salt. "Top
Dog," he said. "Top Dog."

Wailing Well

M. R. JAMES

(This leg-pulling horror tale was specially written for the Eton College troop of Boy Scouts by the most famous of ghost story writers, Dr. M. R. James.)

IN the year 19— there were two members of the Troop of Scouts attached to a famous school, named respectively Arthur Wilcox and Stanley Judkins. They were the same age, boarded in the same house, were in the same division, and naturally were members of the same patrol. They were so much alike in appearance as to cause anxiety and trouble, and even irritation, to the masters who came in contact with them. But oh how different were they in their inward man, or boy!

It was to Arthur Wilcox that the Head Master said, looking up with a smile as the boy entered chambers, "Why, Wilcox, there will be a deficit in the prize fund if you stay here much longer! Here, take this handsomely bound copy of the *Life and Works of Bishop Ken,* and with it my hearty congratulations to yourself and your excellent parents." It was Wilcox again, whom the Provost noticed as he passed through the playing fields, and, pausing for a moment, observed to the Vice-Provost, "That lad has a remarkable brow!" "Indeed, yes," said the Vice-Provost. "It denotes either genius or water on the brain."

As a Scout, Wilcox secured every badge and distinction for which he competed. The Cookery Badge, the Map-

making Badge, the Life-saving Badge, the Badge for picking
up bits of newspaper, the Badge for not slamming the door
when leaving pupil-room, and many others. Of the Life-
saving Badge I may have a word to say when we come to
treat of Stanley Judkins.

You cannot be surprised to hear that Mr. Hope Jones
added a special verse to each of his songs, in commendation
of Arthur Wilcox, or that the Lower Master burst into tears
when handing him the Good Conduct Medal in its handsome
claret-coloured case: the medal which had been unanimously voted to him by the whole of Third Form.
Unanimously, did I say? I am wrong. There was one dissen-
tient, Judkins *mi.*, who said that he had excellent reasons for
acting as he did. He shared, it seems, a room with his major.
You cannot, again, wonder that in after years Arthur Wilcox
was the first, and so far the only boy, to become Captain of
both the School and of the Oppidans, or that the strain of
carrying out the duties of both positions, coupled with the
ordinary work of the school, was so severe that a complete
rest for six months, followed by a voyage round the world,
was pronounced an absolute necessity by the family doctor.

It would be a pleasant task to trace the steps by which
he attained the giddy eminence he now occupies; but for the
moment enough of Arthur Wilcox. Times presses, and we
must turn to a very different matter: the career of Stanley
Judkins—Judkins *ma.*

Stanley Judkins, like Arthur Wilcox, attracted the attention of the authorities; but in quite another fashion. It was
to him that the Lower Master said, with no cheerful smile,
"What, again, Judkins? A very little persistence in this course
of conduct, my boy, and you will have cause to regret that
you ever entered this academy. There, take that, and that,
and think yourself very lucky you don't get that and that!"
It was Judkins, again, whom the Provost had cause to notice
as he passed through the playing fields, when a cricket ball
struck him with considerable force on the ankle, and a voice
from a short way off cried, "Thank you, cut-over!" "I think,"

said the Provost, pausing for a moment to rub his ankle, "that that boy had better fetch his cricket ball for himself!" "Indeed, yes," said the Vice-Provost, "and if he comes within reach, I will do my best to fetch him something else."

As a Scout, Stanley Judkins secured no badge save those which he was able to abstract from members of other patrols. In the cookery competition he was detected trying to introduce squibs into the Dutch oven of the next-door competitors. In the tailoring competition he succeeded in sewing two boys together very firmly, with disastrous effect when they tried to get up. For the Tidiness Badge he was disqualified, because, in the Midsummer schooltime, which chanced to be hot, he could not be dissuaded from sitting with his fingers in the ink: as he said, for coolness' sake. For one piece of paper which he picked up, he must have dropped at least six banana skins or orange peels. Aged women seeing him approaching would beg him with tears in their eyes not to carry their pails of water across the road. They knew too well what the result would inevitably be. But it was in the life-saving competition that Stanley Judkins' conduct was most blamable and had the most far-reaching effects. The practice, as you know, was to throw a selected lower boy, of suitable dimensions, fully dressed, with his hands and feet tied together, into the deepest part of Cuckoo Weir, and to time the Scout whose turn it was to rescue him. On every occasion when he was entered for this competition Stanley Judkins was seized, at the critical moment, with a severe fit of cramp, which caused him to roll on the ground and utter alarming cries. This naturally distracted the attention of those present from the boy in the water, and had it not been for the presence of Arthur Wilcox the death-roll would have been a heavy one. As it was, the Lower Master found it necessary to take a firm line and say that the competition must be discontinued. It was in vain that Mr. Beasley Robinson represented to him that in five competitions only four lower boys had actually succumbed. The Lower Master said that he would be the last to interfere in any way with the work of the Scouts; but that three of these boys had been valued members of his choir, and both he and Dr. Ley felt that the inconvenience caused by the losses outweighed the advantages of the competitions. Besides, the correspondence with the parents of these boys had become annoying, and even distressing: they were no longer satisfied with the printed form which he was in the habit of sending out, and more than one of them had actually visited Eton and taken up much of his valuable time with complaints. So the life-saving competition is now a thing of the past.

In short, Stanley Judkins was no credit to the Scouts, and there was talk on more than one occasion of informing him that his services were no longer required. This course was strongly advocated by Mr. Lambart: but in the end milder counsels prevailed, and it was decided to give him another chance.

So it is that we find him at the beginning of the Midsummer Holidays of 19— at the Scouts' camp in the beautiful district of W (or X) in the county of D (or Y).

It was a lovely morning, and Stanley Judkins and one or two of his friends—for he still had friends—lay basking on the top of the down. Stanley was lying on his stomach with his chin propped on his hands, staring into the distance.

"I wonder what that place is," he said.

"Which place?" said one of the others.

"That sort of clump in the middle of the field down there."

"Oh, ah! How should I know what it is?"

"What do you want to know for?" said another.

"I don't know: I like the look of it. What's it called? Nobody got a map?" said Stanley. "Call yourselves Scouts!"

"Here's a map all right," said Wilfred Pipsqueak, ever resourceful, "and there's the place marked on it. But it's inside the red ring. We can't go there."

"Who cares about a red ring?" said Stanley. "But it's got no name on your silly map,"

"Well, you can ask this old chap what it's called if you're

"They come peerin' out of the bushes and work their way slow by them tracks towards the middle where the well is."

so keen to find out." 'This old chap' was an old shepherd who had come up and was standing behind them.

"Good morning, young gents," he said, "you've got a fine day for your doin's, ain't you?"

"Yes, thank you," said Algernon de Montmorency, with native politeness. "Can you tell us what that clump over there's called? And what's that thing inside it?"

"Course I can tell you," said the shepherd. "That's Wailin' Well, that is. But you ain't got no call to worry about that."

"Is it a well in there?" said Algernon. "Who uses it?"

The shepherd laughed. "Bless you," he said, "there ain't from a man to a sheep in these parts uses Wailin' Well, nor haven't done all the years I've lived here."

"Well, there'll be a record broken to-day, then," said Stanley Judkins, "because I shall go and get some water out of it for tea!"

"Sakes alive, young gentleman!" said the shepherd in a startled voice, "don't you get to talkin' that way! Why, ain't your masters give you notice not to go by there? They'd ought to have done."

"Yes, they have," said Wilfred Pipsqueak.

"Shut up, you ass!" said Stanley Judkins. "What's the matter with it? Isn't the water good? Anyhow, if it was boiled it would be all right."

"I don't know as there's anything much wrong with the water," said the shepherd. "All I know is, my old dog wouldn't go through that field, let alone me or anyone else that's got a morsel of brains in their heads."

"More fool them," said Stanley Judkins, at once rudely and ungrammatically. "Who ever took any harm going there?" he added.

"Three women and a man," said the shepherd gravely. "Now just you listen to me. I know these 'ere parts and you don't, and I can tell you this much: for these ten years last past there ain't been a sheep fed in that field, nor a crop raised off of it—and it's good land, too. You can pretty well see from here what a state it's got into with brambles and suckers and trash of all kinds. *You've* got a glass, young gentleman," he said to Wilfred Pipsqueak, "you can tell with that anyway."

"Yes," said Wilfred, "but I see there's tracks in it. Some-one must go through it sometimes."

"Tracks!" said the shepherd. "I believe you! Four tracks: three women and a man."

"What d'you mean, three women and a man?" said Stanley, turning over for the first time and looking at the shepherd (he had been talking with his back to him till this moment: he was an ill-mannered boy).

"Mean? Why, what I says: three women and a man."

"Who are they?" asked Algernon. "Why do they go there?"

"There's some p'r'aps could tell you who they was," said the shepherd, "but it was afore my time they come by their end. And why they goes there still is more than the children of men can tell: except I've heard they was all bad 'uns when they was alive."

"By George, what a rum thing!" Algernon and Wilfred muttered: but Stanley was scornful and bitter.

"Why, you don't mean they're deaders? What rot! You must be a lot of fools to believe that. Who's ever seen them, I'd like to know?"

"*I've* seen 'em, young gentleman!" said the shepherd, "seen 'em from near by on that bit of down: and my old dog, if he could speak, he'd tell you he've seen 'em, same time. About four o'clock of the day it was, much such a day as this. I see 'em, each one of 'em, come peerin' out of the bushes and stand up, and work their way slow by them tracks towards the trees in the middle where the well is."

"And what were they like? Do tell us!" said Algernon and Wilfred eagerly.

"Rags and bones, young gentlemen: all four of 'em: flutterin' rags and whity bones. It seemed to me as if I could hear 'em clackin' as they got along. Very slow they went, and lookin' from side to side."

"What were their faces like? Could you see?"

"They hadn't much to call faces," said the shepherd, "but I could seem to see as they had teeth."

"Lor'!" said Wilfred, "and what did they do when they got to the trees?"

"I can't tell you that, sir," said the shepherd. "I wasn't for stayin' in that place, and if I had been, I was bound to look to my old dog: he'd gone! Such a thing he never done before as leave me; but gone he had, and when I came up with him in the end, he was in that state he didn't know me, and was fit to fly at my throat But I kep' talkin' to him, and after a bit he remembered my voice and came creepin' up like a child askin' pardon. I never want to see him like that again, nor yet no other dog."

The dog, who had come up and was making friends all round, looked up at his master, and expressed agreement with what he was saying very fully.

The boys pondered for some moments on what they had heard: after which Wilfred said, "And why's it called Wailing Well?"

"If you was round here at dusk of a winter's evening, you wouldn't want to ask why," was all the shepherd said.

"Well, I don't believe a word of it," said Stanley Judkins, "and I'll go there next chance I get: blowed if I don't!"

"Then you won't be ruled by me?" said the shepherd. "Nor yet by your masters as warned you off? Come now, young gentleman, you don't want for sense, I should say. What should I want tellin' you a pack of lies? It ain't sixpence to me anyone goin' in that field: but I wouldn't like to see a young chap snuffed out like in his prime."

"I expect it's a lot more than sixpence to you," said Stanley. "I expect you've got a whisky still or something in there, and want to keep other people away. Rot I call it. Come on back, you boys."

So they turned away. The two others said, "Good evening," and, "Thank you," to the shepherd, but Stanley said nothing. The shepherd shrugged his shoulders and stood where he was, looking after them rather sadly.

On the way back to the camp there was great argument about it all, and Stanley was told as plainly as he could be told all the sorts of fools he would be if he went to the Wailing Well.

That evening, among other notices, Mr. Beasley Robinson asked if all maps had got the red ring marked on them. "Be particular," he said, "not to trespass inside it."

Several voices—among them the sulky one of Stanley Judkins—said, "Why not, sir?"

"Because not," said Mr. Beasley Robinson, "and if that

133

isn't enough for you, I can't help it." He turned and spoke to Mr. Lambart in a low voice, and then said, "I'll tell you this much: we've been asked to warn Scouts off that field. It's very good of the people to let us camp here at all, and the least we can do is to oblige them—I'm sure you'll agree to that."

Everybody said, "Yes, sir!" except Stanley Judkins, who was heard to mutter, "Oblige them be blowed!"

Early in the afternoon of the next day, the following dialogue was heard. "Wilcox, is all your tent there?"

"No, sir, Judkins isn't!"

"That boy is *the* most infernal nuisance ever invented! Where do you suppose he is?"

"I haven't an idea, sir."

"Does anybody else know?"

"Sir, I shouldn't wonder if he'd gone to the Wailing Well."

"Who's that? Pipsqueak? What's the Wailing Well?"

"Sir, it's that place in the field by—well, sir, it's in a clump of trees in a rough field."

"D'you mean inside the red ring? Good heavens! What makes you think he's gone there?"

"Why, he was terribly keen to know about it yesterday, and we were talking to a shepherd man, and he told us a lot about it and advised us not to go there: but Judkins didn't believe him, and said he meant to go."

"Young ass!" said Mr. Hope Jones, "did he take anything with him?"

"Yes, I think he took some rope and a can. We did tell him he'd be a fool to go."

"Little brute! What the deuce does he mean by pinching stores like that! Well, come along, you three, we must see after him. Why can't people keep the simplest orders? What was it the man told you? No, don't wait, let's have it as we go along."

And off they started—Algernon and Wilfred talking rapidly and the other two listening with growing concern.

At last they reached that spur of down overlooking the field of which the shepherd had spoken the day before. It commanded the place completely; the well inside the clump of bent and gnarled Scotch firs was plainly visible, and so were the four tracks winding about among the thorns and rough growth.

It was a wonderful day of shimmering heat. The sea looked like a floor of metal. There was no breath of wind. They were all exhausted when they got to the top, and flung themselves down on the hot grass.

"Nothing to be seen of him yet," said Mr. Hope Jones, "but we must stop here a bit. You're done up—not to speak of me. Keep a sharp look-out," he went on after a moment, "I thought I saw the bushes stir."

"Yes," said Wilcox, "so did I. Look . . . no, that can't be him. It's somebody though, putting their head up, isn't it?"

"I thought it was, but I'm not sure."

Silence for a moment. Then,

"That's him, sure enough," said Wilcox, "getting over the hedge on the far side. Don't you see? With a shiny thing. That's the can you said he had."

"Yes, it's him, and he's making straight for the trees," said Wilfred.

At this moment Algernon, who had been staring with all his might, broke into a scream.

"What's that on the track? On all fours—O, it's the woman. O, don't let me look at her! Don't let it happen!" And he rolled over, clutching at the grass and trying to bury his head in it.

"Stop that!" said Mr. Hope Jones loudly—but it was no use. "Look here," he said, "I must go down there. You stop here, Wilfred, and look after that boy. Wilcox, you run as hard as you can to the camp and get some help."

They ran off, both of them. Wilfred was left alone with Algernon, and did his best to calm him, but indeed he was not much happier himself. From time to time he glanced down the hill and into the field. He saw Mr. Hope Jones

drawing nearer at a swift
pace, and then, to his great
surprise, he saw him stop,
look up and round about him,
and turn quickly off at an angle!
What could be the reason? He
looked at the field, and there he
saw a terrible figure—something in
ragged black — with whitish patches
breaking out of it: the head, perched on a
long thin neck, half hidden by a shapeless sort
of blackened sun-bonnet. The creature was
waving thin arms in the direction of the rescuer
who was approaching, as if to ward him off: and
between the two figures the air seemed to shake and
shimmer as he had never seen it: and as he looked, he
began himself to feel something of a waviness and confusion
in his brain, which made him guess what might be the effect
on someone within closer range of the influence. He looked
away hastily; to see Stanley Judkins making his way pretty
quickly towards the clump, and in proper Scout fashion;
evidently picking his steps with care to avoid treading on
snapping sticks or being caught by arms of brambles. Evidently, though he saw nothing, he suspected some sort of
ambush, and was trying to go noiselessly. Wilfred saw all
that, and he saw more, too.

With a sudden and dreadful sinking at the heart, he caught
sight of someone among the trees, waiting: and again of
someone—another of the hideous black figures—working
slowly along the track from another side of the field, looking from side to side, as the shepherd had described it.

Worst of all, he saw a fourth—unmistakably a man
this time—rising out of the bushes a few yards behind the
wretched Stanley, and painfully, as it seemed crawling
into the track. On all sides the miserable victim was
cut off.

Wilfred was at his wits' end. He rushed at Algernon and

*The crouched figure behind Stanley sprang at him and caught him
about the waist.*

shook him. "Get up," he said. "Yell! Yell as loud as you
can. Oh, if we'd got a whistle!"

Algernon pulled himself together. "There's one," he said,
"Wilcox's: he must have dropped it."

So one whistled, the other screamed. In the still air the
sound carried. Stanley heard: he stopped: he turned round:
and then indeed a cry was heard more piercing and dreadful
than any that the boys on the hill could raise. It was too late.
The crouched figure behind Stanley sprang at him and caught
him about the waist. The dreadful one that was standing
waving her arms waved them again, but in exultation. The

one that was lurking among the trees shuffled forward, and she too stretched out her arms as if to clutch at something coming her way; and the other, farthest off, quickened her pace and came on, nodding gleefully. The boys took it all in in an instant of terrible silence, and hardly could they breathe as they watched the horrid struggle between the man and his victim. Stanley struck with his can, the only weapon he had. The rim of a broken black hat fell off the creature's head and showed a white skull with stains that might be wisps of hair. By this time one of the women had reached the pair, and was pulling at the rope that was coiled about Stanley's neck. Between them they overpowered him in a moment: the awful screaming ceased, and then the three passed within the circle of the clump of firs.

Yet for a moment it seemed as if rescue might come. Mr. Hope Jones, striding quickly along, suddenly stopped, turned, seemed to rub his eyes, and then started running *towards* the field. More: the boys glanced behind them, and saw not only a troop of figures from the camp coming over the top of the next down, but the shepherd running up the slope of their own hill. They beckoned, they shouted, they ran a few yards towards him and then back again. He mended his pace.

Once more the boys looked towards the field. There was nothing. Or, was there something among the trees? Why was there a mist about the trees? Mr. Hope Jones had scrambled over the hedge, and was plunging through the bushes.

The shepherd stood beside them, panting. They ran to him and clung to his arms. "They've got him! In the trees!" was as much as they could say, over and over again.

"What? Do you tell me he've gone in there after all I said to him yesterday? Poor young thing! Poor young thing!" He would have said more, but other voices broke in. The rescuers from the camp had arrived. A few hasty words, and all were dashing down the hill.

They had just entered the field when they met Mr. Hope Jones. Over his shoulder hung the corpse of Stanley Judkins. He had cut it from the branch on which he found it hanging, waving to and fro. There was not a drop of blood in the body.

On the following day Mr. Hope Jones sallied forth with an axe and with the expressed intention of cutting down every tree in the clump, and of burning every bush in the field. He returned with a nasty cut in his leg and a broken axe-helve. Not a spark of fire could he light, and on no single tree could he make the least impression.

I have heard that the present population of the Wailing Well field consists of three women, a man, and a boy.

The shock experienced by Algernon de Montmorency and Wilfred Pipsqueak was severe. Both of them left the camp at once; and the occurrence undoubtedly cast a gloom—if but a passing one—on those who remained. One of the first to recover his spirits was Judkins *mi*.

Such, gentlemen, is the story of the career of Stanley Judkins, and of a portion of the career of Arthur Wilcox. It has, I believe, never been told before. If it has a moral, that moral is, I trust, obvious: if it has none, I do not well know how to help it.

The arms in the snow-caked overcoat were flailing desperately.

Short Circuit

H. J. GOODYER

I DIDN'T see the other car at first; didn't even see the man until I was almost on top of him. The snow was blinding down in huge flakes and the wipers were heaving great chunks of it from side to side of the windscreen.

He must have seen us coming for some distance, or heard us anyway. By the time he loomed up in front of my headlights the arms in the snow-caked overcoat were flailing desperately, like windmills.

Pat gave a little gasp and instinctively I braked, though gently, or I dare say I should have followed his car into the ditch. But immediately I had second thoughts; there'd been one or two nasty cases of hold-up in the papers recently and I wasn't going to chance anything of that sort with Pat there. I changed down and made to drive round him.

Pat was horrified. "Aren't you stopping, Bill?"

I shook my head. "Too risky."

"But he's had a crash. Bill, you've got to stop."

It was then I saw the car. It had skidded right across the verge on the wrong side of the road and was hanging nose down in the ditch, which like most of them in the fen country hereabouts was pretty deep. I braked again and brought the Mini-Minor gradually to rest about twenty yards on. Above the hum of the engine we could hear his feet thumping on the snow as he ran up.

I slid back my steamy window as he peered dimly in and for the first time I saw that he was bleeding from a cut on his cheek. For some reason it seemed to make the whole thing much more serious, and without quite knowing why I opened the door and got out.

"Are you badly hurt?" I said.

141

"No. Only this." And he pointed to his face.

"Anybody else?"

"No. On my own. If you could give me a lift. . . . Going far?" He spoke with a trace of dialect, but not Midlands. West Country, I thought.

"Only about ten miles," I said. "To Shorely. Do you know it?"

"No," he said again. "But it'll do to be going on with. Thanks, old man." He clambered over my seat into the back and thankfully I got back in and slammed the door. "Whew!" I said. "Turn the heater up, Pat."

The chap in the back was undoing his overcoat and snow was flying all over the place. "Sorry about this, folks. I was beginning to think I was stuck there for the night. Not what you'd call a busy road, is it?"

"Not at twelve o'clock at night," Pat said, turning round to smile at him. "We've been to a dance in Bolingford. Bill didn't want to go, but I made him. He's not a bad brother, really."

I made a face at her. "How did it happen?" I said over my shoulder.

He told us, but I wasn't really listening. I needed most of my concentration for keeping on the road.

"Where were you making for?" Pat asked him.

"Nottingham. But I missed the road back in Bolingford."

I said, "Lord, you missed it all right. Miles out of your way. The trouble is, there's no garage before Shorely and I doubt if you'd get them to turn out tonight."

"The car can wait. I've got to get on to Nottingham. Got an important"—he hesitated—". . . business conference tomorrow. Is there a railway station in this Shorely?"

"There is," I said, "but there's only about one train a week."

"What?"

"Well, say six a week. One a day, except tomorrow. Being Sunday."

He muttered under his breath. "Buses?" he said.

"Can you do it by bus?" I said to Pat.

"Only by going back into Bolingford and getting a Notting-ham Direct. You could do it that way."

He cursed softly. I didn't like it much so I said briefly, "I'm afraid that's the only suggestion we can make," and after that we went on in silence for a bit.

The snow seemed to be easing off slightly. Visibility was still very poor and a lot of the old familiar landmarks had disappeared altogether, but I reckoned another half an hour should see us home.

"What was up with Tony Melford?" Pat said suddenly. I gathered she considered you can overdo the politeness-to-strangers routine.

"Tony Melford?" I said absently.

"Yes, didn't you see him? Suddenly strode across the floor looking tremendously important and buttonholed that new squadron leader. You know, the one without a moustache—what's his name ... ?"

"Rogers?"

"That's right. He was doing a samba with Nellie Walcott. When Tony whispered in his ear, he dropped Nellie like a hot cake and he and Tony did a bunk. Why?"

"Haven't a clue. Some flap or other on the station, I suppose."

It struck me that the chap in the back was listening intently; perhaps a sudden stillness, or a change in the rhythm of his breathing.

"R.A.F. dance, was it?" he said, leaning forward.

"Yes," I said.

He gave the ghost of a laugh. "Maybe somebody pinched a missile."

And that set me thinking. How did he know that Boling-ford was now a missile base? The changeover had only been last month and half the stuff hadn't even arrived. Things got around, I didn't need telling that, but surely a fellow just travelling through would scarcely have had the opportunity of picking up that sort of gossip. If he *had* been just travelling through. But of course he hadn't actually said. . . .

"Come far today?" I said, as casually as I could.

He seemed to hesitate. "From Hull."

"Down the A15, I suppose?"

"That's right."

He certainly wasn't being very forthcoming. "Made it much better," I said, "since they opened the new bridge and took the A15 over the river."

He agreed readily. "Lovely bit of engineering," he added gratuitously.

That clinched it. There was no new bridge over the Humber, nor, so far as I was aware, was anyone contemplating spending several millions on building one. He was lying all the time.

But why? I decided to stick my neck out again.

"Did you hear they caught a turkey rustler last week?" I said to Pat.

"Who did? Where?"

"You know, that police trap they set up just this side of the village. Saturday nights mostly," I added, thinking you can chew that one over, my lad.

Pat wasn't really interested, but she asked a few questions about it and all the time there was that uneasy stillness in the back of the car. He was chewing it over all right.

Suddenly, "Stop all the cars, do they?" he said. His voice was different; higher pitched, tensed.

It had put the wind up him, no doubt of that. The last thing he wanted to do was meet a policeman. I suddenly wondered how far he'd go to avoid meeting one; I thought, if they're after him for something really serious, then he could be desperate. He might well be armed . . . I mustn't push him too far. Once I've forced him to show his hand we're done for.

I felt the sweat breaking out on my forehead but somehow I managed a careless laugh, "They won't be there tonight. Would you be?" The breath whistled out softly between his teeth. I could almost feel his relief.

Pat didn't seem to have noticed anything odd. "If he's going to wait for tomorrow morning's bus, where's he going to stay?" she said. "Neither of the pubs takes people. What about Mrs. Spence? It *is* rather late, of course. . . ."

I suddenly saw a way to handle the whole thing, as plainly as if somebody had mapped out a programme for me. It would be easy enough if only I could have a private word with Pat. If not—then it *was* going to take some handling.

We were just coming into Aubrey. "You couldn't knock up Mrs. Spence," I said, "not at this hour. I suppose we could put him up for the rest of the night, though."

She couldn't really say what she thought, but the look she gave me was expressive enough. I knew she hadn't cottoned on to the man. He, on the other hand, jumped at the idea. "That's good of you," he said. "I certainly shan't turn that offer down."

Pat said firmly, "I don't possibly see how we could, Bill." She turned towards the back seat. "It's only a tiny cottage, you see. I'm sorry, but. . . ."

"I don't mind kipping in the kitchen," he said. It was said almost rudely, the tone of his voice aggressive, over-bearing. I knew Pat. This was no time for her to fly off the handle.

"There's a telephone box just round the corner," I said quickly. "I'll ring up home and ask. How's that?"

She didn't answer. I knew she was going to sulk now, but perhaps that was for the best. The dim glow from the kiosk came uncertainly into view.

I pulled up gently and opened my door. "Shan't be a moment or two," I said. I half expected Pat to insist on coming, too, but it was our passenger who said, following me out, "I'll come and have a word with your folks. Just to make sure—you know." The smile he gave it was intended to say, "To make sure that it's quite convenient," but I knew what he really meant. "To make sure I was up to no tricks," was about it.

I was thinking hard as we squeezed into the box. This was

145

something I hadn't reckoned on. There was about one chance in a thousand now that I should be able to pull it off.

I dialled the number. I could hear it ringing out and the blood pounding in my ears was beating double time to it. Then thankfully I heard Dad's sleepy voice at the other end of the wire.

"It's Bill, Dad. Sorry to get you out of bed." Without

"No, not badly hurt—he wants to have a word with you."

giving him time to answer I went straight on, "We're on the way home but we've got a bit of a problem. Chap has crashed his car just this side of Bolingford and we picked him up. . . ." I glued the receiver to my ear and gave him a second or two but just as he began to speak I cut across him. "No, he's not badly hurt. He's standing beside me as a matter of fact— wants to have a word with you in a moment. The thing is, can you put him up there until the morning? We're in Aubrey —should be home in half an hour or so."

The stranger's eyebrows came down at that. I wasn't surprised; this was the tricky bit. "Half an hour?" he mouthed at me.

Dad's clear voice came again. "Did you say you were in Aubrey?"

"That's right."

"And you want to bring him here?"

"Yes."

A moment's pause, then, "Yes, I think that can be arranged. Has he got any luggage?"

Instinctively I looked at the man leaning against the glass door. His overcoat was still open and his jacket, too. And snug against the white shirt I could just make out the dark shape of a shoulder holster. I looked away quickly. "No," I said.

"No," he repeated. "All right. You say he wants to speak to me?"

"I'll put him on," I said and held out the receiver. He took it roughly, shouldering me out of the way. "Very good of you to have me, I'm sure. Not putting you out at all?"

I heard Dad say, "We'll manage. See you soon, then."

Our guest put down the receiver and said, "Half an hour? You told me it was only ten miles from where you picked me up."

"It is, normally. But tonight we've got to go round the world rather to get there. Drifts," I explained.

We got back into the car. "Well?" Pat said.

"I spoke to Dad," I said carefully. "He says it's all right to put him up there."

I thought she'd hit the roof. "Bill, you don't mean to say we've got to. . . ."

"We've got to squeeze up a bit, that's all. After all, Pat, it's only for one night."

She was gaping like a hungry goldfish. "Bill, have you gone quite bonkers?"

I wanted the next turning to the right and it was bad enough having to navigate in a blizzard without coping with

Pat's obtuseness at the same time, but she had to be stopped.

"I must apologize for my sister," I said. "She's a bit tired, that's all." With any luck now she'd go back into her sulk.

But she didn't. "Look, Bill," she said coldly, "I don't know what's come over you. It was bad enough when you wanted to...."

At that moment I saw the turning, almost too late. I swung hard over and for a moment I thought the little bus was going into a skid. Gently, I told myself, gently does it. Don't brake, don't fight it . . . drive into it. . . . Gallantly the Mini-Minor recovered herself and I breathed again.

"Pat," I said quietly. "I can't drive through this if you're going to talk to me all the time." I felt for her foot with mine and pressed it gently. "If you want us to get home alive, don't talk." I accented the last two words as much as I dared and he was on to it at once. I think his suspicions had been aroused already. "Talk to me, Pat," he said. "What were you saying about what he wanted before?"

I could have told him he wouldn't get anywhere that way. Pat sniffed and said, "I think that's our affair."

He shut up for a bit at that. I knew he was trying to work it out and I went over the thing again in my own mind, wondering if there was any snag. He hadn't spotted anything in the phone box, I was pretty sure. Had I told Dad enough? Was there anything I'd forgotten?

And suddenly I knew there was. The knowledge came in a blinding flash that left me feeling weak and hopeless. How could I have forgotten *that*?

I drove on, my thoughts in a turmoil. There was no turning back, now, but was there any point in going on? Out of the tail of my eye I saw the snow-blanked signpost and turned right again.

"This is a rum sort of route. We seem to be going round in circles." His voice was aggressive again, questioning, suspicious.

Pat flashed back, "My brother's doing his best. Can't you ever be satisfied?"

Almost before we had skidded to a stop, a sentry materialized.

For some reason he was. "All right, little lady. Back seat driving always was a fault of mine. I'll watch it in future."

"Thank you," she said.

Twenty minutes went by. Occasionally he leaned forward to peer through the front windscreen, but for most of the time he was much more relaxed and conversation was negligible. Any moment now, I thought. Any moment now the balloon will go up. My eyes were aching with the strain of peering through the dazzling, dancing flakes, searching, searching. . . .

Then, quite unexpectedly, we were there. I drove directly for the gates and flung open my door as we skidded to a stop. The sentry came running, a Sten gun at the ready. "In the back," I said hoarsely. "Cover him, quick. He's armed."

Then Tony Melford was there, and the rest of the guard, and Dad, looking like a shaggy snowman. They dragged our passenger out and got his gun and then everyone began to relax.

"Half-way here," I said, "I got a frightful flap on. I suddenly remembered the perimeter lights. You can see them for miles, even in this stuff. He was already suspicious, and I knew he'd tumble to it once he saw those glaring ambers. Thank heavens you switched them off."

"*We* didn't," Dad said. "*He* did. Sabotage, that's his game. It was when he fused the lights that we knew something was up. Fortunately he didn't do much damage, but he managed to get clean away. If it hadn't been for you two . . . look, come into the guardroom, there's a nice fire there. There's a nice little cell, too, for your friend. Check him for any more arms, Sergeant, then bring him along."

We went into the guardroom. "Now," Dad said, "tell me how you managed to pull it off. I should have thought this was the last place he'd have let you bring him to."

I said, "That's just the point. He thought we were taking him home. You were staying the night here so all I had to do was dial your private number. He thought I was getting through to the cottage in Shorely—there was no reason for him to think otherwise."

"Then you doubled back without his realizing it?"

"Yes, I came back the top way. That part of it wasn't difficult, he was completely lost anyway. The really tricky part was speaking to you with him able to hear every word you said."

Pat had been in a state of complete bewilderment ever since we reached the gates. "How on earth *did* you two fool him?" she said, looking from Dad to me.

Dad grinned at me. "Well, Bill started off by answering a question I hadn't asked. Then he said you were making for home but would *I* put the man up. Then he told me you were in Aubrey and would be home in half an hour. That was the best hint—it's a ten minutes' run even in a blizzard. Of course," he said, "we were pretty well on our toes, you know."

They were taking the prisoner through to the cells. Half-way across the room he stopped and gave me a look of such distilled hatred that my scalp began to tingle.

"You twisting little . . ."

Suddenly I felt on top of the world. It had worked! A thousand to one chance and I'd pulled it off.

"But you asked my father for accommodation yourself," I said sweetly. "I didn't feel bound to explain that he was speaking from R.A.F., Bolingford. Or that he was the Commanding Officer."

The Raiders

SHOWELL STYLES

I

Beneath the hurrying clouds of the October sky the Mediterranean waves were blue-green and capped with white. On the horizon, seen through a haze of driven spray, the French coast stood ever higher against a ragged line of pale-blue heaven that told of clearing weather, like a tapestry backcloth to the wind-whipped stage of sea on which a drama of chase and battle was fast nearing its climax. His Britannic Majesty's frigate *Oread*, thirty-eight guns, lay over close-hauled on the port tack as she foamed through the water, her towers of white canvas taut and straining, in the wake of the French frigate she had been chasing since dawn that morning. It was plain even to the inexperienced eye of Mr. Midshipman Howard that she was overhauling the Frenchman hand over fist.

"Mr. Fraser!" came Captain Strang's bellow from the quarterdeck. "See that the matches in your tubs are alight."

"Aye, aye, sir."

Lieutenant Fraser, tall and thin-faced, strode past Midshipman Howard's post near the mainmast as he hastened to obey. The midshipman gulped convulsively. The order was merely a precaution; the spray flying across the rail and in through the open gunports might spoil the action of the flint-lock triggers, and the coiled slow-match in the tubs on deck must be kept burning in reserve. But to Robert Howard, sixteen years old and facing his first sea-fight, it was yet another reminder that he was soon to take his chance of death or horrible mutilation by an eighteen-pounder cannon-ball.

From where he stood by the mainmast Howard could look aft to the quarterdeck with its group of white-breeched officers and the two quartermasters at the wheel; for'ard along the sanded deck where the gun-crews, stripped to the waist, stood ready behind the wooden carriages that supported the gleaming guns. Bryant, the senior midshipman, was standing near the foremast, gazing eagerly at the flying enemy while his big body swayed easily to *Oread*'s jerky pitching. Howard envied his obvious nonchalance. And envy smouldered into resentment as he remembered the humiliations of the past weeks.

Midshipman Robert Howard had joined the *Oread* at Portsmouth fresh from his father's quiet Sussex rectory and had been whirled at once into the bustle of a frigate ordered to sea. *Oread* was to proceed for a fortnight's independent cruising off Marseilles before reporting to Vice-Admiral Lord Nelson's blockading fleet off Toulon. No enemy vessel had been encountered on the long voyage out, but Howard had found—or made—an enemy in the senior midshipman. Bryant was the third son of a baronet, had two years' sea experience, and possessed a naturally arrogant manner which added to Howard's feeling of inferiority. In the hours of deck duty, in the classes of instruction, during the off-duty periods in the stinking 'tween-decks cubby that was the midshipmen's quarters, Bryant's jests about the new junior officer's seasickness and his contempt for his ignorance had reduced Howard to a sullen misery. If Bryant got to know his present state of terror (Howard was thinking now) life aboard the *Oread* would become totally unbearable.

"Ten minutes should see us in action, Mr. Howard. We're gaining on her fast."

Lieutenant Fraser's voice with its faint Scottish accent brought Howard out of his meditations with a jerk.

"Y-yes, sir," he stammered.

Fraser shot a keen glance at his pallid face and tight lips and lingered for further speech. He was not so old and hardened that he had forgotten his own first days at sea.

"She's running for the shelter of the batteries on Cap Croisette. Not often one of Boney's frigates ventures out so far from Marseilles. It's odd, I'm thinking, that she's making so close inshore towards Cap Roux—that's the dark head-land on our starboard bow. See it?"

"Yes, sir."

Howard's voice was steadier. The lieutenant's cool, conversational tone was having its effect. Fraser nodded at him.

"Our object's to fight and take her before we come within range of the Croisette batteries. Keep your object in the forefront of your mind, Mr. Howard, and leave no room for anything else. That's a good rule for sea officers."

He walked on along the tilted deck. Midshipman Howard felt slightly better. Then his glance fell on the enemy frigate ahead of them and he swallowed hard again. She was much closer now. He could see the tricolor at her yardarm, the tiny figures of men on her quarterdeck, a group clustered round something at the stern rail—and a sudden jet of smoke that hid the group from sight. She had tried a shot with her stern-chaser. He held his breath, releasing it in shuddering relief as a white column of water rose a pistol-shot away on the starboard beam. A miss—but the range had been good. The next shot might strike true, here amidships where he stood, tearing him into red fragments. . . . Fear caught him in its grip once more.

The slight alteration of course she had made to allow that gun to bear had slowed the Frenchman slightly. It was sufficient to bring the chase to an end. Faster now the long bowsprit of the British vessel crept up on the stern of the

Fear caught him in its grip once more.

other frigate. Howard, watching in fascinated terror, saw the dark line of Cap Roux, a crouching rocky headland jutting far out from the French mainland, slide out of sight behind the enemy's hull as *Oread* drew level. In a moment they would be racing side by side.

"Broadsides, Mr. Fraser. Stand by."

Captain Strang's matter-of-fact voice scarcely penetrated Howard's mind. He could not take his eyes from the grinning gunports that now fronted him across a short interval of tossing water, each with its gun-muzzle waiting to spout death. The French captain was also holding his fire for a broadside.

Suddenly the whole vision of racing vessel and intervening sea vanished in an eruption of smoke and flame. The roar of sixteen guns fired simultaneously, the hideous screeching of the heavy shot hurtling overhead, the twang and clatter of severed rigging—Midshipman Howard heard them as from the depths of some frightful nightmare. His eyes were tight shut and his nails biting into the palms of his clenched

155

fists. The thunderous crash of *Oread's* answering broadside made the deck lurch beneath his feet and nearly flung him over. Involuntarily he opened his eyes.

Smoke, thick and acrid-smelling, hid everything for a moment and then blew clear, revealing the French frigate. Howard saw that a gap had appeared in her rail and that her main courses were holed. His wild hope that she would strike her colours and end the fight was shattered instantly by the roar of her second broadside. Every instinct told him to crouch, to grovel—to protect himself somehow against the flying spheres of iron that this time must surely hurl him into eternity. With an inarticulate cry he closed his eyes and clasped both arms above his head, crushing his cocked hat down on his skull.

The screaming of the shot ended in thuds and crashes and discordant human screams, drowned instantly by the explosion of *Oread's* second broadside. Eddying smoke was in his nose and throat, a long-drawn creaking in his ears. The creaking ended in a shuddering crash that shook the frigate from stem to stern. Voices broke through the tumult. *"Foremast gone, sir.... Hands to the braces, there! ... Mr. Bryant! Take a party and clear that tangle!"*

Howard, still with his eyes shut and his arms over his head, felt a hard fist smite into his back. Bryant's voice yelled savagely at him.

"Come *on,* damn you! Lend a hand!"

Dazedly he stumbled through the smoke, following Bryant for'ard. There was blood on the deck. One of the 'midship guns lay on its side and half its crew was torn into red unrecognizable fragments. Across the foredeck lay the wreckage of the mast, snapped off at one-third of its height by a direct hit. Someone thrust an axe into his hand.

"Cut those weather shrouds clear!"

He toiled through a maze of tangled rigging and flapping canvas. There was no more firing. The *Oread* had lost all way and was swinging helplessly head to wind. Beyond the foremasthead where it trailed in the waves he glimpsed the

French frigate, already half a mile away and diminishing fast towards the mainland and safety. Howard's terror left him as he hewed grimly with the others to clear away the hamper of cordage. It was over now. They could never catch the Frenchman.

From the corner of his eye he saw a tall fountain of water hoist itself from the surface a cable's length from the frigate. Seconds later there came a deep *boom*! from landward.

"Gawd 'elp us!" grunted one of the toiling men near Howard. "'Oo'd ha' thought the Frogs would put a gun on Cap Roux?"

"That's it, sure enough," said another. "Forty-two-pounder, what's more. Leadin' us on, was that frigate——"

"Stick to it, men!" Lieutenant Fraser's high cool voice broke in. "They can't hit us at that range."

In fact, his assertion was more comforting than true. Before the *Oread*'s seamen had cleared the wreckage and rigged jury-mast and sail, the new giant gun on Cap Roux had fired seven times, and its last shot fell so close that its fountain rose close alongside and deluged men on the foredeck. But by then she was under way and heading out to sea before a failing breeze, to complete her repairs and bury her three dead in safer waters beyond the horizon.

At nightfall, however, the frigate was creeping back into the eastern curve of the Gulf of Lions, holding the light westerly wind that had succeeded the strong nor'-wester of the morning. Down in the candle-lit 'tween-decks of the midshipmen's berth Fellows, the oldest of the five midshipmen, was holding forth on the reason for this manoeuvre.

"Stands to reason," he was saying, "that we can't let 'em keep that gun on Cap Roux. It'll cover the merchantmen that slip out to get along the coast to Sanary with supplies for Toulon. It's my opinion Captain Strang's going to have a shot at putting it out of action."

"Just the night for it!" exclaimed Midshipman Bryant, flexing his biceps. "By glory, I hope they pick on me for the landing party!" He turned a contemptuous eye on Midshipman Howard, who was sitting silently a little apart from the others. "Like to come along, Mr. Howard? There's a good chance of a French musket-ball in your belly. Bit smaller than an eighteen-pounder."

Howard muttered something inaudible. He had spent the latter part of the day dreading Bryant's revelation of his behaviour.

Bryant's lip curled. "Not your line of country, eh?" he said with a grin. "We'll have to think about changing your name. Just the initial letter, I fancy—to a C."

Howard looked round the circle of grinning faces desperately. He knew it was true. He was a coward—that morning had shown it. But if he let this pass it would have been better if he had been killed in the fight. Bryant's silly jest would follow him all through his service life. He swallowed hard and took a deep breath.

"You all heard that," he said shakily. "Mr. Bryant insulted me. For that I must—must demand an apology or satisfaction."

There was a gasp from the others. Bryant stared and laughed.

"I never apologize," he said scornfully. "And if you think I'll fight a duel——"

"Mr. Howard is perfectly correct," Fellows interrupted sharply. "You insulted him, Bryant. Do you refuse to give him the satisfaction necessary between gentlemen?"

Bryant flushed. "No, by glory! I'll fight him. Next time we get ashore together, with any weapons he——"

He checked himself suddenly as a step sounded in the alleyway and Lieutenant Fraser entered. All five midshipmen rose to their feet, stooping their heads under the low deckbeams. The lieutenant looked keenly from one to another.

"Mr. Bryant," he rapped, "and Mr. Howard. Get your boat-cloaks and dirks and come on deck. You'll be served out pistols and cutlasses. You're coming with me to deal with that forty-two-pounder on Cap Roux."

"Mr. Bryant insulted me—I demand an apology or satisfaction."

II

An elongated patch of black on the silken darkness of the sea, the *Oread*'s longboat slid silently closer and closer beneath the loom of low cliffs overhead. The gentle lapping of water on the rocks of Cap Roux was clearly audible to the twenty-three men in her, for the oars were muffled with strips of sacking and the order for absolute silence was being strictly observed.

Lieutenant Fraser, in the sternsheets with the two midshipmen, had done all the talking that was necessary half an hour ago, when they had begun the long pull from the frigate. Captain Strang had observed the rocky headland minutely through his glass that morning, and no strong fortifications had been visible on Cap Roux. There were, however, huts and buildings indicating that a considerable force of infantry and gunners were stationed there. From the

159

chart he had learned that a small cove below the eastward
cliffs should offer a landing-place, and with a moonless night
and a surprise attack the chance was worth taking. Since a
large force made premature discovery more likely, the captain had detailed Lieutenant Fraser in command, with eight
marines under Captain Bell, ten seamen, Fletcher the gunner's mate, and the two midshipmen, for the expedition.

For equipment, besides firearms and cutlasses, they had
with them four stout six-foot spars and a carefully-prepared
explosive charge which Fletcher was nursing like a baby.
The plan was simple. Bell's marines were to create a diversion by an attack on the barrack buildings while the seamen
dealt with the great gun. Fletcher's explosive charge was
enough to lift it from its mounting and damage it severely,
but if (as was likely) it had been mounted near the cliff edge
the spars would be used to lever it over on to the rocks below.

"'Vast pulling," came Fraser's whisper, and the longboat
glided towards a small pale patch of shingle at the foot of
the black crags.

Midshipman Howard's teeth bit hard into his lower lip.
He was afraid—horribly afraid—of what was to come. But
it was no longer a blind and formless terror that gripped him.
He could face the fact that he was afraid and set it in front
of him like an enemy. It was himself that he must fight, he
saw—his lesser, animal self that wanted to run and hide
from danger that had to be encountered boldly. In challenging Bryant he had taken his ground for another and more
vital duel.

The longboat's forefoot ground gently into the shingle.
The bowmen stepped cautiously overside into three feet of
water and pulled her up a yard or so. Two minutes later the
party was mustering on the tiny slope of beach under the
over-arching fifty-foot cliffs.

Lieutenant Fraser returned from a swift investigation of
the base of the crags.

"There's a gully cutting in on the right," he whispered.
"Masters and Wright will stay with the boat, and keep silence.

Mr. Bell, you'll follow me. Your men had better sling their muskets until we reach the top. Mr. Howard, bring up your four seamen next. Then you, Fletcher. Then Mr. Bryant and his four men. Ready? March."

The lower part of the gully was easy enough. It narrowed above, necessitating the use of hands as well as feet. Midshipman Howard, groping for handhold in rear of the marine ahead of him, winced each time a musket-butt or one of the spars carried by the seamen struck against the rock. But no shot or shout of alarm followed these slight noises. If sentries were posted, it was not on this edge of the cape.

The gully ended in a short steep section as narrow as a chimney, which ejected them into a thorny hollow on the brow of the cliff. There were smothered oaths, checked instantly by Fraser, as thorns found tender spots. The lieutenant crawled to the upper rim of the hollow. His head and shoulders showed in blacker silhouette as he raised himself to look over. They saw his arm raised, waving them forward, and followed him to the higher ground on the top of the headland.

The narrow plateau above the sea was hardly a quarter of a mile across; so much they knew from the chart. Midshipman Howard, crouched behind Lieutenant Fraser and peering above a thornbush, saw an almost level blackness with small shapes studding its farther rim in outline against the paler sky—to the right the oblongs of buildings, to the left a raised and pointing finger that could only be the 42-pounder brought with such labour across the inland crags to menace intruding frigates. The shapes seemed to be about three hundred paces away.

Fraser whispered orders. They were to move forward in two files headed by himself and Captain Bell, seamen in the left-hand file and marines on the right. They would keep together until they were close to the emplacement. There was a pause while the marines unslung and loaded their muskets —a task for experts in that darkness—and then the two files moved forward across the plateau.

Howard groped and stumbled immediately behind the lieutenant, striving to conquer the feeling of sick emptiness that set his knees shaking at every step. If one of the marines beside him accidentally pulled trigger, if a seaman fell and struck his cutlass against a rock, if the French were even now mustering silently behind a hidden redoubt—then the darkness might hurl flame and death at them in the next moment. The heavy pistol in his side-pocket and the cutlass that rasped against the bushes as he passed were small comfort when he thought of that leaden hail from enemy muskets. For a shameful few seconds he thought of feigning a twisted ankle so as to be left behind, safe with a sound excuse, among the rocks and bushes until the fight was over. Then he recognized the thought for an enemy thrust in the duel he was fighting against himself, and parried it with another thought: Mr. Fraser had chosen him from four others to bear a part, with Bryant, in this raid. That helped him a good deal as the two files came nearer to the French position.

The two or three oblong shapes were a long stone's throw on their right now, and the 42-pounder, squatly foreshortened, about the same distance on their left front. Fraser gave the word, and the party of marines made off stealthily towards the buildings while the lieutenant led his men towards the gun. He had not taken a dozen paces more when he tripped and fell violently forward on his face. Almost at the same time a faint jangling noise sounded from the direction of the barracks.

"What is it, sir—are you hurt?" Howard demanded anxiously, helping Fraser to his feet.

"No. It's a ditch and a trip-wire in it. The alarm's given." The lieutenant raised his voice in a shout. "Bell! At the double!" To his own party he added coolly: "Straight for the gun, men—no need for silence now."

This last injunction was scarcely necessary. As the seamen broke into a run the dark buildings came noisily to life. Whistles blew, lights flared, voices screamed orders in rapid French. Midshipman Howard, stumbling forward with the

rest, had to fight hard against the impulse to turn and run
for the longboat. There had been no surprise—the raid was
doomed to failure. Whatever the enemy force that manned
and guarded the great gun, it was bound to outnumber the
score of British. At any moment the French muskets would
mow them down. . . .

*Keep your object in the forefront of your mind, Mr.
Howard, and leave no room for anything else.* Lieutenant
Fraser's words sprang suddenly into his mind. The gun—
that was his object; to destroy it. Nothing else must matter
to him. He set his teeth and lurched on over the rough ground
at Fraser's heels.

A musket banged close on their right, and then two more
in quick succession. Then a scattered volley and a cheer—
that would be Bell's marines attacking. A bank or rampart
just ahead, and beyond it the black finger of the huge gun.
Bright orange flame stabbed at them from the rampart and
Howard felt the flick of wind on his cheek as a musket-ball
whistled past. The crash of the discharge was followed by
groans and a thud just behind him. Next moment he nearly
tripped over the lieutenant. who had dropped with a cry of
pain. Howard was bending over him when Bryant came
dashing past.

"On—get *on*!" yelled the senior midshipman.

Howard ran forward again, leaving the lieutenant. A few
yards away a musket flared and banged. The flash showed
him Bryant's tall figure leaping in mid-air, to fall in a heap.
Then the seamen ahead of him were over the rampart and
laying about them with their cutlasses. He sprang over after
them. Dark figures were reeling all about him, striking and
yelling. He broke through, running for the gun twenty paces
away. Right in his path a man rose up, leaving another pros-
trate on the ground. Howard's cutlass was still in his belt
—he had quite forgotten to draw it—and there was no time
to pull out and cock his pistol. Somehow he swerved from
the downstroke that hissed past his head and smote with
clenched fist at the pale disc of a face. His knuckles jarred

Right in his path a man rose up, and there was no time to cock his pistol.

on hard bone and the Frenchman went down.

He was about to race on towards the gun when a gasping cry stopped him.

"Mister—Howard, sir —the charge!"

It was Fletcher, lying mortally wounded, thrusting a package at him.

Howard snatched it and ran for the gun.

A score of yards behind him the fight in the darkness still raged, but there was no one by the 42-pounder. The long mass of it on its mounting rose before him, as high as his shoulder.

With shaking fingers he tore open the oiled canvas of the wrapping and felt the coil of fuse attached to the powder canister inside. Flint and steel was here too. He pushed the canister along the base of the mounting until it was directly below the gun where the huge barrel swelled from the breechblock, straightened the short fuse, and fumbled with flint and steel. All the time he felt a shrinking between his shoulder-blades where bullet or cutlass-thrust would come, but he concentrated on his task. *Keep your object in the forefront of your mind. . . .*

It was done. The spark flashed life into the powder-grains and the thin fuse began to splutter furiously. Howard waited a second to see that the fire was travelling along the fuse and then turned and ran. As he flung himself on his face there was a vivid flash and the ground beneath him shook to the explosion.

164

III

It was several seconds before Midshipman Howard could collect his senses after that shattering report. He sat up, and above the singing in his ears he heard the distant rattle of musketry and the long shrill note of a whistle. He got shakily to his feet—and cowered with raised arm as a bulky figure loomed over him.

"Mr. Howard?" It was Bushey, one of the seamen. "These Frogs is all done for, sir—but Mr. Bell's drawin' off the marines an' there's another lot o' sojers comin' at us from the barracks. What's the order, sir?"

The order? It took Howard a moment to realize his position. Lieutenant Fraser was dead or disabled; so was Bryant. Captain Bell was withdrawing his little force, or what was left of it, back to the longboat. He, Robert Howard, was in command—and the object, the complete destruction of the great gun, was not fully achieved.

He forced himself to think coolly and fast. And behind his racing thoughts hovered a wraith of wonder—wonder at the fact that there was now no room for fear in his mind.

"How many seamen left?" he demanded.

"Cripps is dead an' Brown's got a ball in 'is shoulder, sir. That leaves six of us."

Shouts and the sounds of many men approaching from the direction of the barracks gave Howard little time for thought now.

"Leave two men with Brown at the rampart," he snapped. "Give them all the pistols there are and tell 'em to hold the French back. Get the others and join me at the gun—and bring those spars."

"Aye aye, sir!"

As Bushey ran back, Howard raced to the gun. The explosion had lifted it from its mounting and it lay with its long barrel resting on the low seaward rampart and its heavy breechblock on the concrete platform. He leaned over the stone rampart. The murmur of the sea came to his ears from

165

The breech end rose slowly and the gun began to slide.

far below. Beyond the gun position the drop was sheer to the invisible rocks at the cliff foot. A medley of shots and yells broke out behind him—the French had come upon the defenders of the landward rampart. In the same instant Bushey and his three men arrived panting beside him, carrying the four spars.

"We'll use three spars." Howard made himself speak quickly and calmly. "Bushey, get one under the barrel. Two men to each of the others, here under the breech. We've got to lift the after end on to the rampart—and don't let it roll back. Ready? *Heave!"*

He and one of the seamen were tugging at the middle spar. The big gun shifted and rolled a little. Behind them muskets banged between the sharp crack of pistol-shots.

"Another—all you've got!" Howard gasped.

The breech end rose slowly. Bushey whipped his spar out from under the barrel and slipped it under the breech. His muscles tipped the scale. The 42-pounder rolled slowly on to the top of the low rampart, seemed to hesitate, and then vanished with a thud. There was a grinding sound; then a pause; and then a heavy crash from far below.

"Done it!" Howard's shout was triumphant. "Back to the other rampart—cutlasses!"

He remembered his own weapon this time. It was out and in his fist as they dashed past the shattered mounting. The French—there were a dozen or so and more coming up—had realized the smallness of the force opposing them and were running at the rampart. The sudden charge of the five men who leaped the rampart and rushed yelling upon them took them by surprise. Some turned, others stood their ground. A musket flashed and roared in Howard's face, half-blinding him, but the bullet sang past and the swinging blow of his cutlass felled the man who had fired. The irregular mass of dark figures was giving back, uncertain of the attackers' numbers

"Make for the boat. men!" Howard yelled above the uproar.

167

He turned and ran, with the seamen bounding over the rocks and thorns beside him. It was likely, he thought, that the pursuit would hesitate long enough to give them a chance. Suddenly, as he ran, he realized that he was not afraid. *He was not afraid!* Triumph surged in him—and ebbed as he thought of Lieutenant Fraser, killed or wounded at the beginning of the action. It was impossible to leave him lying in the thorn-bushes. He had begun to check his pace when he saw a man stumbling towards him from in front and discerned the white crossbelts of a marine.

"Mr. Howard?" panted the man as he came up. "We've got Mr. Fraser, sir—Cap'n Bell's taking him to the boat now."

"Very good. Get back quick as you can—they're coming after us."

The marine vanished towards the edge of the cliffs. Howard, who had halted to speak to him, cast a final glance over his shoulder before following. Two or three black figures —the foremost of the pursuers—were bobbing up and down against the night sky less than two hundred paces away. From farther away two muskets flashed and banged in quick succession, but the shots went wide. As he ran on, he saw that he was the last in the retreat. And then he remembered Bryant. But he could do nothing for Bryant, even if the senior midshipman was still alive. His duty now was to get the remainder of the party safely to the longboat.

The ground dipped suddenly in front of him, and he saw the blackness of space beyond the cliff verge and the notch where the gully started down to the cove and the longboat.

"You all right, sir? We're all down 'cep' you."

It was Bushey's voice. His head was protruding from the chimney at the top of the gully.

"Get down yourself, and look sharp!" Howard said.

He spoke sharply because every second brought the French muskets nearer; but his heart warmed at the thought that Bushey had waited for him. He was on the point of dropping down to the entrance of the chimney when a faint voice

168

called his name and he turned to peer into the darkness behind him. A man was crawling out of the bushes a few yards away, dragging one leg and pulling himself along with desperate energy.

"Can you help me?" he gasped, his breath coming in great sobs. "I'm done. Bullet in the groin."

It was Bryant. Howard glanced quickly beyond the crawling figure. The nearest of the pursuers was a scant hundred paces away. He grabbed at Bryant's collar and hauling with all his strength got him to the rim of the little hollow above the gully.

"Get yourself into the chimney if you can," he said quickly. "It's eight feet vertical, then easier. Lower yourself on your hands."

Groaning, Bryant wriggled his way downward. Howard turned and knelt just below the rim. The French soldier was pounding towards him, near enough now for the midshipman to make out the musket he carried. Howard pulled out his pistol, cocked it, and waited. The man was less than ten paces away when he fired and saw him fall headlong without a cry. There was a shout from another of the pursuers—the only other Frenchman within a hundred yards of the cliff edge. The rest, Howard saw, were strung out well behind him. He crammed the now useless pistol into his pocket and hurled himself down the slope to the mouth of the chimney.

Bryant's voice came up to him as he lowered himself into the narrow opening.

"I'm down—all in, though—can't go any farther."

Howard checked his own descent. With both of them down in the gully, a man above with a musket would have them at his mercy. They would not have time to gain the cover of the rocks lower down. He crushed himself close into the very gut of the chimney, clutching the roots of the thorn-bushes that overhung its rim. So steep was this first descent that a man who wished to look down must come to the very edge.

He had only a few seconds to wait. Heavy boots crashed in the bushes overhead and halted right above him. There was a chuckle of triumph, followed by the loud click of a musket being cocked. Howard reached one hand cautiously upward and forward. His fingers touched the cloth of a trouser-leg. A moment later the Frenchman gave a hoarse cry as he was pulled off his balance. He flew down past the midshipman, nearly knocking him from his precarious holds, his musket exploding harmlessly in mid-air before he crashed to his death on the sharp rocks of the gully.

Howard slid down the chimney as fast as he could and stooped above Bryant.

"On my back!" he panted. "Hang on somehow and I'll get you down."

Bryant's arms in a stranglehold round his neck nearly choked him, but he needed both hands for the scramble down the gully. Slipping, reeling, staggering down the ankle-twisting rocks, he got his awkward burden to the easier part just above the beach, and saw the glimmer of the sea—saw, too, men running up the shingle towards them. Then Bryant's weight was taken from him and he was being hustled between two seamen down the beach. There was a flash from the cliff-top and a musket-ball thudded into the gunwale close to him as he scrambled into the longboat.

"Shove off—oars—give way!"

The familiar orders were inexpressibly comforting. And it was Lieutenant Fraser's voice that gave them. Again a musket banged from the cliff, and again, the bullets plopped harmlessly into the water astern. The longboat was foaming through the little waves now, and any damage the French could do with their muskets was a matter of luck. But the shots and the vengeful shouting continued long after the victorious raiders were out of range.

Ten minutes later Lieutenant Fraser, at the tiller with his head swathed in bandaging, received Midshipman Howard's report.

"Very good, Mr. Howard," he commented when the midshipman had finished. "I shall leave Captain Strang to compliment you. Well, Mr. Bryant?"

Pulled off his balance, the Frenchman gave a hoarse cry.

Midshipman Bryant was lying stretched on a thwart while
Bushey bandaged his upper thigh. He was weak from loss of
blood and his voice was just audible.

"I've an apology to make to Mr. Howard, sir, if he'll
accept it."

"It's accepted, Mr. Bryant," Howard said quickly. "Say
no more."

"And—and the duel's cancelled?"

Midshipman Howard smiled to himself in the darkness

"Let's say it's fought and won, Mr. Bryant," he said.

171

A Man from Glasgow

W. SOMERSET MAUGHAM

I T is not often that anyone entering a great city for the first
time has the luck to witness such an incident as engaged
Shelley's attention when he drove into Naples. A youth ran
out of a shop pursued by a man armed with a knife. The man
overtook him and with one blow in the neck laid him dead on
the road. Shelley had a tender heart. He didn't look upon it
as a bit of local colour; he was seized with horror and indignation. But when he expressed his emotions to a Calab-
rian priest who was travelling with him, a fellow of gigantic
strength and stature, the priest laughed heartily and attempted to quiz him. Shelley says he never felt such an
inclination to beat anyone.

I have never seen anything so exciting as that, but the first
time I went to Algeciras I had an experience that seemed to
me far from ordinary. Algeciras was then an untidy,
neglected town. I arrived somewhat late at night and went
to an inn on the quay. It was rather shabby, but it had a fine
view of Gibraltar, solid and matter of fact, across the bay.
The moon was full. The office was on the first floor, and a
slatternly maid, when I asked for a room, took me upstairs.
The landlord was playing cards. He seemed little pleased to
see me. He looked me up and down, curtly gave me a num-

172

ber, and then, taking no further notice of me, went on with his game.

When the maid had shown me to my room I asked her what I could have to eat.

"What you like," she answered.

I knew well enough the unreality of the seeming profusion.

"What have you got in the house?"

"You can have eggs and ham."

The look of the hotel had led me to guess that I should get little else. The maid led me to a narrow room with white-washed walls and a low ceiling in which was a long table laid already for the next day's luncheon. With his back to the door sat a tall man, huddled over a *brasero,* the round brass dish of hot ashes which is erroneously supposed to give sufficient warmth for the temperate winter of Andalusia. I sat down at the table and waited for my scanty meal. I gave the stranger an idle glance. He was looking at me, but meeting my eyes he quickly turned away. I waited for my eggs. When the maid brought them he looked up again.

"I want you to wake me in time for the first boat," he said.

"Si, señor."

His accent told me that English was his native tongue, and the breadth of his build, his strongly marked features, led me to suppose him a northerner. The hardy Scot is far more often found in Spain than the Englishman. Whether you go to the rich mines of Rio Tinto, or to the bodegas of Jerez, to Seville or to Cadiz, it is the leisurely speech of beyond the Tweed that you hear. You will meet Scotsmen in the olive groves of Carmona, on the railway between Algeciras and Bobadilla, and even in the remote cork woods of Merida.

I finished eating and went over to the dish of burning ashes. It was midwinter and the windy passage across the bay had chilled my blood. The man pushed his chair away as I drew mine forwards.

"Don't move," I said. "There's heaps of room for two."

I lit a cigar and offered one to him. In Spain the Havana from Gib is never unwelcome.

173

"I don't mind if I do," he said, stretching out his hand.

I recognized the singing speech of Glasgow. But the stranger was not talkative, and my efforts at conversation broke down before his monosyllables. We smoked in silence. He was even bigger than I had thought, with great broad shoulders and ungainly limbs; his face was sunburned, his hair short and grizzled. His features were hard; mouth, ears and nose were large and heavy and his skin much wrinkled. His blue eyes were pale. He was constantly pulling his ragged, grey moustache. It was a nervous gesture that I found faintly irritating. Presently I felt that he was looking at me, and the intensity of his stare grew so irksome that I glanced up expecting him, as before, to drop his eyes. He did, indeed, for a moment, but then raised them again. He inspected me from under his long, bushy eyebrows.

"Just come from Gib?" he asked suddenly.

"Yes."

"I'm going tomorrow—on my way home. Thank God."

He said the last two words so fiercely that I smiled.

"Don't you like Spain?"

"Oh, Spain's all right."

"Have you been here long?"

"Too long. Too long."

He spoke with a kind of gasp. I was surprised at the emotion my casual inquiry seemed to excite in him. He sprang to his feet and walked backwards and forwards. He stamped to and fro like a caged beast, pushing aside a chair that stood in his way, and now and again repeated the words in a groan. "Too long. Too long." I sat still. I was embarrassed. To give myself countenance I stirred the *brasero* to bring the hotter ashes to the top, and he stood suddenly still, towering over me, as though my movement had brought back my existence to his notice. Then he sat down heavily in his chair.

"D'you think I'm queer?" he asked.

"Not more than most people," I smiled.

"You don't see anything strange in me?"

"Do you think I'm queer?" he asked.

He leant forward as he spoke so that I might see him well.

"No."

"You'd say so if you did, wouldn't you?"

"I would."

I couldn't quite understand what all this meant. I wondered if he was drunk. For two or three minutes he didn't say anything and I had no wish to interrupt the silence.

"What's your name?" he asked suddenly. I told him.

"Mine's Robert Morrison."

"Scotch?"

"Glasgow. I've been in this blasted country for years. Got any baccy?"

I gave him my pouch and he filled his pipe. He lit it from a piece of burning charcoal.

"I can't stay any longer. I've stayed too long. Too long."

He had an impulse to jump up again and walk up and down, but he resisted it, clinging to his chair. I saw on his

face the effort he was making. I judged that his restlessness
was due to chronic alcoholism. I find drunks very boring,
and I made up my mind to take an early opportunity of
slipping off to bed.

"I've been managing some olive groves," he went on. "I'm
here working for the Glasgow and South of Spain Olive Oil
Company, Limited."

"Oh, yes."

"We've got a new process for refining oil, you know.
Properly treated, Spanish oil is every bit as good as Lucca.
And we can sell it cheaper."

He spoke in a dry, matter-of-fact, business-like way. He
chose his words with Scotch precision. He seemed perfectly
sober.

"You know, Ecija is more or less the centre of the olive
trade, and we had a Spaniard there to look after the business.
But I found he was robbing us right and left, so I had to turn
him out. I used to live in Seville; it was more convenient for
shipping the oil. However, I found I couldn't get a trust-
worthy man to be at Ecija, so I went there myself. D'you
know it?"

"No."

"The firm has got a big estate two miles from the town,
just outside the village of San Lorenzo, and it's got a fine
house on it. It's on the crest of a hill, rather pretty to look at,
all white, you know, and straggling, with a couple of storks
perched on the roof. No one lived there, and I thought it
would save the rent of a place in town if I did."

"It must have been a bit lonely," I remarked.

"It was."

Robert Morrison smoked on for a minute or two in silence.
I wondered whether there was any point in what he was
telling me.

I looked at my watch.

"In a hurry?" he asked sharply.

"Not particularly. It's getting late."

"Well, what of it?"

"I suppose you didn't see many people?" I said, going back.

"Not many. I lived there with an old man and his wife who looked after me, and sometimes I used to go down to the village and play *tresillo* with Fernandez, the chemist, and one or two men who met at his shop. I used to shoot a bit and ride."

"It doesn't sound such a bad life to me."

"I'd been there two years last spring. By God, I've never known such heat as we had in May. No one could do a thing. The labourers just lay about in the shade and slept. Sheep died and some of the animals went mad. Even the oxen couldn't work. They stood around with their backs all humped up and gasped for breath. That blasted sun beat down and the glare was so awful, you felt your eyes would shoot out of your head. The earth cracked and crumbled, and the crops frizzled. The olives went to rack and ruin. It was simply hell. One couldn't get a wink of sleep. I went from room to room, trying to get a breath of air. Of course I kept the windows shut and had the floors watered, but that didn't do any good. The nights were just as hot as the days. It was like living in an oven.

"At last I thought I'd have a bed made up for me downstairs on the north side of the house in a room that was never used because in ordinary weather it was damp. I had an idea that I might get a few hours' sleep there at all events. Anyhow it was worth trying. But it was no damned good; it was a washout. I turned and tossed and my bed was so hot that I couldn't stand it. I got up and opened the doors that led to the veranda and walked out. It was a glorious night. The moon was so bright that I swear you could read a book by it. Did I tell you the house was on the crest of a hill? I leant against the parapet and looked at the olive-trees. It was like the sea. I suppose that's what made me think of home. I thought of the cool breeze in the fir-trees and the racket of the streets in Glasgow. Believe it or not, I could smell them, and I could smell the sea. I'd have given every bob I had

"I jumped over the parapet and ran down towards the sound."

in the world for an hour of that air. They say it's a foul
climate in Glasgow. Don't you believe it. I like the rain and
the grey sky and that yellow sea and the waves. I forgot that
I was in Spain, in the middle of the olive country, and I
opened my mouth and took a long breath as though I were
breathing in the sea-fog.

"And then all of a sudden I heard a sound. It was a man's
voice. Not loud, you know, low. It seemed to creep through
the silence like—well, I don't know what it was like. It
surprised me. I couldn't think who could be down there
in the olives at that hour. It was past midnight. It was a chap
laughing. A funny sort of laugh. I suppose you'd call it a
chuckle. It seemed to crawl up the hill—disjointedly."

Morrison looked at me to see how I took the odd word he
used to express a sensation that he didn't know how to describe.

"I mean, it seemed to shoot up in little jerks, something like shooting stones out of a pail. I leant forward and stared. With the full moon it was almost as light as day, but I'm dashed if I could see a thing. The sound stopped, but I kept on looking at where it had come from in case somebody moved. And in a minute it started off again, but louder. You couldn't have called it a chuckle any more, it was a real belly laugh. It just rang through the night. I wondered it didn't wake my servants. It sounded like someone who was roaring drunk.

" 'Who's there?' I shouted.

"The only answer I got was a roar of laughter. I don't mind telling you I was getting a bit annoyed. I had half a mind to go down and see what it was all about. I wasn't going to let some drunken swine kick up a row like that on my place in the middle of the night. And then suddenly there was a yell. By Jove, I was startled. Then cries. The man had laughed with a deep bass voice, but his cries were—shrill, like a pig having his throat cut.

" 'My God,' I cried.

"I jumped over the parapet and ran down towards the sound. I thought somebody was being killed. There was silence and then one piercing shriek. After that sobbing and moaning. I'll tell you what it sounded like, it sounded like someone at the point of death. There was a long groan and then nothing. Silence. I ran from place to place. I couldn't find anyone. At last I climbed the hill again and went back to my room.

"You can imagine how much sleep I got that night. As soon as it was light, I looked out of the window in the direction from which the row had come and I was surprised to see a little white house in a sort of dale among the olives. The ground on that side didn't belong to us and I'd never been through it. I hardly ever went to that part of the house and so I'd never seen the house before. I asked José who lived there. He told me that a madman had inhabited it, with his brother and a servant."

"Oh, was that the explanation?" I said. "Not a very nice neighbour."

The Scot bent over quickly and seized my wrist. He thrust his face into mine and his eyes were starting out of his head with terror.

"The madman had been dead for twenty years," he whispered.

He let go my wrist and leant back in his chair panting.

"I went down to the house and walked all round it. The windows were barred and shuttered and the door was locked. I knocked. I shook the handle and rang the bell. I heard it tinkle, but no one came. It was a two-storey house and I looked up. The shutters were tight closed, and there wasn't a sign of life anywhere."

"Well, what sort of condition was the house in?" I asked.

"Oh, rotten. The whitewash had worn off the walls and there was practically no paint left on the door or the shutters. Some of the tiles off the roof were lying on the ground. They looked as though they'd been blown away in a gale."

"Queer," I said.

"I went to my friend Fernandez, the chemist, and he told me the same story as José. I asked about the madman and Fernandez said that no one ever saw him. He was more or less comatose ordinarily, but now and then he had an attack of acute mania and then he could be heard from ever so far laughing his head off and then crying. It used to scare people. He died in one of his attacks and his keepers cleared out at once. No one had ever dared to live in the house since.

"I didn't tell Fernandez what I'd heard. I thought he'd only laugh at me. I stayed up that night and kept watch. But nothing happened. There wasn't a sound. I waited about till dawn and then I went to bed."

"And you never heard anything more?"

"Not for a month. The drought continued and I went on sleeping in the lumber-room at the back. One night I was fast asleep, when something seemed to happen to me; I don't exactly know how to describe it, it was a funny feeling as though someone had given me a little nudge, to warn me, and suddenly I was wide awake. I lay there in my bed and then in the same way as before I heard a long, low gurgle, like a man enjoying an old joke. It came from away down in the valley and it got louder. It was a great bellow of laughter. I jumped out of bed and went to the window. My legs began to tremble. It was horrible to stand there and listen to the shouts of laughter that rang through the night. Then there was the pause, and after that a shriek of pain and that ghastly sobbing. It didn't sound human. I mean, you might have thought it was an animal being tortured. I don't mind telling you I was scared stiff. I couldn't have moved if I'd wanted to. After a time the sounds stopped, not suddenly, but dying away little by little. I strained my ears, but I couldn't hear a thing. I crept back to bed and hid my face.

"I remembered then that Fernandez had told me that the madman's attacks only came at intervals. The rest of the time he was quite quiet. Apathetic, Fernandez said. I wondered if the fits of mania came regularly. I reckoned out how long it had been between the two attacks I'd heard. Twenty-eight days. It didn't take me long to put two and two together; it was quite obvious that it was the full moon that set him off. I'm not a nervous man really and I made up my mind to get to the bottom of it, so I looked out in the calendar which day the moon would be full next and that night I didn't go to bed. I cleaned my revolver and loaded it. I prepared a lantern and sat down on the parapet of my house to wait I felt perfectly cool. To tell you the truth, I was rather pleased with myself because I didn't feel scared. There was a bit of a wind, and it whistled about the roof. It rustled over the leaves of the olive trees like waves swishing on the pebbles of the beach. The moon shone on the white walls of the house in the hollow. I felt particularly cheery.

"At last I heard a little sound, the sound I knew, and I almost laughed. I was right; it was the full moon and the attacks came as regular as clockwork. That was all to the good. I threw myself over the wall into the olive grove and

ran straight to the house. The chuckling grew louder as I
came near. I got to the house and looked up. There was no
light anywhere. I put my ears to the door and listened. I
heard the madman simply laughing his head off. I beat on
the door with my fist and I pulled the bell. The sound of it
seemed to amuse him. He roared with laughter. I knocked
again, louder and louder, and the more I knocked the more
he laughed. Then I shouted at the top of my voice.

" 'Open the blasted door, or I'll break it down.'

"I stepped back and kicked the latch with all my might.
I flung myself at the door with the whole weight of my body.
It cracked. Then I put all my strength into it and the damned
thing smashed open.

"I took the revolver out of my pocket and held my lantern
in the other hand. The laughter sounded louder now that the
door was opened. I stepped in. The stink nearly knocked me
down. I mean, just think, the windows hadn't been opened
for twenty years. The row was enough to raise the dead, but
for a moment I didn't know where it was coming from. The
walls seemed to throw the sound backwards and forwards. I
pushed open a door by my side and went into a room. It was
bare and white and there wasn't a stick of furniture in it.
The sound was louder and I followed it. I went into another
room, but there was nothing there. I opened a door and found
myself at the foot of a staircase. The madman was laughing
just over my head. I walked up, cautiously, you know, I
wasn't taking any risks, and at the top of the stairs there
was a passage. I walked along it, throwing my light ahead
of me, and I came to a room at the end. I stopped. He
was in there. I was only separated from the sound by a thin
door.

"It was awful to hear it. A shiver passed through me and I
cursed myself because I began to tremble. It wasn't like a
human being at all. By Jove, I very nearly took to my heels
and ran. I had to clench my teeth to force myself to stay.
But I simply couldn't bring myself to turn the handle. And
then the laughter was cut. cut with a knife you'd have said,

"They were torturing him . . . I flung open the door and burst in."

and I heard a hiss of pain. I hadn't heard that before, it was too low to carry to my place, and then a gasp.

" 'Ay.' I heard the man speak in Spanish. 'You're killing me. Take it away. O God, help me!'

"He screamed. The brutes were torturing him. I flung open the door and burst in. The draught blew a shutter back and the moon streamed in so bright that it dimmed my lantern. In my ears as clearly as I hear you speak and as close, I heard the wretched chap's groans. It was awful, moaning and sobbing, and frightful gasps. No one could survive that. He was at the point of death. I tell you I heard his broken, choking cries right in my ears. And the room was empty."

Robert Morrison sank back in his chair. That huge solid man had strangely the look of a lay figure in a studio. You felt that if you pushed him he would fall over in a heap on to the floor.

"And then?" I asked.

He took a rather dirty handkerchief out of his pocket and wiped his forehead.

"I felt I didn't much want to sleep in that room on the north side so, heat or no heat, I moved back to my own quarters. Well, exactly four weeks later, about two in the morning, I was waked up by the madman's chuckle. It was almost at my elbow. I don't mind telling you that my nerve was a bit shaken by then, so next time the blighter was due to have an attack, next time the moon was full, I mean, I got Fernandez to come and spend the night with me. I didn't tell him anything. I kept him up playing cards till two in the morning, and then I heard it again. I asked him if he heard anything. 'Nothing,' he said. 'There's somebody laughing,' I said. 'You're drunk, man,' he said, and he began laughing too. That was too much. 'Shut up, you fool,' I said. The laughter grew louder and louder. I cried out. I tried to shut it out by putting my hands to my ears, but it wasn't a damned bit of good. I heard it and I heard the scream of pain. Fernandez thought I was mad. He didn't dare say so, because he knew I'd have killed him. He said he'd go to bed, and in the morning I found he'd slunk away. His bed hadn't been slept in. He'd taken himself off when he left me.

"After that I couldn't stop in Ecija. I put a factor there and went back to Seville. I felt myself pretty safe there, but as the time came near I began to get scared. Of course I told myself not to be a damned fool, but you know, I damned well couldn't help myself. The fact is, I was afraid the sounds had followed me, and I knew if I heard them in Seville I'd go on hearing them all my life. I've got as much courage as any man, but damn it all, there are limits to everything. Flesh and blood couldn't stand it. I knew I'd go stark staring mad. I got in such a state that I began drinking, the suspense was so awful, and I used to lie awake counting the days. And at last I knew it'd come. And it came. I heard those sounds in Seville—sixty miles away from Ecija."

I didn't know what to say. I was silent for a while.

"When did you hear the sounds last?" I asked.

"Four weeks ago."

I looked up quickly. I was startled.

"What d'you mean by that? It's not full moon tonight?"

He gave me a dark, angry look. He opened his mouth to speak and then stopped as though he couldn't. You would have said his vocal cords were paralysed, and it was with a strange croak that at last he answered.

"Yes, it is."

He stared at me and his pale blue eyes seemed to shine red. I have never seen in a man's face a look of such terror. He got up quickly and stalked out of the room, slamming the door behind him.

I must admit that I didn't sleep any too well that night myself.

The
Three Blackbirds
of Monsieur Castelet

HUGH PATERSON

THE little French town of Ste-Amélie basked in the afternoon sun. Behind it in a snow-capped line swept the 10,000 foot peaks of the Pyrenees.

An open grey sports car with British number plates slid smoothly and unobtrusively into the flower-bright, strollerfilled central square.

On the sunlit pavement to one side stood the glittering figure of a very senior police official. Black-uniformed motorcyclists hovered in attendance. Local constables fringed the group; deferential subordinates surrounded him.

His eye fell on the sports car's driver. He started. He stared. He stiffened.

His hand flew up, pointing. His voice rang out like a pistol-shot.

"*Fetch me*," he shouted, "*that man!*"

Whistles shrilled, exhausts roared. Police exploded into the road. The sports car skidded to a stop. Before the eyes of the astounded passers-by, the driver—a long, lean Briton—was extracted by many hands and hustled across, protesting.

"No, Monsieur," said the official, smiling cat-like up at him. "There is no mistake—I have waited twenty years for this arrest."

* * *

The night was dark, so dark that the boy who was guiding them was almost invisible.

Sergeant Roberts stumbled, rather noisily. They all three stopped, rigidly listening, but no dog, no stir of alarm broke the black hush.

Very cautiously they moved on and up again.

"Sorry, sir," whispered Roberts. "It's that leg."

"Take it easy," said Captain Kent, steadying him.

He and the sturdy, stocky Sergeant Roberts had met for the first time twelve hours ago, in the loft of a friendly farm-house to which separate French Resistance units had channelled them. Roberts had been badly wounded before capture, and under the stresses of escape his wound was troubling him. It would have been better if he could have had a day or two to rest, but there were rumours of a new and strict police search—Higher Authority was determined to please the Germans—and so the two of them were creeping forward, this autumn night of 1942, towards the mountain crossing and the Spanish frontier.

They had arrived, Kent saw, outside a building. It loomed black against the darker bulk of the hillside. Somewhere below was a smell of wood smoke, a chink of light—they were on the outskirts of a village. He heard the boy scratch at a shutter; a pause, and then a door-hinge creaked. An inky space opened cavernously.

The boy melted like a shadow whence he had come and Roberts and Kent moved forward softly into the unknown.

Behind them a door closed heavily.

A light flared up. By the glow of a stump of candle they saw that they were in a low, earth-floored room. Behind the light, regarding them, was a small, dark, active, leathery man —the smuggler who was to guide them across the frontier. the man called Juan.

He stared at them long and keenly.

"You will undertake it?" said Kent hesitantly into the lengthening silence. "As was arranged?"

Juan nodded.

"Oh, yes. But I warn you, we must start at once. They know you are on the move—they are after you. You will already have been told that someone high up is out to please the Boche—the lesser ones must conform, you understand? For you, if you are taken, not so good. For me—the finish." He gestured briefly. "And now, eat quickly while I make ready."

He brought out bread and cheese and rough country wine, and while they ate ravenously, Juan bundled himself into a short, thick coat and put his scanty things together. By the time they had finished, he was ready. He pinched out the guttering candle and listened at the heavy, barred door. There was no one, nothing.

They passed into the cold mountain air.

Dawn, breaking chill and grey, found them climbing slowly through a narrow, cliff-walled ravine choked with chestnut scrub and thorny, bramble-filled undergrowth. Far behind them lay the villages and the low ground. Ahead, a stony goat-track wound to a pass.

They halted among the thickets to rest. Juan leaned easily against a rock; Roberts sat down on a flat stone and massaged his leg.

"And how——?" said Juan.

"Not too bad," said Roberts cheerfully, and went on rubbing.

To give him time, Kent propped himself as though tired against a tree and looked round at the line of distant snows, the skyline, the climbing spurs, the shallow nick of the pass. A movement there caught his eye—he saw men, two men.

"What's that?" he said to Juan, pointing.

Juan detached himself from his rock. He stared a long moment at the pass. "They are before us," he said, his voice suddenly dead and flat.

"For you, if you are taken, not so good. For me—the finish."

"And now——?" said Kent.

But there was a stir down at the mouth of the ravine, a sound of voices, a trampling over the dead leaves and bracken. A close-set line of uniformed men stretched from cliff to cliff and, as they watched, it moved slowly forward towards them, sweeping the rift as closely and effectively as a net.

"We are betrayed," said Juan.

"Who by?" said Kent.

"The boy, perhaps—does it matter? We are finished."

And, thought Kent, it didn't matter.

They turned and ran like hunted animals. They zig-zagged up the hillside through the chestnut woods, running swiftly, silently. They reached the foot of the cliffs. They hurried along them, looking for a crack, a cranny, a cleft, a way out, a hole among the boulders, a hiding-place. The grey rocks rose unbroken. There was nothing but the thin undergrowth and the litter of old rock-falls.

The search was drawing closer.

They flung themselves down among the dead leaves, burrowing deep among drifts and hollows, lying still—desperately—behind the narrow boles of the chestnuts and the leafless autumn brambles.

A crackling sounded a little way off. It came nearer, louder, clearer. A uniform kepi showed, bobbing briskly over the rough ground.

The searcher came in sight. He was a policeman, young, dark and athletic. He scrambled forward over the boulders, and then stopped in mid-stride, staring full at them.

Then, astonishingly, he winked and put a conspiratorial finger to his lips.

A stentorian hail came up at him from farther down the hillside.

"Castelet! What can you see there?"

"Nothing at all but three blackbirds!" returned the unabashed Castelet.

"Imbecile!" said the distant voice.

Castelet came grinning to attention, and saluted it; he marched on smartly between the fugitives, stepping carefully over the legs of Juan. As he passed, he whispered swiftly: "After dark." Then he was gone, crashing exuberantly through the bushes.

The three waited. There was nothing else to do.

"Raoul Castelet?" said Juan, in answer to Kent's query. "An

honest policeman, yes. In this affair—who knows?"

They heard the searchers reach the head of the ravine and exchange shouts with the watchers in the pass. They listened to their empty-handed retreat, stumbling and gossiping and clattering along the rocky bottom among the trees. One came quite close to them—not Raoul; they flattened themselves among the leaves and he passed, grumbling to his neighbour, smoking, the sharp scent of his tobacco hanging long in the air after him.

He winked at them.

The twilight gathered, and the mountain side grew chill. It was after eight when there came a low whistle down among the trees. Juan responded cautiously.

The dead leaves crackled. Then a figure loomed up out of the darkness, hesitated, and sank down with them. It was Castelet again, in shabby black beret and peasant clothes.

"Monsieur," said Kent, "you understand the position?"

"Oh, perfectly—Captain Kent, is it not?—you see, they furnished us with the description. And your companion is Sergeant Roberts." He bowed politely, and shook hands formally with them in the darkness. "Oh, yes, I understand fully. But it did not seem convenient that you should be arrested just now—it is not in accordance with public sentiment. It would be bad for the reputation of the police. So I felt it advisable to take action. And now to business." He turned with a rustle of leaves, facing Juan. "As you guess, someone has talked. Never mind who—he will be dealt with. My senior officer—" he described him in a few terse words "—who will also be dealt with one day, has had the passes blocked. Now up here are Bonnet and Pichon. The rift has been searched without finding you; they will not be expecting anyone. I will move up on the left of the approach and try to create a diversion. They are sure to chase me, and I can out-distance them. Meantime you slip through on the

191

right; you can go on by the Val d'Enfer and the Col d'Ardet. There's no one up there."

Kent tried to speak his thanks, but Raoul cut him short with—"At your service, Monsieur. *En avant!*"

They set off along the goat-track through the dark woods, Raoul in the lead and Juan bringing up the rear. Roberts, whose leg had stiffened, moved clumsily.

Raoul turned, clicking his tongue in sympathy.

"M'sieur the sergeant is wounded? They did not tell us that—but courage, the pass is not difficult. Juan, moreover, is a good guide."

"Oh, I can make it," said Roberts, who spoke his own brand of fluent but execrable French, picked up in his wanderings. "Don't worry about me, chum."

They threaded the woods, moving slowly at first, till Roberts's leg thawed, when they travelled more quickly and silently. Now Kent could see the nick of the pass ahead of them, silhouetted against the lighter night sky. The mountains, he realized, swept up steeply on either hand, making any low detour impossible. The pass, or over the top— there was no other way.

Now they were creeping out of the stony head of the ravine, moving softly, hand and foot, behind Raoul. They topped a rise, and saw in the distance a pinpoint of light— the sentries' fire. Raoul and Juan joined in whispered colloquy. Then Raoul tugged his beret down tighter and turned up his coat-collar.

"Good luck," he said, and then he was gone into the night.

They were left no time to think of him, for Juan immediately led them on a back-breaking all-fours crawl over rock and grit and shifting scree along the right-hand side of the gully. The farther they went, the smaller grew the boulders and the less the cover, till they were creeping belly-flat from rock to rock. They could now see the two sentries; they sat, heavily wrapped, behind their watch-fire, looking down the stony alley of the pass towards the darkness of the ravine.

Juan stopped not thirty yards from them.

Automatic fire went licking and hose-piping after Raoul.

"When Raoul draws them off," he breathed, "run quickly, bent double—make a dash for it."

They lay there, taut.

There was a long rattle of scree on the far side. In the dimness at the edge of the firelight Kent saw Raoul. Miraculously his beret, scrugged down, had acquired a British Army angle. His jacket, tucked in, looked like battle-dress. A crouching, hesitant figure, he stared at the sentries for a minute; then he turned and fled at a zigzag run.

The nearer of the two men started after him. The other jerked him back and said something they could not catch. Then he pulled some object from under his cloak, and a savage spray of automatic fire went licking and hose-piping after Raoul. It followed the fleeing figure brutally, knocking up stones, whining in ricochets.

There was the distant clatter of a fall, and then only darkness and silence.

When their retreat brought them back to the goat-track

and the shelter of the ravine, Juan was weeping openly.

There was a soft, slightly shaky whistle. Raoul rose like a shadow almost at their feet.

Juan stopped sobbing, and swore.

"Are you hurt?" said Kent.

"Bumps and scratches merely," said Raoul. "You heard me slide? That animal Pichon! He nearly had me. Who would have thought he would fire? And I relieve him at eight o'clock tomorrow!" He began to laugh, shaking silently. "Picture it, my friends! What a scene when he found he'd shot his relief!"

"Be sensible, Raoul," said Juan. "What now?"

"What now?" said Raoul. "Why, if we can't get through the pass, we must go over. There will be snow, but not impassable. But we shall have to go a long way round—there's no short cut out of the ravine—we must go down, and up again by the spur, and the sergeant——"

"Oh," said Roberts stoutly—but Kent could feel him, in the blackness, leaning over to ease his leg—"I like walking —to Spain."

"Be quiet," said Juan.

They stood there silently. Juan moved away from them; they heard the soft click of stones under his feet. He was scouting slowly along the towering crag-face to their right. It rose above them, tall and smooth and unscalable. Kent could have sworn that Juan sniffed like a hound, smelling his way.

Then he said with sudden confidence, "Here."

It was a wholly unsuspected crack, a hidden, hairline rift winding from ledge to infinitely small ledge. Juan, agile as a goat, led the way up to it. Roberts followed, more awkwardly; Kent and Raoul came gingerly behind, clinging to next to nothing, over nothing, two flies on a wall, suspended over gulfs of space.

"Juan," said Raoul breathlessly. "I thought I knew everything—but not this."

"Ah!" said Juan, and chuckled hoarsely somewhere

above them. "This is outside the normal course of business. You'll have to forget this, Raoul. I wouldn't have used it but for the emergency."

"Oh, certainly, certainly," said Raoul, who had momentarily attained a ledge. "But tell me—what d'you bring up it?"

"Who knows?" said Juan.

Kent saw Roberts disappear up and over, one moment a shape against the sky, and the next gone. Then Juan's sinewy hand came down to him. There was a terrifying moment, hanging out over the black and giddying void. Then he, too, was over the overhang and sprawling on the cliff top beside Roberts, and a panting, freely-commenting Raoul was being hauled up.

Kent looked about him. They were on a steep, slanting ledge of the hillside. Far to his left—lower down than they, he saw—glimmered the sentries' fire. Below them lay shadowy darkness, and around and about and over them reared the dimly-seen immensities of the mountains.

They picked themselves up and went on.

"I'll see you part of the way," said Raoul from the tail of the line. "And then I must go back—I relieve that Pichon at eight. I shall spend most of tomorrow looking for my body. I shall believe his story—oh, how I shall believe his story!" He waved at the distant watch-fire. "*A bientôt,* Pichon."

The clouds were breaking and a wan half-moon showed through. They were mounting a steep and shale-covered slope which seemed to go on for ever. At first it was tree-dotted, and then the trees thinned out and grew fewer till the last outliers were gone, and the four were scrambling and slithering up raw, bare scree. The air was bitter and chill. Now and then in the fitful moonlight enormous, snowy peaks looked distantly down on them and vanished again into blanketing cloud. They were climbing and winding, small as ants, up the shoulder of some unknown mountain.

The first white snow patch showed.

The next was larger and, as they rose, there were more and more of them. The four struggled, almost abreast, over the rocky skyline.

They stopped together.

Immense and glimmering, a vast, white, undulating plain, the snow-fields stretched untrodden before them. Away in the blackness beyond the moonlight, beyond the last, wind-rippled rise, lay the cloudy remoteness of Spain.

They started down from the ridge. The snow was shallow at first, crunching sharply under their feet. They were in single file again, Raoul once more in the lead. All of a sudden the snow was deeper. A cloud slid over the moon and, as though in token of what the mountains could do, a wind eddy threw stinging ice particles in their faces. Then the snow grew shallower again as they reached a stretch of high ground, and for a while the going was easier, though there were treacherous, wind-polished ice patches.

The ground fell away again.

Without the least warning they blundered headlong, as though they had stepped into water, into a deeply snow-filled gully. Raoul and Roberts were tumbling and sprawling. Kent sank in to his knees, but scrambled out again. Juan, forewarned, stopped in time.

Raoul floundered out, spluttering and swearing, his clothes and hair plastered with snow. Roberts struggled half-way, and fell back again. He struggled and fell once more.

Kent and Raoul plunged in. They lifted him.

"My leg," said Roberts. "I twisted it." He paused, and ended, "It's broken."

They hauled him out between them to solid ground. There was no doubt about the break—a clean snap of the shin. They had little with which to improvise splints, but, crouching in the dark, they did what they could.

"Look here," said Roberts, sitting up. "You take me back a bit. You put me where I can holler to the sentries. I'll wait till you've gone on, and then yell till they pick me up. Raoul here's going that way—he'll squat behind a rock and keep an eye on me. I'll be all right. You just get on with it."

"Don't be an ass," said Kent.

"Impossible!" said Juan harshly. "After that performance by Pichon—what chance have you?"

"You'll get to Spain," said Raoul. "We'll carry you."

Juan looked sharply at Raoul. He caught him by the arm and pulled him aside, and said something swiftly and vehemently in a *patois* Kent couldn't follow.

Kent, kneeling by Roberts, stared up at them. Juan's face was in shadow; but the moon had come out again, and lit Raoul's. He was cool, set and unruffled. His dark brows were drawn down.

He pushed Juan away, answering briefly. Then he was stooping over Roberts, saying cheerfully: "On our way. Will the captain carry you first, or shall I?"

It was Kent who, helped by Raoul, hoisted the protesting Roberts up pick-a-back and, Raoul leading, they set off again. Now their course was winding and roundabout. With the laden Kent in mind, Raoul picked his way cautiously among the hazards. Detour after detour, up-down, round, up-down, he took them on a more-or-less easy path among clefts and craggy outcrops and slippery ice.

"To me," said Juan, seeing Kent sway.

But Juan was too lightly built, wiry as he was, to carry Roberts's muscular bulk for long. Raoul took over. The weather was worsening now. The moon showed only briefly, the wind was colder and stronger. From time to time snow-squalls swept at them. And still they tramped doggedly, endlessly, over that nightmare extent of snow-clad mountain, crawling up, staggering down, between the white and terrible towers of the peaks. Presently Kent hardly knew when he carried Roberts, or when Raoul did. At first he made himself go from point to point, from this rock to that, from here to the snow-patch three hundred yards away, but at last he could only concentrate on putting one foot after the other—the left, the right—again—again, again. . . .

The blur dissolved suddenly. It was daybreak. In the

Raoul leading, they set off again . . . picking a way among the hazards.

thin, grey light before sunrise they were stumbling—Raoul carrying Roberts—down a snow-free, grassy slope into a deep, inhabited valley. Before them wound a road—a Spanish road.

They dropped exhausted on the verge.

Kent roused himself. He looked at the others; they were sunken-eyed, wan and drawn, and he had no doubt he was too. Juan ferreted in his clothing and brought out a squat, black bottle. They each took a pull at it; it was raw, locally-distilled brandy, so harsh and strong it made them gasp. But a little life began to come back into them.

Somewhere down in the valley they heard the grinding approach of an aged, slow-moving lorry.

Raoul got to his feet. He straightened his coat and jerked his beret to its normal gallant angle.

"*Au revoir,*" he said. "I'm late for my appointment with Pichon."

And with a quick wave of the hand he was gone.

striding swiftly up the hill and back to the mountains.

"A brave man, that," said Juan.

Kent and Roberts looked at him.

"He goes," said Juan quietly, "to face a firing-squad."

* * *

For a long moment the driver of the sports car and the glittering official stared in silence at one another.

Then the Briton hurled himself at the Frenchman.

But even as the constables leapt to seize him, they saw—amazingly, incredibly—that the two were not locked in combat. Their "captive", with howls of joy, was hugging their distinguished superior; and he, with equal fervour was embracing what they had hitherto supposed to be an international criminal.

"*Raoul!*" said Kent, holding the new and gorgeous figure at arm's length. "But how—but how—we thought they'd shoot you!"

"I thought the same myself," said the still unruffled Raoul. "I therefore gave that Pichon the go-by. I returned not to the police force, but to the Resistance. And now, my friend, we must celebrate. The hotel here is tolerable. My men will see to your car. We will send for Juan, who is not at the moment in jail—and we will drink to Sergeant Roberts."

And they walked off arm in arm along the pavement.

The Bus Conductor

E. F. BENSON

MY friend, Hugh Grainger, and I had just returned from a two days' visit in the country, where we had been staying in a house of sinister repute which was supposed to be haunted by ghosts of a peculiarly fearsome and truculent sort. The house itself was all that such a house should be, Jacobean and oak-panelled, with long dark passages and high vaulted rooms. It stood, also, very remote, and was encompassed by a wood of sombre pines that muttered and whispered in the dark, and all the time that we were there a south-westerly gale with torrents of scolding rain had prevailed, so that by day and night weird voices moaned and fluted in the chimneys, a company of uneasy spirits held colloquy among the trees, and sudden tattoos and tappings beckoned from the window-panes. But in spite of these surroundings, which were sufficient in themselves, one would almost say, to generate spontaneously occult phenomena, nothing of any description had occurred. I am bound to add, also, that my own state of mind was peculiarly well adapted to receive or even to invent the sights and sounds we had gone to seek, for I was, I confess, during the whole time that we were there, in a state of abject apprehension, and lay awake both nights through hours of terrified unrest, afraid of the dark, yet more afraid of what a lighted candle might show me.

Hugh Grainger, on the evening after our return to town, had dined with me, and after dinner our conversation, as was natural, soon came back to these entrancing topics.

"But why you go ghost-seeking I cannot imagine," he said, "because your teeth were chattering and your eyes starting out of your head all the time you were there, from sheer fright. Or do you like being frightened?"

"Why, of course, I like being frightened," I said. "I want to be made to creep and creep and creep. Fear is the most absorbing and luxurious of emotions. One forgets all else if one is afraid."

He got up and lit a cigarette, and, looking at him, somehow my mind went back to a certain period in his life, when, from some cause unknown, he had become a mere quivering mass of disordered nerves. Oddly enough, at the same moment and for the first time, he began to speak of it himself.

"You, for all your apprehensions and expectancy, have never seen a ghost. But I have, though I am the last person in the world you would have thought likely to do so, and, though my nerves are steady enough again now, it knocked me all to bits."

He sat down again in his chair.

"No doubt you remember my going to bits," he said, "and since I believe that I am sound again now, I should rather like to tell you about it. But before I couldn't; I couldn't speak of it at all to anybody. Yet there ought to have been nothing frightening about it; what I saw was certainly a most useful and friendly ghost. But it came from the shaded side of things; it looked suddenly out of the night and the mystery with which life is surrounded."

I put on more coal and poked up the fire. "Go on, please, and slowly," I said.

Hugh began: "It was the 24th of June, just eighteen

201

months ago," he said. "I had let my flat, you may remember, and came up from the country to stay with you for a week. We had dined alone here——"

"Did you see the ghost here?" I asked.

"I was in the house when I saw it."

I hugged myself in silence.

"We had dined alone here in Graeme Street," he said, "and after dinner I went out to some party and you stopped at home. At dinner your man did not wait, and when I asked where he was, you told me he was ill, and, I thought, changed the subject rather abruptly. You gave me your latch-key when I went out, and on coming back, I found you had gone to bed. So I suppose it was rather late when I went upstairs.

"You had put me in the front room, on the third floor, overlooking the street, a room which I thought you generally occupied yourself. It was a very hot night, and on my return the whole sky was cloud-covered, and it both looked and felt as if we might have a thunderstorm before morning. I was feeling very sleepy and heavy, and it was not till after I had got into bed that I noticed by the shadows of the window-frames on the blind that only one of the windows was open. But it did not seem worth while to get out of bed in order to open it, though I felt rather airless and uncomfortable, and I went to sleep.

"What time it was when I awoke I do not know, but it was certainly not yet dawn, and I never remember being conscious of such an extraordinary stillness as prevailed. There was no sound of either foot-passengers or wheeled traffic; the music of life appeared to be absolutely mute. But now, instead of being sleepy and heavy, I felt, though I must have slept an hour or two at most, since it was not yet dawn, perfectly fresh and wide-awake, and the effort which had seemed not worth making before, that of getting out of bed and opening the other window, was quite easy now, and I pulled up the blind, threw it wide open, and leaned out, for somehow I parched and pined for air.

"Then I heard suddenly and not very far away the sound

202

of some approaching vehicle; I could distinguish the tread of two horses walking at a slow foot's pace. They were, though not yet visible, coming up the street, and yet this indication of life did not abate that dreadful sense of loneliness which I have spoken of.

"Then the vehicle came into sight. At first I could not distinguish what it was. Then I saw that the horses were black and had long tails, and that what they dragged was made of glass, but had a black frame. It was a hearse.

"It was moving up this side of the street. It stopped at your door.

"Then the obvious solution struck me. You had said at dinner that your man was ill, and you were, I thought, unwilling to speak more about his illness. No doubt, so I imagined now, he was dead, and for some reason, perhaps because you did not want me to know anything about it, you were having the body removed at night. This, I must tell you, passed through my mind quite instantaneously, and it did not occur to me how unlikely it really was, before the next thing happened.

"I was still looking out of the window, and I remember also wondering, yet only momentarily, how odd it was that I saw things—or rather the one thing I was gazing at—so very distinctly. Of course, there was a moon behind the clouds, but it was curious how every detail of the hearse and the horses was visible. There was only one man, the driver, with it, and the street was otherwise absolutely empty. It was at him I was looking now. I could see every detail of his clothes, but from where I was, so high above him, I could not see his face. Suddenly he looked up at me. He had a rather long thin face, and on his left cheek there was a mole with a growth of dark hair on it. All this was as distinct as if it had been noonday, and as if I was within a yard of him.

"Then he touched his hat to me, and jerked his thumb over his shoulder.

"'Just room for one inside, sir,' he said.

"There was something so odious, so coarse, so unfeeling

about this that I instantly drew my head in, pulled the blind down again, and then, for what reason I do not know, turned on the electric light in order to see what time it was. The hands of my watch pointed to half past eleven.

"It was then for the first time, I think, that a doubt crossed my mind as to the nature of what I had just seen. But I put out the light again, got into bed, and began to think. We had dined; I had gone to a party, I had come back and written letters, had gone to bed and had slept. So how could it be half past eleven? . . . Or—*what* half past eleven was it?

"Then another easy solution struck me; my watch must have stopped. But it had not; I could hear it ticking.

"There was stillness and silence again. I expected every moment to hear muffled footsteps on the stairs, footsteps moving slow and small under the weight of a heavy burden, but from inside the house there was no sound whatever. Outside, too, there was the same dead silence, while the hearse waited at the door. And the minutes ticked on and ticked on, and at length I began to see a difference in the light in the room, and knew that the dawn was beginning to break outside. But how had it happened, then, that if the corpse was to be removed at night it had not gone, and that the hearse still waited, when morning was already coming?

"Presently I got out of bed again, and with a sense of strong physical shrinking I went to the window and pulled back the blind. The dawn was coming fast; the whole street was lit by that silver hueless light of morning. But there was no hearse there.

"Once again I looked at my watch. It was just a quarter past four. But I would swear that not half an hour had passed since it had told me that it was half past eleven.

"And then I told myself that the whole thing had been a dream. But if you ask me whether I believed what I told myself, I must confess that I did not.

"Your man did not appear at breakfast next morning, nor did I see him again before I left that afternoon. I think if I had, I should have told you about all this, but it was still

"Just room for one inside, sir!"

possible, you see, that what I had seen was a real hearse, driven by a real driver, for all the ghastly gaiety of the face that had looked up to mine, and the levity of his pointing hand. I might possibly have fallen asleep soon after seeing him, and slumbered through the removal of the body and the departure of the hearse. So I did not speak of it to you."

"Don't tell me it was all a dream," I said.

"I don't know whether it was or not. I can only say that I believe myself to have been wide awake. In any case the rest of the story is—odd.

"Exactly a month afterwards I was in London again, but only for the day. I arrived at Victoria about eleven, and took the underground to Sloane Square in order to see if you were in town and would give me lunch. It was a baking hot morning, and I intended to take a bus from the King's Road as far as Graeme Street. There was one standing at the corner just as I came out of the station, but I saw that the top was full, and the inside appeared to be full also. Just as I came up to it the conductor, who, I suppose, had been inside, collecting fares or what not, came out on to the step within a few feet of me. I saw his face; *it was the face of the driver of the hearse, with a mole on the left cheek*. Then he spoke to me, jerking his thumb over his shoulder.

" 'Just room for one inside, sir,' he said.

"At that a sort of panic terror took possession of me, and I know I gesticulated wildly with my arms, and cried, 'No, no!' But at that moment I was living not in the hour that was then passing, but in that hour which had passed a month ago, when I leaned from the window of your bedroom here just before the dawn broke. What I had seen there had some significance, now being fulfilled, beyond the significance of the trivial happenings of today and tomorrow. The Powers of which we know so little were visibly working before me. And I stood there on the pavement shaking and trembling.

"I was opposite the post office at the corner, and just as the bus started my eye fell on the clock in the window there. I need not tell you what the time was.

"Just room for one inside, sir!"

"Perhaps I need not tell you the rest, for you probably conjecture it, since you will not have forgotten what happened at the corner of Sloane Square at the end of July, the summer before last. The bus pulled out from the pavement into the street in order to get round a van that was standing in front of it. At the moment there came down the King's Road a big motor going at a hideously dangerous pace. It crashed full into the bus, burrowing into it as a gimlet burrows into a board."

He paused.

"And that's my story," he said.

Live Cargo

RICHARD ARMSTRONG

JOE CORNFORTH served his time in a steamer called the *Limpopo*. She was a bluff-nosed old scow in the River Plate trade; general cargo out to Buenos Aires and then homeward from Rosario or one of the other up-river ports with grain and the by-products of the canning factories—green hides for the tanneries, horns and hoofs for the glue manufacturers and crushed bones for making into fertilizer. Each leg of a voyage lasted a month and covered over 6,000 miles but it was a quiet, uneventful sort of seafaring and Corny was beginning to feel a bit cheesed off by the end of his third trip.

"Dreary, that's what I call it!" he said to Jake Blyth.

"What are you cribbing about?" demanded Jake. He was Corny's room-mate and fellow apprentice, a big bull of a fellow two years his senior. "She's a happy ship and the grub's good."

"I know, I know! But nothing ever happens. I mean to say for all the excitement we get we might as well be

208

in a ferry boat or a stinking old mud-hopper."

"There's nothing about excitement in the Articles," retorted Jake. "You signed on to learn the business of a seaman. That means work, not fun and games."

"We get plenty of that all right!" Corny didn't go much on work, claiming he wasn't built for it. Snub-nosed, frecklefaced and tubby, he preferred eating or sleeping and had developed the business of dodging the column into a fine art.

"You're going to get more work still next voyage. The bosun's just tipped me off. We're taking a consignment of live-stock on deck and, if I know anything, you and me, we'll have the privilege of doing the feeding and watering of them; and the mucking out too."

"No!" Corny let out a howl of anguish. "Suffering catfish! Who wouldn't sell a farm and go to sea!"

He was more interested than he cared to admit, however, and when the live cargo came aboard in the London Docks, he made sure of a prominent place for himself in the front rank of the gawpers

The consignment was in three lots. First came a herd of seventy-five long-wooled Lincoln sheep which turned out to be all rams; then two dozen each of White Sussex cocks and hens; and finally, a racehorse which was just about the most noble animal Corny had ever seen. It was a chestnut, a powerful-looking creature with four white stockings, a proudly arched neck and a wild gleam in his eye.

"I rather care for that!" said Corny, sucking his teeth appreciatively. "Tell you what, I'll do the horse and the chickens and you can look after the sheep."

"Like stink, I will!" snorted Jake. "This is going to be fair do's. We'll take it turn about and toss for first pick."

"I didn't know you were crazy about horses."

"I'm not. But I don't like sheep all that much either; so you're going to do your share of both."

"Fine shipmate you are, I must say!" growled Corny reproachfully; then his face brightened as another thought struck him. "But maybe we won't have to do any of it; maybe we're shipping a couple of swede-bashers to do the mucking out and the watering."

"You've got a hope!" answered Jake. "I told you, didn't I? We're already elected."

And he was right. They did ship a stockman who was responsible for all the animals but, so far as Jake and Corny were concerned, he was only another boss and the graft was all theirs.

There was plenty of it too. The chickens were the least trouble. They were stowed in specially constructed coops up on the boat deck—the hens in threes and the cocks singly so they couldn't fight. A scoopful of grain and one bucket of water a day did them all. The horse, which was kept in a loose-box built for the voyage under the break of the bridge-deck aft, was a tougher proposition, particularly the mucking out. But the real pain in the neck was the sheep. They lived on the after deck in a wooden pen divided up into compartments each holding eight or ten of them. There was no roof to the pen but they were protected from the steel deck-plates by a litter of straw about two feet thick. Each section had a drinking trough made out of a forty-gallon cask sawn in two through the bung-hole. Because they fouled the water with the droppings from their long wool, these troughs had to be emptied out and refilled every day. That, with every drop having to be pumped up by hand, made quite a job.

"Sheep!" growled Corny on the third day out. "Noah wanted his brains examined for letting them into the Ark. What beats me is why anybody should be so daft as to ship them all the way out to the Argentine. Haven't they got any of their own?"

"Of course they have," answered Jake. "But these are special ones; prize animals to improve the native breeds. Every one of them's worth more than you'll earn between now and your twenty-first birthday."

"And the horse? What's he worth?"

"Dunno exactly." Jake shook his head. "But the Mate

told me it's insured for more than ten thousand pounds."

"Ten thousand!" Corny whistled through his teeth. "Suffering snakes! There wouldn't half be a stink if anything happened to him."

"That's part of our job, you nit—seeing nothing does happen to him. Now for Pete's sake, belt up and start pumping. We've got to finish watering the sheep."

Corny blew a raspberry, ducked neatly under the swipe Jake aimed at his jaw, then yelled "skinch" and got to work.

The *Limpopo* had now cleared the English Channel and was well across the Bay of Biscay, running on a course a little west of south which, unaltered, would take her all the way to Lobos Island in the mouth of the Rio del Plata. With the weather holding fine, she drove on steadily to the southward and the boys quickly got the extra duties connected with the live cargo hammered into the routine. The animals were fed and watered at sun-up and sun-down, and every forenoon the soiled straw in the pens and loose-box was dumped overboard and fresh stuff laid. As Jake had predicted, the stockman—a short, bandy-legged Irishman called Rafferty who had lived so much with horses he had begun to look like one—reckoned on them doing the work. All he did was to measure out the feed for the horse each day. In consequence Corny took as dim a view of him as he did of the sheep. But the horse was different He had taken a shine to it from the start and, inside a week, they were pals. It was a fierce, wild creature and most of the ship's company kept a respectful distance from him, but Corny could do anything he liked with him. He was a five-year-old with a French name nobody could get his tongue round. Corny called him Rastus, stole knobs of sugar out of the pantry for him, groomed him voluntarily every day and spent most of his spare time around the loose-box just being matey.

It had begun to look like another uneventful passage and then one morning, south of Tenerife, Corny rolled up to breakfast with a face as long as a wet week-end and, being asked what was eating him, said it was Rastus.

211

"That horse is sickening for something," said Corny.

"He's gone a bit queer over night somehow. Looks as if life wasn't much fun for him any more."

"I expect it's the warmer weather," said Jake. "You know, the sudden change upsetting him like."

Rafferty, the stockman, thought the same and didn't seem in the least bit worried. "Race horses are highly bred," he said. "That makes them sensitive and temperamental. Any sort of change sets them back."

"But can't you give him anything for it?" demanded Corny. "Something to buck him up, I mean."

"No, I can't," answered Rafferty harshly. "I'm not a vet, and I don't carry any medicines anyhow. He'll be okay in a couple of days."

Corny had to leave it at that, but instead of getting better Rastus got worse as the day wore on. At first it seemed more like a loss of condition than an actual illness. He still ate normally but his coat lost its silky sheen and became dull and ragged-looking. Then the gleam went out of his eye; and his head, instead of being carried on a proudly arching neck, drooped miserably as if he lacked the strength to hold it up.

"That horse is sickening for something," said Corny at nightfall; and when they found Rastus sweating profusely next morning, even Rafferty had to agree.

"I've been travelling with horses all my life," he said, scratching his head, "but I never saw one go this way. He's sick all right. Some sort of a bug must have got into him."

"Well, aren't you going to do anything about it?" snapped Corny.

"There's nothing we can do but wait for him to throw it off, whatever it is."

"And if he doesn't?"

"That'll be too bad." The stockman shoved his face close to Corny's and stared at him out of a pair of opaque eyes. "If he doesn't throw it off, bud, that means he's had it."

And as the *Limpopo* pushed on through the Cape Verde Islands towards the Equator, it began to look as if he was right. Day by day, hour by hour it seemed, Rastus got steadily worse. He still ate his feed regularly and drank buckets of water; but none of it did him any good. In fact, he threw most of it up again. So quite soon he began to waste and his ribs showed so sharply through his hide he looked like a washboard. Also he seemed to have increasing difficulty with his breathing.

Everybody on board was worried to some degree about him. The Mate examined him carefully from head to tail, looked wise and told Corny to keep him clean and dry as if he had been a bale of soft goods damaged in transit. Then the Old Man looked him over, shook his head and said nothing. Even the bosun, who knew more about most things than a man in his position has any right to do, was baffled.

"He never did look like ten thousand smackers to me," he said, sucking his teeth, "but you'd have a job to raise a fiver on him now."

This was no comfort to Corny, who was inconsolable and,

because he was spending more time with the animal than he could really spare, becoming haggard with anxiety and want of sleep. Two things irked him above all else. One was his inability to do anything for Rastus, and the other the attitude of Rafferty.

"I don't like that guy," he said morosely. "And I never will. His face makes my feet ache."

"Oh, I don't know," said Jake. "He's all right. A bit of a layabout maybe, but you're the last one who should blame anybody for that!"

"I know, I know. But why doesn't he do something for Rastus? He's supposed to know about animals, isn't he? Well, you watch him. Either he's a phoney or he just doesn't care. That's what gets up my nose. Sometimes I even feel he wants the poor old hoss to croak."

"Don't talk so daft," snorted Jake. "What good would that do him?"

Corny had no answer to that one. He piped down and Rastus, with no one able to help him, continued to weaken and waste away. It was quite clear now that whatever the sickness was, he would never throw it off and, at the rate he was going, he couldn't last much longer.

Then, the morning the *Limpopo* crossed the Line, Jake got a touch of the sun. It wasn't much—a lousy headache mostly—but the Old Man ordered him to lie up for the rest of the day and Corny was left with all the animals to see to on his own.

Naturally, he cribbed about it. But that was pure force of habit; and though his protests were loud and long, he didn't really mind all that much. Corny was like that. He would duck any sort of routine job if he saw only half a chance of getting away with it; but in an emergency he would drive himself till he dropped.

This he reckoned was an emergency and he acted accordingly; but by sundown the day had begun to look more like a disaster to him.

The trouble began with his getting behind the clock in the

forenoon. As a result, he hadn't even started to muck out the sheep by midday and, tackling the job immediately after lunch, he tried to rush it to catch up. Unfortunately the sheep refused to co-operate. When he climbed into the first pen, he had to push them out of his way and then, as he stooped to tip over the drinking trough, one of them butted him in the stern. Down he went, full length on his face in the filthy straw; and every ram in the section promptly walked all over him. Those in the other pens when he got among them tried to do the same and though he didn't go down again and finished the job all in one piece, it took him three times as long as he had reckoned on.

The sun had set and it was almost dark before he was done; and by that time he was a sight for sore eyes, plastered from head to foot with sheep-droppings and straw. It wasn't the way he looked that bothered him, however, for he couldn't see himself anyhow; it was the smell. Polecats and skunks had nothing on him; he well and truly stank.

Grimly now he dragged himself up on to the boat-deck to tend the poultry. The corn for the birds was kept in a bucket stowed in a corner of the lifebelt locker and to crown everything, it ran out on him while two of the cocks were still unfed. The idea of tooling his aching bones all the way aft and down into the lazarette to replenish the bucket seemed just then to have whiskers on it. Instead, he nipped down to the loose-box and, grabbing off a couple of handfuls of grain out of the horse's feed-trough, threw them to the last two roosters and called it a day.

"Brother!" said Jake, when he got back to their quarters. "I hate to be personal, but you stink. And how! What happened?"

Corny told him. "And after this," he concluded, reaching for soap and towel, "nobody's going to make me believe that yarn about sheep being stupid. It was all planned. They'd got it worked out and were laying for me. I'll never be able to face a sheep again—not even if it's disguised as mutton stew or lamb chop!"

He stuck the pants and vest he was wearing into a bucket of water with a dollop of disinfectant in it and spent the next forty-five minutes in the bathroom, alternately lathering and rinsing himself under the shower. Even after that he kept on sniffing at himself and weeks later swore he could still smell sheep in his hair, which was either imagination or a bare-faced lie. Anyhow, Jake gave him a clean bill that very night and he turned in.

Having quite recovered from the sun-stroke next morning, Jake turned to as usual and, after drawing a bucket of corn out of the store, went up on to the boat-deck to feed the poultry. In about thirty seconds flat he was back with his eyes popping and his mouth opening and shutting like a stranded catfish.

"The roosters!" he yammered. "Two of them are dead! Look!" He held them up for Corny to stare at.

"All right, so what?" snapped Corny. "You'd better go and tell the Mate but don't expect me to shed any sad tears."

He was too much taken up with Rastus just then to bother about a couple of foolish birds even if they had won prizes; but Jake couldn't get them out of his mind.

"Shook me rigid, it did!" he said at breakfast time. "There they were—ten of them crowing their stupid heads off as usual and the last two in the line lying on their backs with their toes turned up."

Corny put down his knife and fork and swallowed hard, then stared across the table at his room-mate. "Which two did you say?"

"The last two. The ones farthest aft, I mean. Why?"

"I dunno. It's a bit queer, that's all." Corny was thinking fast. "You're sure about it, I suppose?"

"Of course I'm sure. What's on your mind?"

"Nothing. Only those two happen to be the ones I gave the horse's corn to last night."

"Well, don't sit there like one bell half struck," snapped Jake. "What's queer about that?"

"Do I have to draw you a diagram?" demanded Corny.

*"So what?" snapped Corny. "You'd better go and tell the Mate
but don't expect my tears."*

He loaded a slice of bread with marmalade and continued
with his mouthful. "Look, Rastus suddenly becomes a very
sick horse for no reason at all and now a couple of birds that
happened to eat some of his corn go and die on us. Isn't that
queer?"

Jake scratched his head and scowled and you could almost
hear his brain working; then the penny dropped and his face
brightened. "You mean there's something wrong with the
corn?"

"I don't see what else it could be."

"But if you're right, why only two dead roosters? Why
haven't they all curled up?"

"Because only two of them had corn out of the horse's
feed-trough, you nit '

"Okay, so what?" Jake still didn't get it. "It's all the same
corn, isn't it?"

"Yes, to start with it is. Only it doesn't all follow the
same course. Not exactly. Rastus gets his by way of

Rafferty." Corny shoved himself on to his feet, took a long swig of coffee and made for the door. "Come on! This wants looking into. You can think it out later."

With Jake at his heels still carrying the roosters and protesting about his interrupted breakfast, Corny took the shortest way up on to the boat-deck. Ignoring the living birds, he dropped on his knees before the two empty coops and rooted round inside them.

"Look in there and tell me what you see," he said presently, backing out and squatting on his haunches. And when Jake declared he could see nothing but a little chaff and a few grains of corn, he urged him to look again a little closer.

"I've told you there's nothing," protested Jake, but he stuck his head back in the coop. "Wait a minute though. There's some sort of white powdery stuff. Is that what you mean?"

"Could be. It all depends."

"Depends on what?"

"Whether it's in all the coops or only in these two empty ones," answered Corny. "Come on, let's check it."

This proved to be quite a job, for it involved shifting the hens and roosters round from one coop to another and back again. Jake, who still couldn't see what it was all in aid of, wanted to pack it in and go back to his breakfast; but Corny insisted and each of the coops was examined in turn. Only the two in which the roosters had died carried traces of the white powder which Corny now scraped together and stowed in a used envelope he took from his jacket pocket.

"Well," demanded Jake. "Where do we go from here?"

"I'll show you," said Corny. Sliding down the ladder to the main-deck, he hurried to the loose-box, grabbed the horse's feed-trough, brought it out into the light and scraped around with a fingernail in the corners of it. For a moment or two he was tense, silent, then he grunted and pointed. "There you are! See it? That's the same stuff as we found in those two coops, isn't it?"

"Yes, that's it all right," agreed Jake, staring into the trough. "But what is it? What does it mean?"

Corny carefully raked some of the powder-coated chaff into another envelope and refused to say another word until they were back in their own quarters. By then he had it all worked out and was ready to lay it off.

"That white powder is some sort of poison," he said. "That's what killed the roosters and it's slowly killing Rastus."

"But how ... I mean to say, who ..." spluttered Jake.

"Rafferty! It's him that's working it. He mixes the horse's feed so it can't be anybody else...."

As he saw it the whole business was crystal clear. Insurance swindle. He had read about them somewhere. A bloke gets hold of a racehorse. It's a nice animal but it's never won any races so doesn't cost him much—two or three hundred pounds maybe. He keeps it for a little while then ships it out to be sold in the Argentine, insuring it in transit for £10,000. It isn't worth anything like that amount, as the bosun, who knows something about horses, has pointed out. But that doesn't matter because it will never be put up for sale. In fact, it will never reach its destination because it is doomed to die on the passage and be buried at sea where nobody can ask any awkward questions afterwards. To make sure it dies convincingly and not too obviously, the owner bribes the stockman to mix small doses of poison in its feed. Then when the ship's log and the Mate's report have confirmed the death, he collects the insurance money and is left sitting on velvet.

"You read too many thrillers," said Jake cautiously, "but you could be right all the same."

"You bet I'm right," snorted Corny. "But what we've got isn't enough to prove it. If only we could catch him putting the stuff into the feed!"

"He'll watch it. But he must keep the poison somewhere. If we found it in his room that would pin it on him all right."

"Maybe we will."

"But he's never out of the place long enough for anybody to search it, so that's off."

"Wait a bit!" said Corny, his eyes suddenly gleaming. "What's wrong with getting him out long enough?"

"How do you mean?"

"The sheep, that's what I mean. Listen, brother! You're going to see that about twenty of them get loose on the after-deck and while he's putting them back in the pen with your help—it'll take him an hour if you play it right—I'll be searching his room and his gear. Come on, let's go!"

Jake was game.

Corny's plan worked like a charm. Jake borrowed a crowbar from the bosun's locker and, picking a moment when nobody was about, made a hole in the sheep-pen by levering off a couple of planks.

"I don't like it," he said anxiously. "The Mate's going to fillet us when he finds out about this!"

"Not if we're right about Rafferty, he won't," retorted Corny. "Anyhow stop cribbing and get on with it. I'm off to plant myself round the corner of his room."

He slipped away and Jake, leaning over the top of the pen, set about staging the stampede. The rams were suspicious and he had practically to drag the first one out; but once he was through the gap the others followed and in a matter of seconds the after deck was choked with milling sheep. Composing his face into what he fondly imagined was an expression of innocence, Jake then roused out the stockman who, cursing luridly, began the thankless task of getting them back into the pen.

And now, with Rafferty safely tangled up among the sheep, Corny nipped into his room and began his search.

It was a big gamble, a real long shot; but it came off. In the first drawer he opened, Corny's groping fingers encountered a large glass jar with a screw top. It was tucked away in a corner under a couple of shirts; and, pulling it out, he almost dropped it with excitement, for it was two-thirds full of white powder and labelled *Poison*.

At last the stampede was over and the milling sheep driven back.

"The dirty, low-down spiv!" he muttered. "The pie-faced, murdering hoodlum!"

But he had all he needed now and a few minutes later he was telling his story to the Mate, who wasted no time arguing about it and sent for Rafferty right away. The stockman tried to brazen it out at first, but when the Mate confronted him with the evidence Corny had collected, he caved in and came clean. He was promptly relieved of his duties and placed under arrest.

Then, while the bosun was concocting an antidote to the poison and feeding it to the horse, the Mate had Corny and Jake up on the carpet for turning the rams loose. He tore them off a strip about that, but then thanked them for what they had done and said he was going to see they were suitably rewarded.

He did, too, and eventually the insurance people presented each of them with a super sextant, suitably engraved on the case. As for Rastus, in the care of the bosun he made a complete recovery and was landed in Buenos Aires sound in wind and limb. So everything ended okay; but though Corny was often shipmates with live cargo after that, he never got over his dislike of sheep.

The Roar in the Night

ARTHUR CATHERALL

THERE was something wrong. The night was too quiet. For two or three hours the countryside had been bathed in the warm magic of African darkness and the only sound had been the fretful wailing of a hyena. The scavenger was prowling unhappily on the north side of the village. The hyena was hungry, yet even he seemed to sense some mystery in the air.

Each time he sent his blood-curdling wail into the silence he waited, yet nothing happened. That was the frightening thing, for in every African village there are cur-dogs who go mad at the howl of a hyena. In normal circumstances, they would have been howling their heads off at the hyena, even if they had huddled closer to their master's hut. Yet not a single dog answered the frightful wailing howl. It almost seemed as if all life in the native village had fled.

The stars above looked like great lamps shining from a cloudless sky, and a sliver of moon cast a pale, silvery radiance over the scene. A patch of mealies, waving gently in the faint breeze, took on the appearance of a slightly ruffled sheet of silver, while the two tents pitched some fifty yards from each other on the edge of a *donga* looked like toys in the mystic moonlight.

As if taking his courage between his powerful, bone-cracking jaws, the hyena crept even closer, and again loosed his spine-chilling wail.

In one of the tents two game wardens were sitting listening. They, too, felt that all was not well.

"I've never known anything like this," George Sandys murmured, feeling for his pipe and tobacco pouch. "I'm half inclined to get up and see what's wrong. Do you realize, Dave, that not one single dog has barked? Not one. It isn't natural."

Before Dave Brown could comment, the strange silence was shattered completely, and this time it was not by the lone hyena. From beyond the eight-foot-high cattle *boma* (a thorny shelter) came the terrifying roar of a lion. It was a mighty, heart-chilling challenge, threatening and full of blood lust. What was even more terrifying was its volume. It was louder than the roar of any lion either of the game wardens had ever heard in all their years of experience.

Within thirty seconds of that roar there was pandemonium. Inside the *boma* the cattle began to mill round, lowing in terror at the continued roaring of the beast they most feared.

From the grass-thatched huts within the palisade which guarded the village, there was sudden commotion, too. Sleepy-eyed men tumbled out, grabbing spears and shields. The one man left on guard shook the drowsiness from his eyes and quickly kicked his watch-fire to life, so that a myriad of sparks shot up into the night like startled fireflies.

Above the clamour of humans and frightened cattle the continued roaring of the lion went on, booming and reverberating like thunder, far louder than even the natives had ever heard. It added to their terror.

In the tent the two game wardens were also on the move. They dragged on half-knee boots and, grabbing rifles and torches, hurried out into the open.

"Is he near enough to attack us?" Dave asked, pushing the safety catch of his rifle to the "off" position, and making sure there was a round in the breech.

"He's not interested in us," George Sandys assured him. "It's an old trick adopted when lions hunt in troops. One gets his head close to the ground and roars, and keeps on roaring until the cattle in the *boma* get so terrified they stampede and break down the thorn fencing. When they rush out the other lions are waiting. Come on, let's see if we can——"

But before he finished speaking the cattle did stampede from their thorn-protected stockade. Too terrified to realize they were safe so long as they kept behind the high walls of wait-a-bit thorn, they pressed madly away from the sound of the continuous roaring, and the wall of thorn brush gave way.

One or two cattle were trodden underfoot, but the rest streamed out into the pale moonlit night, and for a few moments they could be seen, tails high, heads down as they raced for what they thought was safety.

Almost at once the continuous roaring of the unseen lion ceased as if it had been shut off by a tap, and the bellowing of the terrified cattle seemed louder in consequence.

"You'll hear the end of this little episode in a few moments," old George murmured. "There'll be a few short, sharp roars, then the screams of one or two cows as they go down with a broken neck. After that there'll be silence, and no more panic until the poor natives go out tomorrow to try to round up their beasts."

Old George Sandys knew his Africa well, but for once he was mistaken in almost everything. The quiet did come. The cattle streamed madly away, but there were no coughing grunts of triumph, no screams as cattle died. The terrified bellowing of the herd grew less, the thunder of hoofs died away, and the night became suddenly ominously quiet again Even the hyena seemed too puzzled to wail his hunger to the moon.

There was not even a sound from the village. It seemed a

if the men, women and children were all listening; wondering why the lions had not made a kill.

"That," George said soberly, as he started to walk towards the kraal, "is about the queerest thing I've ever known. It isn't often an attack of this kind fails, yet there doesn't seem to have been a kill." At that moment, from the stockaded kraal came a sudden wail of horror, followed within moments by a chorus of voices, men, women and children, all shouting or wailing at once.

The two game wardens ran, and entered the kraal only a few yards ahead of Bir Mohammed, an Arab trader whom they had arrested the previous afternoon for encouraging the natives to kill elephants and rhinoceros for their tusks and horns. There was no need to guard their captive. They had simply immobilized his lorry. Without the lorry he could not get away.

Torches were already being lit as the three men rushed into the kraal, and it seemed as if everyone was crowding round the largest hut—the chief's hut. In a matter of moments the reason for the pandemonium was clear. The headman was gone—no doubt taken in his sleep by a lion, and his three wives were lying as if dead on the floor of the hut.

The Africans were terrified. No one had heard the lion. There had been no scream from the man, or the three women. What was more, and this made the women huddle together in terror, the gates of the kraal had been closed. What manner of lion was it that could leap an eight foot fence with a dead man in its jaws?

George Sandys shone his torch beam into the hut, and frowned. The three women did not much look as if slain by an animal. Their mats had not even been disarrayed.

"They don't even look dead to me," Dave muttered, and pushing aside the headman's son, he knelt by the nearest woman. In an electric silence he felt her wrist pulse. It was steady as a rock, though rather slow.

He shook her, and got a mumbled protest, but the moment

There were moans of horror at the blood splashes.

he ceased shaking her she relapsed into sleep. The two other
women were the same, and Dave stood up, a deep frown
wrinkling his brow.

"There's something queer here, George. It seems to
me——"

"Ah-ha . . . look!" Bir Mohammed was shining his torch
on the ground, and there were moans of horror as the
brilliant white beam showed up blood splashes.

The three women were forgotten as men followed the
Arab. It was not difficult to see the splashes of blood on the
hard-packed ground, and they led right to the gate of the
kraal. There were murmurs of amazement and fear when
it became obvious that the lion had not jumped over the
gate, but had *gone through the gateway!* Eyes rolled in
terror at the thought that the mysterious lion had not only
carried off their chief, but had been able to open the kraal

gate, and also close it again afterwards. Witchcraft alone could have done this.

"Never mind that," Bir Mohammed said, "if we follow the blood trail we might even be able to save him, if he is not already dead."

That made the natives anxious, and they pressed on. George and Dave used their torches to help show up the trail of blood. It was leading down towards their tent, which puzzled them; for they had definitely been awake when the lion first began to roar.

They were even more puzzled when the blood trail stopped at their tent, and look how they would no one could find any more blood beyond the tent door.

There followed a few moments of horrified silence, and the men with their spears drew back a few paces and stared at the game wardens. Bir Mohammed switched off his torch and turning to George and Dave in great agitation demanded,

"What have you done with him? You must be mad. They'll kill us for this, you fools."

"What have *we* done with him?" George Sandys roared. "Why. you lunatic, if we'd——"

Bir Mohammed was not listening. He turned to the sullen natives and in a sudden babble of words said,

"A blood trail cannot lie. These men are in league with a ghost lion. They are witch doctors. They can bring back your chief. Make them bring him back alive."

Old George Sandys was too late to stop Dave. The younger game warden turned and punched the Arab between the eyes, a knock-down blow which drew blood from his hooked beak of a nose and puffed both his eyes. The foulness of the accusation had stung Dave to action, but it was a mistake. An instant later both wardens were borne down in a sudden rush of angry natives, and if George had not yelled to Dave to surrender without a fight, both men might have died in the next few seconds.

Mauled and breathless they were dragged back to the kraal. There the women had built a huge fire which lit up

"Bring my father back alive . . ." roared the headman's son.

the beehive type huts and revealed the big-eyed children, silent and fearful.

It took only a matter of minutes to bind the two men hand and foot. Then, as more and more men lit torches to cast a flickering red glow over the scene, the headman's son demanded that his prisoners bring back the missing man. They were a frightened crowd, and the terrific roaring of the lion which had started the night's events had not been forgotten. No ordinary lion could roar like that. The natives were sure it was a ghost lion, conjured up by the two white men.

"Bring back my father, and slay the ghost lion, or die!" It was as simple as that, nor would Bir Mohammed help when appealed to. Eyes puffed until they were almost closed, he stood on one side and refused to add his weight to George's threat that there would be plenty of trouble for the villagers if they did not immediately release their two prisoners.

"Bring my father back alive," roared the headman's son. "And show us that you have killed your ghost lion. Do that and we shall set you free. If you don't bring back my father —you shall both die."

"We can't do anything while we are tied up," Dave yelled back.

"Hold it, hold it, Dave," George counselled. "They believe this Arab, so we'll have to promise to bring back the dead man and deal with the ghost."

"Oh, come off it, George," Dave pleaded. "How can we?"

"You've got to use your head, Dave," George said, and turning to the headman's son he said, "All right. We have listened to you. Now listen to me. Your father can be brought back, and the ghost lion killed, but you must set my friend free. He cannot bring back your father while he is in bonds."

The idea made sense even to the headman's son, and he gave orders for Dave to be set free.

"But what am I supposed to do?" Dave asked. "For Pete's sake, George, I can't bring a dead man to life—and I don't even know the first thing about this so-called ghost lion."

"You forget both of them," George urged. "Get to the lorry and try and bring help. I'll try and stall these fellows; but you'll have to hurry."

"Look, I'm not going to do it," Dave snapped. "I won't leave you."

"You'll do as you are told," George said firmly. "I'm talking sense. One of us can get away, and you *might* be able to bring help. But don't try any single-handed rescue stunts. These people are scared, and when they are scared they are dangerous."

Bir Mohammed tried to persuade the headman's son not to let either of his prisoners free but without success. Dave was freed and even allowed to take his rifle; but Bir Mohammed was no fool. When Dave reached their lorry the Arab was waiting for him, his rifle at the ready.

"Your rifle, please, Mr. Game Warden. Thank you! Now you can *walk* for help. I have done for your lorry what you did for mine—taken the distributor off, so the engine will not work. You have only about fifty miles to cover; but by the time you have brought help I think I shall be a long way from here. Goodbye!"

Dave did not argue. If the Arab was taken before a magistrate he faced a prison sentence and lost his lorry and the ivory. Dave's only hope was that by some miracle he might meet either a party of friendly natives, or maybe a white man on safari. The odds were against it, and Dave began the hopeless task of trying to cover fifty miles and bring help for old George.

His luck seemed stone dead, for he had covered no more than three miles and was crossing a donga when the coughing grunt of a lion made him *freeze*. A few moments later the thud-thud-thud of dainty hoofs down the donga was stopped by the sudden rush of a hidden lion. There was a scream, then silence.

Dave needed no one to explain to him what had happened. A lion had startled one of the smaller antelope, and his first

Sound of dainty hoofs down the donga . . . then the rush of a lion.

spring had brought him a meal. The kill had been made so close to where Dave crouched that he simply dared not attempt to get away. Only the fact that the wind was blowing from the lion to him saved him.

For an hour which seemed an age, he sat and listened while the lion fed. Then, full and happy, the killer moved down to a small pool nearby, and in the breathless silence Dave heard him lapping up the water.

Finally his thirst was satisfied, and Dave listened anxiously for some sound which would tell him the lion had gone. He could hear his own heart beat in the silence. Then without warning the silence was broken by the same terrifying roar that he and George had heard before the village cattle broke out of their *boma*. It was a full-throated, terrible roar, telling all who cared to hear that the king of beasts had killed, eaten, and was satisfied.

As the last vague echoes died away something clicked in Dave's brain. Old George Sandys, who knew almost everything there was to be known about African animals, hunters and hunted, had once said: "You can tell by a lion's roar exactly what he's doing. When he gives short, sharp grunting roars, that's to frighten the tommys and gazelles into running. They know by those short grunts that he's out for a kill, and they panic. When he has killed, he roars, and it's an excited, triumphant roar. When he's eaten all he wants, he roars in a bellowing, bragging way, a sort of I'm-boss-round-here, and-I-don't-care-who-knows-it."

"And that was exactly how the ghost lion roared," Dave whispered thoughtfully. "It wasn't a hunting roar, and yet he was apparently just outside the *boma,* trying to scare the cattle into stampeding. And then, when they did break out, there was no kill. Davy," he said to himself, "that lion in the night gave the wrong kind of roar. Think—think hard. If you get the answer you might save old George."

Old George Sandys had thought he could hold off the judgment of the chief's son for a few hours, but it was the dead man's wives who brought things to a head. After lying all night as if dead, or drugged, they came to life about an hour after the sun rose. And when they heard the story of how their husband had been carried off, and how the blood trail led to the white men's tent, they began to scream for vengeance.

George argued, threatened, warned them what would happen if they killed him, but the three women were screaming for ven-

His thirst was satisfied.

geance on the killer, and George was tied to a post. The headman's son was uneasy, but he knew that the whole village looked on him now to force the white man to work a miracle and bring the missing headman back, or else to avenge their loss with his spear.

The village drummer was pounding away and the throbbing fury of it worked them all to a fever heat of excitement. The warriors began to dance, and every few moments one would race over and brandish his spear within a few inches of George Sandys' face. The moment of killing was drawing near.

Suddenly the drumming ceased. The shouting died away and the headman's son snatched up his father's spear. Rushing across he held the point of the broad blade a foot from the white man's chest.

"For the last time," he screamed, "will you bring back my father—alive?"

"I have said you must wait." Somehow, though his face was beaded with drops of perspiration, George managed to speak calmly. "You must wait until my friend returns. He will. . . . Wait . . . W-a-i-t!" he commanded sternly as he saw the young man's arm muscles tighten. "That spear must not drink my blood. If it does——"

"Kill . . . kill . . . kill!" the wives of the dead headman screamed.

The spear was drawn back, the eyes of the headman's son blazed, and then in the tense silence a lion began to roar. Harsh, threatening, and much louder than any ordinary lion roars, the sound came from just outside the kraal gates. Men and women who a few moments earlier had been screaming for George Sandys' blood stood petrified.

All eyes turned towards the gate, and suddenly as the roaring ceased the gate was shaken violently. Then the voice of Dave Brown was heard, loud and commanding:

"Open this gate—and *let your headman return to his hut.*"

George closed his eyes with relief, and when he opened them again it was to see Dave Brown climbing over the kraal

If Dave had not stopped the machine the whole crowd would have vanished in a matter of seconds.

gate, since none of the villagers had the courage to move. Dave dropped lightly to the sunbaked ground, waved a hand to George, then, opening the big creaking gate, he helped in the "dead" man, who looked sleepy and half dazed.

After the initial hubbub had died down—and George had been set free—Dave called the villagers together. From outside the kraal he wheeled in a cinematograph.

"This," he said, "belonged to the Arab who persuaded you to kill rhino and elephants. He showed you magic pictures on a white sheet. Now, sit still and listen, and do not be afraid."

He started the battery-operated machine. There was a low purring, then as the sound track on a film came into operation the air shook again as the loudspeaker amplified the roaring of a lion. It was so real that if Dave had not stopped the machine the whole crowd would have vanished in a matter of seconds.

"That is your lion," he explained. "Last night, because we had arrested him for illegally obtaining elephant tusks and rhino horns, the Arab did three things. He gave the headman and his wives a drink, in which there was a powder to make them sleep heavily. He fed the village dogs and in the food he gave them was the same powder, so that they, too, slept heavily. Then, when all were at rest, he killed a chicken and sprinkled a blood trail from the chief's hut to our tent. Finally—and it seems as if your night watchman does not keep his eyes open—he went into the chief's hut and carried that sleeping man away. He tied him securely and hid him. Then he made the ghost lion roar."

"Why did he do all these things, bwana?" the headman's son asked fearfully.

Dave smiled ruefully.

"Because he knew he had done wrong, and he wanted *you* to kill my friend and me. If you had done that, he would have been able to get away. And I daresay he would have worked more *magic*, by bringing your headman back to life."

"Where is this dog?"

"Never mind where he is," George said, stepping forward. "We will see that he is punished."

Heads nodded and eyes rolled. The native Africans did not really understand what had happened; but their headman was back, alive, and they had been assured the ghost lion would not roar again.

Back in their tent, enjoying what to George was the best mug of coffee he had ever tasted, Dave told how it had all been unravelled.

"It was hearing a real lion roar which put me on to it," he explained. "I didn't quite know what had gone on; but I came back and I just gave Bir Mohammed twenty seconds to tell me the truth, or die. Maybe that isn't the way a real policeman would do things, but he could see I meant business, and with his own rifle muzzle only a foot from his stomach he talked. If I hadn't heard that real lion roaring— well, I don't know what would have happened."

"You don't," and George grinned as he poured himself a second mug of coffee. "I know . . . and it doesn't need a detective to find the answer. I'd have got six inches of spear through me . . . and that would have been plenty. Dave . . . I'm glad you don't believe in ghosts, human or lion. The drinks are on me when we get back to base."

Journey to the End
of a Rope

NORBERT CASTERET

*(No name in the annals of "pot-holing" is better known than that
of the French explorer, Norbert Casteret, who from boyhood
was attracted by the mysteries of underground tunnels, caverns,
abysses and waterways. This extract from his* Ten Years Under
the Earth *gives us the full flavour of descending into chasms
of unknown depth and of the hair-raising peril that arose from
one such venture.)*

ONE day I was making the rounds of a series of these
funnels. Happening to look down one smaller than the
rest, I saw a black hole big enough to let a man in, with a
thin mist rising from it to show its great depth. Against
just such a discovery I had brought along my outfit for preliminary work. I let down into the hole a thin, strong rope,
sixty-five feet long, first making the upper end fast to a
rocky projection. I slid through the narrow opening of the
chasm, and stopped thirty feet down on a stone chunk
caught in the narrow well. Thus far the shaft had had the

shape and dimensions of a chimney, and descending it was a matter of scraping hard against the sides. Below the rock the chimney was considerably larger. I swung the rope in all directions without hitting anything.

Now for a simple trick of my trade. I unfolded a newspaper, set fire to it, and dropped it into the blackness. The paper spiralled slowly down, lighting a bell-shaped chamber. It came to rest, and burned out near the end of the rope, which dangled a yard from the floor.

I slid down to bottom sixty-five feet below ground. Then I stood motionless, listening. Underground the sense of hearing is almost one's chief reliance. Nothing could have pleased and excited me more just then than the mournful plaint which rose to my ears. There was a sighing and wailing, amplified by echoes, distorted by the strange acoustics of caverns—the voice of the Albe torrent.

Another burning newspaper brushed down an almost vertical shaft, and stopped thirty feet below me. I descended with the candle in my teeth, clinging to projections of the rock instead of using a rope. At the end of this third stage, nearly a hundred feet below ground, I set foot on a pile of boulders. Under them I heard the stream, and in spots saw it hastening ever deeper into the bowels of the mountain. My candle dimly showed me a vast sloping gallery filled with boulders, a regular ante-room of hell. I worked my way cautiously downward. I was delighted to have got so far, and at the same time fearful of being lost alone in an unknown abyss. Embracing the rocks as I slid, I reached a point where the torrent vanished through a sluice under a heap of enormous blocks that almost touched the slanting roof. It was certainly not impossible to scale the pile, but careful scrutiny showed me that the blocks were precariously balanced, and the least weight might upset tons of boulders.

Nevertheless that was the spot I returned to a few days later, this time using a rope ladder. I had with me the two assistants, Cabalet and Lledo, a pair as unlike as possible in looks and disposition, but alike in courage and devotion.

We stood in a row at the foot of the boulders while I studied the menacing structure. The presence of companions did not diminish the danger, of course, but still I felt more courageous. Fumbling cautiously and respectfully, I ventured over the gigantic mantrap. Agility and lightness of foot were my sole reliance as I climbed to the top and down on the other side, but nothing stirred. I was delighted at my luck, and hardly less so to find the torrent still hurrying down the steep corridor. My companions, emboldened if not re-assured, passed in their turn.

In quick succession we went down two cascades twelve or fifteen feet high, to find ourselves stopped on the brink of a third. Our burning paper showed us that this one fell a hundred feet in two cascades. My only rope ladder remained at the mouth of the shaft, linking us to the outside world. We had only a rope with us. I slid down it, supported from above by Cabalet and Lledo, who exerted themselves to keep me out of the centre of the waterfall and spare me a rough and icy ducking. The farther down I went, the more the water spread, and I got my shower-bath anyway.

At the bottom of the precipice I let go the rope, and followed the leaping torrent over heaps of rocks down the great sloping tunnel. The gallery was long and steep, and I was like an ant in the underground maze. I had to skirt huge blocks fallen from the ceilings; some of them must have been forty or fifty cubic yards in volume. The farther I went, the larger grew the cavern, and the steeper the slope. My progress was a disorderly scramble down Titan pitches where the water splashed and foamed. I began to lose all sense of time, distance and depth. Still I descended; I was determined to go on until some insuperable obstacle put a stop to my exploration.

Finally, five hundred feet below ground, I halted on the brink of a perpendicular precipice over which the cataract fell with a deafening roar. My burning sheets of paper were instantly snatched and drowned in the waterspout. I rolled down boulders which disappeared without a distinguishable sound or an echo to tell me the depth of the abyss. For a long time I stood dreaming and dazed before the cataract. I forgot what I was there for, forgot my companions anxiously waiting above. I was leaning alone over the mouth of hell.

At that time my outfit consisted of but a hundred feet of rope ladder and some ropes. But some days later, by acrobatic feats, my faithful porters and I managed to carry to the brink of the last abyss a 325-foot rope belonging to the power company.

Leaving early in the morning, we had climbed under crushing loads from the works to the mouth of the funnel (altitude 9,225 feet). Then the painful descent of 500 feet, with repeated wettings, had taxed us severely. I now made the mistake of asking a further effort from the men, which they were rash enough not to refuse. For want of rope ladders—absolutely indispensable for such work—I had planned to be let down on the rope. As we were about to do this Cabalet objected that the rope was not strong enough. So we doubled it, and tied it under my arms. I was loaded with a bag containing the acetylene lamp and various impedimenta. I had on my old trench helmet in case of falling stones, an electric lamp in my hand and a whistle in my mouth. We arranged a system of whistle signals.

Then I slid over the brink of the abyss, as far as possible from the cataract, and my assistants let me down rapidly hand over hand. There was an overhang; I swung free in a void. The electric light showed me an ugly black wall, which I kicked at each swing of the rope, knocking off stones. Occasionally also I brushed the waterfall. I kept blowing the whistle to direct my descent.

At a depth of sixty feet I saw sticking out from the wall a little horizontal slab just big enough for my feet. I managed to get a foothold, whistled twice as a signal to stop, and perched on the terrifying balcony. Below me I could see nothing but the column of the waterfall, piercing the gloom to an unknown depth. I managed to kick down a big stone, which fell with the whistle of a cannon-ball to crash far below. Still I could not tell whether it had reached bottom or had merely struck an outcrop. In any case the rope would not reach that far; there was no use in descending farther. For a long time I watched the plume of water roar from the top, where the men's lamps lit it up, to its disappearance in the depths.

I whistled three times, and then waited with muscles tensed for the hoist. The rope tautened and vibrated. I repeated the signal; the rope tautened still more, and I was raised a little. Now I could feel the trembling of the rope as it rubbed on the projection overhead. I began to revolve in space; then my upward movement stopped. I whistled; I felt a hesitation; I went up three feet. Then I went down six. I could see what was happening: the men above were exhausted, and my weight and the friction set their efforts at naught. I began to spin like a top. Now and then I dangled under the waterfall, which hammered me, and made me still heavier. I could have wished myself elsewhere!

I whistled frantically, but the rope must have been caught. Perhaps it was wearing through. I continued to dangle, as if hanged, in the abyss. By a desperate effort I managed to swing towards the wall. I tried to catch hold of it, but the wet, slippery rock offered no grip, and I dangled again at the end of my line.

I heard anguished voices; in every nerve I felt the frightful tension on the rope. Slowly, very slowly, I went up by short, feeble tugs. But I went up. There were long pauses, but gradually I neared the overhang, and at last my head rose over the edge. The overhang added to the friction, and there was another stop, during which I stared at the demon-faced figures struggling to wrench me from the abyss. Instinctively I looked at their shaking hands on the rope. There was a groan from Cabalet, one last yank, and I sprawled over the edge, landing on my knees at the feet of my exhausted saviours.

After resting from the worst of the shock and strain, we

I could imagine what was happening: the men above were ex-hausted, and my weight and the friction set their efforts at naught.

started for the surface. It took us three hours to cover that five hundred feet. The moonlight outside was magnificent. By the time we finished the endless descent to the works (bent double as we were under loads of stiff wet rope) it was 10 p.m., and there was considerable uneasiness over our absence.

The Fog Horn

RAY BRADBURY

O UT there in the cold water, far from land, we waited every night for the coming of the fog, and it came, and we oiled the brass machinery and lit the fog light up in the stone tower. Feeling like two birds in the grey sky, McDunn and I sent the light touching out, red, then white, then red again, to eye the lonely ships. And if they did not see our light, then there was always our Voice, the great deep cry of our Fog Horn shuddering through the rags of mist to startle the gulls away like packs of scattered cards and make the waves turn high and foam.

"It's a lonely life, but you're used to it now, aren't you?" asked McDunn.

"Yes," I said. "You're a good talker, thank the Lord."

"Well, it's your turn on land tomorrow," he said, smiling. . . .

"What do you think about, McDunn, when I leave you out here alone?"

"On the mysteries of the sea." McDunn lit his pipe. It was a quarter past seven of a cold November evening, the heat on, the light switching its tail in two hundred directions, the Fog Horn bumbling in the high throat of the tower. There

wasn't a town for a hundred miles down the coast, just a
road which came lonely through dead country to the sea,
with few cars on it, a stretch of two miles of cold water out
to our rock, and rare few ships.

"The mysteries of the sea," said McDunn thoughtfully.
"You know, the ocean's the biggest snowflake ever? It rolls
and swells a thousand shapes and colours, no two alike.
Strange. One night, years ago, I was here alone, when all of
the fish of the sea surfaced out there. Something made them
swim in and lie in the bay, sort of trembling and staring up
at the tower light going red, white, red, white across them so
I could see their funny eyes. I turned cold. They were like a
big peacock's tail, moving out there until midnight. Then,
without so much as a sound, they slipped away, the million
of them were gone. I kind of think, maybe, in some sort of
way, they came all those miles to worship. Strange. But think
how the tower must look to them, standing seventy feet above
the water, the God-light flashing out from it, and the tower
declaring itself with a monster voice. They never came back,
those fish, but don't you think for a while they thought they
were in the Presence?"

I shivered. I looked out at the long grey lawn of the sea
stretching away into nothing and nowhere.

"Oh, the sea's full." McDunn puffed his pipe nervously,
blinking. He had been nervous all day and hadn't said why.
"For all our engines and so-called submarines, it'll be ten
thousand centuries before we set foot on the real bottom of
the sunken lands, in the fairy kingdoms there, and know
real terror. Think of it, it's still the year 300,000 Before
Christ down under there. While we've paraded around with
trumpets, lopping off each other's countries and heads, they
have been living beneath the sea twelve miles deep and cold
in a time as old as the beard of a comet."

"Yes, it's an old world."

"Come on. I got something special I been saving up to
tell you."

We ascended the eighty steps, talking and taking our time

At the top, McDunn switched off the room lights so there'd be no reflection in the plate glass. The great eye of the light was humming, turning easily in its oiled socket. The Fog Horn was blowing steadily, once every fifteen seconds.

"Sounds like an animal, don't it?" McDunn nodded to himself. "A big lonely animal crying in the night. Sitting here on the edge of ten billion years calling out to the Deeps, I'm here, I'm here, I'm here. And the Deeps *do* answer, yes, they do. You been here now for three months, Johnny, so I better prepare you. About this time of year," he said, studying the murk and fog, "something comes to visit the lighthouse."

"The swarms of fish like you said?"

"No, this is something else. I've put off telling you because you might think I'm daft. But tonight's the latest I can put it off, for if my calendar's marked right from last year, tonight's the night it comes. I won't go into detail, you'll have to see it yourself. Just sit down there. If you want, tomorrow you can pack your duffel and take the motorboat in to land and get your car parked there at the dinghy pier on the cape and drive on back to some little inland town and keep your lights burning nights, I won't question or blame you. It's happened three years now, and this is the only time anyone's been here with me to verify it. You wait and watch."

Half an hour passed with only a few whispers between us. When we grew tired waiting, McDunn began describing some of his ideas to me. He had some theories about the Fog Horn itself.

"One day many years ago a man walked along and stood in the sound of the ocean on a cold sunless shore and said, 'We need a voice to call across the water, to warn ships; I'll make one. I'll make a voice like all of time and all of the fog that ever was; I'll make a voice that is like an empty bed beside you all night long, and like an empty house when you open the door, and like trees in autumn with no leaves. A sound like the birds flying south, crying, and a sound like November wind and the sea on the hard, cold shore. I'll make a sound that's so alone that no one can miss it, that whoever hears it will weep in their souls, and hearths will seem warmer, and being inside will seem better to all who hear it in the distant towns. I'll make me a sound and an apparatus and they'll call it a Fog Horn and whoever hears it will know the sadness of eternity and the briefness of life.' "

The Fog Horn blew.

"I made up that story," said McDunn quietly, "to try to explain why this thing keeps coming back to the lighthouse every year. The Fog Horn calls it, I think, and it comes. . . ."

"But——" I said.

"Sssst!" said McDunn. "There!" He nodded out to the Deeps.

Something was swimming toward the lighthouse tower.

It was a cold night, as I have said; the high tower was cold, the light coming and going, and the Fog Horn calling and calling through the ravelling mist. You couldn't see far and you couldn't see plain, but there was the deep sea moving on its way about the night earth, flat and quiet, the colour of grey mud, and here were the two of us alone in the high tower, and there, far out at first, was a ripple, followed by a wave, a rising, a bubble, a bit of froth. And then, from the surface of the cold sea came a head, a large head, dark-coloured, with immense eyes, and then a neck. And then—not a body—but more neck and more! The head rose a full forty feet above the water on a slender and beautiful dark neck. Only then did the body, like a little island of black coral and shells and crayfish, drip up from the subterranean. There was a flicker of tail. In all, from head to tip of tail, I estimated the monster at ninety or a hundred feet.

I don't know what I said. I said something.

"Steady, boy, steady," whispered McDunn.

"It's impossible!" I said.

"No, Johnny, *we're* impossible. *It's* like it always was ten million years ago. *It* hasn't changed. It's *us* and the land that've changed, become impossible. *Us!*"

It swam slowly and with a great dark majesty out in the

The fog horn blew and the monster roared again.

icy waters, far away. The fog came and went about it, momentarily erasing its shape. One of the monster eyes caught and held and flashed back our immense light, red, white, red, white, like a disc held high and sending a message in primeval code. It was as silent as the fog through which it swam.

"It's a dinosaur of some sort!" I crouched down, holding to the stair rail.

"Yes, one of the tribe."

"But they died out!"

"No, only hid away in the Deeps. Deep, deep down in the deepest Deeps. Isn't *that* a word now, Johnny, a real word, it says so much: the Deeps. There's all the coldness and darkness and deepness in the world in a word like that."

"What'll we do?"

"Do? We got our job, we can't leave. Besides, we're safer here than in any boat trying to get to land. That thing's as big as a destroyer and almost as swift."

"But here, why does it come *here?*"

The next moment I had my answer.

The Fog Horn blew.

And the monster answered.

A cry came across a million years of water and mist. A cry so anguished and alone that it shuddered in my head and my body. The monster cried out at the tower. The Fog Horn blew. The monster roared again. The Fog Horn blew. The monster opened its great toothed mouth and the sound that came from it was the sound of the Fog Horn itself. Lonely and vast and far away. The sound of isolation, a viewless sea, a cold night, apartness. That was the sound.

"Now," whispered McDunn, "do you know why it comes here?"

I nodded.

"All year long, Johnny, that poor monster there lying far out, a thousand miles at sea, and twenty miles deep maybe. biding its time, perhaps it's a million years old, this one creature. Think of it, waiting a million years; could *you* wait that long? Maybe it's the last of its kind. I sort of think that's true. Anyway, here come men on land and build this lighthouse, five years ago. And set up their Fog Horn and sound it and sound it out toward the place where you bury yourself in sleep and sea memories of a world where there were thousands like yourself, but now you're alone, all alone in a world not made for you, a world where you have to hide.

"But the sound of the Fog Horn comes and goes, comes and goes, and you stir from the muddy bottom of the Deeps. and your eyes open like the lenses of two-foot cameras and you move, slow, slow, for you have the ocean sea on your shoulders, heavy. But that Fog Horn comes through a thousand miles of water, faint and familiar, and the furnace in your belly stokes up, and you begin to rise, slow, slow. You feed yourself on great slakes of cod and minnow, on rivers of jellyfish, and you rise slow through the autumn months, through September when the fogs started, through October with more fog and the horn still calling you on, and then, late in November, after pressurizing yourself day by day, a few feet higher every hour, you are near the surface and still alive. You've got to go slow; if you surfaced all at once you'd explode. So it takes you all of three months to surface, and then a number of days to swim through the cold waters to the lighthouse. And there you are, out there, in the night, Johnny, the biggest damn monster in creation. And here's the lighthouse calling to you, with a long neck like your neck sticking way up out of the water, and a body like your body, and, most important of all, a voice like your voice. Do you understand now, Johnny, do you understand?"

The Fog Horn blew.

The monster answered.

I saw it all, I knew it all—the million years of waiting alone, for someone to come back who never came back. The million years of isolation at the bottom of the sea, the insanity of time there, while the skies cleared of reptile-birds, the swamps dried on the continental lands, the sloths and sabre-tooths had their day and sank in tar pits, and men ran like white ants upon the hills.

The Fog Horn blew.

"Last year," said McDunn, "that creature swam round and round, round and round, all night. Not coming too near, puzzled I'd say. Afraid, maybe. And a bit angry after coming all this way. But the next day, unexpectedly, the fog lifted, the sun came out fresh, the sky was as blue as a painting. And the monster swam off away from the heat and the silence and didn't come back. I suppose it's been brooding on it for a year now, thinking it over from every which way."

The monster was only a hundred yards off now, it and the Fog Horn crying at each other. As the lights hit them, the monster's eyes were fire and ice, fire and ice.

"That's life for you," said McDunn. "Someone always waiting for someone who never comes home. Always someone loving some thing more than that thing loves them. And after a while you want to destroy whatever that thing is, so it can't hurt you no more."

251

I had a glimpse of its gigantic paw....

The monster was rushing at the lighthouse.

The Fog Horn blew.

"Let's see what happens," said McDunn.

He switched the Fog Horn off.

The ensuing minute of silence was so intense that we could hear our hearts pounding in the glassed area of the tower, could hear the slow greased turn of the light.

The monster stopped and froze. Its great lantern eyes blinked. Its mouth gaped. It gave a sort of rumble, like a volcano. It twitched its head this way and that, as if to seek the sounds now dwindled off into the fog. It peered at the lighthouse. It rumbled again. Then its eyes caught fire. It reared up, threshed the water, and rushed at the tower, its eyes filled with angry torment.

"McDunn!" I cried. "Switch on the horn!"

McDunn fumbled with the switch. But even as he flicked it on the monster was rearing up. I had a glimpse of its gigantic paws, fishskin glittering in webs between the finger-like projections, clawing at the tower. The huge eye on the right side of its anguished head glittered before me like a cauldron into which I might drop, screaming. The tower shook. The Fog Horn cried; the monster cried. It seized the tower and gnashed at the glass, which shattered in upon us.

McDunn seized my arm. "Downstairs!"

The tower rocked, trembled, and started to give. The Fog Horn and the monster roared. We stumbled and half fell down the stairs. "Quick!"

We reached the bottom as the tower buckled down toward us. We ducked under the stairs into the small stone cellar. There were a thousand concussions as the rocks rained down; the Fog Horn stopped abruptly. The monster crashed upon the tower. The tower fell. We knelt together, McDunn and I, holding tight, while our world exploded.

Then it was over, and there was nothing but darkness and the wash of the sea on the raw stones.

That and the other sound.

"Listen," said McDunn quietly. "Listen."

We waited a moment. And then I began to hear it. First a great vacuumed sucking of air, and then the lament, the bewilderment, the loneliness of the great monster, folded over upon us, above us, so that the sickening reek of its body filled the air, a stone's thickness away from our cellar. The monster gasped and cried. The tower was gone. The light was gone. The thing that had called to it across a million years was gone. And the monster was opening its mouth and sending out great sounds. The sounds of a Fog Horn again and again. And ships far at sea, not finding the light, not seeing anything, but passing and hearing late that night, must've thought: There it is, the lonely sound, the Lonesome Bay horn. All's well. We've rounded the cape.

And so it went for the rest of that night.

The sun was hot and yellow the next afternoon when the rescuers came out to dig us from our stoned-under cellar.

"It fell apart, that is all," said Mr. McDunn gravely. "We had a few bad knocks from the waves and it just crumbled." He pinched my arm.

There was nothing to see. The ocean was calm, the sky blue. The only thing was a great algaic stink from the green matter that covered the fallen tower stones and the shore rocks. Flies buzzed about. The ocean washed empty on the shore.

The next year they built a new lighthouse, but by that time I had a job in the little town and a wife and a good small warm house that glowed yellow on autumn nights, the doors locked, the chimney puffing smoke. As for McDunn, he was master of the new lighthouse, built to his own specifications, out of steel-reinforced concrete. "Just in case," he said.

The new lighthouse was ready in November. I drove down alone one evening late and parked my car and looked across the grey waters and listened to the new horn sounding, once, twice, three, four times a minute far out there, by itself.

The monster?

It never came back.

"It's gone away," said McDunn. "It's gone back to the Deeps. It's learned you can't love anything too much in this world. It's gone into the deepest Deeps to wait another million years. Ah, the poor thing! Waiting out here, and waiting out there, while man comes and goes on this pitiful little planet. Waiting and waiting."

I sat in my car, listening. I couldn't see the lighthouse or the light standing out in Lonesome Bay. I could only hear the Horn, the Horn, the Horn. It sounded like the monster calling.

I sat there wishing there was something I could say.

ACKNOWLEDGEMENTS

Editor and Publishers would like to thank the authors, their representatives, and other publishers with whom arrangements have been made to include in this collection certain copyright stories: Henry Treece for "The Visitor" from *I Cannot Go Hunting Tomorrow*; John Kruse and *Argosy* for "Murder Fish"; the Executors of Lieutenant-Colonel Oreste Pinto and Panther Books Ltd. for "He Talked in the End" from *Spycatcher*; the Executors of H. G. Wells and Ernest Benn, Ltd. for "The Remarkable Case of Davidson's Eyes" from *The Short Stories of H. G. Wells*; Gerald Kersh and William Heinemann, Ltd. for "The Extraordinarily Horrible Dummy" from the book of the same title; David Walker and *Argosy* for "Old Warrior"; Elleston Trevor and William Heinemann, Ltd. for "Moonrise" (somewhat abridged) from *The Killing-Ground*; Edward Arnold, Ltd. for "Wailing Well" from *The Collected Ghost Stories of M. R. James*; W. Somerset Maugham and William Heinemann, Ltd. for "A Man from Glasgow" from *Creatures of Circumstance*; the Copyright Owner of "The Bus Conductor" (somewhat abridged) from *The Room in the Tower* by E. F. Benson; Norbert Casteret and J. M. Dent and Sons, Ltd. for "Journey to the End of a Rope" from *Ten Years Under the Earth*; and Ray Bradbury and Rupert Hart-Davis, Ltd. for "The Fog Horn" from *The Golden Apples of the Sun*.

BIG BOOK OF BOYS' ADVENTURE STORIES

Volume Two

Open-Air Adventure Stories for Boys

Contents

No Medal for Matt

WALTER MACKEN

IT WAS a beautiful morning. The cliff top, at the western edge of the island, which lay some miles off the Irish coast, was a green carpet of closely cropped grass. Five hundred feet below, the water broke indolently over black jagged rocks. Its sinister sound was almost soothing. Westward, the Atlantic stretched calmly away to a limitless light-blue horizon.

Matt came toward the cliff from the village, walking on the enormous slabs of flat rock that covered the fields, which sloped steeply upward. The rocks were warm to the soles of his bare feet. Homespun trousers ending at the shin and a heavy knitted red jersey were making him sweat under the June sun. A canvas schoolbag flopped up and down on his hip as he journeyed, reminding him and bringing a frown between his brown eyes.

The climb up the slope was hard enough. He had to leap at times, and try to dodge the briars lurking in the crevices of the rocks. Sometimes the thorns scraped at the brown skin of his feet, leaving behind a scarlet scratch of blood. On both sides of him, small black-faced sheep, the kind that make such tender mutton, raised their heads to look at him and then moved cautiously away, following him with their eyes for a little, after he had passed, and then resuming the search for their meagre forage.

Matt was filled with a sense of guilt and injustice, and between the two of them his heart was very heavy. You are in school, see, just as he was yesterday. Near the end of the day, the sleepy part, the fellow beside him in the desk, young Pat Mullen, suddenly gives him a fierce puck in the ribs. Matt turns to clatter him, but before he can land even one blow on him, down the master comes and belts Matt. Matt protests that he is being belted in the wrong, and the master belts him again. Matt still protests, and the master, his face as red as the comb of a Christmas turkey, belts him once again and asks him does he want more. Matt says he doesn't want more. On his way home from school, burning with the injustice of it all, Matt tells himself that his father will right this wrong. His father is noted for his justice. "All right," says his father when Matt explains to him, "so the master was in the wrong. What do you want me to do, go up and hit the man? If every father did that, there would be not a school left in the universe." Couldn't he just tell him that he was in the wrong? Matt asks. No, he could not, his father says. Maybe the poor fellow was having trouble with his wife, or maybe he had an interior ailment that was persecuting him. Well, you will just have to tell him he was in the wrong, Matt says. His father gets angry then and shouts that he'll be damned if he will do anything of the sort, and even if this time Matt has been belted in the wrong, it will do him no harm, because there were times when he wasn't belted before and should have been. Matt denies this, and his father walks out of the house saying, "If I don't go, I'll belt you, and where will

you be then?" His father is upset, because he doesn't like
to think of Matt's being belted, right or wrong, but, being
civilized, he can't go and hammer the poor teacher.

So now Matt saw that the whole world was a place of
great injustice for boys; that there was no equity in it at all
when even your father refused to stand up for you. That
was why he had walked past the schoolhouse door this
morning, just as if it wasn't there, and had headed for the
tall cliffs. He had never done this before, because he liked
school, except on Mondays and the first day after holidays.
And even though he knew that he was right—it is necessary
for every man to make some protest against injustice—he
felt that he was wrong, and it seemed to him that some of
the beauty had gone out of the day, and that this freedom
he had chosen had, in some odd way, a chain on it.

When he had cleared the last obstacles barring his way to
the cliff top, he stood there and looked back. He could see
the whole island sloping away from his feet. It was shaped,
he thought, like the kidney of a pig. He could see the
golden beaches, and the sea beyond them reaching toward
the distant mainland, which was hidden in a blue haze. He
couldn't see his own house, but he could see the schoolhouse, and was sorry he was out of it, because just about
now they would be chanting the multiplication tables, and
he liked that. He also liked going into the yard at lunch-
time and wolfing his jam sandwiches, so that he would
have more time to play *capaillini conemara*, a game in
which small boys, mounted on the backs of larger boys,
raced each other.

He sighed and his heart was heavy, but his stomach was
empty, so he sat on the grass and, after removing the books
from his schoolbag, took the sandwiches his mother had
made for his lunch and proceeded to eat them, and it was
miraculous how the seagulls knew that there was food
around. They thronged about him, screaming, from the
sky and from the cliffs, and he amused himself by throwing crusts into the void and watching the wonderful swerv-

ing and twisting, the grace and the beauty of the gulls as they caught the crusts in flight.

My father will kill me, Matt thought then, and he looked over the water, thinking he might see his father's lobster boat if his father was doing this side of the island today. No boat was in sight. His father wouldn't actually kill him, Matt thought. He never raised a hand to him. It was his mother who always held the threat of him over Matt's head. Someday your father will kill you, Matt, she'd say. All the same, Matt knew that his father would be hurt by what he had done, and this made him feel a bit sad. He rolled on his stomach with his face over the cliff and looked down at the waves breaking on the rocks far, far below.

It was some while before he saw the movement—a fluttering movement, about fifty feet below him, on a ledge. He thought at first it might be a young gull, but then, as he watched closely, he saw that what moved was a rabbit, a plump young rabbit. He raised himself to his knees in surprise. A rabbit

*They swerved and twisted and caught
the crusts in flight.*

fifty feet down the face of the cliff! How could he have got there? Did a big bird claw him and lose him, or was he chased by a fox so that he fell and landed on that ledge below, or what?

Will I climb down and get the rabbit? was the next thought that came into his head. A terrible thought. His eyes narrowed as he looked over every inch of the cliff to the ledge. Suppose I fall, he wondered, looking farther, to the cruel black rocks waiting below. Who would miss me? Isn't everyone against me? Even so, his heart had begun to thump excitedly. It would be a famous climb. He stood up straight now, his hands on his hips, his eyes very bright. If the rabbit was left there, he would die and become a skeleton, or a bird would scoop him. If Matt saved his life, what a hero Matt would be! I climbed down cliffs when I was smaller, he thought, but never this cliff. This was the highest on the island.

He was still standing up when the boat came around a promontory behind him. He didn't see it, of course, and he didn't hear it. The chug-chug of its diesel engine was not loud, because the boat was going slowly as it negotiated a channel through some rocks toward a cluster of bobbing buoys that marked lobster pots.

The man at the tiller raised his eyes and saw the figure of the boy up there on the cliff top. He took his pipe out of his mouth, which remained open in amazement. "Here, Tom!" he called to the other man, who was coiling a rope in the waist. "For the love of God, is that my Matt up there?"

Tom came back to him, shaded his eyes with his hand, and said, "By all that's holy, it is!"

"What's he doing up there?" Matt's father asked. "He should be at school."

Then Matt's father opened his lungs to let a shout out of them, but it was never emitted, because Tom suddenly clapped a hard hand over his mouth and the shout died in a strangled gurgle. Tom took his hand away, and the two of them stood there, looking up, petrified with fear,

the hair rising on the back of their necks at the sight of
the boy casually letting himself down over the cliff.

"Oh, my God!" groaned Matt's father.

"If you shouted, you would have startled him," Tom
whispered.

"He'll fall! He's mad! What's come over him?" Matt's
father asked in anguish, his eyes glued painfully to the
small figure slowly descending the sheer face. In that red
jersey of his, it was all too easy to see him.

"Birds' eggs or something," said Tom. "I never saw
anybody climbing that bit. He'll be kilt!"

Matt's father swung the tiller to bring the boat in
toward the foot of the cliff. Tom struggled with him, and
forced the tiller so that the boat turned out again. He
switched off the engine.

"Are you mad?" he asked. "You can't get within fifty
yards of the place. The tide is low. Will you kill us as well?"

"He'll fall! He'll fall!" said Matt's father.

"Well, if he falls now," said Tom, annoyed at the boy,
"you'll only get his body. The rocks are up."

"Oh, my God!" said Matt's father.

Matt's heart was thumping and his mouth was dry.
Even so, there was a soaring in his breast. He was glad
he was in his bare feet. His big toes were wonderful, the
way they could feel, gauge, and grip a narrow crevice. The
cliff face was almost solid granite, which, for all its height,
had many times been washed by enormous waves. The sea
water had sought every weakness, and here and there had
scooped out the poor spots in the stone. So there were
cracks for Matt's thin fingers and his hardened toes. All
the same, you could be frightened, he thought, if you
hadn't climbed down cliffs before. He knew where he was
going, but he didn't want to look down to see. Clinging
like a fly, he lowered himself bit by bit, until below him,
out of the corner of his right eye, he could see the end of
the ledge where the rabbit crouched.

Down in the boat, Matt's father, who was in the middle
of a prayer, thought he could feel the hairs turning grey

"For the love of God, is that my Matt up there?"

on his head. He relaxed a little as he saw his son's feet feeling for a ledge and then resting there firmly.

Matt was happy to feel his feet on solid rock, though it was a very narrow ledge. The rabbit went to the far end of it, on the right, but he was still within reach of Matt's hand. Matt lowered his body slowly, gripping the surface of the cliff with the nails of his left hand and reaching for the rabbit with his right.

He grabbed the rabbit's fur. Don't struggle, don't struggle, Matt shouted at him in his heart, or you'll have the two of us over. He gripped him tightly. The animal stiffened. Slowly, Matt lifted him, and then carefully inserted him in the open schoolbag on his hip and strapped the flap shut.

Matt rested for a moment. He felt good now. Then he took a few deep breaths and started the climb up. The rabbit remained very still in the bag.

By now, Matt's father was kneeling, his hands covering his eyes. "What's he doing now, Tom?" he asked. "What in the name of God is he doing now?"

"He's on his way up," Tom said quietly. "He'll likely make it. What scoundrels boys are! What did he do it for? He got something. I wouldn't do that to rescue a king. That fellow will be a famous man or he'll end up hung."

"God bring him to the top," said Matt's father.

On the cliffside, Matt whispered to himself, "Going up is not as bad as going down." Because you can see. It looked fierce far just the same. The granite had torn his fingers. The middle ones were bleeding. And the sides of his toes were bleeding, too. He could feel them. Above, he could see a few slivers of green grass on the very top, beckoning to him. I'm coming, he silently called up to them, laughing. Wait'll you see. But it seemed a long time to him, before his hand rested on the coolness of the grass, and he paused, breathless, and then pulled himself over the top.

It seemed a lifetime to his father before he heard Tom's pent-up breath expelled and his voice saying, with a sigh,

"He is over. He is over now." Matt's father couldn't say anything.

Matt was now lying on the grass, feeling it with one cheek. His fist was beating the ground. "I did it! I did it!" he said out loud. What a tale to tell, he thought, but who will believe me? But what does it matter if nobody believes me? It was a great and famous climb, so it was.

Then, from the depths below, he heard a voice hailing and hailing, so he stood up and looked over the edge. Oh, it was his father and Tom. He hoped they hadn't seen him climbing down to the ledge. His father would murder him!

"What you doing? What the hell you think you're doing?" he faintly heard Tom saying.

So they *had* seen him! Then he remembered the rabbit. The rabbit would change things. Because of the rabbit, his father would be pleased with him. He'd be pleased, you'd see, and forget all about his dodging school. He opened the schoolbag and, reaching for the rabbit with his left hand, caught him by the hind legs and extracted him. Then he expertly hit him on the back of the neck with the edge of his right hand, so that the rabbit died, swiftly executed, in a second.

And Matt waved the body of the rabbit above his head, leaning out perilously over the cliff, and, with one hand curved around his mouth, shouted down, "Hey, Father! Father! You'll have rabbit stew tonight. You hear that? Rabbit stew tonight!"

He laughed as he waved the rabbit, because his father loved rabbit stew, he really did. Then Matt gathered up his schoolbooks and put them back in his bag, along with the rabbit, and hurried down the slope, over the long fields of great flat rocks, toward home.

And his father still sat, completely drained, completely exhausted, in the bottom of the lobster boat.

Indian Medicine

A. B. GUTHRIE

THE MIST along the creek shone in the morning sun, which was coming up lazy and half-hearted, as if of a mind to turn back and let the spring season wait. The cottonwoods and quaking aspens were still bare and the needles of the pines old and dark with winter, but beaver were prime and beaver were plenty. John Clell made a lift and took the drowned animal quietly from the trap and stretched it in the canoe with three others.

Bill Potter said, "If 'tweren't for the Injuns! Or if 'tweren't for you and your notions!" For all his bluster, he still spoke soft, as if on the chance that there were other ears to hear.

Clell didn't answer. He reset the trap and pulled from the mud the twig that slanted over it and unstoppered his goat-horn medicine bottle, dipped the twig in it and poked it back into the mud.

"Damn if I don't think sometimes you're scary," Potter went on, studying Clell out of eyes that were small and set close. "What kind of medicine* is it makes you smell Injuns with nary one about?"

"Time you see as many of them as I have, you'll be scary too," Clell answered, slipping his paddle into the stream. He had a notion to get this greenhorn told off but he let it slide. What was the use? You couldn't put into a greenhorn's head what it was you felt. You couldn't give him the feel of distances and sky-high mountains and lonely winds and ideas spoken out of nowhwere, ideas spoken into the head by medicines a man couldn't put a name to. Like now. Like here. Like this idea that there was brown skin about, and Blackfoot skin at that.

"I seen Blackfeet enough for both of us," he added. His mind ran back to old comrades and a time that seemed long ago because so much had come between; to days and nights and seasons of watching out, with just himself and the long silence for company; to last year and a hole that lay across the mountains to the south, where the Blackfeet and the Crows had fought, and he had sided with the Crows and got a wound in the leg that hurt sometimes yet. He could still see some of the Blackfeet faces. He would know them, and they would know him, being long-remembering.

He knew Blackfeet all right, but he couldn't tell Bill Potter why he thought some of them were close by. There wasn't any sign he could point to; the creek sang along and the breeze played in the trees, and overhead a big eagle was gliding low, and nowhere was there a footprint or a movement or a whiff of smoke. It was just a feeling he had, and Potter wouldn't understand it, but would only look at him and maybe smile with one side of his mouth.

"Ain't anybody I knows of carries a two-shoot gun but you," Potter said, still talking as if Clell was scared over nothing.

Clell looked down at it, where he had it angled to his hand. It had two barrels, fixed on a swivel. When the top one was fired, you slipped a catch and turned the other up.

* "Indian Medicine"—his special knowledge, "know-how" and artfulness.

One barrel was rifled, the other bigger and smooth-bored, and sometimes he loaded the big one with shot, for birds, and sometimes with a heavy ball, for bear or buffalo, or maybe with ball and buck both, just for what-the-hell. There was shot in it this morning, for he had thought maybe to take ducks or geese, and so refresh his taste for buffalo meat. The rifle shone in the morning sun. It was a nice piece, with a patch box a man wouldn't know to open until someone showed him the place to press his thumb. For no reason at all, Clell called his rifle Mule Ear.

He said, "You're a fool, Potter, more ways than one. Injuns'll raise your hair for sure, if it don't so happen I do it myself. As for this here two-shooter, I like it, and that's that."

Bill Potter always took low when a man dared him like that. Now all he said was "It's heavy as all hell."

Slipping along the stream, with the banks rising steep on both sides, Clell thought about beaver and Indians and all the country he had seen—high country, pretty as paint, wild as any animal and lonesome as time, and rivers unseen but by him, and holes and creeks without a name, and one place where water spouted hot and steaming and sometimes stinking from the earth, and another where a big spring flowed with pure tar; and no one believed him when he told of them, but called him the biggest liar yet. It was all right, though. He knew what he knew, and kept it to himself now, being tired of queer looks and smiles and words that made out he was half crazy.

Sometimes, remembering things, he didn't see what people did or hear what they said or think to speak when spoken to. It was all right. It didn't matter what was said about his sayings or his doings or his ways of thinking. A man long alone where no other white foot ever had stepped got different. He came to know what the Indians meant by medicine. He got to feeling like one with the mountains and the great sky and the lonesome winds and the animals and Indians, too, and it was a little as if he knew what they knew, a little as if there couldn't be a secret but was whispered to him, like the secret he kept hearing now.

"Let's cache," he said to Potter. The mist was gone from the river and the sun well up and decided on its course. It was time, and past time, to slide back to their hidden camp.

"Just got one more trap to lift," Potter argued.

"All right, then."

Overhead the eagle still soared close. Clell heard its long, high cry.

He heard something else, too, a muffled pounding of feet on the banks above. "Injuns!" he said, and bent the canoe into the cover of an overhanging bush. "I told you."

Potter listened. "Buffalo is all. Buffalo trampin' around."

Clell couldn't be sure, except for the feeling in him. Down in this little canyon a man couldn't see to the banks above. It could be buffalo, all right, but something kept warning, "Injuns! Injuns!"

Potter said, "Let's git on. Can't be cachin' from every little noise. Even sparrers make noise."

"Wait a spell."

"Scary." Potter said just the one word, and he said it under his breath, but it was enough. Clell dipped his paddle. One day he would whip Potter, but right now he reckoned he had to go on.

It wasn't fear that came on him a shake later, but just the quick knowing he had been right all along, just the holding still, the waiting, the watching what to do, for the banks had broken out with Indians—Indians with feathers in their hair, and bows and war clubs and spears in their hands; Indians yelling and motioning and scrambling down to the shores on both sides and fitting arrows to their bow strings.

Potter's face had gone white and tight like rawhide drying. He grabbed at his rifle.

Clell said, "Steady!" and got the pipe that hung from around his neck and held it up, meaning he meant peace.

These were the Blackfeet sure enough. These were the meanest Indians living. He would know them from the Rees and Crows and Pierced Noses and any other. He

"Don't point that there rifle 'less you want a skinful of arrows."

would know them by their round heads and bent noses and their red-and-green leather shields and the moccasins mis-matched in colour, and their bows and robes not fancy, and no man naked in the bunch.

The Indians waved them in. Clell let go his pipe and stroked with his paddle. Potter's voice was shrill. "You fool! You gonna let 'em torment us to death?"

That was the way with a mouthy greenhorn—full of himself at first, and then wild and shaken. "Steady!" Clell said again. "I aim to pull to shore. Don't point that there rifle 'less you want a skinful of arrows."

There wasn't a gun among the Indians, not a decent gun, but only a few rusty trade muskets. They had battle axes, and bows taken from their cases, ready for business, and some had spears, and all looked itching for a white man's hair. They waited, their eyes bright as buttons, their faces and bare forearms and right shoulders shining brown in

276

the sun. Only men were at the shore line, but Clell could see the faces of squaws and young ones looking down from the bank above.

An Indian splashed out and got hold of the prow of the canoe and pulled it in. Clell stepped ashore, holding up his pipe. He had to watch Potter. Potter stumbled out, his little eyes wide and his face white, and fear showing even for an Indian to see. When he stepped on the bank, one of the Indians grabbed his rifle and wrenched it from him, and Potter just stood like a scared rabbit, looking as if he might jump back in the canoe any minute.

Clell reached out and took a quick hold on the rifle and jerked it away and handed it back to Potter. There was a way to treat Indians. Act like a squaw and they treated you bad; act like a brave man and you might have a chance.

Potter snatched the gun and spun around and leaped. The force of the jump carried the canoe out. He made a splash with the paddle. An arrow whispered in the air and made a little thump when it hit. Clell saw the end of it, shaking from high in Potter's back.

Potter cried out, "I'm hit! I'm hit, Clell!"

"Come back! Easy! Can't get away!"

Instead, Potter swung around with the rifle. There were two sounds, the crack of the powder and the gunshot plunk of a ball. Clell caught a glimpse of an Indian going down, and then the air was full of the twang of bow-strings and the whispered flight of arrows, and Potter slumped slowly back in the canoe, his body stuck like a pincushion. An Indian splashed out to take the scalp. Two others carried the shot warrior up the bank. Already a squaw was beginning to keen.

Clell stood quiet as a stump, letting only his eyes move. It was so close now that his life was as good as gone. He could see it in the eyes around him, in the hungry faces, in the hands moving and the spears and the bows being raised. He stood straight, looking their eyes down, thinking the first arrow would come any time now, from any place,

277

and then he heard the eagle scream. Its shadow lazed along the ground. His thumb slipped the barrel catch, his wrist twisted under side up. He shot without knowing he aimed. Two feathers puffed out of the bird. It went into a steep climb and faltered and turned head down and spun to the ground, making a thump when it hit.

The Indians' eyes switched back to him. Their mouths fell open, and slowly their hands came over the mouth holes in the sign of surprise. It was as he figured in that flash between life and death. They thought all guns fired a single ball. They thought he was big medicine as a marksman. One of them stepped out and laid his hand on Mule Ear, as if to draw some of its greatness into himself. A murmur started up, growing into an argument. They ordered Clell up the bank. When he got there, he saw one Indian high-tailing it for the eagle, and others following, so's to have plumes for their war bonnets, maybe, or to eat the raw flesh for the medicine it would give them.

There was a passel of Indians on the bank, three or four hundred, and more coming across from the other side. The man Clell took for the chief had mixed red earth with spit and dabbed it on his face. He carried a bird-wing fan in one hand and wore a half-sleeved hunting shirt made of bighorn skin and decorated with coloured porcupine quills. His hair was a wild bush over his eyes and ears. At the back of it he had a tuft of owl feathers hanging. He yelled something and motioned with his hands, and the others began drifting back from the bank, except for a couple of dozen that Clell figured were head men. Mostly, they wore leggings and moccasins, and leather shirts or robes slung over the left shoulder. A few had scarlet trade blankets, which had come from God knew where. One didn't wear anything under his robe.

The squaws and the little squaws in their leather sacks of dresses, the naked boys with their potbellies and swollen navels, and the untried and middling warriors were all back now. The chief and the rest squatted down in a half circle, with Clell standing in front of them. They passed a

*He heard the eagle scream . . . and shot without knowing
he aimed.*

pipe around. After a while they began to talk He had some of the hang of Blackfoot, and he knew, even without their words, they were arguing what to do with him. One of them got up and came over and brought his face close to Clell's. His eyes picked at Clell's head and eyes and nose and mouth. Clell could smell grease on him and wood smoke and old sweat, but what came to his mind above all was that here was a man he had fought last season while siding with the Crows. He looked steadily into the black eyes and saw the knowing come into them, too, and watched the man turn back and take his place in the half circle and heard him telling what he knew.

They grunted like hogs, the Blackfeet did, like hogs about to be fed, while the one talked and pointed, arguing that here was a friend of their old enemies, the Crows. The man rubbed one palm over the other, saying in sign that Clell had to be rubbed out. Let them stand him up and use him for a target, the man said. The others said yes to that, not nodding their heads as white men would, but bowing forward and back from the waist.

Clell had just one trick left. He stepped over and showed his gun and pointed to the patch box and, waving one hand to catch their eyes, he sprang the cover with the other thumb. He closed the cover and handed the gun to the chief.

The chief's hands were red with the paint he had smeared on his face. Clell watched the long thumbnail, hooked like a bird claw, digging at the cover, watched the red fingers feeling for a latch or spring. While the others stretched their necks to see, the chief turned Mule Ear over, prying at it with his eyes. It wasn't any use. Unless he knew the hidden spot to press, he couldn't spring the lid. Clell took the piece back, opened the patch box again, closed it and sat down.

He couldn't make more medicine. He didn't have a glass to bring the sun down, and so to light a pipe, or even a trader's paper-backed mirror for the chief to see how pretty he was. All he had was the shot at the eagle and the patch box on Mule Ear, and he had used them both and had to take what came.

Maybe it was the eagle that did it, or the hidden cover, or maybe it was just the crazy way of Indians. The chief got up, and with his hands and with his tongue asked if the white hunter was a good runner.

Clell took his time answering, as a man did when making high palaver. He lighted his pipe. He said, "The white hunter is a bad runner. The other Long Knives think he runs fast. Their legs are round from sitting on a horse. They cannot run."

The chief grunted, letting the sign talk and the slow words sink into him. "The Long Knife will run." He pointed to the south, away from the creek. "He will run for the trading house that the whiteface keeps among the Crows. He will go as far as three arrows will shoot, and then he will run. My brothers will run. If my brothers run faster—" The chief brought his hand to his scalp lock.

The other Indians had gathered around, even the squaws and the young ones. They were grunting with excitement. The chief took Mule Ear. Other hands stripped off Clell's hunting shirt, the red-checked woollen shirt underneath, his leggings, his moccasins, his small-clothes, until he stood white and naked in the sun, and the squaws and young ones came up close to see what white flesh looked like. The squaws made little noises in their throats. They poked at his bare hide. One of them grabbed the red-checked shirt from the hands of a man and ran off with it. The chief made the sign for "Go!"

Clell walked straight, quartering into the sun. He walked slow and solemn, like going to church. If he hurried, they would start the chase right off. If he lazed along, making out they could be damned for all he cared, they might give him more of a start.

He was two hundred yards away when the first whoop sounded, the first single whoop, and then all the voices yelling and making one great whoop. From the corner of his eye he saw their legs driving, saw the uncovered brown skins, the feathered hair, the bows and spears, and then he was running himself, seeing ahead of him the far tumble and roll of high plains and hills, with buffalo dotting the distances and a herd of prairie goats sliding like summer mist, and everywhere, so that not always could his feet miss them, the angry knobs of cactus. South and east, many a long camp away where the Bighorn River joined the Roche Jaune, lay Lisa's Fort, the trading house among the Crows.

He ran so as to save himself for running, striding long and loose through the new-sprouting buffalo grass, around the cactus, around the pieces of sandstone where snakes were likely to lie. He made himself breathe easy, breathe deep, breathe full in his belly. Far off in his feelings he felt the cactus sting him and the spines pull off to sting again. The sun looked him in the face. It lay long and warm on the world. At the sky line the heat sent up a little shimmer. There wasn't a noise anywhere except the thump of his feet and his heart working in his chest and his breath sucking in and out and, behind him, a cry now and then from the Indians, seeming not closer or farther away than at first. He couldn't slow himself with a look. He began to sweat.

A man could run a mile, or two or three, and then his breath wheezed in him. It grew into a hard snore in the throat. The air came in, weak and dry, and burned his pipes and went out in one spent rush while his lungs sucked for more. He felt as if he had been running on forever. He felt strange and out of the world, a man running in a dream, except that the ache in his throat was real and the fire of cactus in his feet. The earth spread away forever, and he was lost in it and friendless, and not a proper part of it any more; and it served him right. When a man didn't pay any mind to his medicine, but went ahead regardless, as he had done, his medicine played out on him.

Clell looked back. He had gained, fifty yards, seventy-five, half a musket shot; he had gained on all the Indians except one, and that one ran as swift and high-headed as

He was 200 yards away when the first whoop sounded.

a prairie goat. He was close and coming closer.

Clell had a quick notion to stop and fight. He had an idea he might dodge the spear the Indian carried and come to grips with him. But the rest would be on him before he finished. It took time to kill a man just with the hands alone. Now was the time for the running he had saved himself for. There was strength in his legs yet. He made them reach out, farther, faster, faster, farther. The pound of them came to be a sick jolting inside his skull. His whole chest fought for air through the hot, closed tunnel of his throat. His legs weren't a part of him; they were something to think about, but not to feel, something to watch and to wonder at. He saw them come out and go under him and come out again. He saw them weakening, the knees bending in a little as the weight came on them. He felt wetness on his face, and reached up and found his nose was streaming blood.

He looked over his shoulder again. The main body of Indians had fallen farther back, the the prairie goat had gained. Through a fog he saw the man's face, the chin set high and hard, the black eyes gleaming. He heard the moccasins slapping in the grass.

Of a sudden, Clell made up his mind. Keep on running and he'd get a spear in the back. Let it come from the front. Let it come through the chest. Let him face up to death like a natural man and to hell with it. His feet jolted him to a halt. He swung around and threw up his hands as if to stop a brute.

The Indian wasn't ready for that. He tried to pull up quick. He made to lift his spear. And then he stumbled and fell ahead. The spear handle broke as the point dug in the ground. Clell grabbed at the shaft, wrenched the point from the earth and drove it through the man. The Indian bucked to his hands and knees and strained and sank back. It was as easy as that.

Bending over him, Clell let his chest drink, let his numb legs rest, until he heard the yells of the Indians and, looking up, saw them strung out in a long file, with the closest of them so close he could see the set of their faces. He turned and ran again, hearing a sudden, louder howling as the Indians came on the dead one, and then the howling dying again to single cries as they picked up the chase. They were too many for him, and too close. He didn't have a chance. He couldn't fort up and try to stand them off, not with his hands bare. There wasn't any place to hide. He should have listened to his medicine when it was talking to him back there on the creek.

Down the slope ahead of him a river ran—the Jefferson Fork of the Missouri, he thought, while he made his legs drive him through a screen of brush. A beaver swam in the river, its moving head making a quiet V in the still water above a dam. As he pounded closer, its flat tail slapped the water like a pistol shot, the point of the V sank from sight, and the ripples spread out and lost themselves. He could still see the beaver, though, swimming under water, its legs moving and the black tail plain, like something to follow. It was a big beaver, and it was making for a beaver lodge at Clell's right.

Clell dived, came up gasping from the chill of mountain water, and started stroking for the other shore. Beaver lodge! Beaver lodge! It was as if something spoke to him, as if someone nudged him, as if the black tail pulled him around. It was a fool thing, swimming under water and feeling for the tunnel that led up into the lodge. A fool thing. A man got so winded and weak that he didn't know medicine from craziness. A fool thing. A man couldn't force his shoulders through a beaver hole. The point of his shoulder pushed into mud. A snag ripped his side. He clawed ahead, his lungs bursting. And then his head was out of water, in the dark, and his lungs pumped air.

He heard movement in the lodge and a soft churring, but his eyes couldn't see anything. He pulled himself up, still hearing the churring, expecting the quick slice of teeth in his flesh. There was a scramble. Something slid along his leg and made a splash in the water of the tunnel, and slid again and made another splash.

His hands felt sticks and smooth, dry mud and the softness of shed hair. He sat up. The roof of the lodge just cleared his head if he sat slouched. It was a big lodge, farther across than the span of his arms. And it was as dark, almost, as the inside of a plugged barrel. His hand crossing before his eyes was just a shapeless movement.

He sat still and listened. The voices of the Indians sounded far off. He heard their feet in the stream, heard the moccasins walking softly around the lodge, heard the crunch of dried grass under their steps. It was like something dreamed, this hiding and being able to listen and to move. It was like being a breath of air, and no one able to put a hand on it.

After a while the footsteps trailed off and the voices faded. Now Clell's eyes were used to blackness, the lodge was a dark dapple. From the shades he would know it was day, but that was all. He felt for the cactus spines in his feet. He had been cold and wet at first, but the wetness dried and the lodge warmed a little to his body Shivering, he lay down, feeling the dried mud under his skin, and the soft fur. When he closed his eyes he could see the sweep of distances and the high climb of mountains, and himself all alone in all the world, and, closer up, he could see the beaver swimming under water and its flat tail beckoning. He could hear voices, the silent voices speaking to a lonesome man out of nowhere and out of everywhere, and the beaver speaking, too, the smack of its tail speaking.

He woke up later, quick with alarm, digging at his dream and the noise that had got mixed with it. It was night outside. Not even the dark dapple showed inside the lodge, but only such a blackness as made a man feel himself to make sure he was real. Then he heard a snuffling of the air, and the sound of little waves lapping in the tunnel, and he knew that a beaver had nosed up and smelled him and drawn back into the water.

When he figured it was day, he sat up slowly, easing his muscles into action. He knew, without seeing, that his feet were puffed with the poison of the cactus. He crawled to the tunnel and filled his lungs and squirmed into it. He came up easy, just letting his eyes and nose rise above the water. The sun had cleared the eastern sky line. Not a breath of air stirred; the earth lay still, flowing into spring. He could see where the Indians had flattened the grass and trampled an edging of rushes, but there were no Indians about, not on one side or the other, not from shore line to sky line. He struck out for the far shore.

Seven days later a hunter at Fort Lisa spotted a figure far off. He watched it for a long spell, until a mist came over his eyes, and then he called to the men inside the stockade. A half-dozen came through the big gate, their rifles in the crooks of their arms, and stood outside and studied the figure too.

"Man, all right. Somep'n ails him. Look how he goes."

"Injun, I say. A Crow, maybe, with a Blackfoot arrer in him."

"Git the glass."

One of them went inside and came back and put the glass to his eye. "Naked as a damn jay bird."

"Injun, ain't it?"

"Got a crop of whiskers. Never seed a Injun with whiskers yet."

"Skin's black."

"Ain't a Injun, though."

They waited.

"It ain't! Yes, I do believe it's John Clell! It's John Clell or I'm a Blackfoot!"

They brought him in and put his great, raw swellings of feet in hot water and gave him brandy and doled out roast liver, and bit by bit, that day and the next, he told them what had happened.

They knew why he wouldn't eat prairie turnips afterward, seeing as he lived on raw ones all that time, but what they didn't understand, because he didn't try to tell them, was why he never would hunt beaver again.

Secret Airstrip

EDWARD LINDALL

ED BARLOW'S broad and sunburnt features were heavy with a mixture of resentment and anger, a vast disquietude, as he stumped down from the house and turned the corner of his implement shed. His brown eyes, narrowed against the late morning sunlight after the shadow of the house, shafted a glare at Charlie Bigtoe and Tommy Tucker, chanting a liquid-sounding native song as they worked unhurriedly at putting a new rail into the stockyard fence.

"Hi, boss," Charlie Bigtoe called, grinning like piano keys across his big black face.

"Good morning," Barlow grunted and didn't mean it, either as a comment or a wish. It was a dark, emotional thunderhead of a morning.

He turned abruptly into the big iron shed that sheltered the machines he had so painstakingly acquired over the years: a small secondhand bulldozer for dam building, a harvester for summer feeding-crops, a couple of old trucks, and a battered but efficient jeep, the motor that supplied electricity for the house and outbuildings and pumped water when the windmill failed. He took a greasegun from a rack nailed to the wall-timbers and advanced on the jeep.

It didn't really need greasing; it was smooth with care, but it was the dirtiest job around the place. And he needed it. He needed a job that he could hate because that way he could work off steam. He would have preferred, of course, to have taken Collie, his wise old stockhorse, and gone riding in the scrub. But the plane had landed out past the hills the previous afternoon. Its purpose was unknown, its presence a mystery. He knew something illegal was going on; something he had either to report or to wink at. He wasn't sure which. So he didn't want to leave the homestead while the plane was down. He might learn too much. People might even think he was involved.

He cursed now, thinking of the plane, and swung his big strong-framed body on to the front seat of the jeep, one long leg swinging, the other anchored to the ground.

Blast the plane! he thought now. He had seen it first seven weeks ago, or rather read its tracks, and Mary, his wife, had been arguing quietly all that time, pushing her viewpoint with the awful inflexibility of someone who knows she is right and cannot appreciate any other rightness than her own. She was tall and rounded, dark-eyed and dark-haired, and with a will like a team of donkeys. She had flared into a new hostility the moment yesterday when she had seen the plane. And he knew she must have been watching for it, because in all the times it must have landed on the airstrip he had never spotted it, a speck against an immensity of sky. She had insisted, almost frantically, that he should tell the police.

Barlow wished again now, as he had wished so many times, that he had kept his mouth shut. But so few unusual things happened in the busily placid life of Brolga Downs, a thousand square miles of cattle country in the lonely northern territory of Australia, that it had been natural to come home and tell of his discovery.

He had been hunting strays with Charlie Bigtoe and Tommy Tucker in the thick scrub on the far side of the low hills fifteen miles north of the homestead, driving them into a rough V-fence preparatory to pushing them back, as a herd, into the main pasture lands. And they had ridden along the old abandoned airstrip, a secret wartime base for the American Liberator bombers that had operated against the Japanese in Timor and Indonesia, until the war rolled farther north.

Charlie Bigtoe, with his radar eyes, had seen them first . . . tyre tracks leading off the strip into one of the many old bays beneath the fringing trees. And the bay had been cleared of its new-grown curtain of bushes. A dozen drums of fuel stood along its edge, and there were the oil drip patches and the fat tyre tracks of a three-ton truck. Charlie Bigtoe and Tommy Tucker could read mechanized tracks as easily as they could identify the age and weight of honey ants, the dimensions of a kangaroo. The tracks were four weeks old. And there were men's tracks too, a few of them big and booted, the majority small and curiously muffled, without heels.

Barlow had filled it in from there. He had heard rumours on his infrequent trips to Darwin of the organized smuggling of Chinese refugees into Australia. And then, at the old airstrip, he knew he had stumbled on the feedline. These muffled tracks were from the sandals of Chinese refugees being smuggled in to work in the market gardens of the southern cities, in Chinese restaurants, in coastal ships. Poor homeless devils, Barlow thought, who should be entering Australia lawfully, given a home in their homeless world.

The plane, he deduced from the tyre tracks and the state of the strip, was some sort of four- or six-seater, doubtless one of those fast American lights. It would carry up to ten thin Chinese, and maybe more, on island-hops down through the back areas of Indonesia and Timor.

"You will radio Sergeant Lawson, of course," Mary had said when he told her, intensely serious across the white-clothed spotlessness of their dinnertable.

Barlow had raised his eyebrows, his big broad face bland, his brown eyes a little wider, and the crowsfeet wrinkles at the corners deeper from the movement.

"Why?"

"These men are breaking the law."

"So what? It's a stupid, cruel law. The few Chinese they bring in don't do any harm and, anyway, the poor devils deserve a break."

Mary shook her head slowly and slightly, her lips touched with a small sadly-wise smile. After an adult lifetime in the territory, it was astonishing how little of the heat and grinding dust showed in her face.

"And you still hate Sergeant Lawson," she said. "You won't side with him on anything. Not even on the law."

Barlow had felt like shaking his head then, too, like a fighter who, having been hit, needs to shake himself back to clarity. This was an old and unresolved conflict. Sergeant Lawson, sitting big and square and pompous in his one-man post sixty miles to the south-west, by the stock route river crossing, was the type of man Barlow never could have liked, even if Lawson hadn't, on that blazing day five years before, arrested him on a baseless charge of cattle stealing.

The circuit judge had dismissed the case for want of evidence; Barlow was freed, but he had been deeply humiliated. He had spent five sweltering days in the police post's lock-up, had been treated like a criminal through sheer stupidity, and he knew that once mud was thrown, some stuck. So he had hated Lawson with a bitter, all-but-consuming hatred which, even though it mellowed with the years, had never really disappeared.

He had tried to convince Mary that it was all forgotten, and for long periods she believed, or pretended to believe him. Then, out of some careless remark, her suspicions would be renewed. She worried about it, the hate and its

291

They took spears and boomerangs and went roaming in the bush.

effects. It was something there, in the back of his mind. But now, with the Chinese, it was out in the open again, worrying Mary and exasperating him.

He had put on a patience he didn't feel, settling his shoulders deliberately, building a cigarette with an unhurried precision of calloused fingers.

"I don't hate Lawson," he said quietly. "I don't like him. That's all."

"Ed." She was suddenly tense, shredding his proffered truce with urgent hands. "Don't play games with me. You're still bitter, and you're letting it sway your judgment."

"All right," he said suddenly, bitingly. "I still hate him. But that doesn't mean I'm not right about the smuggling."

"Ed." Mary's voice became deeper. Beseeching.

"Don't you see? This hate is eating you up. You can't think straight."

"Mary," he said quietly, drawing on the cigarette, looking down his nose at it. "You're reading things into this, the way you always do."

She had leaned across to touch him, then stopped, as though repulsed. She sat up stiffly. "It's your duty, as a citizen, to report this plane."

"I've got other duties," he said shortly. "I'm a man, too. I've got duties as a man, duties to mankind."

Then he had watched the worry deepen on her face and wondered about the expression of his feelings. It was true, but where the words had come from he did not know. They were not the sort of words he used; not cattleman's words. He felt sympathy for the Chinese, thought they were having a rough deal, and somehow those simple feelings had been translated into "duties to mankind".

The phrase could have come from some unremembered book. Duties to mankind. It was true enough, and the pity was that Mary couldn't see it. She could only see his hate for Lawson.

Barlow levered himself off the jeep seat with a sigh, swinging the greasegun easily in his big hand, hearing again the liquid song of Charlie Bigtoe and Tommy Tucker and wondering what they would think of duties to mankind. They had, he thought, with darting envy, a simple and philosophic attitude to life. They took it as it came and adapted to its contours. They were first-class stockmen—he could never run Brolga Downs without them—but whenever the mood came upon them, they shed their boots and jeans and coloured shirts, stripped down to loincloths, took spears and boomerangs, and went roaming in the bush.

They stayed out for days, even weeks, to come back rested, fit and happy, stockmen again, resuming their married lives in the whitewashed cottages where their women waited for them. And now, in the midst of all the white man turmoil, they were getting the urge for walkabout again. Barlow had noticed that they both had boomerangs thrust into their belts, which showed the way their thoughts were tending. No duties to mankind there, Barlow thought ruefully. They *were* mankind.

Then Barlow sensed that he was not alone in the shed. He didn't believe in miracles of sixth sense; skilled bushmen didn't. Everything came through observation and identification, from variations of the normal. Now he stood perfectly still, listening. And it came again, a jagged slur of breathing. He reversed the greasegun in his hand with a quick flip, waited for the sound again, placed it in the deep shadow behind the harvester, and crossed to the doorway on silent feet to sign-talk Charlie Bigtoe and Tommy Tucker. It always paid to stack the odds.

They advanced on padding feet, the three of them, stalking the breather without too much seriousness. Occasionally tramps tottered through, aimless and harmless for the most part, but sometimes with a nuisance value. The men split at the harvester, one going round the front and two round the back. And then they stopped, looking down at the dusty ground, at the scarecrow thing that sprawled there in exhausted sleep. Thin and frail. Shrivelled. Barlow put the greasegun on the sideboard of the harvester, vaguely ashamed to have it in his hand. Charlie Bigtoe and Tommy Tucker leaned far forward, peering with big eyes, their broad black faces sagging with pity and concern.

"Chinese," Barlow said, feeling the stirring of a vast uneasiness, a touch of fate, a sense of arriving at some crossroads of the mind.

"Bin come from dat plane, mine tinkit," Charlie Bigtoe said.

Tommy Tucker pointed at the bare feet, sticking bonily from the torn blue overalls the man wore, and they were black with dried blood.

"Bin walk longtime plenty fast," he said. "Bin someone after 'im, like dust come dis way now."

"What dust?" Barlow demanded sharply.

Tommy Tucker waved a hand towards the hills, the airstrip. "Dat way. Maybe five, maybe six mile out."

Barlow dropped to his knees and shook the Chinaman, softly at first, then more roughly when he did not come awake. But not too roughly. The man was a bag of bones that could easily be shaken into dry component parts. Then the eyes opened slowly, dark slits that grew almost round with fear, and he was trying to scramble away. But Barlow grabbed his right hand and began to shake it, smiling and nodding to make his friendship clear. It worked. The man sat up, was still, a young-old man with a sunken mask of suffering for a face. And then Barlow saw the long angry furrow of a bullet wound across his shaven head.

"What's this?" He pointed.

The Chinaman stared a moment, then used his fingers to make a gun, gesturing in the general direction of the hills. He put two fingertips on the ground, and made the fingers run, stumbling and falling as they went. Someone out there had tried to kill him and he had run away. And that some-one, Barlow guessed, was on the way now to settle the account. What more, what were the rights of the case, the

Barlow shook the Chinaman, whose eyes grew round with fear.

background, he could not guess as yet. The Chinaman could have started it, although from his condition it seemed unlikely. The man was ill, in addition to his exhaustion, and he had obviously been in a bad way before he set out on his desperate flight. Barlow rose abruptly to his feet and stood back, thinking, figuring quickly. He did not know how many men were coming from the plane, but he knew they would be tough. Traffickers in human cargo would not be gentle men.

"Charlie," he said. "Tommy. Take this man into the scrub and keep him hidden. Quickly. Don't leave tracks."

The stockmen didn't hesitate, but stripped off their boots. They moved so quickly it was certain they had anticipated him. They stooped together and hauled the Chinaman to his feet. But he collapsed, so they swung him between them and made for the wide back door. Barlow walked behind them, taut and watchful, saw them pad quickly round and behind the house, their big bare feet like cushions on the hard-baked ground, and disappear into the scrub.

From the front garden of her cottage, Maudie Bigtoe shaded her eyes to stare.

Barlow waved to her and went back to the shed, got a roll of fencing-wire, a pair of heavy pliers, and began unnecessarily strengthening the stockyard fence, working from the outside. He had thought at first to wait on the verandah of the house, but realized that would have brought Mary out to meet the callers—with imponderable results if she should identify them. It was safer at the stockyards, where he could play his cards in simulated innocence, test the men and determine his course of action, free of the sort of storm that Mary might provoke.

Ten minutes later the truck arrived, bursting from the scrub track into the cleared space round the homestead, pulling up in an unmannerly cloud of dust some few feet from the stockyard. Barlow straddled his pliers across the top rail and put down his fencing-wire, like a methodical man about to enjoy a break. His big face was calm but his mind was working swiftly. The truck, complete with canvas canopy, would be the one they used to transport fuel, he reasoned, and take off their Chinese.

The two men who swung down from the cabin were tough, dressed in grubby khaki shirts and slacks, hatless, and with pistols bulky at their hips. The driver was Australian, big, red-faced, and carrot-haired, with a reckless brutality about him. The other, and he had to be the pilot, was slight and dark, with a thin black moustache and a scruff of facial stubble, black eyes, and a hard, cruel mouth. Probably Portuguese, Barlow thought.

"Howdy," the Australian said, stumping to the fence, with the pilot catfooting just behind, darting black eye-shafts at the house and outbuildings.

"Good day," Barlow said.

"We're lookin' for a man," Red-face said curtly. "Thought you might've seen him. Chinese. Got a bullet wound on the scalp."

Barlow rubbed his hands on his trousers, wishing he had a rifle leaning against the fence, but knowing it would have ruined his act of innocence. "I'm Ed Barlow," he said. "This is my place: Brolga Downs."

Red-face nodded shortly. "We reckoned he'd head this way."

No names, Barlow thought. Aloud, he said, "How come the bullet wound?"

"Madman," the Portuguese said in soft but deadly tones. "We take him south to hospital in our truck here, but he grow sick . . . want to fight. We camp out there, past your hills, for tie him up, but he snatch gun . . . my gun." He slapped the pistol at his hip for emphasis. "Thees one. An' try kill himself."

Red-face nodded gravely, pulling his mouth in a grimace. "We tried to grab him, but he run."

The teamwork shrieked rehearsal, and if Barlow had needed anything further to tell him they were lying it was Red-face's spurious gravity. Not a word about the plane; that was to be expected. Smugglers didn't advertise. But they were lying too about the Chinaman, who was very far from mad. And Barlow detected a callousness, almost of contempt, behind their plausibility. He felt a cold rage growing in him, more searing, more bitter than anything he had felt for Sergeant Lawson; for his anger was not about himself, but for others. For all the illegal migrants these men had carried and planned to carry in the future.

These men confirmed what his mind had already constructed without his bidding, a thought-picture of what had happened at the plane. They had tried to kill a sick man because he had been a burden, a risk of disclosure, the way slave-ship captains in the old days had thrown their cargoes overboard at the first sign of capture by a man-o'-war. Or perhaps when the other Chinese had been stowed aboard the truck, they had tried to force him back on to the plane, to be dropped into the smiling Timor Sea.

And Barlow knew then, as he had known instinctively since he had first seen the fugitive, what it was he had to do. Despite his sympathy for the Chinamen, he had to stop the trade. He had to take these men and give them to the police, to Sergeant Lawson of the rock-hard head, who was the sole residence of authority. And he wouldn't be doing it for Mary's reasons, the breaking of the law, but because of their brutality; because it was the only way to protect other men, other hopeless, homeless men who trusted them with their lives.

"And what makes you think he came this way?" he asked evenly.

"He's a town man," Red-face said, "an' this is the only house." He grinned, suddenly, brutally, without humour. "And we found some tracks back at the creek crossing. You know, the one just before you get here."

"Well, that narrows the field," Barlow said. He ran a square hand ruminatively across his jaw, thinking that it was probably the first true thing that they had said, but wanting to appear helpful. He needed to stall. It was one thing to resolve to take them; another to figure how.

"Give me a moment and I'll get my rifle," he said easily.

"I'll help you search."

"Why, thanks," Red-face said. "That's real nice."

"We got the guns," the Portuguese said harshly. "Why you want to bring one?"

"Forget it, Silva," Red-face snapped. "Sure he wants a gun."

Barlow went up to the house, fifty yards away, and took a light repeater from the gun-rack in the hall, moving quietly so as not to attract Mary's attention. He could hear her bumping away at housework somewhere about the kitchen. He loaded the rifle from a box above the rack, held steady for a moment, making sure he was under control, then turned towards the door. He was going to walk down there to the stockyard, bland-faced and pacing steadily, and put the rifle on them before they had time to think about getting out their pistols. But as he went out on to the verandah, eyes searching for their target, they were each side of the door. He was neatly caught between them.

"Well, let's go," he said steadily. "We'll try the out-buildings. See if he's crawled in somewhere."

They combed through the implement shed, the feed barn, and the fuel dump, with Barlow always in the middle. And they did it cleverly. Real professionals. If Barlow had not intended to get the drop on them he would never have noticed their suave positioning. As it was, it grated on him, drove him to anger and frustration. There seemed no way of carrying out his plan, and yet there had to be. They started on the stockmen's homes, those neat whitewashed cottages he had built for Bigtoe and Tucker and their workmates. And there he found his chance.

Maudie Bigtoe, Charlie's wife, was still in her patch of garden, dusting beans against red spider, keeping tabs, a big broad-shouldered woman with a smiling face and a quick intelligence. Barlow touched his throat casually, in the native finger-talk sign for enemies, and saw her black eyes gleam.

"Maudie, you see any strange man today?" He paused, letting her wait for his meaning, balancing on his nerve

He touched his throat casually—the native sign for enemies—and said: "Maudie, you see any strange man today?"

edges. "Like out in the scrub? Any man you see?"

She looked with interest at the men on either side of Barlow, at their watchfulness, at their loosely holstered pistols. "Yair, boss," she said at last. "Dat feller way." And she jerked her head towards the piece of scrub where Charlie, Tommy and the Chinaman were hiding. "Seen strange feller all right dat way."

Barlow took a grip on himself to stop his relief from showing. "Well, gentlemen," he said carefully. "Lead on."

Red-face grinned. Triumphantly. "My honour."

So Barlow followed Red-face with Silva close behind, walking between two guns that would not hesitate to leap out and fire, between two men who had been doing something he had once imagined to be humane, but discovered, face-to-face, to be inhuman, brutal, because these men were so.

He was going to take them into the scrub because he had two trusted helpers there, Charlie Bigtoe and Tommy

Tucker, who did not care a cuss about the issues, but would fight for him. He was taking them into the scrub because he could not handle them in the open. But once inside the trees, the advantage would be his despite all their manoeuvres. He would have as allies two of the finest bushmen in the world, two shadows. . . . Just the same, there was a tight band round his throat. His mouth was dry.

Inside the line of trees the brash light of the day was filtered, and the peopled silence of the homestead became murmurous with small noises. Red-face and Silva took out their pistols, and Barlow had the chilling feel of Silva's pointed right in the middle of his back. There was no sign of the stockmen, but Barlow was certain at least one of them, probably Charlie Bigtoe, was somewhere close. He couldn't know for sure; he could only guess. And it was on that guess that he was going to act. He had to show them he wanted help. And there was only one way to do it.

He eased back the bolt of his rifle. And Silva said quietly, hissingly, from behind, "You do not need that, mister. We have guns."

"Sure," Red-face said, turning and grinning evilly. "You might trip and shoot someone."

Then the dry, throaty rattle of a brush turkey sounded out to the right, fairly close, a little to the rear. And Barlow's senses leapt, for there were no turkeys so near the house. He stepped up close to Red-face.

"What's that?" Silva rasped, jerking his head round.

Barlow saw the head jerk and knew his chance had come. He cocked the rifle swiftly, jumping round in front of Red-face and thrusting the rifle into his belly. "Hold it," he snapped at Silva, watching the boil of fury in the dark face, the trembling brink of violence in the pistol hand.

"So you know," Red-face said flatly, his blue eyes cold and hard. "You crazy fool. We have to kill you now."

"You first," Barlow said. "Tell your pal to drop his gun."

"So you know. You crazy fool! We have to kill you now."

"Like hell," Red-face said. "You won't shoot." He grinned. "You haven't got that sort of guts."

"Maybe I don't need it," Barlow said, and then he was sure of it because the shadow had moved again, not far from Silva. He waited a breath-held moment. Then he heard the whistle of swift flight, saw a dark flash in the air . . . and a boomerang crashed into Silva's head. The man dropped down without a sound, without a kick or flutter, just dropped softly to the ground.

"Turn round," he said to Red-face harshly. "You've got a job to do."

They made a slow procession, Red-face carrying Silva, and the two stockmen cradling the sick Chinaman. And while Bigtoe and Tucker sat on guard with rifle and captured pistols, Barlow went racing into the house.

"Mary," he called. "Mary." She came from the kitchen and met him at the hall door, a rapt, tense expression on her face. "Get on the radio," he said. "Call Lawson and tell him we've got some prisoners."

"I have," she said. "I saw you coming."

"You knew?" He stared at her, seeing her expression for the first time. "You knew what was happening?"

She nodded jerkily. She was under the after-stress of excitement. "I saw the boys carry off that Chinaman, then the two men came—they looked so horrible, I guessed who they were." Then she smiled, a little tremulously, betraying the tension she was trying so hard to hide. "I watched you. I feared you were helping them."

Barlow stared again. He opened his mouth to speak, but she slid her arms round his neck and buried her face in his shoulder.

"Oh, Ed," she whispered. "I prayed you'd see it my way and call the police. And now you have."

"The law's the law," he said. "You were right." He'd even speak nicely to Lawson when he came. Shake his hand. . . . And hope this time the façade of forgotten bitterness would remain intact.

Contents of the
Dead Man's Pocket

JACK FINNEY

AT THE LITTLE living-room desk Tom Benecke rolled two
sheets of flimsy and a heavier top sheet, carbon paper
sandwiched between them, into his portable. *Inter-office
Memo*, the top sheet was headed, and he typed tomorrow's
date just below this; then he glanced at a creased yellow
sheet, covered with his own handwriting, beside the typewriter. "Hot in here," he muttered to himself. Then from
the short hallway at his back, he heard the muffled clang
of wire coat hangers in the bedroom closet, and at this
reminder of what his wife was doing he thought: Hot, hell
—guilty conscience.

He got up, shoving his hands into the back pockets of
his grey wash slacks, stepped to the living-room window
beside the desk and stood breathing on the glass, watching

the expanding circlet of mist, staring down through the autumn night at Lexington Avenue, eleven storeys below. He was a tall, lean, dark-haired young man in a pullover sweater, who looked as though he had played not football, probably, but basketball in college. Now he placed the heels of his hands against the top edge of the lower window frame and shoved upward. But as usual the window didn't budge, and he had to lower his hands and then shoot them hard upwards to jolt the window open a few inches. He dusted his hands, muttering.

But still he didn't begin his work. He crossed the room to the hallway entrance and, leaning against the doorjamb, hands shoved into his back pockets again, he called, "Clare?" When his wife answered, he said, "Sure you don't mind going alone?"

"No." Her voice was muffled, and he knew her head and shoulders were in the bedroom closet. Then the tap of her high heels sounded on the wood floor and she appeared at the end of the little hallway, wearing a slip, both hands raised to one ear, clipping on an earring. She smiled at him—a slender, very pretty girl with light brown, almost blonde, hair—her prettiness emphasized by the pleasant nature that showed in her face. "It's just that I hate you to miss this movie; you wanted to see it too."

"Yeah, I know." He ran his fingers through his hair. "Got to get this done, though."

She nodded, accepting this. Then, glancing at the desk across the living-room, she said, "You work too much, though, Tom—and too hard."

He smiled. "You won't mind, though, will you, when the money comes rolling in and I'm known as the Boy Wizard of Wholesale Groceries?"

"I guess not." She smiled and turned back towards the bedroom.

At his desk again, Tom lighted a cigarette; then a few moments later as Clare appeared, dressed and ready to leave, he set it on the rim of the ash tray. "Just after seven," she said. "I can make the beginning of the first feature."

305

She was dressed and all set for the movies.

He walked to the front-door closet to help her on with her coat. For an instant he was tempted to go with her; it was not actually true that he had to work tonight, though he very much wanted to. This was his own project, un-announced as yet in his office, and it could be postponed. But then they won't see it till Monday, he thought once again, and if I give it to the boss tomorrow he might read it over the week-end. . . . "Have a good time," he said aloud. He gave his wife a little swat and opened the door for her, feeling the air from the building hallway, smelling faintly of floor wax, stream gently past his face.

He watched her walk down the hall, flicked a hand in response as she waved, and then he started to close the door, but it resisted for a moment. As the door opening narrowed, the current of warm air from the hallway, channelled through this smaller opening now, suddenly rushed past him with accelerated force. Behind him he heard the slap of the window curtains against the wall and the sound of paper fluttering from his desk, and he had to push to close the door.

Turning, he saw a sheet of white paper drifting to the floor in a series of arcs, and another sheet, yellow, moving towards the window, caught in the dying current flowing through the narrow opening. As he watched, the paper struck the bottom edge of the window and hung there for an instant, plastered against the glass and wood. Then as the moving air stilled completely the curtains swinging back from the wall to hang free again, he saw the yellow sheet drop to the window ledge and slide over out of sight.

He ran across the room, grasped the bottom of the window and tugged, staring through the glass. He saw the yellow sheet, dimly now in the darkness outside, lying on the ornamental ledge a yard below the window. Even as he watched, it was moving, scraping slowly along the ledge, pushed by the breeze that pressed steadily against the building wall. He heaved on the window with all his strength and it shot open with a bang, the window weight rattling in the casing. But the paper was past his reach and, leaning out into the night, he watched it scud steadily along the ledge to the south, half plastered against the building wall. Above the muffled sound of the street traffic far below, he could hear the dry scrape of its movement, like a leaf on the pavement.

The living-room of the next apartment to the south projected a yard or more farther out towards the street than this one; because of this the Beneckes paid seven and a half dollars less rent than their neighbours. And now the yellow sheet, sliding along the stone ledge, nearly invisible in the night, was stopped by the projecting blank wall of the next apartment. It lay motionless, then, in the corner formed by the two walls—a good five yards away, pressed firmly against the ornate corner ornament of the ledge, by the breeze that moved past Tom Benecke's face.

He knelt at the window and stared at the yellow paper for a full minute or more, waiting for it to move, to slide off the ledge and fall, hoping he could follow its course to the street, and then hurry down in the elevator and retrieve it. But it didn't move, and then he saw that the paper was caught firmly between a projection of the convoluted corner ornament and the ledge. He thought about the poker from the fireplace, then the broom, then the mop—discarding each thought as it occurred to him. There was nothing in the apartment long enough to reach that paper.

It was hard for him to understand that he actually had to abandon it—it was ridiculous—and he began to curse. Of all the papers on his desk, why did it have to be this one in particular! On four long Saturday afternoons he had stood in super-markets, counting the people who passed certain displays, and the results were scribbled on that yellow sheet. From stacks of trade publications, gone over page by page in snatched half-hours at work and during evenings at home, he had copied facts, quotations and figures on to that sheet. And he had carried it with him to the Public Library on Fifth Avenue, where he'd spent a dozen lunch hours and early evenings adding more. All were needed to support and lend authority to his idea for a new grocery-store display method; without them his idea was a mere opinion. And there they all lay, in his own improvised shorthand—countless hours of work—out there on the ledge.

For many seconds he believed he was going to abandon the yellow sheet, that there was nothing else to do. The work could be duplicated. But it would take two months, and the time to present this idea, damn it, was *now*, for use in the spring displays. He struck his fist on the window ledge. Then he shrugged. Even though his plan were adopted, he told himself, it wouldn't bring him a raise in pay—not immediately, anyway, or as a direct result. It won't bring me a promotion either, he argued—not of itself. . . .

But just the same, and he couldn't escape the thought, this and other independent projects, some already done and others planned for the future, would gradually mark him out from the score of other young men in his company. They were the way to change from a name on the payroll to a name in the minds of the company officials. They were the beginning of the long, long climb to where he was determined to be, at the very top. And he knew he was going out there in the darkness, after the yellow sheet fifteen feet beyond his reach.

By a kind of instinct, he instantly began making his intention acceptable to himself by laughing at it. The mental picture of himself sidling along the ledge outside was absurd—it was actually comical—and he smiled. He imagined himself describing it; it would make a good story at the office and, it occurred to him, would add a special interest and importance to his memorandum, which would do it no harm at all.

To simply go out and get his paper was an easy task— he could be back here with it in less than two minutes— and he knew he wasn't deceiving himself. The ledge, he saw, measuring it with his eye, was about as wide as the length of his shoe, and perfectly flat. And every fifth row of brick in the face of the building, he remembered—leaning out, he verified this—was indented half an inch, enough for the tips of his fingers, enough to maintain balance easily. It occurred to him that if this ledge and wall were only a yard above ground—as he knelt at the window staring out, this thought was the final confirmation of his intention—he could move along the ledge indefinitely.

On a sudden impulse, he got to his feet, walked to the front closet and took out an old tweed jacket; it would be cold outside. He put it on and buttoned it as he crossed the room rapidly towards the open window. In the back of his mind he knew he'd better hurry and get this over with before he thought too much, and at the window he didn't allow himself to hesitate. . . .

He swung a leg over the sill, then felt for and found the ledge a yard below the window with his foot. Gripping the bottom of the window frame very tightly and carefully, he slowly ducked his head under it, feeling on his face the sudden change from the warm air of the room to the chill outside. With infinite care he brought out his other leg, his

mind concentrating on what he was doing. Then he slowly
stood erect. Most of the putty, dried out and brittle, had
dropped off the bottom edging of the window frame, he
found, and the flat wooden edging provided a good gripping surface, a half inch or more deep, for the tips of his
fingers.

Now, balanced easily and firmly, he stood on the ledge
outside in the slight, chill breeze, eleven storeys above the
street, staring into his own lighted apartment, odd and
different-seeming now.

First his right hand, then his left, he carefully shifted his
finger-tip grip from the puttyless window edging to an
indented row of bricks directly to his right. It was hard to
take the first shuffling sideways step then—to make himself move—and the fear stirred in his stomach, but he did
it, again by not allowing himself time to think. And now—
with his chest, stomach, and the left side of his face pressed
against the rough cold brick—his lighted apartment was
suddenly gone, and it was much darker out here than he
had thought.

Without pause he continued—right foot, left foot, right
foot, left—his shoe soles shuffling and scraping along the
rough stone, never lifting from it, fingers sliding along the
exposed edging of brick. He moved on the balls of his feet,
heels lifted slightly; the ledge was not quite as wide as he'd
expected. But leaning slightly inward towards the face of
the building and pressed against it, he could feel his
balance firm and secure, and moving along the ledge was
quite as easy as he had thought it would be. He could hear
the buttons of his jacket scraping steadily along the rough
bricks and feel them catch momentarily, tugging a little,
at each mortared crack. He simply did not permit himself
to look down, though the compulsion to do so never left
him; nor did he allow himself actually to think. Mechani-
cally—right foot, left foot, over and again—he shuffled
along crabwise, watching the projecting wall ahead loom
steadily closer. . . .

Then he reached it and, at the corner—he'd decided how

With infinite care he brought out his other leg.

he was going to pick up the paper—he lifted his right foot and placed it carefully on the ledge that ran along the projecting wall at a right angle to the ledge on which his other foot rested. And now, facing the building, he stood in the corner formed by the two walls, one foot on the ledging of each, a hand on the shoulder-high indentation of each wall. His forehead was pressed directly into the corner against the cold bricks, and now he carefully lowered first one hand, then the other, perhaps a foot farther down, to the next indentation in the rows of bricks.

Very slowly, sliding his forehead down the trough of the brick corner and bending his knees, he lowered his body towards the paper lying between his outstretched feet. Again he lowered his fingerholds another foot and bent his knees still more, thigh muscles taut, his forehead sliding and bumping down the brick V. Half squatting now, he dropped his left hand to the next indentation and then slowly reached with his right hand towards the paper between his feet.

He couldn't quite touch it, and his knees now were

pressed against the wall; he could bend them no farther. But by ducking his head another inch lower, the top of his head now pressed against the bricks, he lowered his right shoulder and his fingers had the paper by a corner, pulling it loose. At the same instant he saw, between his legs and far below, Lexington Avenue stretched out for miles ahead.

He saw, in that instant, the Loew's theatre sign, blocks ahead past Fiftieth Street; the miles of traffic signals, all green now; the lights of cars and street lamps; countless neon signs; and the moving black dots of people. And a violent, instantaneous explosion of absolute terror roared through him. For a motionless instant he saw himself externally—bent practically double, balanced on this narrow ledge, nearly half his body projecting out above the street far below—and he began to tremble violently, panic flaring through his mind and muscles, and he felt the blood rush from the surface of his skin.

In the fractional moment before horror paralysed him, as he stared between his legs at that terrible length of street far beneath him, a fragment of his mind raised his body in a spasmodic jerk to an upright position again, but so violently that his head scraped hard against the wall, bouncing off it, and his body swayed outwards to the knife edge of balance, and he very nearly plunged backwards and fell. Then he was leaning far into the corner again, squeezing and pushing into it, not only his face but his chest and stomach, his back arching; and his finger-tips clung with all the pressure of his pulling arms to the shoulder-high half-inch indentation in the bricks.

He was more than trembling now; his whole body was racked with a violent shuddering beyond control, his eyes squeezed so tightly shut it was painful, though he was past awareness of that. His teeth were exposed in a frozen grimace, the strength draining like water from his knees and calves. It was extremely likely, he knew, that he would faint, slump down along the wall, his face scraping, and then drop backwards, a limp weight, out into nothing. And to save his life he concentrated on holding on to con-

He looked down—an explosion of terror roared through him.

sciousness, drawing deliberate deep breaths of cold air into his lungs, fighting to keep his senses aware.

Then he knew that he would not faint, but he could not stop shaking nor open his eyes. He stood where he was, breathing deeply, trying to hold back the terror of the glimpse he had had of what lay below him; and he knew he had made a mistake in not making himself stare down at the street, getting used to it and accepting it, when he had first stepped out on to the ledge.

It was impossible to walk back. He simply could not do it. He couldn't bring himself to make the slightest movement. The strength was gone from his legs; his shivering hands—numb, cold and desperately rigid—had lost all deftness; his easy ability to move and balance was gone. Within a step or two, if he tried to move, he knew that he would stumble clumsily and fall.

Seconds passed, with the chill faint wind pressing the side of his face, and he could hear the toned-down volume of the street traffic far beneath him. Again and again it slowed and then stopped, almost to silence; then presently, even this high, he would hear the click of the traffic signals and the subdued roar of the cars starting up again. During a lull in the street sounds, he called out. Then he was shouting *"Help!"* so loudly it rasped his throat. But he felt the steady pressure of the wind, moving between his face and the blank wall, snatch up his cries as he uttered them, and he knew they must sound directionless and distant. And he remembered how habitually, here in New York, he himself heard and ignored shouts in the night. If anyone heard him, there was no sign of it, and presently Tom Benecke knew he had to try moving; there was nothing else he could do.

Eyes squeezed shut, he watched scenes in his mind like scraps of motion-picture film—he could not stop them. He saw himself stumbling suddenly sideways as he crept along the ledge and saw his upper body arc outwards, arms flailing. He saw a dangling shoe-string caught between the ledge and the sole of his other shoe, saw a foot start to move, to be stopped with a jerk, and felt his balance leaving him. He saw himself falling with a terrible speed as his body revolved in the air, knees clutched tight to his chest, eyes squeezed shut, moaning softly.

Out of utter necessity, knowing that any of these thoughts might be reality in the very next seconds, he was slowly able to shut his mind against every thought but what he now began to do. With fear-soaked slowness, he slid his left foot an inch or two towards his own impossibly distant window. Then he slid the fingers of his shivering left hand a corresponding distance. For a moment he could not bring himself to lift his right foot from one ledge to the other; then he did it, and became aware of the harsh exhalation of air from his throat and realized that he was panting. As his right hand, then, began to slide along the brick edging, he was astonished to feel the yellow paper pressed to the bricks underneath his stiff fingers, and he uttered a terrible, abrupt bark that might have been a laugh or a moan. He opened his mouth and took the paper in his teeth, pulling it out from under his fingers.

By a kind of trick—by concentrating his entire mind on first his left foot, then his left hand, then the other foot, then the other hand—he was able to move, almost imperceptibly, trembling steadily, very nearly without thought. But he could feel the terrible strength of the pent-up horror on just the other side of the flimsy barrier he had erected in his mind; and he knew that if it broke through he would lose this thin, artificial control of his body.

During one slow step he tried keeping his eyes closed; it made him feel safer, shutting him off a little from the fearful reality of where he was. Then a sudden rush of giddiness swept over him and he had to open his eyes wide, staring sideways at the cold rough brick and angled lines of mortar, his cheek tight against the building. He kept his eyes open then, knowing that if he once let them flick outwards, to stare for an instant at the lighted windows across the street, he would be past help.

He didn't know how many dozens of tiny sidling steps

he had taken, his chest, belly and face pressed to the wall; but he knew the slender hold he was keeping on his mind and body was going to break. He had a sudden mental picture of his apartment on just the other side of this wall —warm, cheerful, incredibly spacious. And he saw himself striding through it, lying down on the floor on his back, arms spread wide, revelling in its unbelievable security. The impossible remoteness of this utter safety, the contrast between it and where he now stood, was more than he could bear. And the barrier broke then, and the fear of the awful height he stood on coursed through his nerves and muscles. . . .

A fraction of his mind knew he was going to fall, and he began taking rapid blind steps with no feeling of what he was doing, sidling with a clumsy, desperate swiftness, fingers scrabbling along the brick, almost hopelessly resigned to the sudden backward pull and swift motion outward and down. Then his moving hand slid on to not brick but sheer emptiness, an impossible gap in the face of the wall, and he stumbled.

His right foot smashed into his left ankle-bone; he staggered sideways, began falling, and the claw of his hand cracked against glass and wood, slid down it, and his finger-tips were pressed hard on the puttyless edging of his window. His right hand smacked gropingly beside it as he fell to his knees; and, under the full weight and direct downward pull of his sagging body, the open window dropped shudderingly in its frame till it closed and his wrists struck the sill and were jarred off.

For a single moment he knelt, knee bones against stone on the very edge of the ledge, body swaying and touching nowhere else, fighting for balance. Then he lost it, his shoulders plunging backwards, and he flung his arms forward, his hands smashing against the window casing on either side; and—his body moving backwards—his fingers clutched the narrow wood stripping of the upper pane.

For an instant he hung suspended between balance and falling, his finger-tips pressed on to the quarter-inch wood

316

strips. Then, with utmost delicacy, with a focused concentration of all his senses, he increased even further the
strain on his finger-tips hooked to these slim edgings of
wood. Elbows slowly bending, he began to draw the full
weight of his upper body forward, knowing that the instant his fingers slipped off these quarter-inch strips he'd
plunge backwards and be falling. Elbows imperceptibly
bending, body shaking with the strain, the sweat starting
from his forehead in great sudden drops, he pulled, his
entire being and thought concentrated in his finger-tips.
Then suddenly, the strain slackened and ended, his chest
touching the window-sill, and he was kneeling on the ledge,
his forehead pressed to the glass of the closed window.

Dropping his palms to the sill, he stared into his living-
room—at the red-brown davenport across the room, and
a magazine he had left there; at the pictures on the walls
and the grey rug; the entrance to the hallway; and at his
papers, typewriter and desk, not two feet from his nose.

*At that moment the window slammed shut and his body
swayed outwards, fighting for balance.*

A movement from his desk caught his eye, and he saw that it was a thin curl of blue smoke; his cigarette, the ash long, was still burning in the ash-tray where he'd left it— this was past all belief—only a few minutes before.

His head moved, and in faint reflection from the glass before him, he saw the yellow paper clenched in his front teeth. Lifting a hand from the sill he took it from his mouth; the moistened corner parted from the paper, and he spat it out. . . .

For a moment, in the light from the living-room, he stared wonderingly at the yellow sheet in his hand and then crushed it into the side pocket of his jacket.

He couldn't open the window. It had been pulled not completely closed, but its lower edge was below the level of the outside sill; there was no room to get his fingers underneath it. Between the upper sash and the lower was a gap not wide enough—reaching up, he tried—to get his fingers into; he couldn't push it open. The upper window panel, he knew from long experience, was impossible to move, frozen tight with dried paint.

Very carefully observing his balance, the finger tips of his left hand again hooked to the narrow stripping of the window casing, he drew his right hand, palm facing the glass, and then struck the glass with the heel of his hand.

His arm rebounded from the pane, his body tottering, and he knew he didn't dare strike a harder blow.

But in the security and relief of his new position, he simply smiled; with only a sheet of glass between him and the room just before him, it was not possible that there wasn't a way past it. Eyes narrowing, he thought for a few moments about what to do. Then his eyes widened, for nothing occurred to him. But still he felt calm: the trembling, he realized, had stopped. At the back of his mind there still lay the thought that once he was again in his home, he could give release to his feelings. He actually *would* lie on the floor, rolling, clenching tufts of the rug in his hands. He would literally run across the room, free to move as he liked, jumping on the floor, testing and revelling in its absolute security, letting the relief flood through him, draining the fear from his mind and body. His yearning for this was astonishingly intense, and somehow he understood that he had better keep this feeling at bay.

He took a half-dollar from his pocket and struck it against the pane, but without any hope that the glass would break and with very little disappointment when it did not. After a few moments of thought he drew his leg up on to the ledge and picked loose the knot of his shoelace. He slipped off his shoe and, holding it across the instep, drew back his arm as far as he dared and struck the leather heel against the glass. The pane rattled, but he knew he'd been a long way from breaking it. His foot was cold and he slipped the shoe back on. He shouted again, experimentally, and then once more, but there was no answer.

The realization suddenly struck him that he might have to wait here till Clare came home, and for a moment the thought was funny. He could see Clare opening the front door, withdrawing her key from the lock, closing the door behind her and then glancing up to see him crouched on the other side of the window. He could see her rush across the room, face astounded and frightened, and hear himself shouting instructions: "Never mind how I got here! Just open the wind—" She couldn't open it, he remembered, she'd never be able to; she'd always had to call him. She'd have to get the building superintendent or a neighbour, and he pictured himself smiling and answering their questions as he climbed in. "I just wanted to get a breath of fresh air, so—"

He couldn't possibly wait here till Clare came home. It was the second feature she'd wanted to see, and she'd left in time to see the first. She'd be another three hours or— He glanced at his watch; Clare had been gone eight minutes. It wasn't possible, but only eight minutes ago he had kissed his wife good-bye. She wasn't even in the theatre yet!

It would be four hours before she could possibly be

home, and he tried to picture himself kneeling out here, finger-tips hooked to these narrow strippings, while first one movie, preceded by a slow listing of credits, began, developed, reached its climax and then finally ended. There'd be a newsreel next, maybe, and then an animated cartoon, and then interminable scenes from coming pictures. And then, once more, the beginning of a full-length picture—while all the time he hung out here in the night.

He might possibly get to his feet, but he was afraid to try. Already his legs were cramped, his thigh muscles tired; his knees hurt, his feet felt numb and his hands were stiff. He couldn't possibly stay out here for four hours, or anywhere near it. Long before that his legs and arms would give out; he would be forced to try changing his position often—stiffly, clumsily, his co-ordination and strength gone —and he would fall. Quite realistically, he knew that he would fall; no one could stay out here on this ledge for four hours.

A dozen windows in the apartment building across the street were lighted. Looking over his shoulder, he could see the top of a man's head behind the newspaper he was reading; in another window he saw the blue-grey flicker of a television screen. No more than twenty-odd yards from his back were scores of people, and if just one of them would walk idly to his window and glance out. . . . For some moments he stared over his shoulder at the lighted rectangles, waiting. But no one appeared. The man reading his paper turned a page and then continued his reading. A figure passed another of the windows and was immediately gone.

In the inside pocket of his jacket he found a little sheaf of papers, and he pulled one out and looked at it in the light from the living-room. It was an old letter, an advertisement of some sort; his name and address, in purple ink, were on a label pasted to the envelope. Gripping one end of the envelope in his teeth, he twisted it into a tight curl. From his shirt pocket he brought out a book of matches. He didn't dare let go the casing with both hands but, with

The blazing fragment fell.

the twist of paper in his teeth, he opened the match-book with his free hand; then he bent one of the matches in two without tearing it from the folder, its red-tipped end now touching the striking surface. With his thumb, he rubbed the red tip across the striking area.

He did it again, then again, and still again, pressing harder each time, and the match suddenly flared, burning his thumb. But he kept it alight, cupping the match-book in his hand and shielding it with his body. He held the flame to the paper in his mouth till it caught. Then he snuffed out the match flame with his thumb and forefinger, careless of the burn, and replaced the book in his pocket. Taking the paper twist in his hand, he held it flame down, watching the flame crawl up the paper, till it flared bright. Then he held it behind him over the street, moving it from side to side, watching it over his shoulder, the flame flickering and guttering in the wind.

There were three letters in his pocket and he lighted each of them, holding each till the flame touched his hand and

321

then dropping it to the street below. At one point, watching over his shoulder while the last of the letters burned, he saw the man across the street put down his paper and stand—even seeming, to Tom, to glance towards his window. But when he moved, it was only to walk across the room and disappear from sight. . . .

There were a dozen coins in Tom Benecke's pocket and he dropped them, three or four at a time. But if they struck anyone, or if anyone noticed their falling, no one connected them with their source, and no one glanced upwards.

His arms had begun to tremble from the steady strain of clinging to this narrow perch, and he did not know what to do now and was terribly frightened. Clinging to the window stripping with one hand, he again searched his pockets. But now—he had left his wallet on his dresser when he'd changed clothes—there was nothing left but the yellow sheet. It occurred to him irrelevantly that his death on the sidewalk below would be an eternal mystery; the window closed—why, how, and from where could he have fallen? No one would be able to identify his body for a time, either—the thought was somehow unbearable and increased his fear. All they'd find in his pockets would be the yellow sheet. *Contents of the dead man's pockets,* he thought, *one sheet of paper bearing pencilled notations— incomprehensible.*

He understood fully that he might actually be going to die; his arms, maintaining his balance on the ledge, were trembling steadily now. And it occurred to him then with all the force of a revelation that, if he fell, all he was ever going to have out of life he would then, abruptly, have had. Nothing, then, could ever be changed; and nothing more— no least experience or pleasure—could ever be added to his life. He wished, then, that he had not allowed his wife to go off by herself tonight—and on similar nights. He thought of all the evenings he had spent away from her, working; and he regretted them. He thought wonderingly of his fierce ambition and of the direction his life had taken; he thought of the hours he'd spent by himself, filling the yellow sheet that had brought him out here. *Contents of the dead man's pockets*, he thought with sudden fierce anger, *a wasted life.*

He was simply not going to cling here till he slipped and fell; he told himself that now. There was one last thing he could try; he had been aware of it for some moments, refusing to think about it, but now he faced it. Kneeling here on the ledge, the finger-tips of one hand pressed to the narrow strip of wood, he could, he knew, draw his other hand back a yard perhaps, fist clenched tight, doing it very slowly till he sensed the outer limit of balance, then, as hard as he was able from the distance, he could drive his fist forward against the glass. If it broke, his fist smashing through, he was safe; he might cut himself badly, and probably would, but with his arm inside the room, he would be secure. But if the glass did not break, the re-bound, flinging his arm back, would topple him off the ledge. He was certain of that.

He tested his plan. The fingers of his left hand claw-like on the little stripping, he drew back his other fist until his body began teetering backwards. But he had no leverage now—he could feel that there would be no force to his swing—and he moved his fist slowly forward till he rocked forward on his knees again and could sense that his swing would carry its greatest force. Glancing down, however, measuring the distance from his fist to the glass, he saw that it was less than two feet.

It occurred to him that he could raise his arm over his head, to bring it down against the glass. But, experimenting in slow motion, he knew it would be an awkward girl-like blow without the force of a driving punch, and not nearly enough to break the glass. . . .

Facing the window, he had to drive a blow from the shoulder, he knew now, at a distance of less than two feet; and he did not know whether it would break through the heavy glass. It might; he could picture it happening, he could feel it in the nerves of his arm. And it might not;

he could feel that too—feel his fist striking this glass and being instantaneously flung back by the unbreaking pane, feel the fingers of his other hand breaking loose, nails scraping along the casing as he fell.

He waited, arm drawn back, fist balled, but in no hurry to strike; this pause, he knew, might be an extension of his life. And to live even a few seconds longer, he felt, even

With every last scrap of strength he struck.

out here on this ledge in the night, was infinitely better than to die a moment earlier than he had to. His arm grew tired, and he brought it down and rested it.

Then he knew that it was time to make the attempt. He could not kneel here hesitating indefinitely till he lost all courage to act, waiting till he slipped off the ledge. Again he drew back his arm, knowing this time that he would not bring it down till he struck. His elbow protruding over Lexington Avenue far below, the fingers of his other hand pressed down bloodlessly tight against the narrow stripping, he waited, feeling the sick tenseness and terrible excitement building. It grew and swelled towards the moment of action, his nerves tautening. He thought of Clare —just a wordless, yearning thought—and then drew his arm back just a bit more, fist so tight his fingers pained him, and knowing he was going to do it. Then with full power, with every last scrap of strength he could bring to bear, he shot his arm forward towards the glass, and he said, "*Clare!*"

He heard the sound, felt the blow, felt himself falling forward, and his hand closed on the living-room curtains, the shards and fragments of glass showering on to the floor. And then, kneeling there on the ledge, an arm thrust into the room up to the shoulder, he began picking away the protruding slivers and great wedges of glass from the window frame, tossing them in on to the rug. And, as he grasped the edges of the empty frame and climbed into his home, he was grinning in triumph.

He did not lie down on the floor or run through the apartment, as he had promised himself; even in the first few moments it seemed to him natural and normal that he should be where he was. He simply turned to his desk, pulled the crumpled yellow sheet from his pocket and laid it down where it had been, smoothing it out; then he absently laid a pencil across it to weight it down. He shook his head, wonderingly, and turned to walk towards the closet.

There he got out his topcoat and hat and, without waiting to put them on, opened the front door and stepped out, to go find his wife. He turned to pull the door closed and the warm air from the hall rushed through the narrow opening again. As he saw the yellow paper, the pencil flying, scooped off the desk and, unimpeded by the glassless window, sail out into the night and out of his life, Tom Benecke burst into laughter and then closed the door behind him.

The Rockslide

DON KNOWLTON

THE BOY stood in the doorway of the shack on the side of the mountain, looking down, away down, across the valley. He held a cup of coffee. He had come up early that Saturday morning in the old jeep and cooked breakfast. He wanted to get in another weekend on the mountain before school started again.

It was his mountain. Oh, he didn't own it. The range, most of it, was inside the national park boundaries. The shack was right on the line. But just the same, the mountain belonged to him; or rather, he belonged to the mountain.

They said in Pinedale, down below, where his father taught in the college, that Kit Sherry was a strange lad. Bright enough, but shy. Solitary sort of an individual. He knew what they said, and he did not care. He was in love with the mountain.

Kit knew that mountain as a city boy knows his back-
yard. He knew it in rain and in sunshine, in moonlight, in
mist, in driving snow.

There was the long slope that purple flowers covered in
July. There were the reaches of open pines, with grass
underfoot. There were the brooks, two on his side of the
mountain, that came tearing down in a rush through
tangles of brush. There was the high, placid pond, where
the beavers worked. There was the clearing with the dead,
blackened stumps where the fire had gone through four
years before; berries and fireweed grew there now. There
was the little wood, tucked away in a fold, where there still
stood tall spruces that the timbermen had spared. There
was the meadow, up above, scattered with larches, where
the anemones put on their white beards after they blos-
somed.

There was the clear spring in a little pocket right on the
timber line where columbine bloomed in August. And,
above and beyond all else, the rocks.

There were ways to get up and over, to twist in and
round, those rocks. There were bypasses to sheer cliffs,
curious ways along knife edges, ladderlike steps to spots
that looked inaccessible—if you knew them. And Kit did.

It was the end of August. There had been the nightly
nip of cold—at daybreak there had probably been a film
of ice on the water bucket that hung by the spring—but as
yet no hard frost to turn the aspens yellow.

Kit finished his coffee and began washing his breakfast
dishes. As he did so he turned on his portable radio. The
music suddenly broke off. The announcer said, "We interrupt this programme again to repeat a special news bul-
letin. This morning Barney Zucco, the notorious Chicago
gangster, held up the Pinedale Bank. He shot down the
cashier and a clerk in cold blood, scooped up some eleven
thousand dollars, and made his getaway in a green Cadillac.
Both men are dead.

"Zucco, known as the Muscle, contrived two days ago
to escape from an FBI squad who thought they had him

cornered in Chicago. He is wanted on charges of dope smuggling and extortion, and is presumed to have been the man behind a series of killings in South Chicago.

"Zucco is reported to have headed south on Route 168. Police throughout the state have been alerted. Zucco is over six feet tall, broad-shouldered, and powerfully built. He has black hair, black eyes, and regular, handsome features. He was wearing a brown checked suit, brown tie, brown shoes, and no hat. He carries a gun in his right-hand coat pocket. We return you now to the regular programme."

By that time the few dishes were done, and Kit turned off the radio. As he did so, he heard the whine of a high-powered car coming up the road.

That's strange, he thought. He stepped to the door—and as he did so there pulled up, beside his parked jeep, a green Cadillac convertible.

The man who got out was over six feet tall, broad-shouldered, and powerfully built. He had black hair, black eyes, and regular, handsome features. He wore a brown checked suit, brown tie, brown shoes, and no hat. His right hand was thrust into his right coat pocket—and in that pocket there was a bulge.

The man looked at the tall, skinny youngster in blue jeans and open shirt who stood in the doorway.

"Say, kid," he said, "where does this road go?"

"It doesn't go anywhere," answered Kit. "It just goes to here. This is where it ends."

The regular, handsome features of the man in the brown suit contorted in a sort of spasm.

"Well, how do I get out of here?"

"Only back the way you came."

"But I can't—hell, there must be some way to get from here to some place else—"

"Not by road," said Kit.

"What do you mean, not by road?"

There was a long pause, while they stared at each other. Finally Kit took a deep breath.

"You'd better come inside, Mr. Zucco," he said. "Somebody might come along and see you."

In a flash the man's gun was out of his pocket. He held it before him, motioning Kit to step back into the shack, following him in, and closing the door. Kit sat down at the table, and Zucco sat opposite him, holding the gun.

"Kid," said Zucco, "I've *got* to get out. I've got to get away. You understand that, don't you?"

Kit nodded.

"Those damn fools at that bank—I *had* to do it. I didn't have time in Chicago to get money. A man has to have money, doesn't he?"

Kit said nothing.

"You know how to get me out of here. All right—do it, see? Either you get me out or—"

He gestured with the gun. "Get the idea?"

"I get it," said Kit. "But there's only one way. Up over the mountain."

"What do you mean, up over—on *foot*?"

Kit nodded. "Look, Mr. Zucco," he said, "you've got to understand just where you are and what you're up against. Here, have some coffee, and I'll explain to you."

"There's no time—"

"You don't want to get caught, do you?"

Moving slowly, while Zucco fiddled with the gun, Kit poured him a cup of coffee. Then he got from the wood-box an old piece of wrapping paper, and from a shelf a stubby pencil. He sat down next to Zucco, spreading the paper on the table.

"I'll draw you a map. Here's Pinedale. Now, south-west of Pinedale runs the Pinion Mountain range. We're on the side of it, here. It runs for miles. It's high.

"Now you took Route 168 out of Pinedale. It runs up through a narrow valley and turns a bit right, like this— and crosses the Pinion range at Harper's Pass, about fifty miles from Pinedale. You see, it heads right into the range. There are mountain spurs on both sides. None of these sideroads go anywhere. They just lead up to places like

"Kid, I've got to get out—I've got to get away."

this one, and then come to a dead end. When you don't show up at the pass, the police will know you turned up one of these sideroads. They'll search them, one by one, until they find your car. Sooner or later—"

"O.K., O.K.," said Zucco. "So what do we do?"

"Like I said. We go up over the mountain."

Kit drew another line on the map. "On the other side of the range," he said, "there's a main highway running from south-west to north-east. Nobody would ever dream of looking for you over there. And there are through buses on that road. There's a bus stop by an old mine. We go up over the top and down to that bus stop."

"But—"

"There are some old clothes of Dad's in the cupboard that will fit you well enough," Kit said. "Of course, you can't wear his shoes, but you'd better get into some slacks and a shirt of his. You'd look funny at that old mine getting into a bus with those city clothes of yours, especially after the broadcast this morning. If I were you, I'd burn them up in the stove."

"But—"

"Think it over."

"You sit right where you are," commanded Zucco. Taking his gun with him, he rummaged in the cupboard. He swore as he rammed his brown checked suit into the stove. He swore some more as he put on an old pair of khaki slacks, a dirty flannel shirt, and a torn hat.

"That's better," Kit said. "Now, drive your car on past my jeep and right into that thicket of young pines. They might hunt for a week before they'd find it there."

"You drive it. I'll sit in the back seat."

Kit did. Behind him was Zucco, with the gun.

When they got back to the shack, Zucco was carrying a canvas bag labelled PINEDALE BANK. Kit did not have to ask what was in it.

Kit put a big hunk of cheese, a loaf of bread, and a canteen of water in a light knapsack.

"What's that for?" asked Zucco.

"Grub. It's all I've got, and it's all we'll get to eat for the rest of the day. We'll be lucky if we get down to that other road by dark. You'd better put that moneybag in my pack and let me carry it. It'll get in your way."

Zucco laughed nastily.

"Fat chance! The dough and the gun stay with me—*you* go ahead."

"Naturally I'll go ahead," Kit said politely, "because you don't know where to go."

They started along a faintly traced zigzag path at the back of the shack. Suddenly Kit stopped. "There's one thing that worries me, Mr. Zucco," he said. "Tell me—have you ever climbed a big mountain?"

"No, why?"

"I'm just wondering whether you can make it."

"What do you mean!"

"Well, it's a long way up and it isn't like walking on a trail. There *isn't* any trail. We've got to crash through the brush, and we've got to do some rough climbing on the rocks. If you're not used to mountains—"

"So what's a mountain?" Zucco gestured his contempt for mountains. "Listen, kid," he said, "I could break you in two with one hand. You think they call me the Muscle just for fun? Now get going."

He was indeed a big brute of a man, thought Kit: thick-shouldered, deep-chested, with the arms of a prize fighter and the legs of a wrestler. Big—heavy. He would weigh, Kit guessed, at least fourteen stone.

"O.K.," agreed Kit. "Here we go."

And he turned uphill, off the path, and struck straight up the mountainside.

It was a thicket of brambles and scrub, that first stretch. Branches snagged them. Stumps scratched them. Loose stones tripped them up on the steep slope. Kit squeezed up and through. Zucco, gun in one hand and moneybag in the other, kept getting caught like a fly in a web.

"Hey, wait for me!" he yelled.

The gun, Kit noticed, had gone into his pocket. Zucco

now had one free hand to grab with. Even so, he kept slipping and sliding.

"Don't go so fast!" he called.

At the end of an hour, Zucco was panting hard. Sweat was running down his face.

"We'll take a rest," he said.

"We just can't, Mr. Zucco, if we're going to make it."

Then they entered the old burn. Fire had gone through there years before and killed the timber. The dead trees had fallen—and a new crop of pines had sprouted up. They were now about twenty-five feet tall, standing very thick, with interlaced branches extending at shoulder height. The ground was covered with tall ferns—and concealed beneath them, lying like jackstraws in all directions, were the still-undecayed trunks of the fallen trees.

The place was a succession of booby traps. Zucco kept falling down. He fell forwards, backwards, and sideways. His face was a mass of scratches. Sometimes, when he fell, the moneybag would go flying off into the ferns, and he would have to make a frantic search for it.

"Why don't you tie that bag round your neck?" suggested Kit. Zucco did.

Up, always up, and rather steeply they went, until finally they came upon a brook that leapt down over mossy rocks. Zucco drank deeply and washed his hot face.

"How much farther?" he asked.

"Mr. Zucco, you don't seem to realize that this is a big mountain. We'd better keep going."

And Kit started right up the bed of the roaring brook.

"That way?"

"Yes," Kit explained, "we have to go up the brook, because that's the only way up this part of the mountain. To the right there's an impassable cliff, and to the left there's an overhang."

Zucco groaned and followed.

It became obvious at once that Zucco had never balanced himself upon the irregular stones of a creek bed. He teetered, fell, and was soon splashed from head to foot.

"Can't you push on a little faster, Mr. Zucco?" asked Kit.

Then they came to a stretch that was really steep. The creek slid down a shale slope, slippery with slime, with nothing to hold on to except the tips of willow branches. Kit scrambled up, and from the top called down impatiently.

Three times Zucco almost made it to the top—and three times he and his moneybag cascaded to the bottom.

"We're losing precious minutes, Mr. Zucco," Kit complained. On the fourth try Zucco reached the top of the shale. He lay flat on his belly in the bed of the brook and tried to get back his breath.

"Let's be on our way," insisted Kit. "It's getting late."

A few moments later they emerged upon a vast slope of broken rock. They were above the timber line. Looking out from the side of the mountain, towards the valley, Pinedale was just a blob on a plain of yellow and blue.

"Up there," said Kit, "is where we're going."

Zucco looked up—and up and up. The green gave way to the grey, and there were cliffs and great outcropping masses of rocks, and here and there little pockets of snow. They were at the foot of a broken rock slope beneath a vertical rampart.

"We go up to the base of the cliff," Kit said.

Rocks with sharp, uneven edges. Rocks that were loose and turned when one stepped on them. And steeper than a gangway. Slip, tumble, scrabble on all fours. Zucco's breath came in great gasps. His windpipe was getting raw. The sun burnt fiercely.

"Can't you step on it a little?" asked Kit. "I'm really getting worried."

They reached the foot of the cliff. There was a tiny shady patch of almost level land—and Zucco flung himself upon it.

"Well," Kit said cheerfully, "let's rest here a bit and have lunch. We'll need to stoke up. We've got a hard climb just ahead of us."

He opened the knapsack and took out the bread, cheese, and canteen. He handed the canteen to Zucco. "Drink plenty of water," he advised him. Zucco did.

"Nothing like cheese to keep you going on a climb," Kit observed.

"I'm not hungry," Zucco said.

"Hungry or not, you'd better eat. You'll need it. Plenty of bread too."

"It's awful dry."

"Wash it down with water. Get some food into you!"

With urging, Zucco took in a considerable load of cheese, bread, and water.

"O.K.," Kit said. "Now let's go."

They skirted the base of the cliff, to the left, until they came to a fissure that was little less than vertical.

"Here's where we go up," Kit announced. "There are good handholds and footholds, but you have to watch your step."

"It's the only way up this part of the mountain," said Kit.

It was as steep as a ladder. One look told Zucco that it could not be climbed. But there was the boy, above him.

They began working their way up. The moneybag flapping from Zucco's neck caught on the rocks and got in the way of his hands.

"Hey!" he yelled. "Put this damn thing in your pack!" And he handed it up to Kit.

It was work, gruelling work, that rock climb. Zucco could hardly make his muscles obey. There was, too, inside him, a feeling that something was very wrong indeed.

"I've got to stop for a while!" he called to Kit.

He stopped—and looked down. Looked down, and screamed. For he was falling off the mountain! He pressed himself against it. He held on to the rocks with an iron grip.

"Help!" he yelled. "I can't hang on!"

Kit came back down to him.

"You're all right," he said. "Just don't look down. Now, put your left foot here—"

"No, no!"

"And your right hand here—"

"No, I can't!"

It took five minutes to persuade Zucco to loosen one hand. Kit literally put Zucco's hands and feet in the right places. Zucco was trembling. He babbled incessantly that he couldn't, he couldn't, he couldn't.

"Just one more tricky place, and we will be on a ridge," Kit said. They managed it—and came out on the top of a broken-rock hogback, not more than five feet wide. On both sides it dropped off, off, off.

Zucco looked down to the right, he looked down to the left, and with a groan he lay down and threw up cheese, bread, and water for a long time.

"That's too bad," said Kit.

After a while Zucco sat up. "I'm not going any farther," he said.

Kit looked out over the vast panoramas that unfolded on both sides of the ridge—wave after wave of spurs from the main range, which topped them to the north-east.

"It gets awfully cold up here at night," he remarked.

No response.

"After the fourth day you'll get pretty hungry—"

"Shut up!"

After a moment Kit started up the narrow hogback.

"Hey, don't leave me!" There was panic in that voice.

"Mr. Zucco," Kit said, "if you want to stay up here and die slowly all by yourself, that's your business. But I want to get down off this mountain before it gets dark." And again he headed up the hogback.

"Stop right where you are!"

Kit turned. Zucco had his gun out.

"Now, Mr. Zucco!" Kit protested. "Does that make any sense? If you shoot me you can never find your way down."

Zucco put the gun back into his pocket.

He could not walk; he crawled, mumbling, gasping, swearing. Thus, after a long time they came to the spot where the hogback joined the main divide. Here all was rock, bare rock.

"Climbing's about over," Kit called out cheerfully. "Come up here and take a look down the other side."

Zucco wriggled his way up the final slope and looked over the edge. He looked down, straight down, two thousand feet. The drop-off was as vertical as the side of a building.

And, for Zucco, the earth began to turn. It whirled slowly round and round, oscillating meanwhile up and down. Valleys rose, peaks sank, in rotation. And Zucco sprawled grotesquely, in the grip of wave after wave of the most horrible nausea.

"We walk along the edge of this drop-off for a way," Kit began.

"Oh no!"

"It's easy. Almost level. Then we cross the rockslide. Beyond it one short push up, and then we're over the hump and down we go to the other road."

But Zucco did not move. He was muttering. "Mary,

337

As Kit showed him how, Zucco gazed and trembled.

Mother of God, save me," Kit heard. And incoherent mumbling about people and places. "I *had* to shoot them." Spasms of tears and retching.

Kit saw the gun sticking half out of Zucco's pocket. He slipped it out and put it in his own. He helped Zucco to his feet. "Hang on to me," he said.

The path was almost like a city pavement, about four feet wide, between the drop-off on the left and a towering straight-up cliff on the right. The sun was getting low in the west when they rounded a corner of a high buttress and came to a steep smooth slope surmounted by walls of rock that rose high towards the sky.

"That's the top of the main peak up there," Kit explained. "We have to go round it. To do that we have to cross this rockslide. Do you know about rockslides?"

But Zucco was sitting down, eyes closed. Kit shook him and slapped his face. "Come on!" he said, and there was a most peculiar expression on his face as he said it. "You've got to listen to me. This rockslide is formed by the stones that fall off the big cliffs above it. It goes all the way down the side of the mountain. See?"

He pointed. As far down as the eye would carry, the slide extended, down, down, past side escarpments, down and through the timber, down to where its bottom was lost in mistiness.

"The minute anything lands on that rockslide it starts to move. If you just stand in it, it moves and you move with it—and that starts a rock avalanche and you get caught in it. Understand?"

Zucco nodded in an idiotic sort of way.

"So to cross a rockslide, you have to run—and you have to lift your knees way up high. You can't stand still. Get the idea?"

Zucco said nothing.

"All right; now watch me, and do what I do. It's only about a hundred feet across, this high up. It's easy, if you do it right."

And Kit headed across the slide. He ran, bringing his

knees up high. With each step the stones and gravel started to slide—but with each step, running, he got his foot out again before the slide could gain momentum. In no time at all he was across.

"Now *you* do it."

Zucco braced himself, tested the edge of the slide with a trembling foot and stepped out into it.

"Run!" yelled Kit. "Bring your knees up high!"

But Zucco did not run. The movement of the gravel, every time he put his foot in it, seemed to paralyse him. With each step he took, he sank deeper.

About a third of the way across he tried in vain to free a leg—and he stood still. He began to move downhill. The whole hillside began to tremble; the whole slide began to move.

Deeper and deeper Zucco sank; faster and faster down he went. The growing rumble turned into a roar. There was one last scream from Zucco—and then the avalanche, gathering momentum and picking up rocks half as big as a house, thundered on down into the valley far below.

Kit dusted his hands, as if to rid them of dirt. He hurried on a bit, turned sharply down a short, steep slope and came to the well-beaten trail that led to the shack. He went down it at a dogtrot. When he got near the shack, in the dusk, he slowed and began to whistle a loud tune. He kept his eyes on the alert.

Sure enough, when he was still just round the corner from the shack, a loud voice yelled, "Come out with your hands up!"

Kit did—and at the clearing was confronted by three state policemen with levelled guns. So they had found Zucco's car.

"Oh, it's you," one said. "We thought so, but we weren't taking any chances. Where's Zucco?"

"He's up on the mountain under about a thousand tons of rock," answered Kit. "What I need is some coffee."

Until he had started the fire and boiled a pot, he would not say a word. Then, with steaming cups before them,

"Here's his gun and here's the 11,000 dollars."

the four sat round the table in the shack.

In detail, and interrupted by many questions, Kit re-
counted everything that had happened that day. . . .

"Well I'll be damned," finally said the big policeman
with the black moustache. "But how did you come to
think of it?"

"Chicago," answered Kit. "I reckoned anybody who'd
lived at lake level all his life would be likely to get the
mountain sickness. I got out of him that he'd never been
on a big mountain. I felt sure that if I could just get him
up high enough—"

"The idea of taking him up through the old burn and the
creek bed and the chimney climb, and the hogback!" exclaimed the little policeman with the blue eyes. "When all
the time there was a trail—"

"Well," explained Kit, "I reckoned I'd better condition
him. I had to get him sick and all tired out, or he *might*
have got across the rockslide."

"What gets me," said the big one, "is the way you
dreamed up that cock-and-bull story about a road on the

341

other side and a bus stop at an old mine. What if he *knew* there wasn't any such road? What if he knew there was nothing in that direction but wilderness, for miles and miles?"

"It was a chance I had to take. There wasn't much time, and I had to think of something that would get him *up* there."

"Up the rockslide?"

Kit nodded.

"That's what you were aiming for, from the start?"

Kit said nothing.

"Well, let's go," said the big officer. "We'd better get down to a phone and turn in a report. Coming down with us, Kit?"

Kit shook his head.

"O.K. We'll be back in the morning."

The police got into their car.

"Wait a minute!" called Kit from the shack doorway. "Here's his gun—and here's the eleven thousand dollars." He tossed them out.

"Well I'll be double damned," said the big officer. He got out of the car and came back to Kit. "Boy," he said, "you ought to be mighty proud of this day's work." And he put his arm round Kit's shoulders.

"Somehow," Kit said, and his voice almost broke, "somehow I can't feel that way."

"He would have killed you."

"I know."

The big policeman shrugged—and then off they all went, down the road.

Kit stood in the doorway of the shack, looking down, way down, across the valley. And then he looked at the mountain—his mountain. The moon was just rising over the pines.

I ought to cook supper, he thought. But somehow he was not hungry. He sat down, with his head in his hands.

"I warned him," he said finally, aloud. "I told him to run, and to lift his knees up high."

The Case of the
Submerged Aircraft

CAPTAIN W. E. JOHNS

BIGGLES TOOK a second glance at the expression on the face
of his chief, Air Commodore Raymond of the Special Air
Police at Scotland Yard, as, in response to an order, he
walked into the headquarters office.

"Why are you looking at me like that?" inquired the
Air Commodore.

Biggles smiled. "I was wondering why *you* were looking
like that."

"Sit down and I'll tell you. What would you say if I told
you there is reason to believe that an aeroplane is standing
on the bottom of a Highland loch?"

"I hope the pilot finds it comfortable," returned Biggles
evenly. "What is this? Has some crank designed an aircraft
for underwater aviation?"

"It may not turn out to be funny," said the Air Commodore, seriously. "I want you to fly up to confirm the
report."

"Who told you about this, sir?"

"I've just had a phone call from an official of the Highland Hydro-Electric Board. He thought we'd like to know."

"What type of machine is this—military or civil?"

"He doesn't know. That's what I want you to find out. If it's an R.A.F. type the Air Ministry can take over. This is what I'm told. There is, in the north-west corner of the Cairngorms, a sheet of water called Lochnaglash. As a matter of detail, and this should help you to find it, it is the lowest of a string of three lochs deep in the mountains, each taking the spill-over of the one above it. Lochnaglash is the source of a small river called the Glash, which is a tributary of the Spey, twelve miles away. A rough track leads to a village called Balashlin. That's fourteen miles."

"Sounds like pretty wild country," remarked Biggles.

"It is. For some months of the year snow makes the place inaccessible. The land was once a deer forest. But deer-stalking is now out of fashion, and with the death of the laird the place came into the market. It was bought by the Forestry Commission who have made some experimental plantings but are no longer working there. Apparently the hydro-electric people have had an eye on the water. The lochs are fed by snow melting on the high tops. Anyway, they sent a man up to check the height of the water at summer level. As a result of the recent drought he found the water exceptionally low. Showing above the surface is an object that looks like the top of an aeroplane rudder. There's no question of it being a tree because there are no trees near except the small stuff planted by the Forestry people and they're some distance away."

"If it is a machine it must have been there for some time," stated Biggles. "It must be years since we had a record of an aircraft disappearing without trace."

The Air Commodore nodded. "It could be a relic of the war. But the easiest way to settle the matter is for you to fly up and have a look. I suggest you take the Otter and land on the loch; otherwise you'd have to get a boat from somewhere to reach the object. There isn't one on the spot, which is why the hydro-electric man could do nothing there."

344

"Okay, sir." Biggles looked at his watch. "I'll get off right away while the weather's fine. The Cairngorms, with cloud about, are no place for low flying. It shouldn't take us long to get this sorted out."

Biggles returned to his own office, where his police pilots were waiting.

"What's the drill?" asked Ginger.

Biggles grinned. "The Loch Ness monster, sick of being ridiculed, has popped up in a place called Lochnaglash. It looks like an aircraft. We're flying up in the Otter to catch it by the tail. We shall need the large-scale map of Banff-shire and, I suppose, our bathing costumes. And Ginger, you might bring along the file on post-war machines that have disappeared, for possible identification."

"How long is this job going to take?" asked Algy.

"It shouldn't take long—why?"

"Hadn't we better take something to eat in case we get stuck there for the night?"

"Yes," agreed Biggles. "There's nothing to be had on the spot. Let's get mobile. I'll tell you what I know about this business on the way up."

Four hours later, in clear weather, the Otter, an amphibious aircraft on the establishment of the Air Police, was losing height as it circled over the objective, which had not been difficult to find. But it was not such an easy matter to get down, on account of the towering hills which held the three lochs in a long narrow valley, with the result that while Lochnaglash had plenty of length it hadn't much width. In fact, it was only after three attempts to get down had failed that Biggles succeeded by flying through the only break, a narrow funnel through which the overflow of the lochs escaped during the spring thaw, to form a minor tributary of the Spey.

Even before the keel had kissed the water, dark and sinister even under a summer sky, Ginger could see the object that had brought them to the spot. It was the only mark to break the unruffled surface, on which the sur-rounding hills were reflected with the faithfulness of a .

Their objective was easy to find, but it

mirror. Only a few inches of the object showed, some fifty yards or so from a strip of detritus, the only feature that bore any resemblance to a beach. For the rest, the heather-clad slopes of the hills, with forbidding outcrops of rock, fell sheer into the water. A white streak showed where a sunless corrie still held its snow. There was not a soul, or a living creature, in sight, except an eagle, high overhead. Nor was there a tree, although a small clump of shrubby birch had managed to gain a foothold at one end of the beach. In a word, it was a typically remote Highland scene.

"A dismal sort of place to finish up," remarked Bertie.

"About as wild a spot as you'd find," returned Biggles, taxi-ing on slowly towards the mark which Ginger had pointed out. "If it's like this in summer think what it must be like in the winter, with snow everywhere and the loch a sheet of ice."

"That's an aircraft rudder all right," asserted Algy, as they approached the object. "Who on earth could have *was not such an easy matter to get down.*

tried to get down here?"

"We should soon know," answered Biggles as, with the Otter edging towards the mark, he switched off. "Stand by with the anchor, Ginger, as we come alongside. The water can't be deep or nothing would show above the surface."

"I'd say that rudder belongs to a Gipsy Moth," said Algy.

"Then it has probably been here for a long time," replied Biggles. "De Havillands must have made hundreds of Gipsys, but you don't see so many about nowadays."

The Otter drifted nearer and came silently to rest. When it was so close to the rudder that Ginger could have touched it he lowered the anchor, slowly, so as not to disturb the water.

They all leaned over the side to wait for the ripples to settle down, but even before this occurred the shape of an aircraft could be seen clearly through the crystal water. It appeared to be on even keel but slightly down by the nose, for which reason the tail unit was the only part to break the surface. The upper side of the top plane was about six feet down. The machine stood in a position parallel with the beach on a slightly shelving bottom of broken rock.

"It's a Gipsy," said Biggles definitely. "I fancy this is an old story."

There was silence for a minute as they continued to stare down. "There's no one in it," said Ginger. "I'm pretty sure both seats are empty."

"Thank goodness for that," muttered Bertie. "Corpses give me the willies."

"Can anyone make out the identification letters?" inquired Biggles. Not even when the water was dead still could the letters be seen, this being due, apparently, to a slight coating of silt, or weed.

"The pilot, whoever he was, must have been out of his mind to try to get down here," declared Bertie.

"Not necessarily," returned Biggles.

"You think it was an accident?"

"One would assume that, but I'm by no means sure."

"What do you mean?" queried Ginger.

"Let's look at it like this," suggested Biggles. "Had that machine gone in out of control surely it would have broken up when it hit the water. In such cases the wings are buckled, if not actually torn off at the roots; yet as you can see for yourselves, this aircraft is not only intact but is on even keel. Again, had the machine crashed there would have been a body in at least one of the seats. There seems to be something unnatural about this."

"The pilot, with engine trouble, might have been making for that bit of a beach and undershot," offered Ginger.

"In which case the nose would be pointing to the beach. I doubt if he'd see that beach from up topsides, anyway. Put yourself in the pilot's position. You're in trouble. Which would you choose, to ditch yourself miles from anywhere or take a chance on dry land, even if that meant a crack-up?"

"I'd go for the heather."

"So would I," asserted Biggles. "Remember the job I had to get down even with a machine in good order. The way I came was the only way in, but I wouldn't care to try it with a groggy engine."

"But half a mo', old boy," protested Bertie. "The alternative to what you're saying is, the pilot put the machine here *deliberately*. Does that make sense?"

"No," admitted Biggles. "But neither do a lot of things that happen. I can't believe this machine crashed, by which I mean hit the water hard. The pilot could of course have done a belly-flop. But why here, knowing he'd have to swim for it? I have a feeling this machine came here for a definite purpose, although what that could be I haven't a clue. I can see only one possible alternative. This might have happened in the winter, when the loch was ice-bound. When the ice melted the machine would go down quietly in the position in which we now see it. There are two arguments against that. The pilot would have to know the loch was frozen over, and secondly, having got down, would he just walk away and abandon the machine without reporting it?"

"In winter conditions it wouldn't be possible to get a rescue party here," put in Algy. "He might have died from exposure trying to reach help."

"In which case the body should have been found when the snow went. The Forestry people have been working about here, don't forget, testing the soil."

"He might have been drowned," put in Ginger.

"Even so the body would come to the surface. He wasn't trapped in the cockpit. But why are we wasting time guessing? How many Gipsy Moths have you in that file of missing machines, Ginger? I saw you going through it on the way up."

"I can only recall three," answered Ginger, producing the file. "One went west on a flight to the Cape. Another, belonging to a planter flying back to Malaya, either went down in the Channel or disappeared somewhere in Europe."

"Neither of those would come this way. Carry on."

"The other was the case of that man whom the police wanted to interview in connexion with a murder. A fellow named Alva Murray, an ex-commando, was thought to have shot his wife. He took off in a Gipsy and was never seen again. We helped in the search for him. You decided he'd found a hideout on the Continent."

Biggles frowned. "I remember that business. It must have been seven or eight years ago. It was in June, so we can forget the ice theory should this turn out to be the machine. If ever there was a deliberately planned job that was it. Murray joined a flying club to get his 'A' licence—as he said. Even then he must have known what he was going to do because while he was under instruction he drew all his money from the bank, about four thousand pounds, a few hundreds at a time. Then he shot his wife, took off in a club machine and vanished. It turned out he was a jealous type and thought she'd been playing him up. At least, that was what it looked like. What were the registration letters?"

"GB-XKL."

Biggles got up. "This could be it. If it is, it's no wonder we never found it. But we'll soon settle that. A man planning to disappear could hardly find a better place, or devise a more cunning method. I'll go down. The sides of the fuselage, being vertical, should be clear of muck."

He got into his bathing costume, lowered himself gently into the water and swam down. For half a minute the others could see him working his way along the side of the fuselage; then he shot to the surface.

"Brr. That water's cold!" he exclaimed, as he climbed back on board. "No matter. At last we know where GB-XKL ended its career. But that's still a long way from knowing where Murray finished up. While I'm getting my togs on run the machine up on the beach. We'll stretch our legs and eat a sandwich while we think about this."

In a few minutes they were sitting on dry stones, in warm sunshine. "Are we going to try to haul the Gipsy ashore?"

asked Ginger.

"Not for the moment," decided Biggles. "It's better where it is."

"Why?"

"I'm assuming Murray is still alive. If this story gets out he'll hear about it and take fright. After all this time he must think he's sitting pretty. If he learns that the machine has been found he'll be more difficult to find than he may be at present. By thunder! He must have brains, and nerve, to work out a scheme like this."

"Then you think he ditched the machine here deliberately?" questioned Bertie.

"If you remember, I suspected someone had done just that before we knew who it was," returned Biggles. "Everything pointed to that. But one or two things still puzzle me. Murray must have known exactly what he was going to do, in which case he would have made the necessary prepara-

First, he had to identify the sunken plane.

tions. That implies that he knew all about this place—the beach, the depth of the water, and so on. Obviously, he had been here before. His name tells us he was a Scot so he may have come from these parts. The ambition of every Highlander who leaves home is to get back to his beloved heather. It's in the blood. Murray may have come home."

"These preparations you talk about," put in Ginger. "I don't see that he would have to make any. Having ditched the machine all he had to do was swim ashore."

"He had to get other things ashore beside himself. If he intended to lie low for a while he'd need food. He'd want to dry his clothes. He also had a little matter of four thousand pounds with him. He'd have more sense than to go straight to the village, knowing that in these parts the arrival of a stranger is a subject for conversation and conjecture." Biggles got up and walked towards the clump of birch.

"What are you going to do?" asked Algy.

"I'm going to see if Murray left behind any signs of his arrival here. He wouldn't leave anything on the beach and there aren't many hiding places."

They all walked to the bushes.

Almost at once they came upon a spot where, long ago, a fire had been lighted.

"I'd say that's where he dried his clothes," remarked Biggles. "Hello! What's this?" Stooping, he lifted from the tangle of encroaching heather a length of window cord. As he pulled on it more and more came to light until there must have been fifty yards of it. At the end was an object so strange that it produced ejaculations of astonishment from all except Biggles. It was the deflated remains of a pair of water-wings, sometimes used for swimming instruction.

"So he couldn't swim," said Ginger.

"As a commando he'd have to be able to swim," reminded Biggles. "But he had other things to get ashore beside himself. A kit-bag, for instance. I've never tried swimming with one but I imagine it would be awkward.

Don't forget he had four thousand in notes. He wouldn't want to get them soaking wet. I'd say these wings kept his luggage afloat while he hauled it ashore with the cord. I told you this chap had his scheme cut and dried. If he put the machine down carefully it wouldn't sink at once. He'd have time to take off some of his clothes and put them in a bag brought for the purpose. All he had to do then was inflate the wings, tie them on, swim ashore with the cord and pull his luggage after him. Well, this answers one question. All we have to do now is follow his trail, but after all this time that won't be easy. Let's go back."

Biggles thrust the cord into the heather where he had found it and led the way back to the machine.

"You'll never catch up with him now," asserted Algy. "This chap was too smart to leave a trail."

"Don't you believe it," argued Biggles. "Even the smartest murderers usually make one slip. This chap has already made one by leaving that cord there. No doubt he was in a hurry to get away."

"It was thousands to one against anyone finding it," said Ginger.

"That may be what he thought, but as you see, a thousand to one chance can come off. The trouble with these rural jobs is, there's no one on the spot to question," concluded Biggles, as, seated on the stones, they finished their meal with biscuits and cheese and coffee from the thermos.

"There's someone coming now," observed Ginger.

They all looked up. Striding down a deer track from the hill behind them came a powerfully built man, black-bearded, wearing a kilt of Lovat tweed, carrying in his hand a Highland *cromach* —a long, strong, ash stick with a crook at the end, an instrument that serves many useful purposes in such country. On his head he wore a Laggan bonnet, sometimes called a deer-stalker. With the handle of a *skean-dhu*, the Highland name for a dagger, showing above the top of his stocking, where it is usually carried, he fitted into the scene perfectly.

"I wonder what he's doing here," said Biggles. "He doesn't look like a Forestry worker. Might be a shepherd looking for lost sheep—no, if he was a shepherd he'd have a dog. So he would if he was a gamekeeper."

The man came up. Biggles spoke. "Good morning, Mr.—"

"Macrae's the name. I saw the plane circling and came to see what ye were at."

"What did you think we might be doing?"

"I thought ye might be after the eagles' eggs."

Biggles smiled faintly. "I'd never have thought of that. Do people come after eagles' eggs?"

"Aye, they do that, with yon devils of collectors in London paying five pounds a time, and up to fifty pound for a clutch."

"So you take care of the eagles," prompted Biggles.

"Aye. For the Scottish Bird Protection Society."

"An interesting job. How long have you been doing that?"

"Five years."

"Do you live here all the year round?"

"Aye."

"How do you manage in the winter?"

"I manage fine."

"Then you have a house here?"

Macrae pointed with his stick. "I have a wee place doon the glen. In the old days it was the stalker's hoose."

"It must be the only house this side of Balashlin."

"Aye. It is."

"What about the big place I noticed over there, standing in some trees, as I flew over?" Biggles pointed.

"Och, ye mean the old lodge. It's a ruin. The laird didna do a thing about it, tho' they say he should have done."

"Why, if there's no more deer-stalking?"

"He had money from the Government to put it right. They took it over in the war."

"For what purpose?"

"They put some troops in, and they knocked the place

354

"I thought ye might be after the eagles' eggs."

to pieces like they always do."

"What troops did they put in?"

"I couldna tell ye that. But you're free with your questions, mon. What might ye be doing here?"

"As you see, having a picnic. I imagine it's the first time a plane has landed on the loch."

"Aye. I'd think that. Ah weel. I'll awa' an' look to me nests. Good dee to ye."

"Good morning, Mr. Macrae. We shan't touch your eagles."

"I'll be after ye if you do. They're protected by law, ye ken." The man strode off at the long, ground-covering gait of a man born in the hills.

"Well, old boy, there's one man not likely to die in a road accident," remarked Bertie. Biggles lit a cigarette.

"What do we do next—go home?" queried Ginger.

"No."

"But there's nothing else we can do here."

"There's one thing I'm going to do. I want to cast an

eye over this empty lodge."

"Then let's get on with it."

"Not yet."

"Why?"

"Because that chap on the hill will be watching us. I don't want word to get around that we're poking about here."

"You think Murray might still be in the district?"

"He might."

Algy stepped in. "But what are you expecting to find at the lodge?"

"According to Macrae the Government requisitioned it during the war. They put troops in it. I want to know what troops they were."

"What troops have you in mind?" inquired Ginger.

"The place might have been a Commando Training School," returned Biggles. "I don't say it was, but there were some in the Highlands in the war. If I'm right it would give us a line on how Murray knew about the loch. He was a commando. We'll wander round presently. There's no point in going home only to come back again tomorrow. Fetch the torch from the machine, Ginger. We may need it."

They waited until the sun sank behind the hills, throwing the valley into gloom, and then set off at a brisk pace.

It was a long walk over hard going, and Ginger was thankful when the stand of Scots pines that hid the lodge loomed darkly against the sky.

The once smart lodge, now silent and dilapidated, with rotting hutments accompanying it to ruin, presented a depressing spectacle in an atmosphere of melancholy which the interior, when Biggles opened the door and went in, did nothing to dispel. All furniture had been removed. Some foolscap sheets of type-written matter hung from the wall in the empty hall.

Biggles walked over. "Number Seven Commando Training unit. Daily Routine Orders," he read aloud. Turning to face the others he went on. "So now we know. Murray was stationed here during the war That's how he knew of the place. What a hide-out! I'd say he came back here."

Followed by the others Biggles went down a corridor to the kitchen. A cheap frying pan and kettle were rusting on the stove. An enamel plate, with a knife and fork on it, were in the sink. He opened the back door and went out. In a corner was a heap of brown, long-dead heather. He kicked away some of it to expose a pile of empty cans. "These weren't army rations," he said, picking up a sardine tin. "Yes," he went on. "This was Murray's objective when he ditched his aircraft."

"Is there any reason why he shouldn't still be here?" asked Ginger, looking slightly alarmed.

"Plenty of reasons, one of which being the Forestry Commission people have been here." He pointed to a row of long-handled brushes: "There is some of their fire-fighting equipment. No. Murray only came here while the hue and cry was on, long enough perhaps for him to change his appearance. He couldn't bring a lot of food. Enough to last him a week or two at the outside. Then he'd have to go where some was available, to lay in a fresh stock."

"So it's a question of where did he go from here," said Ginger.

"Exactly."

"There might still be fingerprints on the handle of that frying pan," observed Algy.

"Even if they turned out to be his they wouldn't help us to find him. We needn't bother with that at this juncture."

"What are you going to do?"

"We'll go back to the machine and spend the night in the cabin. In the morning we'll have a look round. Murray might not be far away."

The walk back to the loch, in the dark, was tiring work, and would have been dangerous had they not had the advantage of a moon, nearly full. As they trudged along the stony beach towards the machine suddenly Ginger stopped, gazing out across the star-reflecting water.

"Can you see what I can't see?" he exclaimed, in a

puzzled voice.

"What can't you see?" asked Algy.

"The rudder."

"Well, blow me down!" muttered Bertie. "The water must be rising."

"Either that or Biggles caused the machine to move when he went down to it," opined Algy, casually.

"That could have happened," agreed Biggles. He walked on towards the bushes.

"Where are you going?" asked Ginger.

"I want to have another look at that cord," replied Biggles. "Give me the torch." He went on alone, but was soon back.

"That's enough for today," he said. "Let's turn in."

The next day dawned with the weather still clear and fine.

"Where do we start looking for Murray?" asked Ginger.

Biggles, who had been somewhat preoccupied, answered: "For a start I'm going down the glen to have another word with Macrae. His cottage will be by the river so it shouldn't be hard to find."

Presently they set off, taking an old deer track that skirted the loch. This soon brought them to a rock shelf over which a trickle of water spilled to form the little river Glash. Following the stream, sparkling in the sunshine, a walk of twenty minutes revealed, a little way ahead, a stone cottage nestling in a stand of wind-warped pine and silver birch. Beyond it ran a cart track, following the river. Macrae, apparently having seen them coming, was waiting, hands on hips.

"What can I do for ye?" he greeted.

"You can answer some questions," returned Biggles. "You say your name is Macrae?"

"That's richt."

"We are police officers," stated Biggles. "I have reason to believe you are the Alva Murray who we have been anxious to interview in connexion with the murder of his wife seven years ago. I must warn you that anything you say—"

Biggles got no farther. Never did a man move faster than the one who called himself Macrae. In a flash he had whipped up his *skean-dhu*. With this in his hand he backed towards the house. "Don't come near me," he growled. "Ye'll no tak me alive."

"Don't be a fool, Murray," said Biggles curtly. "That sort of talk won't help you."

Murray dashed into the house and slammed the door.

"Watch out!" cried Ginger urgently, as a window was opened and the barrels of a twelve-bore appeared.

They dashed to the nearest cover, a dilapidated venison larder. The gun blazed, shot spattering against the wall of the building.

"If we try to get to that house someone will be killed," said Biggles calmly. "I should have taken into account that we're dealing with a man who has had commando training. He can't get away and he must know it; but being guilty of murder he won't care who else he kills. I was prepared for trouble, but not a twelve-bore."

"What are we going to do?" asked Algy, anxiously. "It would be suicide to face that gun."

"He's armed and resisting arrest," Bertie pointed out. "We should be justified in using our guns."

"I'd rather not," said Biggles. "There's only one thing to do. We shall have to fetch help. Algy, go back to the machine. Fly south until you can contact the Yard on the high-frequency. Tell the chief what's happened and ask him to notify the county police. Make it snappy."

Algy ran off. The others settled down to wait, and watch.

The day wore on. The sun climbed over its zenith. High overhead an eagle soared on rigid wings. From time to time a cock grouse croaked a warning to his kind.

Late in the afternoon the gun crashed again, showing that Murray was still within.

"Who's he shooting at?" queried Bertie.

"Just letting us know he's still about, I imagine."

"I can hear a vehicle coming up the track," said Ginger.

Presently it appeared. From a jeep stepped four police officers, one an inspector.

"Watch your step," called Biggles.

The inspector ignored the warning. He walked straight to the door of the house. "Come out of that, Murray," he shouted. "Let's have no nonsense."

Finding the door locked he walked round the house and looked in a window. Then, turning, he beckoned.

Biggles and his party joined him at the window. Inside, on the floor, in a crumpled heap lay Murray, the gun beside him.

Biggles' eyes opened wide. "We didn't do that," he told the inspector. "He must have shot himself. We heard a shot."

"Aye, I'd think that," said the inspector, without emotion. "It's the sort of thing I'd expect him to do when he realized he hadn't a chance. He'd choose to die in the heather rather than be hanged in a city gaol."

Biggles, rather pale, shook his head. "Well, there it is. I'll leave this to you, now, Inspector, if you don't mind," he said, glancing up as the Otter roared past on the way to the loch. "You'll find an aeroplane in Lochnaglash, near the beach, the one Murray used to get here. It's hardly worth salvaging but you may need it for evidence. We'll get along. Thanks for your help."

Biggles turned away, and followed by the others walked back to the loch to find the Otter on the beach.

"Thanks," Biggles told Algy. "It's all over. He shot himself. For him, probably, it was the best way out. We'll get along home. I'm afraid I didn't handle that too well."

"What beats me is how you knew Macrae was Murray," said Ginger.

"You saw what I saw, and heard what I heard," stated Biggles. "I told you it needs a very smart murderer never to make a mistake. Murray made several. The first was coming near us, otherwise we might never have known he was there. He couldn't keep away. He saw us coming down

The gun blazed as they dashed to the nearest cover.

and a guilty conscience and anxiety to know what we were doing brought him along. Then he made the fatal blunder of lying. He said his was the only house between here and Balashlin. He only admitted the lodge was there when I said I'd seen it. Then he said he didn't know what troops had been there. A regiment always leaves its mark, so that was asking me to believe that in the years he had lived here he had never been to the place. I was already suspicious when I noticed the black handle of the commando knife which he carried as a *skean-dhu*. That was silly. Maybe he had grown careless over the years."

"And I didn't notice a thing," said Bertie, sadly.

"There was more to it than that," went on Biggles. "I don't think he had realized that the water had dropped so low. Did he hope we hadn't noticed the rudder? He must have seen it as we stood here talking. Any man with nothing to fear would have called attention to it. During the hours we were away at the lodge I fancy he swam out to it and either pushed it under or cut it off. I knew he'd been here."

"How?"

"He was worried about us, and in his natural anxiety wondered if he had left anything about. He remembered that cord and the water-wings. When I went along there last night on our return from the lodge it was to see if they were still there. I wasn't surprised to find they'd gone. Only Murray could have known they were there. That was all I needed to know to confirm my suspicions. Maybe I was silly to confront him as I did but I hoped the shock would cause him to give himself away, as in fact it did. I should have guessed that having been a commando he'd show fight. But let's get home. We can just do it before dark."

Subsequent inquiries revealed that Murray had served at Lochnaglash Lodge during the war. He must have lived there for some time, in hiding, for it was not until some months after his arrival that he had bought the cottage from the owner, paying for it in cash. In the interval he had grown a beard and taken to wearing Highland dress. Then, feeling safe from recognition, he had made periodical visits to the village for stores, making his excuse for living far up the glen that he was an eagle-watcher for the Bird Protection Society, as in fact he was, having offered his services in a voluntary capacity—presumably as a cover.

It was a clever scheme that might never have come to light had it not been for the drought which exposed the tail of the Gipsy. Weather conditions were outside the murderer's calculations, but, as Biggles remarked, on this occasion they proved the old saying that "Murder will out."

The Ghost Tent

SHOWELL STYLES

"GETTING late, Mike!" muttered Colin.

"Pipe down, can't you?" hissed Mike impatiently.

The two boys were crouched uncomfortably in the rushes at the edge of a moorland pool. For miles all round them the wild bleak upland of Thirlby Moss stretched away in bog and heather and shaly ridge, invisible now in a grey mist that was already darkening with the early twilight of a March evening. Mike had the binoculars glued to his eyes, watching the reeds fifty feet away along the curving edge of the pool. Fifty feet was about as far as he could see, for the mist hid everything beyond that.

Something soft and wet and cold floated down through the mist and landed on Colin's nose. A snowflake. He glanced at the intent Mike and decided to say nothing; a keen bird-watcher doesn't like chatter when he's hoping for an identification. And Mike, who had Irish blood in him, was apt to be snappy when disturbed. All the same,

364

they were a long way from their tent and night was coming on—to say nothing of the threat of snow. Colin shifted his cramped position very slightly, causing the camera that was slung round his neck to bump against his chest. Useless to hang on here, he thought. The light's far too bad now for a photo, even if it *does* turn out to be a Red-necked Phalarope. A photo was essential to prove their identification, because a Red-necked Phalarope had never been positively identified in this area. Both boys were members of the British Trust for Ornithology, and it was the rumour that someone had seen a bird resembling the Phalarope on the moor a few days ago that had brought them here, to camp for a wintry weekend in early March and confirm the rumour. If they succeeded—put the identification beyond all doubt—they would have added one more bit to the knowledge of birds and their movements. Almost like making history, thought Colin, shivering as two more large snowflakes settled on his face.

There was a slight movement in the reeds twenty feet away. Mike stiffened, motionless, the binoculars steady in his gloved hands. A small brown-grey bird waded perkily out into the shallow water at the edge of the pool, made a quaint bobbing bow, and waded back out of sight— exactly as though it had come out to receive their applause. It got no applause from Mike.

"A blighted, ordinary Common Sandpiper!" he exclaimed wrathfully, not bothering to whisper. "Greenish legs, wing-bar, underparts white. Come on—we'll turn it in now."

Colin was glad to agree. They got up stiffly from their "hide" in the rushes and edged their way to more solid ground. The grey mist hemmed them in on every side, revealing only a narrow circle of uneven heather.

"Snow!" Mike said, turning his face upward. "Lucky we've got anoraks." He laced the hood of his windproof round his chin. "We can't be in for much of a snowstorm this time of year, though."

"I won't be sorry to get back to the tent and brew up

some hot soup," said Colin. "We must've come three miles. Think you can find it?"

Mike snorted. "Easy. That first tarn we tried was due east from the tent. This pool was south from the other, with a bit of west in it. We've only got to reverse the bearings."

As he spoke he was putting the binoculars into his rucksack and getting out a compass. He held the compass for a moment for the needle to stop swinging, got his direction— a little east of north—and started off across the heather into the mist, with Colin plodding close behind him. As if it had been waiting for them to move, the snow began to float down more thickly out of the greyness.

"Be nice to snug-up in the old Ant tonight," Mike said over his shoulder.

"The Ant" was their name for the Antarctic Junior tent which they owned jointly, a type of tent extremely popular with people who liked camping in the remoter places of Britain. Colin thought of their little green shelter with its sewn-in groundsheet and the two warm sleeping-bags and felt he would be very glad to get there. For as the minutes of their plodding progress through the mist lengthened to fifteen and twenty and then to half an hour the falling snow became gradually thicker and thicker. Down by the marshy pool—one of many on Thirlby Moss—there had been little wind, but Mike was heading up slightly rising ground and the mist began to blow about them, with the snow swirling out of it in spirals of big soft flakes. The short springy heather they were treading began to whiten, seeming to lighten the growing darkness. Only when Colin noticed that Mike's red anorak looked black against the mottled grey of mist and snow did he realize that night was close upon them now.

"Sort of weather to bring out the Grey Man," he shouted, trying to sound more cheerful than he felt.

He had to shout to overcome the increasing *whoo-oosh* of wind and snow. Mike only grunted in reply, and Colin remembered his Irish superstition. The Grey Man of

Thirlby Moss was an age-old ghost who was supposed to haunt the moorland at twilight. The old folk in Thirlby village still believed in it. Colin wished he hadn't mentioned the Grey Man.

He almost blundered into Mike, who had halted to peer at the compass, and then they were moving on again with a slight downhill slope beneath their feet. Ten paces was the utmost limit of visibility now, and the snow whirling in their faces made it worse. Their anoraks and woollen gloves were plastered with snow. Colin felt the cold seeping into his very bones. They had been out all day in a cold mist, crouching motionless for hours at a time to watch for the Red-necked Phalarope, and hadn't taken much food with them. Unwillingly he remembered stories of walkers who had died from exposure on this very moor. But that wouldn't happen to them, of course—they'd be safe in the tent in another twenty minutes or so.

Mike, who had been walking more and more slowly, suddenly halted again.

"We ought to have struck that other tarn by now," he said, "but the ground's starting to rise again."

"We've got a bit too high," Colin suggested. "If we head downhill to the left—"

"All right."

Both of them spoke casually, but each could hear the apprehension in the other's voice. To be off course in a snowstorm on Thirlby Moss, with night creeping fast through the drifting mist, was to be in grave danger, and they knew it. Down over the whitening heather they plodded. Though the snow now drove at them from the right flank instead of in their faces, so that it was easier to look ahead, the circle of darkness was closing in. It was like being blind. The wind was rising, too, numbing their cheeks and fingers. Colin felt very cold and tired—and a bit frightened.

Once again Mike came to a sudden halt, and this time Colin cannoned into him heavily. He felt Mike's fingers shaking as they clutched his arm.

"A m man," Mike chattered. "Over there—t-to the left."

The tall shape that had loomed up a few paces away through the snowstorm could have been the Grey Man waiting for them. But Colin knew better.

"We're all right!" he cried joyfully. "It's that rock spike—remember? Only two or three minutes from the tent."

Mike recovered himself. "That's it! The little stream's on the other side of this low rise. Come on!"

Going as fast as they could, they passed the rock pinnacle protruding from its pile of boulders. Uphill for a few paces over the snowy heather, then more steeply down.

"By gum!" Colin shouted, a bit shakily. "I'll be glad to see that tent!"

They came to the little stream gurgling in its narrow bed and turned down it. A pool, black in the white carpet that now covered everything, showed just ahead.

"There's our washing-place!" exclaimed Mike. "But—" He stopped. "We must have passed the tent—it was just above that pool."

"Can't have done. The Ant was right by the stream."

The wind howled derisively, hurling the snow at them as they turned and went slowly back beside the stream. There was a flat place at the burnside, whitened now but obviously a good camp-site. Both of them recognized it as the place where they had camped the previous night, where they had left the little tent to go searching the misty moorland for the Red-necked Phalarope.

But the tent was gone.

Mike was the first to find his voice, and it was a very shaky voice.

"It can't be the place—it's the wrong stream."

Colin left him and hurried back to the little pool. When he returned he was clutching something in his hand.

"It *is* the place, Mike," he said, trying to stop his teeth

Their tent was gone, and with it their hope of shelter.

from chattering. "Look—my toothbrush. I left it by the pool this morning."

There was a short silence, while the driving snow fled past them into the darkness.

"The tent blew down," Mike said suddenly, "That's what happened—we'll find it a few yards downstream."

He started down along the bank of the burn. Colin followed without a word. He knew how strongly those pegs had been put in; and the wind, fierce though it was, wasn't nearly violent enough to carry the Ant away. A little below the camp-site the stream curved sharply between its low banks of heather. There were rocks, snow-whitened, here. If the tent had indeed broken from its moorings it would have been caught up on those rocks.

"It's—it's uncanny!" muttered Mike, stopping by the rocks; and Colin knew he was thinking of the Grey Man of Thirlby Moss. "Who'd move the tent? And—what are we going to do? The snowstorm's blowing straight down this watercourse. We can't stay here. If we don't find some kind of shelter—"

He left the sentence unfinished. Colin had a sudden mental picture of the two of them wandering the moor in the snowstorm until they fell exhausted, to be found days later stiff and dead. He made himself speak firmly.

"Cross the moor and get on the track to Thirlby village. It's our only chance."

"It's a good eight miles," Mike said slowly. "And remember the track, Colin? We could hardly spot it in the mist yesterday, when there was no snow. We'd never find it now—even if we'd got the strength to get that far. And I'm pretty well done."

"So am I," Colin confessed miserably; and suddenly saw a ray of hope. "Peat-hags! I've read about people finding shelter under a peat-hag in a winter storm, and coming through safely. D'you remember when we were looking for a camp-site yesterday—"

"That's it!" Mike shouted. "Half a mile from camp, wasn't it—that peat bog we walked round? Good man.

Must be almost due south from here."

He got the compass out of his pocket. It was too dark to read the dial now, but there was a small torch in the rucksack. Mike got his direction and they climbed wearily up the side of the watercourse and set off once more across the storm-swept moorland into the night.

It should have been easier going with the snow driving from behind them, but both boys were rapidly becoming exhausted and stumbled frequently as they toiled across the snow-laden heather. Only half a mile, only half a mile —Colin found the comforting words going through and through his mind. Not long ago the snug little "Ant" had been his goal; now all his hopes were centred on the black, damp undercurve of a peat-hag where they might huddle shivering for the long hours of night. And he knew well that it meant the difference between life and death for both of them.

Mike had kept the torch in his hand so that he could consult the compass at intervals. The circle of light, when it flashed on, lit a dark-grey wall of mist with the whirl of white flakes racing past to vanish in it. When the torch went out again the night seemed utterly black for a few minutes until their eyes got accustomed to the dark once more and could see the same ceaseless turmoil of snow in front. Colin, numbed and leg-weary, forced himself to stagger on behind Mike's dark figure. He began to feel as if he was dreaming, and somehow the Red-necked Phalarope kept coming into his dream. *"Very small . . . bill black, longer and finer than grey phalarope's . . . rare inland in Britain . . . very tame . . ."*—phrases from the Bird Recognition book repeated themselves in his mind. Vaguely he knew that they should have reached the peat-bog by now—that they were going downhill, not up as they ought to do; but he was too weary to call out to Mike and tell him. Too weary to do anything beyond going on until he dropped. . . .

From just in front came a splash and a startled exclamation. Next moment Colin, too, had stumbled into the

371

shallow water at the edge of a reedy pool. As he followed Mike's faltering steps to drier ground a gust of wind and snow smote him in the face. He reeled and nearly fell. He was at the end of his tether, and there was no shelter here.

And then Mike gave a shout. His torch shone on the snow-powdered pebbles at the pool's edge and on the level ground a pace or two above. Beyond the veil of snow a triangular shape hovered ghostlike, showing a familiar green through the white. It was the tent.

Comparing notes with Mike afterwards, Colin found that his friend had experienced the same feelings as himself. Utter astonishment at finding the "Ant" safely pitched by a pool far from where they had left it; then a most eerie sensation—partly fright at the uncanny business, partly a sudden memory of the Grey Man of Thirlby Moss; and lastly the realization that here, by a miracle, was shelter and safety. Whether the tent had got there by witchcraft, or whether this was the ghost of their vanished "Ant", didn't matter to a pair of half-frozen bird-watchers who had come very near to deadly peril. They reeled up to the tent, managed to undo the door-lacings with nerveless fingers, and fairly fell inside. Colin had a dim recollection of fumbling at boot-laces and stripping off wet socks and stockings. The sleeping-bag he struggled into didn't feel like his; probably it was Mike's, but it wasn't important. His friend was fastening the tent door and muttering something or other. Good old Mike! Colin felt warmth creeping back into his body. Outside, the snow whirled on and the wind pushed at the tent fabric. Inside it was snug— and safe. A wave of weariness and relief swept over him, and before Mike had crawled into the sleeping-bag beside him Colin was asleep.

According to Mike, they slept for eleven hours that night on Thirlby Moss. At any rate, when Colin woke and stretched stiff and aching limbs the sun had come over the low horizon and the tent was glowing with morning light. Mike had just woken up and was talking excitedly.

."Wh-what?" mumbled Colin sleepily

"I said the mystery's partly explained," Mike repeated forcibly. "Look!" He pointed to some objects in a corner of the tent. "Tinned sausage—we didn't bring any. And these sleeping-bags. Blue covers, and ours are brown. *This isn't our tent!*"

"Great Godfrey!" Colin sat up and stared round him. "And you're right, too. It's an Antarctic Junior, same as ours, but it *isn't* ours. Whose is it, then? And where's our tent?"

"Don't ask me," said Mike. "Maybe it's a ghost tent. It was a snowstorm when we got into it—now the sun's shining. What's the betting we've been spirited away to a tropical island or somewhere? Let's have a look."

He said it lightly, but his fingers shook with excitement as he unfastened the tent door and pulled the fabric aside. The Irish in him was uppermost at that moment. Even Colin stared eagerly, wondering what he would see.

The opened door revealed a morning sky from which the sun was already clearing the slight haze, and a little moorland tarn with new-fallen snow sparkling on its shores. Wind and snowstorm had passed and left a wonderful morning of early spring. The pebbly beach of the tarn was a stride or two from the tent doorway, with brown rushes fringing the shining blue water. And just emerging from the rushes were five very small wading-birds with long, slim, black bills.

Mike froze motionless with his hand holding the tent curtain.

"Camera! Exposure-meter! *Quick*, man!"

He spoke under his breath and out of one corner of his mouth. Colin groped for the camera, hardly daring to breathe. The light-meter was in his anorak pocket. It'd have to be a hundredth of a second—f. 1·9 would just do it. As he raised the little camera he looked almost incredulously at the five small waders who were now pottering about and probing busily with their long beaks as if there was no tent twenty feet away from them. "*Very*

373

tame," said the bird book. That fitted right enough—and there was the dark-grey back with whitish streaks, the prominent wing-bar, and—yes! One of the waders, starting his summer plumage early, had the faintest hint of an orange band on his neck and upper breast. They were Red-necked Phalaropes!

The camera clicked. A swift wind-on and a second exposure to make sure. The colour-film would clinch this miraculous identification. A moment later Mike, who had been screwing his face into horrible contortions, let out a resounding sneeze and the five phalaropes instantly took wing. "*Whit-whit-whit!*" they piped as they vanished, continuing their long journey northward to the breeding-grounds in the Polar Sea.

Three hours later Colin and Mike were striding down in the March sunshine to Thirlby village in the valley below them. The "ghost tent" was strapped on Mike's rucksack and Colin was carrying the sleeping-bags and stores. A tough-looking lad who was plodding up the steep lane, which led to Thirlby Moss, halted and stared at the two as they approached.

"Good morning," he said hesitantly. "I—er—I suppose you don't happen to have my tent?"

"Camera! Exposure meter! Quick man!"

Mike glanced quickly at Colin and then grinned.

"I shouldn't wonder," he replied. "I suppose you don't happen to have ours?"

After that, it took only a moment for the other boy to identify "the ghost tent" as his. And two sets of explanations were exchanged.

"I'm dead keen on bird-watching," said their new acquaintance, "and I got hold of that chap who thought he'd seen a Red-necked Phalarope on the Moss a few days ago. He agreed to go up and camp with me, by the pool where he'd seen it. Well, it was very misty yesterday, as you know, and this chap woke up feeling ill. I could see he was really bad—malaria, it turned out to be—and I had to get him down to a doctor. It was a fearful game getting him down to Thirlby, because he got so feeble he could hardly stand. The doctor took him over and I went to the Thirlby Hostel, where I'm staying. Some of the chaps there volunteered to go up and bring my tent down—I was just about all in, you see—and I gave them some pretty vague directions—"

"And they brought down the wrong tent," Mike broke in. "That comes of the Antarctic Junior being so popular."

"Yes—and you being a pair, same as we were. I was just going up to bring in my tent. Yours is safe at the Hostel, by the way."

The three boys went down the lane together.

"Bad luck for you," Colin said thoughtfully as they walked, "but—in a way—good luck for us. Because we've not not only eaten your tinned sausages, but also bagged your Red-necked Phalarope."

"Cracking good sausages they were, too," grinned Mike; he glanced at Colin. "I reckon we owe you something for them—*and* for the use of your ghost tent."

And that is why, in the records of the British Trust for Ornithology, the credit for the first positive identification of the Red-necked Phalarope on Thirlby Moss is given to four people instead of two.

The Boy and the Salmon

NEIL M. GUNN

KENN MUMBLED and grumbled and kept his eyes shut, for being rudely wakened out of sleep was a thing that often happened to him. He had been up late last night because everyone had been busy over the departure of the boats in the morning for the distant fishing. There had been such comings and goings and preparations that the excitement had kept sleep away much longer than usual. In this little Highland community young boys were not sent to bed early, and though he might be shouted at to take himself off at ten o'clock, Kenn would often hang out until eleven. Last night it had been nearly midnight before sleep had curled him up in a corner of the kitchen, and his father had had to carry him to bed.

It was only when his mother's voice said something about the boats going away that he knew he must get up, so he muttered, "What are you wanting?" His mother told him that she wanted fresh water from the well. What an excuse for wakening a fellow! He could almost have cried. And when he did stagger out of bed and found from the greyness of the light that it could not be much more than six o'clock, his vexation became bitter. He stood in his shirt, whimpered moodily as he scratched himself, then slowly pulled on his trousers and his blue fisherman's gansey.

In the kitchen his father and mother were talking. He paid no attention to them, but picked up the bright tin pail and made it clatter against the jamb of the door as he went out.

The dawn air was cold and the touch of frost in the ground was such a shock to his bare feet that he nearly cried out. He should have put on his boots, holed as they were. He hoped his parents were watching him through the window and seeing what he had to endure.

In this mood he arrived at the well, which was at the foot of a steep bank by the side of the river. Carelessly he bumped the pail down on the flat stone, and at the sound, as at a signal in a weird fairy tale, the whole world changed. His moodiness leapt right out of him and fear had him by the throat.

For from his very feet a great fish had started ploughing its way across the river, the king of fish, the living salmon.

Kenn had never seen a living salmon before, and of those he had seen dead this was beyond all doubt the all-father.

When the waves faded out on the far side of the stream, where the bed was three feet deep, Kenn felt the great silence that lay upon the world and stood in the midst of it trembling like a hunted hare.

His eyes shot hither and thither, along horizons, down braes, across fields and wooded river-flats. No life moved; no face was watching.

Out of that noiseless world in the grey of the morning, all his ancestors came at him. They tapped his breast until the bird inside it fluttered madly; they drew a hand along his hair until the scalp crinkled; they made the blood within him tingle to a dance that had him leaping from boulder to boulder before he rightly knew to what desperate venture he was committed.

For it was all in a way a sort of madness. The fear was fear of the fish itself, of its monstrous reality, primal fear; but it was also infinitely complicated by fear of gamekeepers, of the horror and violence of law courts, of our modern social fear. Not only did his hunting ancestors of the Caledonian Forest come at him, but his grown-up brothers and his brothers' friends, with their wild forays and epic stories, a constant running the gauntlet against enemy forces, for the glory of fun and laughter and daring —and the silver gift of the salmon. A thousand influences had his young body taut as a bow, when at last, bending over a boulder of the old red sandstone, he saw again the salmon.

Fear rose at him afresh, for there was a greyness in its great dark-blue back that was menacing and ghostly. . . . He could see the eyes on each side of the shapely head and knew the eyes must see him. Still as a rock and in some mysterious way as unheeding, the salmon lay beneath him. Slowly he drew his head back until at last the boulder shut off sight of the salmon and released his breath.

As before, he looked all around him, but now with a more conscious cunning. Tiptoeing away from the boulder, he went searching downstream until he found a large flattish stone, and returned with it pressed against his stomach.

When he had got the best grip, he raised it above his head, and, staggering to the upper edge of the sandstone boulder, poised it in aim. Then he did not let it drop so much as contrive, with the last grain of his strength, to hurl it down on the fish.

Though untouched, the salmon was very clearly astonished and, before the stone had right come to rest, had the pool in a splendid tumult. For it was not one of those well defined pools of gradual depths. There were gravel banks in it and occasional boulders forming little rest

With all his might he hurled it down on the fish.

pools behind them. The tail was wide and shallow.

It was a sea-trout rather than a salmon pool, as became apparent in that first blind rush, when the fish thrashed the water to froth in a terrific boil on top of the gravel bank, cleared the bank, and, with back fin showing, shot across the calm water towards the well where he had been resting. So headlong was his speed that he beached himself not two yards from Kenn's pail. Curving from nose to tail, the great body walloped the stones with resounding whacks. So hypnotized was Kenn by this extraordinary spectacle, that he remained stiff and powerless, but inwardly a madness was already rising in him, an urgency to rush, to hit, to kill. The salmon was back in the shallow water, lashing it, and in a moment, released, was coming straight for him. Right at his feet there was a swirl, a spitting of drops into his face. The fish saw him and, as if possessed by a thousand otters, flashed up the deep water and launched himself, flailing wildly, in the rushing shallows of the neck.

And then Kenn went into action, caution and fear forgotten. It was in truth a madness not unlike the salmon's. In his blind panic, the fish had no regard for bodily stress; in his blind exaltation, neither had Kenn.

Less than a hundred yards beyond the shallows of the neck was a long dark pool, and in it lay escape. If the brute had been calm, been travelling by night, it could have made the passage with ease. But now, having lost its head, it defeated itself by its own strength and added to its panic by bashing its nose against boulders.

Kenn approached the scene with such speed that before one toe could slip on slime the other was forward to thrust him on. Landing knee-deep in the final jump, he tore a stone from the bed of the stream and, blinded by the salmon's splashings, let drive.

He missed by over a foot and there followed a jumble in which, in his excitement, he lunged fiercely and recklessly, to be left grovelling on his back as the salmon shot downward.

In his leap for the bank Kenn stumbled and was thrown

severely. But he had no consciousness of pain, only of loss of time, of awful fear lest the salmon should escape.

And running down the bank it seemed to him as if the salmon had escaped. No trace of "way" on the pool. Nothing. . . . Was that a swirl—far down? Making his way out of the pool!

On his toes again, Kenn sped downward, came in below the fish, and picking up a stone half the size of his head, went straight to the attack.

The water was now growing narrower and deeper, but it was tortured by boulders and sloping flagstones. Twice the salmon flashed past him, and now Kenn was not merely wading into the water, but falling and crawling and choking in it, yet ever with his dark head rising indomitably.

If the salmon had possessed an instinct for an enemy at all, it must have been for some animal like the otter, swift and sure in attack and deathly in grip. This rushing, sprawling, stone-throwing inhabitant of another world had fingers that slid off the back like caressing fingers of seaweed. Unable to bite yet pursuing relentlessly. Shake him off! A rush and a heave and the salmon bared his girth on a sloping flagstone. From the bottom, Kenn had raked a stone barely the size of his small fist, but he threw it with all his vigour and it scored a first direct hit. . . .

Back off the flagstone came the salmon with his nose pointing upstream, and he followed his nose. At the best of times it is awkward for a salmon to go downstream, but upstream, given depth and shoulder room, speed becomes a frenzy. This fish turned it into a debauch and reached the Well Pool like a demented torpedo.

Kenn had chosen his battleground and laid down the conditions of the fight.

And it was a saga of a fight. For Kenn had no weapons of attack other than his fists and what they could grab from the river bottom; no rod, hook, net, or implement of constraint or explosion. It was a war between an immature human body on the one side, and a superbly matured body

*He beached himself, walloped the stones and was
back in the river.*

of incredible swiftness and strength on the other. In physical length, laid out side by side, there would have been
little difference between them.

But neither of them was laid out yet! Indeed so far there
had been little more than the courteous slap on the cheek
as gage of battle, and it had been delivered by Kenn.

The initial strategy, however, for such warfare could be
summed up in the words "keep him on the run". All his
tactics brought this about as their natural result, whether
he was careering wildly up and down the bank, pausing to
hurl a stone, or dashing into shallows to get at close
quarters. The frenzy of both had first to be worn down,
before the cunning brain could stalk the tired body.

A curious mood of fatalism comes upon a salmon that
has committed its life to a pool. Up and down it will go,
round this boulder, by the side of that, turning here, turn-

ing back again there, but never making any attempt to leave the known ground. No barrage of stones will drive it forth, however successfully timed. The dangers of the shallows are the dangers of the unknown, of death. If the pool be just deep enough a salmon will pass between swimming human legs rather than be driven forth, and in this restless fashion will ultimately tire out its enemies.

But if the Well Pool had not sufficient depth over a wide enough area to permit of this endless swimming, it had on the other hand its own suggestions for escape. The water was amber-coloured, for it was the tail-end of a mighty spate, and drained from peat-banks in distant moors; being for the most part shallow, it had a considerable flow; and the scattered pieces of rock against the ground inequalities offered a tired fish many a natural hiding place.

Indeed several times Kenn had his heart in his mouth when it seemed that the salmon had altogether vanished. In the dark shadow of a leaning stone where the amber water gurgled past, a dark-blue back was but a darker shadow. Then Kenn would spot the tail or the curve of the nose or the pallor of a fin; would be overcome with an emotion keener in its thrust than ever; would back away and hunt his stone. Splash! and the salmon was on its journey once more, betrayed by its great size.

This phase of the battle went on for a long time, until Kenn knew all the resting places and there began to grow in him a terrible feeling of power, terrible in its excitement, in its realization that he might be successful, and even more terrible in its longing.

There came a time when Kenn, having got the fish resting where he wanted him, went downstream to choose his stone, but no longer in blind urgency. He handled two or three before lifting one against his breast.

The salmon lay by the outer edge of a greenish underwater slab. By approaching it on a slant towards its tail, he could keep its head out of sight. Warily he did this until he came to the edge of the stream. But now he knew that however he stooped while wading in, the eyes would be disclosed. He did not hesitate; he let himself down into the water and, the stone against his stomach, slithered over the gravelly bottom on his stern. It was an autumn morning, after a night of hoar-frost, but when the water got fully about his body he felt it warm. Foot by foot he thrust himself on, until at last he could have put out a hand and touched the tail; and the tail was deep as his face and as taut.

Slowly he reared up on his knees, fighting down the sinking sensation that beset him, his hands fiercely gripping the stone. Anxiety now started shouting in him to heave the stone and be done, but, though trembling, he rose with infinite care, little by little, disclosing the back fin, the nape of the neck where the otter bites, and at last the near eye. The fish did not move. Inch by inch the stone went up. Then in one thrust he launched stone and body at the fish.

The thud of the stone on the great back was a sound of such potency that even in that wild drenching moment it sang above all else. For the stone had landed; the stone had got him! Spewing the river water forth, stumbling and falling, he reached the bank. Then both of them went berserk.

This great fish had not the slippery cunning, the evasiveness, of a small salmon or grilse. It tore around like a bull in a ring. Kenn began to score direct hits more often. He was learning the way. He could throw a stone ahead; he could madden; he could stalk warily and hear ever more exultingly the singing thud.

The fatal part for a salmon is the nape of the neck. The time came when Kenn landed there heavily with the narrow stone edge; the salmon circled and thrashed as if half paralysed or blinded; Kenn with no more stones at hand launched a body attack and received one wallop from the tail that sent him flat on his back; the salmon was off again.

The end came near the neck of the pool on the side opposite the well. Here the low bank of the river widened out into a grassy field. The tired fish, with pale mouth

In the grip of human hands the salmon went berserk.

gaping every now and then, went nosing into shallow water, where some upended flagstones might provide a new and dark retreat. But there was no hidden retreat there and Kenn, well down the pool, waited with wild hope. If it lay anywhere thereabouts until he got up, it would be finished! And it lay.

It actually lay in full view between two stone edges, its back fin barely covered. Kenn hit it as it moved and then fell on it. His hands went straight for the gills; one found a grip under a cheek, the other, slipping, tried for a hold on the body, and there and then began the oddest tussle that surely that river could ever have seen.

Under the burning grip of human hands, the salmon went frantic and threw Kenn about as if he were a streamer tied to its neck; the upended stones bashed his arms, his legs, the back of his head; the bony cheek dug into his wrist; but nothing could now dim the relentless instinct in him to roll both bodies from the shallow water on to dry land.

And this in time he accomplished. When his hand was shot from behind the cheek it drew gills with it.

The salmon flailed the dry stones with desperate violence, but Kenn was now in his own element, and ever he brought his body behind the body of the fish and shored it upwards, thrusting at the gills until his hands were lacerated and bleeding.

He dragged that fish over fifty yards into the grass park before he laid it down. And when it heaved in a last convulsive shudder, he at once fell upon it as if the river of escape still lapped its tail.

And now on this busy morning, angered against him for not returning with the well water, his mother suddenly saw him rounding the corner of the house towards the door of the back porch, face down, hands knotted behind his head, dripping wet and staggering. The salmon's nose was under his right ear, its tail was sweeping the ground behind. She gave way to him as he lurched in. Releasing his crooked fingers and heaving with a shoulder, he set the great fish with a mighty thump on the smooth blue flagstone at her feet.

She looked at the frightening size of the fish on the floor; she looked at her son and whispered, "Where did you get that?"

"In the river."

"Yourself?"

"Who else?"

His dark hair was flattened to rat tails. His brown eyes were black against the excited pallor of his face. There was a fighting spirit in him that suddenly pulled at her heart: "You're all wet. Every stitch of you."

At that moment his father came round the house.

"Come here, Davy," said the woman to him quietly.

The father came up. He looked at the fish; he looked at the boy. "God bless me!" he whispered. "Where did you get him?"

"In the Well Pool."

"God bless me, boy!" His features softened in a slow winning smile, touched to the breath of wonder. His son felt it without looking at it, felt it in the breath of his voice, and a weakening warmth ran about his heart.

"Did anyone see you?" asked his mother.

"No," he muttered.

"How did you land him?" asked his father.

"With my hands."

His father looked at the hands. Kenn, seeing for the first time that they had been bloodily combed by the gills, put them behind his back.

"And he's wet to the skin besides," nodded his mother in a rising tone that implied that all this was none of her doing. "You'll go in and change every stitch on you this minute."

Kenn paid no attention to her.

"Was there no one there at all?" his father asked in his quiet voice, still hushed in wonder.

"No."

He staggered home with his load, exultation in his heart.

The man looked at the fish. They all stared at it. It beat everything!

"Do you think," said the mother thoughtfully, "that Sans would like a bit?"

"What's the weight of him, do you think?" said Sans, the merchant.

"He's maybe twenty pounds," said Kenn's father tentatively.

"Twenty! If he's not over twenty-five I'll eat my bonnet!"

On the wooden scales used for weighing bags of meal, the merchant laid the fish. "Twenty, did you say? Very well." He put on twenty pounds—and pressed the beam—and chuckled. He added the seven weight. Nothing happened. Two more to make twenty-nine. Then, gently, one for thirty and the beam trembled.

"Bless me," said Davy softly.

"Thirty good," said Sans. He laughed and brought down his hand on Kenn's shoulder: "Good for you, my little hero!"

Something Lost

JACK SCHAEFER

June

THIS WAS far up in the mountains and still the great peaks climbed, thrusting up and thinning to the bare bones of rock above the timber-line. The high upland valley was lost among them, an irregular pocket caught in the soaring immensity, rimmed by the timeless rock, its glints of meadow green shading into the darker green of forest where it broke into the downward slopes. The figure of the man by the stream near the upper end of the valley, where the water slowed from its rush down the rocks, was un-

believably small in the vastness. He stood stooped by a sandbar where the riffles swung and died in a pool and the slant sunlight flashed on the worn tin in his hands and his shoulders rocked as his arms moved in a circular motion.

The motion stopped and the man bent his head farther to peer into the pan in his hands and the dull gleaming of the flakes there was reflected in the pale hazel irises of his eyes. He straightened and nodded his head in slow satisfaction. He studied the sandbar and the pool where the water slipped into apparent stillness and the silt of years had settled to the bottom. He raised his head and looked at the untouched wilderness about him. The valley lay open around him, a half-mile wide and a mile long, its level floor cut by the swinging course of the stream. At its head the mountain wall rose steeply in huge broken steps that the stream took in rushes and falls as it drove down from the endless snow in the far upper reaches of rock. Along the valley sides the slopes climbed, tree-dotted and thicket-entangled, to stop against the enduring stone, on the near side against a high sharp ridge, on the opposite side against a vast rock buttress towering out to a tremendous cliff edge. Between the ridge and the buttress the valley entrance swept out to open parkland that dropped abruptly into jack pine forest covering the downward slopes and divided by the deepening gorge of the stream as it sought the lower levels. And beyond the ground rose again, rising in ridge upon ridge to the high eastward mountain barrier.

The man nodded his head again in slow satisfaction and the sun shone warm on the broad flat planes of his face beneath the wide squared brim of his hat. He took a leather pouch from a pocket and eased the flakes into it. He strode across the carpet of wild flowers bordering the stream and bent to pick up the trailing lead rope of the grazing burro. By the slope of the near valleyside, where a thickening stand of spruce and juniper fringed the valley floor, he stopped and pulled the rifle and axe and short shovel from under the tie ropes and unfastened the pack and picketed the burro on a twenty-foot rope length. He selected a fallen tree, angling up, the upper end wedged in a crotch of another tree. Using this as his ridgepole, he began building his shelter. He shed his jacket and sweat darkened his shirt as his short broad body swung in steady rhythm and the axe blade bit into the springy wood.

Across the meadow green, across the wild-flower carpet and the stream, half a mile across the stretching expanse of valley floor and two hundred yards up the opposite slope

where bare rock jutted over a flat ledge, the great bear lay
and watched the man. It lay limp on the ledge in the warm
slant sun, hind legs sprawled back, front legs stretched
forward with the big head, broad and dished to the muzzle,
resting on the rock between them. A light breeze ruffled
through the short brown fur made ragged by the remaining
long still unshed hairs touched with silver on the tips. Its
small far-sighted eyes followed the man's every move
among the distant trees.

Eighty-odd miles away, over the mountain barrier to the
east, where a ragged collection of rude log cabins and tents
straggled along the side of an almost dry stream bed, men
worked at their wooden cradles and sluice boxes and
grumbled to themselves and each other. The showings of
colour that had drawn them there to stake their claims

392

It watched his every move.

were dwindling. In the oblong tarpaulin-roofed shack that served as store and bar other men spoke of the one who had left, quietly, speaking to no one, abandoning his slow half-worked claim to disappear with his burro into the high distances to the west. Their talk was tainted with envious wondering. They argued with each other in edged monotones. Unrest and disappointment crawled through the mining camp.

Far up in his valley, as the midnight stars wheeled in their slow course, the man stirred on his bed of spruce boughs and sat up, suddenly alert. The embers of the fire outside the open end of his shelter had faded to a dull glow that meant nothing to the moonless dark under the trees. He heard the burro moving restlessly on its shortened

His eyes searched the pan for hint of gold.

picket rope. In the following silence he felt a familiar prickling on the back of his neck as the short hairs there stiffened in response to some instinct beyond reach of the mind. His right hand moved and took the rifle and he was leaning forward to rise when he heard the burro scream and lunge to the end of the rope. He leaped to his feet and stood in the open end of the shelter, baffled by the unrelenting blackness of the night. Gradually he could make out the darker shapes of the trees. He went cautiously toward the burro and found it half choked by the taut rope. He spoke softly and it pushed against him and together they stood in a silence that lived and breathed around them. There was not a single separate discernible sound, yet the prickling persisted on his neck and the flesh of the burro quivered against him. The prickling died and the burro quieted and they stood in an empty silence. The man returned to the fire and piled wood on it and kneeled to blow until flames sprang and a circle of firelight fought back the dark. He shifted the burro closer to the circle before he lay again on his spruce bed.

In the morning the man found the tracks. Those of the forefeet were nearly seven inches wide and nine long, those of the hind feet eight inches wide and fourteen long. The claw marks of all five toes on each were plain. Apprehension crept along the man's spine. His hands tightened on the rifle. The tracks led in a circle around his camp and close in by the shelter and again by the place where the burro had first been picketed. He crawled inside his shelter to the low diminishing end where his meagre supplies, depleted by weeks of wandering, were cached behind a barrier of short logs. He took a handful of cartridges and dropped them into a jacket pocket. Outside again, he strode off, steady and unhurried, following the tracks away.

They led him across the stream below the pool and across the level of the valley. He lost them on the edge of a field of slide rock near the lower end of the valley. He skirted the field and could find no further trace. He turned back and began a thorough circuit of the valley.

He found signs in many places, old tracks caked where the ground had dried and fresher tracks in soft ground. He found three rubbing trees with bark worn thin and high up, higher than he could reach, gashes where the bark had been torn open crosswise by gripping jaws. He found the trail angling up the far slope to the ledge. Approaching the ledge, he saw the wide and narrowing crevice behind it leading back to blackness under the overhanging rock. No light could penetrate the inner dark depth. He dropped silently back down the trail fifty yards and crouched behind a big stone and shouted and there was no response except the jeering call of a jay. He shouted again and waited. At last he strode down the trail and across the valley. In a few moments he was stooped by the pool, his arms moving in circular motion as the sun glinted on the pan in his hands. But now he looked up at regular intervals and scanned the expanse all around him and the rifle lay within quick reach not more than a yard from his steady hands.

Out of the valley, eight miles around the jagged sweep of the vast rock buttress that towered above the opposite slope, out where the forest of jack pine below the edging parkland flowed unbroken down to the shore of a small lake, the great bear lay in a patch of sunlight on the soft needle carpet. Already it had forgotten the man and the burro. They were new sights, new scents, never before known, tucked away now in the reservoir of experience and would remain untouched until a fresh encounter summoned remembrance into being. They had been seen and smelled and investigated in the caution of the night and dismissed. There was no challenge in them for the bear to understand.

A marten drifted down the trunk of a nearby tree, stretching its small pointed head outward to stare intently at the bear. The scratch of the small claws in the bark was barely audible a few feet away, yet the bear's head rose. The marten scurried back up the tree. The big head dropped and the bear, full-fed and lazy, drowsed in the sunlight. The tree shadows moved slowly and crept to engulf the bear and it rose and padded softly on through the forest.

July

The man strode up the stretch of parkland that edged the forest and led to the valley entrance. The late afternoon sun was full in his face. Behind him the burro trotted obediently, weighted by the big pack, whose new canvas covering gleamed white in the sunlight. Where the parkland levelled to enter the valley he stopped and turned to look back the way he had come, down the long rolling forested slope sliced by the stream gorge and up and over the first high ridge beyond. Satisfied at last that no one followed, he turned again and led the burro up the valley and across the green carpet to his camp in the spruce and juniper fringe. Everything there was as he had left it eight days before. But in the soft ground by the pool he found

Envious rumours declared he had made a rich strike.

the big five-toed tracks crossing the stream toward his camp and going back again. He looked across the valley and up. The steep sideslope curving to the high rock buttress was splendid in the late sunlight and the over-hanging rock and the ledge two hundred yards above the valley floor shone rust-red and grey against the green around them. A hawk floated in the air above the scattered clinging trees. There was no other sign of life. He strode back to his camp and began unpacking the burro.

Far to the eastward, over the mountain barrier, where the rude cabins and tents marred the bank of the stream bed, men talked to the keeper of the tarpaulined store and bar, worrying again the worn questions of four days about the one who had returned with his burro and bought supplies and shaken bright flakes out of a leather pouch in payment and disappeared again into the western heights. Already the legend was growing. He had made a rich strike. He was scooping dust out of rich silt pockets by the handful. He had unlimited wealth in dust and nuggets cached in his mountain hideout. The voice of a lean man with narrow hatchet face gashed by a thin-lipped mouth was tinged with bitterness as he told of his failure in following the boot and hoofmark traces into the mountains. A trail that well hidden must have been deliberately cloaked to cover its destination. The talk warmed and eyes glittered and the storekeeper did good business.

Twice in the night the man awoke, alert and rising to sitting position on his bed of boughs. There was no sound beyond the barrier of logs with which he had closed the open end of his shelter except an occasional soft movement of the burro in the narrow high-poled enclosure he had built for it. In the morning there were no new tracks. It was the same the next night and the next and early during the night after that thunder echoed through the mountains and lightning laced down through the peaks and enough rain fell in the valley to dampen the ground and renew it for fresh writings by any living thing that walked it. In the morning the man took the rifle and made another thorough circuit of the valley. He found no fresh signs, no five-toed tracks except what remained of the old after the erasing action of the rain. But in the moist sand by the stream where it eddied around rolled rocks well below the pool, he found other tracks, split-hooved, deeply indented. He studied these a long moment. He followed them along the stream and when they faded into the firm sod he kept on down the valley. His stride, long for the length of his legs, gnawed steadily into distance.

Half an hour later he was skirting the vast rock buttress, pausing often to scan the sweep of slope opening below him. He was well around, out of sight of the valley entrance, when he saw the elk, three of them, more than a mile away, on the edge of the parkland that slipped abruptly into the jack pine forest. Patient and steady, he began the long approach, angling down the slope to put the light wind directly in his face.

Far ahead where the forest dipped into a deep ravine, a thin column of smoke floated upward from the inside hollow of the shattered stump of a long dead pine. The slow fire, legacy of the lightning, glowed faintly as it ate into the punklike wood. It edged through a split in the old bark and little flames began to flicker along the side of the stump. It worked down and began to creep through the carpet of brown needles. It crept to the tiny outstretched dried twigs of the branch ends of a fallen tree and moved hungrily along them, reaching for the more solid wood.

The man was on his hands and knees, lifting the rifle carefully and setting it down gently with each forward movement of his right hand. He crawled to the top of a slight rise and lay flat to peer over. He was within rifle-shot of the elk. He eased the gun forward and let the sights sink down on the closest of the three. It stood quartering away from him and he aimed a bit behind and below the high foreshoulder and squeezed the trigger. He saw his elk leap a fraction of a second before the others and the three of them swirl and melt like sudden swift shifting shadows into the forest. He rose and went forward and followed. He was well in among the trees when he found the first blood drops, spattered and dark from internal bleeding. He lengthened his stride to follow the trace deeper into the forest. Forty minutes later, winded from climbing over and around down timber, he jumped the wounded elk out of a bushed hollow and his bullet, fired almost without aiming in the instant reflex of long experience, broke the animal's neck as it strove with flagging strength to leap away.

399

Down the slope, farther into the thick of the forest, the great bear prowled, sniffing for rotted logs among a tangle of fallen trees. It heard the second shot, faint yet distinct, a sound foreign and unknown. The big body stopped moving and the big head, unacquainted with fear in any form, rose and turned toward the sound. The bear waited, listening, then the head lowered and the long straight foreclaws sank into the outer shell of a log and, seeming without effort, ripped it open. The tongue, surprisingly small in the big mouth, licked quickly at the scurrying insects and slowed to take the sluggish wriggling white grubs.

The man worked steadily with his knife, quartering the elk carcass. He had already bled and dressed it. The small of his back ached from bending over and he straightened to rest it, and as his head came up he caught the first faint tang in the air. His body stiffened and the tiny premonitions running through him tightened into awareness. Smoke.

Smoke drifting over the forest ceiling and filtering down fine tendrils that could elude the eye but not the nose.

The man stood motionless, testing the breeze. It stirred gently, barely whispering through the branches above him. He started at a right angle to the direction of the breeze, straight up the slope, the shortest path to the edge of the forest and the open parkland. Steadily he hammered on and the breeze freshened and talked in the branches and smoke began weaving among the tree trunks from the left. He angled toward the right, and the smoke thickened, and at last he stopped, listening between the laboured rush of his own breathing. The breeze strengthened and was a wind sighing high overhead, and faint and far he could hear, not so much heard as sensed, the sullen roar of the racing fire. Around him he could fairly feel the hurrying of panic, the small life of the forest moving, unseen but known, past him down the slope. A deer bounded out of the smoke and saw him and swerved and was gone. Without hesitation he turned and struck down the slope.

The smoke thickened and the light dimmed strangely and the roar rose until it was clearly audible and a high crackling breaking over it, and in a short while he was running, using his free hand to help him vault fallen logs, stumbling often and driving downward. The ground levelled and the trees ended and he broke through bushes and tripped full length into the shallow shore waters of a lake. The rifle leaped from his hand and disappeared beneath the surface and he scrambled after it. But the water deepened suddenly a few feet out and he floundered, with his chest heaving for air. He struggled back to the shallow edge and stood quietly while his lungs eased their frantic labour. Smoke rolled around him and he kneeled to keep his head close to the water and the layer of clear air just above it. Fire flared on the rim of the forest to the right and moved toward him and the heat grew until it drove him into the deeper water. He stood stretched upward with his head alone above the surface and looked out over the lake through the rolling smoke clouds. Fifty yards from shore a huge rock showed, humping out of the water like the low ridged back of some vast immobile beast. He swam slowly to it, fighting the drag of his clothes and boots, and crawled up on it and lay flat, while his tired muscles jumped and knotted and relaxed to rest.

The man lay on the rock and watched the fire work its way along the shore. He saw flames spire swiftly up one tree and leap to the next and sometimes, driven by the surge of their own tremendous draught, lunge to engulf several trees at once. The roar of the burning drowned all

He turned his head back to the rock and his body stiffened—the bear was looking at him, its head raised.

possible other sound. It was nothing heard, little more than a slight prickling on the back of his neck, that turned his eyes to the water past the other end of the rock. Only the broad head showed, with the muzzle cutting the water, as the great bear swam toward the rock. Quietly the man slipped into the water, stretching out in it with one hand holding to the stone while the other took the knife from its sheath on his belt. Silent in the water, he saw the bear's head rise over the rock opposite him, not more than twenty feet away, the forepaws stretched for footing, the massive shoulders emerge into view. He watched the bear turn broadside and shake and send the drops spattering clear across the rock. He watched it settle on its haunches, facing the flaming shore-line, and let its forepaws slide forward until the broad belly rested on the rock and the big head sank on them. He moved cautiously to look out over the rest of the lake. Through the clear area just over the surface he saw that it was almost ringed with fire and there was no other haven showing above the water. He turned his head back to the rock and his body stiffened. The bear was looking at him. Its head was raised and swung toward him and the small eyes watched. His knees began to flex under him for a swift thrust outward from the rock but the bear remained motionless and while he waited, taut in tenseness, he saw the big mouth open and stretch in a yawn and the white of the great teeth and the lips drawing lazily back and the muzzle crinkling. The jaws closed and the head swung away and dropped on the forepaws again.

The hot air, uncomfortable but not unendurable, beat against the man's face and the chill of the water sank into his body. Cautiously he reached and put the knife between his teeth and placed both hands on the rock and began to draw himself forward and up on it. The bear's head rose and swung toward him and the small eyes watched. He waited and the bear did not move and he inched forward until at last he was on his hands and knees on the rock. Slowly he shifted position until he was sitting crosslegged, ready for an instant scrambling push striking into the water. The bear watched and when he was settled the big head swung straight again and sank down. Gradually the man's muscles softened and the instant alertness eased out of them. The hot air dried his clothes, and the fingers holding the knife now in his right hand relaxed. The smoke clouds rolled and made a strange unnatural dusk and the fire roared through it along the shore. The man's back and buttocks ached with the strain of his position on the hard rock. Slowly he shifted again until he was stretched full length on his side with his face toward the bear and his head pillowed on his left arm. The bear's ears twitched upright but the big head did not move and in a moment the ears eased limp again. The heat in the air lessened slightly and the fire roared dwindling along the shore. Far off it reached the edge of the gorge of the stream running out of the valley and sought to leap across and failed and fell back and was content with the timber it had taken.

The sun, hidden behind the smoke clouds, dropped behind the westward heights and the remaining flames around the lake sent weird lights dancing in the murky dark over the water. The man's eyes closed and opened abruptly and closed again and at last remained closed. The wind died and the smoke trailed away in wisps and the high stars wheeled in the clearing sky above the two silent figures pinpointed together on their rock in the heart of the soaring immensity of the timeless mountains.

The man woke suddenly in the grey dawn of the light before sunrise. He had rolled over in his sleep on his back and the knife had slipped from his opened hand. As awareness flooded him he fought the stiffness in his muscles to turn quickly on his side and fumble for the knife handle. The seeking fingers halted before they found it. The rock stretched away from him empty and open to the sky. The bear was gone. He pushed to his feet and stooped to take the knife and stood straight. The sound of splashing water turned his head toward the near shore. The bear was emerging from the lake on to a short sandy spit. Against the background of rising slope with charred trunks thrusting above blackened floor and thin wisps of smoke still spiralling lazily, it was a miracle of enduring life, enormous and indomitable in the half-light in defiance of the barren desolation. It started inland and drew back with quick mincing steps. There were hot embers under the ashes and flames ready to break forth flickering strong in many places at the push of any breeze.

The man slipped into the water and swam to the sandy spit. Working from there he made systematic forays into the deeper water until he found the rifle. He washed away the bottom muck and broke it open to blow the barrel and firing chamber clean. Shivering in the first rays of the sun, he moved along the shoreline as the bear had done, stepping slowly but swinging his arms vigorously to warm his muscles.

Hidden in an aspen thicket a short way out on the parkland above the stricken forest, the great bear stood over the carcass of a whitetail doe that had fallen in the flight of fear into the upper gorge and broken its neck. The bear had dragged the carcass to the open of the parkland and into the thicket. The big head lifted and the small eyes peered through the thicket. The man was passing, sixty yards away. A low rumble sounded in the bear's throat, soft and deep, not audible to the man and not meant to be. He strode on with the tireless stride of a man long used to the mountains. The bear watched him, its head turning slowly to follow his passing, and when his figure grew small in the distance the big head dropped to feed again.

August

In the clear light of early morning the man stood by the pool and looked at the shallow pan in his hands. The bottom of it was almost covered with the dull gleaming flakes.

405

The pool silt had become richer as he worked deeper into it. He took the leather pouch from a pocket and shook the flakes into it. This was his third panning of the morning and already the pouch was full. He went to his camp and behind it among the trees and stopped by a flat stone. He heaved at the stone to raise one side and braced it against one leg while he set a piece of stout branch to prop it up. In a hollow underneath lay a five-pound salt bag filled to plumpness and another partly filled. He emptied the pouch into the second bag and lowered the stone into place. He went back by the pool and stood slapping the pan gently against his thigh while he looked out over the valley. The air was fresh on his face and mystic cloud shadows wandered on the mountain wall at the head of the valley. He dropped the pan on the sandbar and took the rifle from the grassbank and strode off down the valley with the sun warm in his face. He was close to the valley entrance,

where the big boulders of an ancient rockslide had rolled out to become bedded in the ageless sod, when he met the bear, suddenly, coming toward him around one of the rocks.

The bear stopped and the man stopped, thirty feet apart. Slowly the man swung up the rifle so that his left hand could grip the barrel and his right forefinger slipped around the trigger. The bear watched him and the low rumble, soft and deep, formed in its throat. Slowly the man stepped to the left, moving in a half-circle, always facing the bear, yielding the right of way. The bear watched him, turning its head to follow him. When he completed the half-circle the man turned, deliberately turned from the bear, and his will clamped hard on his muscles to hold them to a steady walk away. When he had travelled some forty feet he looked back. The bear had gone forward on its own way and its big, ridiculously tiny-tailed rump was toward him as it overturned scattered stones and sniffed for the scuttling insects.

Five hours later, in the early afternoon, the man returned to his camp, back-packing the dressed carcass of a small whitetail buck. Across the valley the great bear lay on the ledge and watched him. He could see it there, a dark shape on the stone, while he skinned the deer and pegged out the hide for drying. He built a big fire of dry wood and while he waited for it to turn down to glowing embers he began cutting the meat into strips. He looked across the valley and saw the bear rise and disappear into the dark recess of the crevice and he nodded to himself. He knew its habits now.

The man raised poles in a rack over the fire and hung the strips of meat on it. He piled green wood on the fire and retreated from the smoke and sat resting with his back against a tree looking out across the valley.

The stream gathered speed as it left the valley and skipped in stony steps down past the edge of the burned-out forest where new green was beginning to rise above blackened ground. It dropped, gaining momentum, into the deepening gorge that took it farther down and where it raced and whirled in rock pools and raced on. The man stood on the low cliff edge overlooking the gorge. Thirty-five feet below him the great bear lay beside the stream. Its new coat was lengthening and a pale silvery cast was beginning to touch the tips of the thick-grown hairs. It lay limp and relaxed on the pebble strand. Suddenly a forepaw darted and flipped a fat trout flashing through the air and the bear leaped from its lying position to seize the fish as it landed flopping a dozen feet away. Lazily the bear fed, then wandered up the stream to where a smooth rock slanted straight into the water. Standing at the top of the

A forepaw darted and flipped a fat trout through the air.

slant, it gave a small bounce and went forward on its belly on the rock with legs outstretched and slid splashing into the stream. The man leaned over the cliff to watch and a soundless chuckle shook him. Lazily the bear climbed again to the top of the smooth rock and rolled over on its back and slid down, tail first, thick legs waving. Its rump struck the water with a spattering smack and the chuckle in the man grew into sound. The bear whirled and rose in the water and looked up. It looked away and inspected the opposite bank in plain pretence that the man was not there. Its head dropped and it shuffled away down the gorge and out of sight around the first turn.

The chill of the night lingered, gradually giving way to the sun's warmth. The morning air was crystal in its distinct clarity. The man stood by the pool and looked at the pan in his hands. There were only a few scattered flakes in it. The pool was almost worked out. He started to walk along the stream, studying its flow and occasional silt banks. His steps slowed and at last stopped and he looked out over the valley. New colour was showing on the clumps of low bushes that dotted the valley floor. Berries were ripening there and along the climbing sides of the valley. Far by the opposite slope he saw the bear rise out of the bushes, settling back on its haunches like a big sitting squirrel, stripping berries into its mouth with its long foreclaws. He strode back to his camp and tossed the pan to one side and lifted the flat stone. Three full salt bags lay there now and a fourth partly filled. He emptied the leather pouch into the fourth bag and lowered the stone in place. Rifle in hand he wandered out through his side of the valley, tasting berries along the way.

September

The green of the valley was changing, darker with a brown cast in barely discernible splotches. The thin cutting edge of fall was invading the air. Among the trees behind the man's camp the flat stone lay undisturbed with grass blades curling over it. The camp itself was neat and orderly. Fire-wood was stacked in a long pile. A little to one side the pan lay, no longer glinting bright, spotted with dirt and rust. Where the tree fringe abutted the open of the valley the man sat, cross-legged in the sun. Across his lap was a deerskin, tanned with lye from wood ashes and worked to fairly smooth flexibility. Carefully he sliced into the leather, cutting doubled patterns for moccasins to replace his worn boots.

Across the valley, working along the base of the slope and up a short way, the great bear was digging for ground squirrels, ripping into the soil several feet with half a dozen powerful strokes and lying flat on its belly for the final reaching, scraping thrust. The increasing richness of the fur with its silver tipping shone in the clear light. Alternately the man bent to his cutting and raised his head to watch the bear. Suddenly, with the suddenness of decision, he rose and strode back among the spruce and juniper and about, until he found a level space between the trees to his liking. Here he laid out a rough rectangle, scratching the lines with his boot heel. He marked off space inside for a bunk and another rectangle, small and against one end of the other, for a fireplace. He studied his design and nodded to himself and looked around, estimating the standing timber close by. He strode to his shelter and crawled to the low end to inspect what remained of his staple supplies. He came out carrying a small pack and closed the open end of the shelter with its log barrier. He strode to the flat stone and filled the leather pouch from one of the bags. A few moments later he was striding eastward out of the valley with the rifle in one hand, the lead rope of the burro in the other.

A cool wind whipped down the valley, whispering of the winter still hidden far up in the soaring peaks. It moved

410

over the changing green that was darker with the brown splotches plainer and spreading. It moved out the valley entrance and down the rolling slope where the man strode steadily forward, facing straight into it. He was leading a loaded pack horse now and the burdened burro trotted behind. At the crest of the slope he stopped and searched his back trail for long minutes. His head rose higher and his stride lengthened as he passed through the valley entrance and the horse and the burro followed.

Three miles away on the ridge overlooking the last slope, ten feet back in the timber that topped the ridge, two men stood in the tree shadows and watched the three figures entering the valley. The taller of the two, lean even in his thick mackinaw jacket, had a narrow hatchet face gashed by a thin-lipped mouth. The other, shorter but bulking thick from shoulders to hips, had burnt-out eyes in a round bullet head. The thin-lipped one snapped his fingers and nodded to the other. Together they went back deeper into the timber and mounted the two horses there and rode out and down the ridge, circling to the right toward the high shoulder of climbing rock that would give them a view out over the valley.

Restless on its rock ledge, the great bear lay on the stone and watched the empty camp across the valley. Its ears twitched and the big head rose and swung to the right. It saw the man entering the valley and the horse and burro following. It saw the man stop and look toward it and wave his arms and start forward again. The low rumbling, soft and deep, rolled out from the ledge and died away in the afternoon wind. Quietly the bear watched the man stride toward his camp and begin untying the packs. Quietly it rose and padded on the stone into the darkness of the crevice.

Vigour flowed through the man. The afternoon air of his valley flooded his muscles with strength. His axe leaped into his hands and he felled four trees of the right foundation size and lopped away the branches and cut the logs to the lengths he wanted and notched them; using the axe handle for a measure he took three pieces of rope and used the three-four-five rule to square the corners as he fitted the logs together. As he straightened from checking the fourth joint he saw first the heavy boots, and as his eyes swept upward he saw the small wicked muzzle of the rifle bearing on his belly and the thin-lipped gash of a mouth in the narrow face.

The two men wasted no time. They asked their questions and when he did not answer they roped him to a thick tree. They searched through his camp and came back by him and built a fire and when this was blazing strong they took his rifle and emptied the magazine and laid it with the barrel reaching into the flames and waited for the metal to heat.

The man stood tight against the tree and the pale hazel of his eyes was startling against the dead bloodless brown of his broad wind-burned face. He stared out over the valley and his gaze moved upward and stopped two hundred yards up the opposite slope, and the beginning of living colour crept into his face. The muscles along his jaw were ridged hard and he waited, cautious in his cunning, until the hot steel was close to his flesh before he spoke. He spoke quickly and bobbed his head toward the far slope. The two others turned. They saw the ledge and the uneven dark outline of the crevice. They spoke briefly together and the burnt-eyed one swung abruptly and started across the valley and the thin-lipped one sat hump-kneed on the ground and picked up his rifle and set it across his lap.

The man tight against the tree and the thin-lipped one hump-kneed on the ground watched the other move out and across the valley floor. They saw him stop at the base of the opposite side and look around for the trail and find it. They saw him start up, hurrying now, and reach the ledge almost running and disappear into the crevice.

Time passed and they watched, each in his own intentness, and nothing moved across the way. The ledge under

They wasted no time—where had he hidden the gold?

its overhanging rock slept in its own quietness in the afternoon sun. The thin-lipped one rose and unloosened the rope holding the man to the tree and ordered him ahead and prodded him in the small of the back with the rifle. The man led and the thin-lipped one followed and they started across the valley floor.

Deep in the crevice darkness the great bear stood over the crumpled body. The big head with the small eyes, red-rimmed now, swung slowly from side to side. The sound of running steps had brought it from sleep into instant alertness. The forward leap out of the inner darkness into the dimness near the crevice entrance and the incredibly swift slashing stroke of forepaw had been instinctive reactions to the challenging affront of invasion. Silently it had dragged the body back into the protective darkness and stepped over it, facing the entrance. The scent of the body, familiar yet unfamiliar, rose in its nostrils and caution at an experience never before known held it waiting in the darkness, listening for further sound.

413

Striding steadily, the man led the way up the trail. His face was a fixed mask and his muscles bunched in tight tension. When the bear broke from the crevice, red-rimmed eyes blinking for swift focus in the sunlight, the man leaped sideways off the trail and down the steep slope, falling and rolling over the sharp rocks and hard against the trunk of a sturdy spruce. He scrambled to his feet and jumped for the first limb and swung his legs in to the trunk and began climbing.

Above him on the trail the thin-lipped one swung up the rifle and fired and the bullet thudded into the bear's left shoulder and scraped the bone and bore back along the side under the skin. In a silent rush the great bear drove down the trail and the thin-lipped one screamed and turned to run and a crashing forepaw crushed his spine forward into his breastbone and raked tearing down through the muscles of his back. The big jaws closed on the already lifeless body and shook it and flung it away.

Close against the trunk, the man peered through the thick branches of the spruce. Below him the great bear quartered the ground like a huge dog on a hunt, moving with a silent flowing deadliness, raising its head often to test the wind. It limped slightly, favouring its left foreleg, and the recurrent pain from the flesh wound in the shoulder swelled the steady rage within and brightened the reddened rims of the eyes. It worked back along the trail near the valley floor and looked across at the man's camp. Abruptly it swung and with steady purpose went up the trail to the ledge and passed along the slopeside and faded into the tangled growth near the head of the valley.

Safe in his spruce, the man watched it go and disappear from his sight. He waited. At last he climbed to the ground and scrambled up to the trail and grabbed the rifle there. Quickly he ejected the spent cartridge shell and pumped another cartridge into the firing chamber. Quickly he checked the magazine and saw it was almost full. Cautious and alert he slipped down and started across the valley.

*As the bear emerged, the captive leaped aside and the
thin-lipped one raised his rifle and fired.*

The packhorse and burro grazed by the camp, quiet now after the brief startling from the single shot across the way. In the fringe of trees behind them and around the camp nothing stirred except the wind whispering its endless murmur through the evergreen branches. As the man approached, downwind, he stopped often to peer forward and swing his head to scan the whole long fringe of trees, searching with his eyes every possible cover. It was the drumming of the horse's hoofs as it pounded to the length of its picket rope and jerked around, strangling, that whirled him toward the sound. The great bear streaked toward him out of thicket shadow and he fired in the instant, instinctively—aiming as rapidly as he could pump the gun. The first shot bored into the junction of neck and right shoulder and shattered the bone there and the second smashed into the massive breast and ripped back through the lungs. The great bear drove ahead, uneven in bounding stride with a deep coughing tearing its throat, and the third shot struck through the mouth and back into the spine. The man leaped aside and the bear's rush took it past and it crumpled forward to the ground. The man stood by the bear's body and stared down. It was smaller with the life gone. The muscles of the man's shoulders shook a little and he swung his head slowly from one side to the other and the flat planes of his face were hard as the rock formations ringing the valley.

He stood by the rectangle of notched logs a long time. Quietly he turned and went to the flat stone and took the plump salt bags from under it and carried them over by his shelter and began to prepare his packs. Half an hour later he strode across the valley floor and the packhorse and the burro followed. The sun, dropping below the far peaks, was behind him. The chill rising wind beat against his back. Unbelievably small in the vastness he strode out of the valley, and with him went a new loneliness and a sense of something lost.

The Shark Cage

JAMES ALDRIDGE

BEN AMINO had lost his left arm—from elbow to wrist—to a shark. The shark had attacked him underwater in a remote Egyptian bay along the Red Sea coast, where he had been taking underwater films for an American film company. By some miracle he had managed to reach the surface of the coral reef in a bloody heap. By some greater miracle, his son Davy had flown him, unconscious, back to Cairo in the small Auster aeroplane.

Apart from the responsibility of getting his father to a hospital, it had been a terrorizing experience for a boy who had never flown a plane by himself before. And Ben Amino had realized it was not going to be easy to change suddenly from a withdrawn and short-spoken father to a grateful but uncertain parent who must try to find a way of penetrating the barrier his son had erected against him.

417

"This time," Ben told his son, "I'm going to build a shark cage."

"What's that?" Davy asked suspiciously, not commenting at all on his father's intention of returning to Shark Bay.

"It's a metal cage," Ben said in his impatient way.

Then he corrected himself. He must try to change even the tone of his voice, although it was going to be difficult for a man of forty to express himself gently when he had never been inclined that way.

"It's a small iron cage big enough for a man to stand up in underwater so that he can photograph sharks in safety," he explained. "You're inside, and they're outside. Cousteau has one on his ship. But mine will have to be much smaller, and light enough to carry in a small aircraft and dismantle too."

"How can you fly with one arm?" Davy asked him.

"It's my left arm that's gone," Ben told him. "Which doesn't matter on the Auster. I can use my right on the throttles. That's what counts. . . ."

"Are you allowed to fly an aeroplane with only one arm?"

"They don't know about it," Ben said. "It's eight months since it happened. And there was no accident to the plane. They have no reason to know I lost an arm. My next medical check isn't due until November, and we'll be gone from Egypt by then. I can get the plane all right whether I have a false arm or not. They won't know. . . ."

He was making it seem so easy, when he suddenly realized that Davy was trying to make it difficult.

Davy did not want to go back to Shark Bay. He did not want to face again the terror of seeing his father rising bloody and mangled from the sea. He did not want to remember his terrified efforts to get his father into the plane, to start the plane, to get it off the ground, to fly it on course; to find the airfield, and finally to put the plane down among the airliners without smashing it to pieces.

"This time," Ben assured him again, trying to be patient

with Davy's desire to retreat from him, "there will be no accidents. I promise. . . ."

How could he promise such a thing? Yet it was the least he could do.

Ben still had only a hazy idea of the whole project. The last time he had photographed sharks under water for the Universal Film Company he had hoped to collect enough money from his shark films to take the boy home, to try to set him up in a decent school, or to arrange for someone to look after him. But eight months of hospitals and doctors and keeping the flat in Cairo until he was out of hospital had eaten away all his stake money. There was not enough left now to pay his and the boy's fares back home, and to live there a few months while he found some sort of work for an ex-bush-pilot with one arm and no wife.

"D'you want to come and see the cage being made?" he asked the boy.

"Yes!" Davy said seriously.

"Come on then," he said, trying to sound light-hearted about it.

Ben had drawn a rough plan of the cage, and he had persuaded a native blacksmith in a big car-repair shop to attempt it. The Greek foreman had agreed (with a pound in his pocket) and the Egyptian smith and his assistant, who was even younger than Davy, began working the angle iron and mild steel strips into four separate walls of a cage.

"It would be better to have the door on top," the smith told him before beginning to weld the flat strips to the angle iron on the greasy garage floor.

"I might not have the strength to push it up under water," Ben argued, making the gesture of pushing above his head with his one and half arms.

"But this door is too big, too long," the smith said with a shrug. "It will be stiff."

"It'll do," Ben insisted.

He tried to explain the construction plan to Davy, but

the boy seemed so uninterested in explanation that Ben did not pursue it, and he allowed the boy to watch with his own eyes. Ben had already noticed that his son observed everything; but he disliked being taught.

Ben kept his eye on it to be sure it was done properly. He watched the smith cutting and welding and drilling, assisted by the Arab boy, Mahmoud, who never said a word, although he worked like a man. The boy had perfected the helper's art. He knew when and where to hold the thin steel strips for the smith to cut and drill. If the smith needed a hammer or a cold-chisel it was in the smith's hand before he could ask for it—like a surgeon being supplied by a well-drilled team of assistants.

As the cage took shape Ben asked his son what he thought of it.

"How will you keep it standing up underwater?" Davy asked.

"I'll weight the floor and lash the sides to the coral," Ben said.

The smith broke a drill with a loud crack, and while he was hunting for another one in his tool box he told Mahmoud to weld the door strips together. Ben and Davy watched the Arab boy light the acetylene torch, adjust the flame to its blue point, adjust his cracked goggles, and begin welding the last of the mild steel strips to the door frames.

"Plenty of weld!" Ben warned the boy.

Mahmoud grinned. "*Iowa, ya bey*," he said.

But Ben watched him carefully to be sure that the welding was not slip-shod. He stood over the boy until he realized that Davy had deliberately walked away. What for? Ben looked at Davy's back and guessed it was a strange act of loyalty to the Arab boy, who was obviously quite capable of welding the door without any adult supervision.

Once it was built, the next problem was transporting the cage in a small hired aeroplane without frightening the

From inside the cage, Ben would photograph the sharks.

people who owned the plane. The less they saw of the strange iron cage the better. Even dismantled, it was far too cumbersome and wide to fit into the fuselage of an Auster.

The only way to carry it would be to lash it along the bottom of the fuselage on the outside. But that would have to be well arranged, otherwise it might shift in flight, with disastrous results.

Ben had his friends among the Egyptian aeroplane riggers at the little airfield, and he explained what he wanted to one of them who was called Salaam by his friends because of his habit of saying: *Ya Salaam* (Good gracious!) to all events, be it a successful operation on an aeroplane or some serious crash on the airfield.

"*Ya Salaam!*" Salaam said to Ben when he saw the cage. "You can't fly that on the Auster."

"Why not?" Ben asked. "She'll lift the weight easily enough. . . ."

Salaam shook his head and "Ya Salaamed" and showed Ben the thin tubular fuselage of the Auster braced only by wooden stringers.

"They must be elastic in flight," Salaam said. "If you lash a rigid steel weight to them you will put too much local strain on the tail. And then . . . *Ya Salaam!*"

Ben might fly it all right, but it would dangerously weaken the whole structure of the plane.

"But there's a Beechcraft in the hangar," Salaam told him. "It will be better."

The Beechraft was an efficient and tough American plane with a big engine. This one had been bought up by the Egyptians from the oil company which Ben had originally worked for. He had been flying oil geologists over the Egyptian deserts in Beechcrafts and Fairchilds, but now they were beat-up and rotting in the hangars.

"Under here, you see?" Salaam said, under the fuselage of one of the Beeches.

Ben saw and remembered the four eyebolts on the fuselage which were used for tying down a plane in the open desert in case of high winds.

"Perfect," Ben said.

Salaam opened a panel in the back of the fuselage and showed him where he could attach two more brackets to which he could lash the cage.

"What about the engine of this one? It used to take oil like a sieve," Ben said.

"It will be all right for another twenty hours, and I have some very heavy oil."

He was safe with Salaam, and he felt half-way there.

It had not been unusual in Ben's Canadian days to fly small planes with long lumps of mining equipment lashed outboard to the fuselage. But this old Beechcraft was very slack on the controls, and its engine lost compression even in take-off, so that he felt as if he were flying the shark cage itself.

"All right?" he asked Davy.

Davy was white, and Ben did not know if that was caused by the hot air bumps over the desert or by Davy's natural fear of aeroplanes, or by some other anticipation of danger yet to come at Shark Bay.

"Can't you go up higher," Davy asked, "where there aren't any bumps?"

"We're climbing as fast as we can," Ben shouted over the unimpressive roar of the worn-out engine. "That shark cage is too far forward. . . ."

Even with full tail-trim adjustment the Beechcraft was nose heavy. Ben held the stick well back, but his false left arm was already cutting into his flesh as a result. He had to keep the plane delicately balanced; if he pulled the stick back too far the nose would suddenly lift, and then she would probably spin out of control.

"There are peppermints in my pocket," Ben said. "Get them out."

Davy put his hand in Ben's shirt pocket and took out the roll of peppermints. He put one in his father's mouth because Ben dare not let anything go.

"Do you feel sick?" Ben asked.

Davy shook his head, and Ben realized he shouldn't have asked that question. It probably invoked bad memories of the last flight, when Davy had been very sick. But this time Ben had given him some air-sick pills.

"Do you want to feel it?" Ben asked, nodding at the stick.

Davy shook his head and looked at his father's aluminium arm, and at the leather-covered alloy hand. Where the false arm joined the real one at the elbow there was already a large red wound which was beginning to bleed. It looked raw; but when Davy glanced at his father's face to see how he could bear it, Ben simply looked back, impassive.

"Like trying to steer a heavy freight train," Ben shouted.

He made light work of it, but he felt as if he were holding the plane aloft in the air with his bad arm, which was beginning to feel the strain.

"There it is," Ben shouted thankfully when they came over a white bay among the ten thousand others along the naked green line of sea and desert.

Ben had heard from an Egyptian marine biologist of this new bay, which was supposed to be full of both sharks and large manta rays. It also was called Shark Bay, as they all were, and like the others it was simply a curved strip of inaccessible coral sand rimmed by featureless desert, impossible to approach except by light plane or from the sea.

"Hold on tight," Ben shouted as they began to go down. "She'll bump. . . ."

The approach was simple. But the moment they levelled off over the white and yellow sand the surface changed aspect from an apparently smooth stretch to an incredibly lumpy one.

The moment the plane touched down, something underneath seemed to slip out of place, and the plane slewed round in a vicious curve. They heard a heavy rip in the

The plane slewed round in a vicious curve.

fuselage, and the crash of something coming through into the after compartment. The plane bumped up once and then came down to a dead stop with another sad crashing noise below. . . .

"Are you all right?" Davy asked his father. "What's happened?"

Ben's false arm had almost been ripped off by the sudden jerk of the stick forward, and he was obviously in pain. He was tearing at the straps which bound the false limb to the real one, and he worked desperately until he had freed his raw flesh from the torture of metal and leather.

"Blast this thing," he said angrily "It's worse than no arm at all."

He was cursing it until he saw his son's face. Then he remembered himself, and he calmed down. But when he saw this old terror in the boy's face, he asked himself if he was doing the right thing—dragging his son back over this frightening experience. Yet, from the beginning, the idea resolved itself into a necessity for both their sakes.

Ben was not a subtle man, and doggedness was the only way he knew of overcoming his difficulties.

"It'll be all right," he told Davy and jumped out to inspect the damage.

It was not serious. The edge of the shark cage had sliced off a large lump of coral protruding from the sand. It was this lump which had smashed through the fuselage and made such a noise. If the coral had not been so neatly sliced off, it might have gone through the tail plane, with irreparable results.

"Nothing much," Ben the improviser said. "We can patch the fuselage. . . ."

But Davy had already gone to the sea's edge, where he was dipping his hot face in the water and rubbing it over his hair and his neck.

"Poor kid," Ben said again.

Then he shook off that feeling. "Poor kidding" his son was not going to help anybody.

The shark cage was slightly bent from the blow on the coral, but with Davy's silent help Ben had assembled it by midday.

They waited until the sun was down, resting under the plane. Then they bolted the pieces together. Davy put the bolts in place and Ben used the wrench with his good arm to make sure that they were tight. They had hung the door on its hinges in time for nightfall.

"Do you think they can get my other arm through that?" Ben joked, admiring the cage.

"Are you going to wear your metal arm under water?" Davy asked.

"No. That's worse than having none at all," Ben said.

He did not say that he could never get the arm back on over his bruised flesh.

They slept under the plane, and this time Ben had thought of everything for his son: soft drinks and even biscuits and tinned fruit, which they ate with their fingers while Ben showed him how to identify the constellations.

In the early morning Ben reconnoitred the best place underwater for the cage, but they found it difficult to roll it over the sand to the edge of the coral reef.

"Better wear your shoes," Ben told Davy, who had cut his foot.

Ben himself was not yet used to being one-armed, and his temper was short by the time the cage was ready to tip over the edge of the reef into the twenty feet of clear water. Davy helped. He did what he was told to do— silently; but he never volunteered a move, as most boys would surely be inclined to.

"When I say push, give it all you've got," Ben told him, "and then jump clear of the ropes. . . ."

He had attached four ropes to the top of the cage. That way the cage would not fall in sideways, but would go down the right way up.

"Now push!" Ben said.

They slipped and struggled until the cage started to topple over the reef.

"Get out of the way," Ben shouted.

But Davy was already clear when the cage went in. The ropes tightened on the stakes which Ben had driven into the sand, and the cage was suspended underwater. Ben put on his mask and went down to take a look at it.

"That's pretty good, Davy," Ben said when he came out after fixing the cage where it should be on the sea floor. "Now I'll lash it to the coral and we're all set. . . ."

He noticed then that Davy had already erected the canvas shelter under which they would spend the hot part of the day. He had also carried down one half of the little air compressor, so that Ben could set it up.

"I'm finally getting somewhere," Ben decided.

The underwater camera which the Universal Film Company had sent him was built to take 35 mm wide screen film and lenses. That was the point of this expedition. The company would pay up to five thousand dollars for a thousand feet of good shark film, and an extra thousand

Ben braced the camera on the side of

dollars for any shot of a big manta ray.

The camera was heavy, but Ben slung it down on one of the ropes, and then pulled on his aqualung.

"You can lie on the coral edge and watch if you like," he told Davy, showing him how he could stretch out in the few inches of water behind a bar of coral and put his face in the water over the deep edge.

"I know," Davy said.

"But don't go in with the aqualung."

Ben had brought along an extra lung. He had already shown Davy how to use it in a safe inlet behind one of the reefs, where the sharks could not enter. Davy was a good swimmer and he had easily mastered the lung.

"I won't be long," Ben said and lowered himself in with the rope.

Once he was under the silver-blue surface, he looked around hopefully to see if any sharks had appeared to *the cage and pushed the trigger button.*

sample his bait of donkey meat. The meat was pouring out thin black streaks of blood into the clear coral sea. There were herds of small fish nosing it curiously, but nothing big in sight. He slid the camera down the rope, and he congratulated himself on his ingenuity when he entered the cage—an almost fool-proof approach and a safe position for shark filming. He closed and lashed the door, and waited.

He had to wait until after he had gone down again in the afternoon before the first sharks appeared. They came, as they always did, from nowhere. One moment there were no sharks, then mysteriously, with a wave of the hand, one was nosing at the donkey meat in front of him. By the time he had raised the camera, there were two more nearby, one of them a tiger shark with two striped pilot fish cruising over his nose bulge. Ben braced the camera on the side of the cage and pushed the trigger button. The nearest

429

shark fled in fright. They had not yet tasted blood. When they did they would be much bolder; so he waited.

He was not upset to be back among these terrors of flesh and blood which had cut him up so badly. He felt very safe in the cage. But he did feel, quite clearly, the memorized pain in his arm where the teeth had slashed him. But he felt it in the part of the arm which was no longer there.

"This is the last time," he was saying to himself. "When I've made this stake I won't come back. It's not fair to the boy. . . ."

He knew he was too much of an improviser. That was all right for bush piloting and the sort of knock-about flying he had been doing in Egypt. In fact, looking back on it, improvisation had almost become his life. How else did a pilot like him operate or even survive? But that was not such a good method of life for a man with a son to bring up. He must (he decided, looking at the wrinkled hide of a shark not six feet away) give it some more serious thought later on. He did not want Davy to grow up the same way.

There were two sharks attacking the meat now, and as they turned away they swam by the cage without fear. He held the camera on them.

"Not me!" he said as one of them came back to look at him. "Not me. . . . ."

He had the choice of five or six in range. Some of them were basking sharks, but two of them were tigers. One was lying on the bottom near a large undersea rock of dead coral, the place where he had hoped to see the big rays. He had also anchored one of the guy ropes to it.

"Take your time," he warned himself.

The inclination was always to make the film sequences too short. He was supporting the camera with his delicate lump of serrated flesh. It hurt, but it worked. Then suddenly one of the larger basking sharks approached the cage very boldly, and when it swung away it slapped the side of the cage with its tail.

The cage teetered back and forth and almost fell over on its side; but it was held up by the ropes which he had lashed to the mushroom coral behind him. He waited for it to settle, and then he decided he had had enough for the time being. He had used up all his film.

"One more and I'm through," he told Davy when he had surfaced.

"Why did the shark knock the cage?" Davy asked.

He had been watching from the top, and Ben shrugged it off.

"Hard to say," he said. "Probably an accident. . . ."

But Davy looked unconvinced, and to encourage him out of his fears Ben told him to start packing up the gear so that they could leave the moment he came out.

He was an unlucky man, he always had been; and though he had learned to live with his bad luck, he was getting too old to survive it much longer.

He had finished filming the sharks. The meat was finished, which meant that most of them had gone. But he still waited doggedly on in the hope of a thousand-dollar manta ray appearing over the coral rock, where they liked to come to be de-loused by the smaller fish.

"Good heavens!" he said. "I'm in luck. . . ."

A shadow, a speckled moving cloud was cruising along the bottom beside the reef. It was a manta with monstrous lobed jaws, flying in a heavy and cumbersome manner as if it were blind or hurt or simply old. It was knocking small lumps of coral off the reef as it came, and the white sand below it was swirling off the bottom as it flapped its giant pointed wings in heavy propulsion.

"Come on you beauty," Ben encouraged.

It was coming right by the cage, and though he was lost in the elation of filming it, he saw that its wings, or its massive head, were going to foul the rope which he had tied from the cage to the coral rock on the sea floor.

Ben rattled the camera on the bars to divert the ray from its course, but it flew on and fouled the rope.

431

"How do I get out of this?" Ben thought.

In the shock of contact, or in the sudden and powerful lashing of the ray's wings, the cage was pulled forward by the guy rope. Ben felt it going over, as if it had been hit by a destroyer. . . .

For a moment he thought that the manta was going to drag the cage and himself out to sea. He was on his side. He knew that the moorings behind had snapped, or the coral had broken, and he felt the cage roll over and over on the bottom under great force. Then, with a sudden jerk, the ray was free of the rope and it blundered away in a fog of sand and coral dust.

"How do I get out of this?" Ben thought.

He was lying on his side in the cage. The door was flat on the sea-bed. The cage had also been pushed out of shape, and the door itself was forced in on one side. He felt like an enormous fish in a bowl. It had been a small enough prison standing up in it, but lying down like this he could hardly manoeuvre.

"If I ever get out of this one, it will be a miracle," he said.

He began to lever the cage by putting his foot through the bars on to the sea floor, trying to turn the cage over to bring the door on top. Impossible. He tried to bend the mild steel strips, but the smithy had made them too strong. He shook the door underneath, in the hope that he could break something, but Mahmoud's welding held.

"I've had it," he told himself at last.

He rolled over to see if Davy was watching. He could not see Davy's mask on the surface. Then he looked at his air gauge and cursed himself for a fool for waiting that extra five minutes—for that thousand miserable dollars.

He had no more than twenty minutes' air left, at the outside.

It was two minutes, it seemed like an hour.

He had tried everything again, and then he looked up and saw Davy's mask. Ben lay on his back and waved. He could see Davy's hand wave back. Ben made the motion with one arm of undoing the nuts which held the cage together, and he tried to show Davy that he needed the spanner.

Davy's face disappeared in an instant.

When he came back Ben saw the spanner in the boy's hand in the water.

"Don't drop it," he bubbled out through his air as if the boy could hear.

Davy dropped it, but he had tied it to a fishing cord, and he guided it by swinging it into the cage. Ben did not wait to untie it but began to reach out for the bolts.

But the round heads of the bolts were on the inside, the square heads outside. No amount of arm-twisting could bring the spanner to play on them. He looked up and shook his head. Davy was not there.

He calculated that he had fifteen minutes of air left, when he saw one of the guy ropes coming his way. Davy was paying it out to him, and he guessed that the boy was going to try his strength at pulling the cage upright. On the surface it would have been impossible, but with the cage underwater he might have a chance.

"Okay!" Ben bubbled out when he had tied the rope to the cage roof. "But hurry!"

Davy's mask disappeared, and in half a minute he saw the rope straining tight, but there was no impression on the position of the cage. This was hopeless, and when Davy's face appeared again Ben whirled his hand around and around.

"The plane," he was saying into the sea. "Start the plane. . . ."

He made the gestures of propellor-turning, of stick, of throttle, until the boy understood and disappeared again. While he waited, Ben tried to calculate what the boy would do: whether he would have enough sense to attach the rope to the tail-wheel, whether he could manage to start the engine with its tendency to flood, whether a thousand things would be done that would be right or wrong or successful, and even though he was underwater he had the

434

As the rope strained, the cage below heaved.

impression that he was sweating.

"Hurry up, Davy," he said and began to worry about the boy now.

If he was left down here Davy would never fly that Beechcraft off the ground. The plane was too old and too difficult for Davy to succeed a second time. This time Davy's life depended entirely on his own.

He felt the tug then.

"He's got it going. . . ."

The rope strained, but he thought it would be cut loose by one of the iron edges. He pushed it off with his good hand. He was cut to pieces already by pinches and slaps from the cage, but now that the plane was straining he knew he had a chance.

"He's got the brakes on," Ben told himself.

If they were old enough the brakes would give, and suddenly something did give.

The cage bounced along the floor, side down, and then the bottom struck the edge of the coral and it began to

435

right itself, not right up, but near enough.

"Hold it!" Ben cried desperately.

Regardless of the results to his good hand, Ben put his arm through the side and held the cage up to the coral. The rope slacked off, and he pulled it down and got a hitch on to a coral projection and tied it roughly on to one of the steel bars.

He could already feel his air valve beginning to drag. His gauge registered less than ten atmospheres, and he was obviously dragging out the last of it.

He pushed on the cage door, but even though it was upright it would not budge. The cage was so out of shape that the door was jammed in beyond hope of moving it by the force of an arm or a leg.

He looked up helplessly again. . . .

"I'm licked," he wept, "I'm licked. . . ."

He felt as if he were losing his head, but when he saw the boy's face again—the mask, the opaque oval of eyes— he showed the boy that he could not push the door open.

It was only when he saw Davy suddenly disappear and then re-appear, body and all, under the surface, that he began to look around anxiously to see what had happened to the sharks.

"Stay up!" he tried to wave at the boy.

Davy came down awkwardly. He was too small and too buoyant for the amount of air in the big lung, but he reached the cage and hung on. Ben wanted the air in that lung badly, but he looked frantically around to be sure that there were no sharks.

There were two, but they were basking a little way off near the rock.

Davy tried to pull the door open with his hands.

Ben thought of a hacksaw, but he knew they did not have one in the tool box.

He was out of ideas and almost out of air. He watched Davy, stupidly mesmerized, as the boy tied the other guy rope to the cage door.

What now?

Davy kicked frantically to dive deeper. Ben saw the boy swimming over towards the rock with all the broken rope he could find. The sharks lying on the floor near the rock could be any kind, as far as Ben could see, and he watched his son swim carefully around the rock dragging the tied length of rope so that it swung right around the rock.

"He's going to use it as a pulley," Ben realized, sucking at the valve and wondering which lungful would be the last.

He wanted to hurry the boy, but he knew he dare not.

He watched Davy's clumsy passage over the sleeping sharks. It was a bitter moment when he realized that youth should not be exposed to danger, even in the interests of life and death. He had always committed his greatest crimes against his son, simply by assuming that everything would be all right. Nothing was all right. Life itself was a trap, and he must guard the boy against it if he ever got out of this. He must guard the boy against even the simplest risks, the remotest dangers. . . .

Ben was dragging the very last gasps out of the lung as Davy completed the circuit safely and began to surface with the length of rope.

"Let me have your lung!" Ben gestured at him.

He pointed to his gauge and shook his head and pointed to his lung and to Davy's, indicating that he must lower it down quickly. . . .

Davy nodded.

Ben felt the valve rattling and resisting heavily with every short breath he took.

He had to suck it in from the depth of his stomach muscles to get the last inch of pressure out of it. He was feeling dizzy, and he wondered what was holding the boy up. He was not going to last, he knew it. . . .

The lung came down on the end of the cord.

Ben ripped off the mouthpiece of his own and pulled the hose of the new one through the bars, jamming his face against the cage so that he could get the mouthpiece through it into his mouth.

The mouthpiece was bubbling air automatically and he felt the first full drag of cold, metallic air enter his lungs.

Yet it seemed too late, because he was too exhausted by his last breathing efforts to do more than hold the side of the cage with his lump of an arm, hold the mouthpiece in with the other, and simply hang on to consciousness.

He was not aware of the tug on the cage until it began to topple over again. The rope, which was now attached to the twisted door and was then passed around the rock, began to tighten. He could see lumps of dead coral flying off the dead rock and the fish flying away and the sharks waking up.

Davy was revving up the Beechcraft and pulling on the rope with it.

Ben got a good grip on the mouthpiece of the lung with his teeth and used his good arm to hold on to the nearest lump of coral.

He could feel the strain on the rope now. He held on, feeling his flesh tearing on the coral.

Everything happened together:

The door was ripped open, the rope broke, and he lost his grip on the mouthpiece of the spare aqualung, which floated away. The cage itself began to teeter over to fall again. . . .

There was a second to get through the half-open door before it fell.

He felt the iron scrape his back as he flung his body forward. He felt the cage crack down on his heels as it fell over. He began to kick his way to the surface with bursting lungs.

Yet he could kill himself, even now.

If he did not remember to let the air in his lungs out, slowly, as he went up—the pressure of the air which he had breathed in would quickly expand as he got nearer the surface, and he would blow his lungs out.

"Let it out," he told himself, "slowly. . . ."

He burst to the top with his lips still whistling out air.

Then he gulped in the first draught of light and sun and air, right down to his diaphragm.

"Hurry!" Davy was shouting, putting his mask on to the water to see what was below. "There's a shark. . . ."

Ben knew real terror, that last of all terrors which drove men to exceed the limited capacities of normal strength and thought, and he thrashed his legs and arms and reached the coral shallows as if he were flying with his arms.

Davy helped him out, and he remembered the empty lung still on his back. He hardly had the strength to fall flat on his stomach in the hot shallow water. . . .

That was all.

He lay still and exhausted with his face in the hot shallows, feeling the sun. He heard Davy asking him, begging to know, if he was all right. He nodded slowly. He could hear the Beechcraft's engine still running. It was probably overheating.

"Turn the engine off, Davy," he managed.

The cage began to teeter over to fall again.

He heard the boy splash off, and then the silence as the rumble of the Beech's engine died in a hot cough. Ben knew he had to get up now or he would never get up.

He pulled the release buckles of the lung and the weight belt, and he crawled out of the harness. He got to his feet and reached the sand, where he lay down again on his back feeling every tear and rent in his body.

He knew then that he was a wasteful man.

But he knew it! That counted. And he would never again risk the life of the boy.

"I'm sorry, kid," he said, looking at the boy. "Are you all right?"

That solemn, frightened face was looking down at him.

"You did the right thing," Ben told him desperately.

It was more than true. Davy was not a willing volunteer, he was not much at anticipation, he would certainly never go around offering anyone generous slices of himself; but he was going to be a good man to have around when you were in a tight spot. Perhaps that was the value of improvisation, the temperament of both father and son; the dogged grip they both had on life.

"I left the camera. . . ." Ben said.

He sat up. The camera was insured and it would be nobody's loss. But the film in it—the sequence of the manta ray—was worth a thousand dollars.

"You're not going back in are you?" Davy said. "Are you?"

Ben knew he still had the pugnacity to do it, to find the other lung and go back under and get the camera. But other values began to intervene.

"I don't think so, Davy," he said. "I don't think so."

The boy was almost smiling in his embarrassment. He was trying to pity or comfort or assure his father—as far as he could.

Ben saw his son's relief, and his heart warmed to him.

Jimmy Goggles the God

H. G. WELLS

IT ISN'T everyone who's been a god," said the sunburnt man. "But it's happened to me. Among other things."

I intimated my sense of his condescension.

"It don't leave much for ambition, does it?" said the sunburnt man.

"I was one of those men who were saved from the *Ocean Pioneer*. Gummy! how time flies! It's twenty years ago. I doubt if you'll remember anything of the *Ocean Pioneer*?"

The name was familiar, and I tried to recall when and where I had read it. The *Ocean Pioneer*? "Something about gold dust." I said vaguely, "but the precise—"

"That's it," he said. "In a beastly little channel she hadn't no business in—dodging pirates. It was before they'd put the kybosh on that business. And there'd been

441

volcanoes or something and all the rocks was wrong.
There's places about by Soona where you fair have to
follow the rocks about to see where they're going next.
Down she went in twenty fathoms before you could have
dealt for whist, with fifty thousand pounds worth of gold
aboard, it was said, in one form or another."

"Survivors?"

"Three."

"I remember the case now," I said. "There was something about salvage—"

But at the word salvage the sunburnt man exploded into
language so extraordinarily horrible that I stopped aghast.
He came down to more ordinary swearing, and pulled
himself up abruptly. "Excuse me," he said, "but—salvage!"

He leant over towards me. "I was in that job," he said.
"Tried to make myself a rich man, and got made a god
instead. I've got my feelings—

"It ain't all jam being a god," said the sunburnt man,
and for some time conversed by means of such pithy but
unprogressive axioms. At last he took up his tale again.

"There was me," said the sunburnt man, "and a seaman
named Jacobs, and Always, the mate of the *Ocean Pioneer*.
And him it was that set the whole thing going. I remember
him now, when we was in the jolly boat, suggesting it all
to our minds just by one sentence. He was a wonderful
hand at suggesting things. 'There was forty thousand
pounds,' he said, 'on that ship, and it's for me to say just
where she went down.' It didn't need much brains to
tumble to that. And he was the leader from the first to the
last. He got hold of the Sanderses and their brig; they were
brothers, and the brig was the *Pride of Banya*, and he it
was bought the diving dress—a second-hand one with a
compressed air apparatus instead of pumping. He'd have
done the diving too, if it hadn't made him sick going down.
And the salvage people were mucking about with a chart
he'd cooked up, as solemn as could be, at Starr Race, a
hundred and twenty miles away.

"I can tell you we was a happy lot aboard that brig,

jokes and drink and bright hopes all the time. It all seemed so neat and clean and straightforward, and what rough chaps call a 'cert'. And we used to speculate how the other blessed lot, the proper salvagers, who'd started two days before us, were getting on, until our sides fairly ached. We all messed together in the Sanderses' cabin—it was a curious crew, all officers and no men—and there stood the diving-dress waiting its turn. Young Sanders was a humorous sort of chap, and there certainly was something funny in the confounded thing's great fat head and its stare, and he made us see it too. 'Jimmy Goggles', he used to call it, and talk to it like a Christian. Asked if he was married, and how Mrs. Goggles was, and all the little Goggleses. Fit to make you split. And every blessed day all of us used to drink the health of Jimmy Goggles in rum, and unscrew his eye and pour a glass of rum in him, until, instead of that nasty mackintosheriness, he smelt as nice in his inside as a cask of rum. It was jolly times we had in those days, I can tell you—little suspecting, poor chaps! what was a-coming.

"We weren't going to throw away our chances by any blessed hurry, you know, and we spent a whole day sounding our way towards where the *Ocean Pioneer* had gone down, right between two chunks of ropy grey rock—lava rocks that rose nearly out of the water. We had to lay off about half a mile to get a safe anchorage, and there was a thundering row who should stop on board. And there she lay just as she had gone down, so that you could see the top of the masts that was still standing perfectly distinctly. The row ended in all coming in the boat. I went down in the diving-dress on Friday morning directly it was light.

"What a surprise it was! I can see it all now quite distinctly. It was a queer-looking place, and the light was just coming. People over here think every blessed place in the tropics is a flat shore and palm trees and surf, bless 'em! This place, for instance, wasn't a bit that way. Not common rocks they were, undermined by waves; but great

443

curved banks like ironwork cinder heaps, with green slime below, and thorny shrubs and things just waving upon them here and there, and the water glassy calm and clear, and showing you a kind of dirty grey-black shine, with huge flaring red-brown weeds spreading motionless, and crawling and darting things going through it. And far away beyond the ditches and pools and the heaps was a forest on the mountain flank, growing again after the fires and cinder showers of the last eruption. And the other way forest, too, and a kind of broken—what is it?—amby-theatre of black and rusty cinders rising out of it all, and the sea in a kind of bay in the middle.

"The dawn, I say, was just coming, and there wasn't much colour about things, and not a human being but ourselves anywhere in sight up or down the channel. Except the *Pride of Banya*, lying out beyond a lump of rocks towards the line of the sea.

"Not a human being in sight," he repeated, and paused.

"*I* don't know where they came from, not a bit. And we were feeling so safe that we were all alone that poor young Sanders was a-singing. I was in Jimmy Goggles, all except the helmet. 'Easy,' says Always, 'there's her mast.' And after I'd had just one squint over the gunwale, I caught up the bogey and almost tipped out as old Sanders brought the boat round. When the windows were screwed and everything was all right, I shut the valve from the air belt in order to help my sinking, and jumped overboard, feet foremost—for we hadn't a ladder. I left the boat pitching, and all of them staring down into the water after me, as my head sank down into the weeds and blackness that lay about the mast. I suppose nobody, not the most cautious chap in the world, would have bothered about a look-out at such a desolate place. It stunk of solitude.

"Of course you must understand that I was a greenhorn at diving. None of us were divers. We'd had to muck about with the thing to get the way of it, and this was the first time I'd been deep. It feels damnable. Your ears hurt beastly. I don't know if you've ever hurt yourself yawning

444

or sneezing, but it takes you like that, only ten times worse. And a pain over the eyebrows here—splitting—and a feeling like influenza in the head. And it isn't all heaven in your lungs and things. And going down feels like the beginning of a lift, only it keeps on. And you can't turn your head to see what's above you, and you can't get a fair squint at what's happening to your feet without bending down something painful. And being deep it was dark, let alone the blackness of the ashes and mud that formed the bottom. It was like going down out of the dawn back into the night, so to speak.

"The mast came up like a ghost out of the black, and then a lot of fishes, and then a lot of flapping red seaweed, and then whack I came with a kind of dull bang on the deck of the *Ocean Pioneer*, and the fishes that had been feeding on the dead rose about me like a swarm of flies from road stuff in summer time. I turned on the compressed air again—for the suit was a bit thick and mackintoshery after all, in spite of the rum—and stood recovering myself. It struck coolish down there, and that helped take off the stuffiness a bit.

"When I began to feel easier, I started looking about me. It was an extraordinary sight. Even the light was extraordinary, a kind of reddy coloured twilight, on account of the streamers of seaweed that floated up on either side of the ship. And far overhead just a moony, deep green blue. The deck of the ship, except for a slight list to starboard, was level, and lay all dark and long between the weeds, clear except where the masts had snapped when she rolled, and vanishing into black night towards the forecastle. There weren't any dead on the decks, most were in the weeds alongside, I suppose; but afterwards I found two skeletons lying in the passengers' cabins, where death had come to them. It was curious to stand on that deck and recognize it all, bit by bit; a place against the rail where I'd been fond of smoking by starlight, and the corner where an old chap from Sydney used to flirt with a widow we had aboard. A comfortable couple they'd been, only a month ago, and now you couldn't have got a meal for a baby crab off either of them.

"I've always had a bit of philosophical turn, and I dare say I spent the best part of five minutes in such thoughts before I went below to find where the blessed dust was stored. It was slow work hunting, feeling it was for the most part, pitchy dark, with confusing blue gleams down the companion. And there were things moving about, a dab at my glass once, and once a pinch at my leg. Crabs I expect. I kicked a lot of loose stuff that puzzled me, and stooped and picked up something all knobs and spikes. What do you think? Backbone! But I never had any particular feeling for bones. We had talked the affair over pretty thoroughly, and Always knew just where the stuff was stowed. I found it that trip. I lifted a box one end an inch or more."

He broke off in his story. "I've lifted it," he said, "as near as that! Forty thousand pounds' worth of pure gold! Gold! I shouted inside my helmet as a kind of cheer and hurt my ears. I was getting confounded stuffy and tired by this time—I must have been down twenty-five minutes or more—and I thought this was good enough. I went up the companion again, and as my eyes came up flush with the deck, a thundering great crab gave a kind of hysterical jump and went scuttling off sideways. Quite a start it gave me. I stood up clear on deck and shut the valve behind the helmet to let the air accumulate to carry me up again—I noticed a kind of whacking from above, as though they were hitting the water with an oar, but I didn't look up. I fancied they were signalling me to come up.

"And then something shot down by me—something heavy, and stood a-quiver in the planks. I looked, and there was a long knife I'd seen young Sanders handling. Thinks I, he's dropped it, and I was still calling him this kind of fool and that—for it might have hurt me serious—when I began to lift and drive up towards the daylight. Just about the level of the top spars of the *Ocean Pioneer*, whack! I came against something sinking down, and a

Down they went, clutching and turning over.

boot knocked in front of my helmet. Then something else, struggling frightful. It was a big weight atop of me, whatever it was, and moving and twisting about. I'd have thought it a big octopus, or some such thing, if it hadn't been for the boot. But octopuses don't wear boots. It was all in a moment, of course. I felt myself sinking down again, and I threw my arms about to keep steady, and the whole lot rolled free of me and shot down as I went up—"

He paused.

"I saw young Sanders's face, over a naked black shoulder, and a spear driven clean through his neck, and out of his mouth and neck what looked like spirits of pink smoke in the water. And down they went clutching one another, and turning over, and both too far gone to leave go. And in another second my helmet came a whack, fit to split, against the niggers' canoe. It was niggers! Two canoes full.

"It was lively times, I tell you! Overboard came Always with three spears in him. There was the legs of three or four black chaps kicking about me in the water. I couldn't see much, but I saw the game was up at a glance, gave my valve a tremendous twist, and went bubbling down again after poor Always, in as awful a state of scare and astonishment as you can well imagine. I passed young Sanders and the nigger going up again and struggling still a bit, and in another moment I was standing in the dim again on the deck of the *Ocean Pioneer*.

" 'Gummy,' thinks I, 'here's a fix! Niggers?' At first I couldn't see anything for it but Stifle below or Stabs above. I didn't properly understand how much air there was to last me out, but I didn't feel like standing very much more of it down below. I was hot and frightfully heady quite apart from the blue funk I was in. We'd never reckoned with these beastly natives, filthy Papuan beasts. It wasn't any good coming up where I was, but I had to do something. On the spur of the moment, I clambered over the side of the brig and landed among the weeds, and set off through the darkness as fast as I could. I just stopped once and knelt, and twisted back my head in the helmet and had

a look up. It was a most extraordinary bright green-blue
above, and the two canoes and the boat floating there very
small and distant like a kind of twisted H. And it made me
feel sick to squint up at it, and think what the pitching and
swaying of the three meant.

"It was just about the most horrible ten minutes I ever
had, blundering about in that darkness—pressure something awful, like being buried in sand, pain across the
chest, sick with funk, and breathing nothing as it seemed
but the smell of rum and mackintosh. Gummy! After a bit,
I found myself going up a steepish sort of slope. I had
another squint to see if anything was visible of the canoes
and boats, and then kept on. I stopped with my head a foot
from the surface, and tried to see where I was going, but,
of course, nothing was to be seen but the reflection of the
bottom. Then out I dashed like knocking my head through
a mirror. Directly I got my eyes out of the water, I saw I'd
come up a kind of beach near the forest. I had a look
round, but the natives and the brig were both hidden by a
big hummocky heap of twisted lava. The born fool in me
suggested a run for the woods. I didn't take the helmet off,
but I eased open one of the windows, and, after a bit of a
pant, went on out of the water. You'd hardly imagine how
clean and light the air tasted.

"Of course, with four inches of lead in your boot soles,
and your head in a copper knob the size of a football, and
been thirty-five minutes under water, you don't break any
records running. I ran like a ploughboy going to work.
And halfway to the trees I saw a dozen niggers or more,
coming out in a gaping, astonished sort of way to meet me.

"I just stopped dead, and cursed myself for all the fools
out of London. I had about as much chance of cutting
back to the water as a turned turtle. I just screwed up my
window again to leave my hands free, and waited for them.
There wasn't anything else for me to do.

"But they didn't come on very much. I began to suspect
why. 'Jimmy Goggles,' I says, 'it's your beauty does it.' I
was inclined to be a little lightheaded, I think, with all

Nothing like a striking appearance to help a man in trouble.

these dangers about and the change in the pressure of the blessed air. 'Who're ye staring at?' I said, as if the savages could hear me. 'What d'ye take me for? I'm hanged if I don't give you something to stare at,' I said, and with that I screwed up the escape valve and turned on the compressed air from the belt, until I was swelled out like a blown frog. Regular imposing it must have been. I'm blessed if they'd come on a step; and presently one and then another went down on their hands and knees. They didn't know what to make of me, and they was doing the extra polite, which was very wise and reasonable of them. I had half a mind to edge back seaward and cut and run, but it seemed too hopeless. A step back and they'd have been after me. And out of sheer desperation I began to march towards them up the beach, with slow, heavy steps, and waving my blown-out arms about, in a dignified manner. And inside of me I was singing as small as a tomtit.

"But there's nothing like a striking appearance to help a man over a difficulty—I've found that before and since. People like ourselves, who're up to diving dresses by the time we're seven, can scarcely imagine the effect of one on a simple-minded savage. One or two of these niggers cut and run, the others started in a great hurry trying to knock their brains out on the ground. And on I went as slow and solemn and silly-looking and artful as a jobbing plumber. It was evident they took me for something immense.

"Then up jumped one and began pointing, making extraordinary gestures to me as he did so, and all the others began sharing their attention between me and something out at sea. 'What's the matter now,' I said. I turned slowly on account of my dignity, and there I saw, coming round a point, the poor old *Pride of Banya* towed by a couple of canoes. The sight fairly made me sick. But they evidently expected some recognition, so I waved my arms in a striking sort of noncommittal manner. And then I turned and stalked on towards the trees again. At that time I was praying like mad, I remember, over and over again: 'Lord help me through with it! Lord help me through with it!' It's only fools who know nothing of dangers can afford to laugh at praying.

"But these niggers weren't going to let me walk through and away like that. They started a kind of bowing dance about me, and sort of pressed me to take a pathway that lay through the trees. It was clear to me they didn't take me for a British citizen, whatever else they thought of me, and for my own part I was never less anxious to own up to the old country.

"You'd hardly believe it, perhaps, unless you're familiar with savages, but these poor misguided, ignorant creatures took me straight to their kind of joss place to present me to the blessed old black stone there. By this time I was beginning to sort of realize the depth of their ignorance, and directly I set eyes on this deity I took my cue. I started a baritone howl, 'wow-wow', very long on one note, and began waving my arms about a lot, and then very slowly and ceremoniously turned their image over on its side and sat down on it. I wanted to sit down badly, for diving dresses ain't much wear in the tropics. Or, to put it different

451

Girls came in and danced about me something disgraceful.

like, they're a sight too much. It took away their breath, I could see, my sitting on their joss, but in less time than a minute they made up their minds and were hard at work worshipping me. And I can tell you I felt a bit relieved to see things turning out so well, in spite of the weight on my shoulders and feet.

"But what made me anxious was what the chaps in the canoes might think when they came back. If they'd seen me in the boat before I went down, and without the helmet on—for they might have been spying and hiding since over night—they would very likely take a different view from the others. I was in a deuce of a stew about that for hours, as it seemed, until the shindy of the arrival began.

"But they took it down—the whole blessed village took it down. At the cost of sitting up stiff and stern, as much like those sitting Egyptian images one sees as I could manage, for pretty nearly twelve hours, I should guess at least, on end, I got over it. You'd hardly think what it meant in that heat and stink. I don't think any of them dreamt of the man inside. I was just a wonderful leathery great joss that had come up with luck out of the water. But the fatigue! the heat! the beastly closeness! the mackintosheriness and the rum! and the fuss! They lit a stinking fire on a kind of lava slab there was before me, and brought in a lot of gory muck—the worst parts of what they were feasting on outside, the Beasts—and burnt it all in my honour. I was getting a bit hungry, but I understand now how gods manage to do without eating, what with the smell of burnt offerings about them. And they brought in a lot of the stuff they'd got off the brig and, among other stuff, what I was a bit relieved to see, the kind of pneumatic pump that was used for the compressed air affair, and then a lot of chaps and girls came in and danced about me something disgraceful. It's extraordinary the different ways different people have of showing respect. If I'd had a hatchet handy I'd have gone for the lot of them—they made me feel that wild. All this time I sat as stiff as company, not knowing anything better to do. And at last, when nightfall came, and the wattle joss-house place got a bit too shadowy for their taste—all these here savages are afraid of the dark you know—and I started a sort of 'Moo' noise, they built big bonfires outside and left me alone in peace in the darkness of my hut, free to unscrew my windows a bit and think things over, and feel just as bad as I liked. And, Lord! I was sick.

"I was weak and hungry, and my mind kept on behaving like a beetle on a pin, tremendous activity and nothing done at the end of it. Come round just where it was before. There was sorrowing for the other chaps, beastly drunkards certainly, but not deserving such a fate, and young Sanders with the spear through his neck wouldn't go out of my mind. There was the treasure down there in the *Ocean Pioneer*, and how one might get it and hide it somewhere safer, and get away and come back for it. And there was the puzzle where to get anything to eat. I tell you I was fair rambling. I was afraid to ask by signs for food, for fear of behaving too human, and so there I sat and hungered until very near the dawn. Then the village got a bit quiet, and I couldn't stand it any longer, and I went out and got some stuff like artichokes in a bowl and some sour milk. What was left of these I put away among the other offerings, just to give them a hint of my tastes. And in the morning they came to worship, and found me sitting up stiff and respectable on their previous god, just as they'd left me overnight. I'd got my back against the central pillar of the hut, and, practically, I was asleep. And that's how I became a god among the heathen—a false god no doubt, and blasphemous, but one can't always pick and choose.

"Now, I don't want to crack myself up as a god beyond my merits, but I must confess that while I was god to these people they was extraordinary successful. I don't say there's anything in it, mind you. They won a battle with another tribe—I got a lot of offerings I didn't want through it—they had wonderful fishing, and their crop of pourra was

454

exceptional fine. And they counted the capture of the brig among the benefits I brought 'em. I must say I don't think that was a poor record for a perfectly new hand. And, though perhaps you'd scarcely credit it, I was the tribal god of those beastly savages for pretty nearly four months.

"What else could I do, man? But I didn't wear that diving-dress all the time. I made 'em rig me up a sort of holy of holies, and a deuce of a time I had too, making them understand what it was I wanted them to do. That indeed was the great difficulty—making them understand my wishes. I couldn't let myself down by talking their lingo badly—even if I'd been able to speak at all—and I couldn't go flapping a lot of gestures at them. So I drew pictures in sand and sat down beside them and hooted like one o'clock. Sometimes they did the things I wanted all right, and sometimes they did them all wrong. They was always very willing, certainly. All the while I was puzzling how I was to get the confounded business settled. Every night before the dawn I used to march out in full rig and go off to a place where I could see the channel in which the *Ocean Pioneer* lay sunk, and once even, one moonlight night, I tried to walk out to her, but the weeds and rocks and dark clean beat me. I didn't get back till full day, and then I found all those silly niggers out on the beach praying their sea-god to return to them. I was that vexed and tired, messing and tumbling about, and coming up and going down again, I could have punched their silly heads all round when they started rejoicing. I'm hanged if I like so much ceremony.

"And then came the missionary. That missionary! It was in the afternoon, and I was sitting in state in my outer temple place, sitting on that old black stone of theirs when he came. I heard a row outside and jabbering, and then his voice speaking to an interpreter. 'They worship stocks and stones,' he said, and I knew what was up, in a flash. I had one of my windows out for comfort, and I sang out straight away on the spur of the moment. 'Stocks and stones!' I says. 'You come inside,' I said, 'and I'll punch your bloom-

"Hullo," I said. "How's the trade in calico?"

ing head.' There was a kind of silence and more jabbering, and in he came, Bible in hand, after the manner of them—a little sandy chap in specks and a pith helmet. I flatter myself that me sitting there in the shadows, with my copper head and my big goggles, struck him a bit of a heap at first. 'Well,' I says, 'how's the trade in calico?' for I don't hold with missionaries.

"I had a lark with that missionary. He was a raw hand, and quite outclassed with a man like me. He gasped out who was I, and I told him to read the inscription at my feet if he wanted to know. Down he goes to read, and his interpreter, being of course as superstitious as any of them, took it as an act of worship and plumped down like a shot. All my people gave a howl of triumph, and there wasn't any more business to be done in my village after that journey, not by the likes of him.

"But, of course, I was a fool to choke him off like that. If I'd had any sense I should have told him straight away of the treasure and taken him into Co. I've no doubt he'd

456

have come into Co. A child, with a few hours to think it over, could have seen the connection between my diving dress and the loss of the *Ocean Pioneer*. A week after he left I went out one morning and saw the *Motherhood*, the salver's ship from Starr Race, towing up the channel and sounding. The whole blessed game was up, and all my trouble thrown away. Gummy? How wild I felt! And guying it in that stinking silly dress! Four months!"

The sunburnt man's story degenerated again. "Think of it," he said, when he emerged to linguistic purity once more. "Forty thousand pounds' worth of gold."

"Did the little missionary come back?" I asked.

"Oh yes? Bless him! And he pledged his reputation there was a man inside the god, and started out to see as much with tremendous ceremony. But there wasn't—he got sold again. I always did hate scenes and explanations, and long before he came I was out of it all—going home to Banya along the coast, hiding in bushes by day, and thieving food from the villages by night. Only weapon, a spear. No clothes, no money. Nothing. My face was my fortune, as the saying is. And just a squeak of eight thousand pounds of gold—fifth share. But the natives cut up rusty, thank goodness, because they thought it was him had driven their luck away."

The Password

V. H THOMAS

I SUPPOSE it would be stretching a point to say that I *won* the war. Lots of others have already claimed that distinction anyway. Let's say rather that, by hesitating over something I ought to have done, I helped preserve one of the vital instruments of our ultimate victory. Still sounds a bit steep, eh? Then read and judge for yourself.

This story begins in an Army camp just outside Reading. I had been in the Army for seven months, and when the Low Countries were swooped upon by Hitler had been all set to join the B.E.F. Now a long spell in the U.K. loomed ahead.

One hot, Friday afternoon the whole camp was detailed to parade on the square. Cooks, defaulters, sick—the lot. The C.O. was there, and the Adjutant, armed with a large notebook and pencil. They passed down the ranks, picking out a man here and a man there, until a full fifty of us were standing "one pace forward".

"Get your teas," said the C.O., "and be back here at 17.00 hours with full kit, arms and blankets."

We piled into a couple of buses, but it wasn't until we were clear of Reading that the officer-in-charge told us that we were on our way to guard the Prime Minister during his week end stay at Chequers. This was tough on the boys who'd been looking forward to the bright lights of Broadway, but promised, nevertheless, to be a break from camp routine.

Chequers stands in the heart of woody Buckinghamshire. A delightful spot at any time, and in that lovely summer of 1940 it was a sheer paradise.

We pitched our tents under the trees about a quarter of a mile from the house. The Prime Minister had arrived already, so we posted sentries and established Bren positions without delay. Apparently the P.M. liked to be seen without seeing and instructions were given that we must move about as unobtrusively as possible. A password was instituted—"Tofrek"—one of the regiment's battle-honours.

I drew the 23.59–02.00 hours shift, and midnight found me skirting the terrace with its lovely formal gardens and quaint old summer-houses. Everyone outside Chequers seemed very much awake, for there had been a constant stream of official cars and dispatch-riders, coming and going since early evening.

But by 01.30 hours the traffic had died down a bit, and I had draped myself in a leisurely fashion round one of the tall trees fringing the croquet-lawn. I thought about a quick smoke, and was just getting out my matches when the door of the house opened and, framed in the light beyond, stood a stout figure in a dinner-suit, flanked on one side by the glowing end of a cigar, and on the other by a glass of something strengthening.

Winston in person it was, and with him was General de Gaulle. They walked across the lawn, engaged in earnest conversation. They were discussing the German Navy, Winston sprinkling his colourful English with pinches of a French all his own and de Gaulle making his contribution in a low, bell-like voice.

They were approaching my tree now, and with a start I realized that my only way out was to scramble noisily up the steep bank behind me. Alternatively, I must move forward and join the party. Both manoeuvres had their disadvantages. Then again, wasn't I supposed to challenge them?

True, I knew they were the P.M. and de Gaulle respectively, but Army regulations made no provision for profoundly intelligent deductions like that. Right then:

"Halt, who goes there?"

I tried to sound masterful, but my voice was curiously high-pitched.

The two stopped in their tracks. Winston spoke:

"Prime Minister here."

"Will you give me the password, please, sir?"

There was an ominous silence, and upon my slim, twenty-two-year-old shoulders there descended an awful responsibility. I had asked for the password, and neither of them knew it! In accordance with my orders, they must, therefore, be shot at. Well, here was a thing.

"Prime Minister here," said Winston again, a bargainer to the last.

Here was a great man, orator, statesman, author and pride of a nation, but nothing could save him. It was all written down in the book, and that was that. I fingered the well-oiled bolt of my rifle. Here we go. . . .

"Tofrek," called a pleasant feminine voice.

"Eh?"

"Tofrek."

"Pass, friend," I gulped weakly.

The P.M. and the General moved toward me, and with them was the Premier's young daughter, Mary, the unseen owner of the voice which had given me the password when the two great men stood dumb.

Winston, in affable mood, patted me on the shoulder, bade me: "Look after me well," and the trio turned and went back to the house.

I learned afterwards that Miss Churchill had moved out to join her father at the moment I was grappling with my great problem under the tree.

Well, there you are. Now what were you saying?

They stopped in their tracks. Winston spoke:
"Prime Minister here."

The Spotted Devil of
Gummalapur

KENNETH ANDERSON

ALTHOUGH EXAMPLES of panthers turned man-eaters are
comparatively rare, when they do occur they depict the
panther as an engine of destruction quite equal to his far
larger cousin, the tiger. Because of his smaller size he can
conceal himself in places impossible to a tiger, his need
for water is far less, and in demoniac cunning and daring,
coupled with the uncanny sense of self-preservation and
stealthy disappearance when danger threatens, he has no
equal.

Such an animal was the man-eating leopard of Gummalapur. This leopard had established a record of some
forty-two human killings and was held in awe throughout
an area of some 250 square miles over which it held
indisputable sway.

Before sundown the door of each hut in every one of the
villages within this area was fastened shut. Not until the
sun was well up in the heavens next morning did the timid
inhabitants venture to expose themselves.

Finding that its human meals were increasingly difficult to obtain, the panther became correspondingly bolder, and in two instances burrowed its way in through the thatched walls of the smaller huts, dragging its screaming victim out the same way, while the whole village lay awake, trembling behind closed doors, listening to the shrieks of the victim as he was carried away. In one case the panther, frustrated from burrowing its way in through the walls, which had been boarded up with rough planks, resorted to the novel method of entering through the thatched roof. In this instance it found itself unable to carry its prey back through the hole it had made, so in a paroxysm of fury had killed all four inhabitants of the hut—a man, his wife and two children—before clawing its way back to the darkness outside and to safety.

Such was the position when I arrived at Gummalapur, in response to an invitation from Jepson, the District Magistrate, to rid his area of this scourge. Preliminary conversation with some of the inhabitants revealed that they appeared dejected beyond hope, and with true eastern fatalism had decided to resign themselves to the fact that this *shaitan*, from whom they believed deliverance to be impossible, had come to stay, till each one of them had been devoured or had fled the district.

Indeed, they spoke in whispers as if afraid that loud talking would be overheard by the panther, who would single them out for revenge.

That night, I sat in a chair in the midst of the village, with my back to the only house that possessed a twelve-foot wall, having taken the precaution to cover the roof with a deep layer of thorns and brambles, in case I should be attacked from behind by the leopard leaping down on me. It was a moonless night, but the clear sky promised to provide sufficient illumination from its myriad stars to enable me to see the panther should it approach.

The evening, at six o'clock, found the inhabitants behind locked doors, while I sat alone on my chair, with my rifle across my lap, loaded and cocked, a flask of hot tea nearby,

463

a blanket, a water-bottle, some biscuits, a torch at hand, and of course my pipe, tobacco and matches as my only consolation during the long vigil till daylight returned.

With the going down of the sun a period of acute anxiety began, for the stars were as yet not brilliant enough to light the scene even dimly, but by seven-fifteen p.m. they shed a sufficiently diffused glow to enable me to see along the whole village street, although somewhat indistinctly. My confidence returned, and I began to think of some way to draw the leopard towards me, should he be in the vicinity. I forced myself to cough loudly at intervals and then began to talk to myself.

By nine p.m. I got tired of it, and considered taking a walk around the streets of the village. After some deliberation I did this, still talking to myself as I moved cautiously up one lane and down the next, frequently glancing back over my shoulder. I soon realized, however, that I was exposing myself to extreme danger, as the panther might pounce on me from any corner, from behind any pile of garbage, or from the rooftops of any of the huts. Ceasing my talking abruptly, I returned to my chair, thankful to get back alive.

Time dragged by. Midnight came and I found myself feeling cold. By two a.m. I found I was growing sleepy. Hot tea and some biscuits, followed by icy water from the bottle dashed into my face, revived me a little, and I fell to talking to myself again, as a means of keeping awake thereafter.

At three-thirty a.m. heavy cloud covered the heavens and obscured the stars, making the darkness intense, and it would have been quite impossible to see the panther a yard away.

Next day I conceived a fresh plan for that night. I explained the plan to the villagers, who, to my surprise, entered into it with some enthusiasm. A hut was placed at my disposal immediately next to that through the roof of which the leopard had once entered and killed the four inmates. A very life-like dummy was rigged up, made of straw, an old pillow, a jacket, and a *sari*. This was placed within the doorway of the hut in a sitting position, the door itself being kept half-open. I sat myself behind a low parapet of boxes, placed diagonally across the opposite end of the small hut, the floor of which measured about twelve feet by ten feet. At this short range, I was confident of accounting for the panther as soon as it made itself visible in the doorway.

The hours dragged by in dreadful monotony. Suddenly the silence was disturbed by a rustle in the thatched roof which brought me to full alertness. But it was only a rat, which scampered across and then dropped with a thud to the floor nearby, from where it ran along the tops of the boxes before me, becoming clearly visible as it passed across the comparatively light patch of the open doorway.

I kept awake, occasionally smoking my pipe, or sipping hot tea from the flask, but nothing happened beyond the noises made by the tireless rats, which chased each other around the room, and even across me, till day dawned, and I lay back to fall asleep after another tiring vigil.

The following night, for want of a better plan, and feeling that sooner or later the man-eater would appear, I decided to repeat the performance with the dummy. Shortly after one a.m. a sharp wind sprang up, and I could hear the breeze rustling through the thatched roof. This rapidly increased in strength, till it was blowing quite a gale. The rectangular patch of light from the partly open doorway practically disappeared as the sky became overcast with storm clouds, and soon the steady rhythmic patter of rain-drops, which increased to a regular downpour, made me feel that the leopard, who like all his family are not over-fond of water, would not venture out on this stormy night, and that I would draw a blank once more.

By now the murmuring voices from the neighbouring huts had ceased or become inaudible, drowned in the swish of the rain. I strained my eyes to see the scarcely perceptible doorway, while the crouched figure of the dummy could not be seen at all, and while I looked I evidently fell asleep,

Suddenly the dummy moved and vanished through the door —
I jumped up but failed to get a shot.

tired out by my vigil of the two previous nights.

How long I slept I cannot tell, but it must have been for some considerable time. I awoke abruptly with a start, and a feeling that all was not well.

The rain had ceased and the sky had cleared a little, for the oblong patch of open doorway was more visible now, with the crouched figure of the dummy seated at its base. Then, as I watched, a strange thing happened. The dummy seemed to move, and as I looked more intently it suddenly disappeared to the accompaniment of a snarling growl. I realized that the panther had come, seen the crouched figure of the dummy in the doorway which it had mistaken for a human being, and then proceeded to stalk it, creeping in at the opening on its belly, and so low to the ground that its form had not been outlined in the faint light as I had hoped. The growl I had heard was at the panther's realization that the thing it had attacked was not human after all.

Switching on my torch and springing to my feet, I hurdled the barricade of boxes and sprang to the open doorway, to dash outside and almost trip over the dummy which lay across my path. I shone the beam of torchlight in both directions, but nothing could be seen. Hoping that the panther might still be lurking nearby and shining my torch-beam into every corner, I walked slowly down the village street, cautiously negotiated the bend at its end and walked back up the next street, in fear and trembling of a sudden attack. But although the light lit up every corner, every roof-top and every likely hiding-place in the street, there was no sign of my enemy anywhere. Although I searched for it through all the streets of Gummalapur that night, it had vanished as mysteriously as it had come.

It was therefore obvious that I would have to change my scene of operations, and so, after considerable thought, I decided to move on to the village of Devarabetta, diagonally across an intervening range of forest hills, and some eighteen miles away, where the panther had already secured five victims, though it had not been visited for a month.

467

The inhabitants were preparing to shut themselves into their huts when I appeared, and scarcely had the time nor inclination to talk to me. However, I gathered that they agreed that a visit from the man-eater was likely any day, for a full month had elapsed since his last visit and he had never been known to stay away for so long.

Time being short, I hastily looked around for the hut with the highest wall, before which I seated myself as on my first night at Gummalapur, having hastily arranged some dried thorny bushes across its roof as protection against attack from my rear and above.

Devarabetta was a far smaller village than Gummalapur, and situated much closer to the forest, a fact which I welcomed for the reason I would be able to obtain information as to the movements of carnivora by the warning notes that the beasts and birds of the jungle would utter, provided I was within hearing.

The night fell with surprising rapidity, though this time a thin sickle of new moon was showing in the sky. The occasional call of a roosting jungle-cock, and the plaintive call of peafowl, answering one another from the nearby forest, told me that all was still well. And then it was night, the faint starlight rendering hardly visible, and as if in a dream, the tortuously winding and filthy lane that formed the main street of Devarabetta. At eight-thirty p.m. a sambar hind belled from the forest, following her original sharp note with a series of warning cries in steady succession. Undoubtedly a beast of prey was afoot and had been seen by the watchful deer, who was telling the other jungle-folk to look out for their lives.

Time passed, and then down the lane I caught sight of some movement. Raising my cocked rifle, I covered the object, which slowly approached me, walking in the middle of the street. Was this the panther after all, and would it walk thus openly, and in the middle of the lane, without any attempt at concealment? It was now about thirty yards away and still it came on boldly, without any attempt to take cover or to creep along the edges of objects in the usual manner of a leopard when stalking its prey. More-over, it seemed a frail and slender animal, as I could see it fairly clearly now. Twenty yards and I pressed the button of my torch, which this night I had clamped to my rifle.

As the powerful beam flashed across the intervening space it lighted a village cur, commonly known to us in India as a "pariah dog". Starving and lonely, it had sought out human company; it stared blankly into the bright beam of light, feebly wagging a skinny tail in unmistakable signs of friendliness.

Welcoming a companion, if only a lonely cur, I switched off the light and called it to my side by a series of flicks of thumb and finger. It approached cringingly, still wagging its ridiculous tail. I fed it with some biscuits and a sand-wich, and in the dull light of the star-lit sky its eyes looked back at me in dumb gratitude for the little food I had given it. Then it curled up at my feet and fell asleep.

Time passed and midnight came. One o'clock, two and then three o'clock passed in dragging monotony, while I strained my tired and aching eyes and ears for movement or sound. Fortunately it had remained a cloudless night and visibility was comparatively good by the radiance of the myriad stars that spangled the heavens, a sight that cannot be seen in any of our dusty towns or cities.

And then, abruptly, the alarmed cry of a plover, or "Did-you-do-it" bird, as it is known in India, sounded from the nearby muddy tank on the immediate outskirts of the village. "*Did-you-do-it, Did-you-do-it, Did-you-do-it, Did-you-do-it,*" it called. No doubt the bird was excited and had been disturbed, or it had seen some-thing. The cur at my feet stirred, raised its head, then sank down again, as if without a care in the world.

It dashed round the corner and charged me.

The minutes passed, and then suddenly the dog became fully awake. Its ears, that had been dropping in dejection, were standing on end, it trembled violently against my legs, while a low prolonged growl came from its throat. I noticed that it was looking down the lane that led into the village from the vicinity of the tank.

I stared intently in that direction. For a long time I could see nothing, and then it seemed that a shadow moved at a corner of a building some distance away and on the same side of the lane. I focused my eyes on this spot, and after a few seconds again noticed a furtive movement, but this time a little closer.

Placing my left thumb on the switch which would actuate the torch, I waited in breathless silence. A few minutes passed, five or ten at the most, and then I saw an elongated body spring swiftly and noiselessly on to the roof of a hut some twenty yards away. As it happened, all the huts adjoined each other at this spot, and I guessed the panther had decided to walk along the roofs of these adjoining

470

huts and spring upon me from the rear.

I got to my feet quickly and placed my back against the wall. In this position the eave of the roof above my head passed over me and on to the road where I had been sitting, for about eighteen inches. The rifle I kept ready, finger on trigger, with my left thumb on the torch switch, pressed to my side and pointing upwards.

A few seconds later I heard a faint rustling as the leopard endeavoured to negotiate the thorns which I had taken the precaution of placing on the roof. He evidently failed in this, for there was silence again. Now I had no means of knowing where he was.

The next fifteen minutes passed in terrible anxiety, with me glancing in all directions in the attempt to locate the leopard before he sprang, while thanking Providence that the night remained clear. And then the cur, that had been restless and whining at my feet, shot out into the middle of the street, faced the corner of the hut against which I was sheltering and began to bark lustily.

This warning saved my life, for within five seconds the panther charged around the corner and sprang at me. I had just time to press the torch switch and fire from my hip, full into the blazing eyes that showed above the wide-opened, snarling mouth. The ·405 bullet struck squarely, but the impetus of the charge carried the animal on to me. I jumped nimbly to one side, and as the panther crashed against the wall of the hut, emptied two more rounds from the magazine into the evil, spotted body.

It collapsed and was still, except for the spasmodic jerking of the still opened jaws and long, extended tail. And then my friend the cur, staunch in faithfulness to his new-found master, rushed in and fixed his feeble teeth in the throat of the dead monster.

And so passed the "Spotted Devil of Gummalapur", a panther of whose malignant craftiness I had never heard the like before and hope never to have to meet again.

I took the cur home, washed and fed it, and named it "Nipper".

Corny's Nightmare

RICHARD
ARMSTRONG

EVERY SEAFARING man has his own private worry, a nagging anxiety about something awkward or crazy or just plain stupid that could easily happen to him but never does. With Joe Cornforth it was the fear of missing his passage, of arriving on the dockhead somewhere and finding his ship gone on without him.

In Corny this was a queer thing because he wasn't the worrying sort. One look at him was enough to convince anybody about that. He was a short, thick-set fellow with a round, fat face and a nose like a three-cornered piece of sponge rubber stuck on it among the freckles. His hair was red and nobody—not even his own mother—had ever accused him of being good looking. He was as tough as he looked but this phobia about losing his ship was real enough and he reckoned he picked it up, like an attack of measles or a family of fleas, in a place called La Spezia.

He was in the *Kariba* at the time, sharing the half-deck with Jonty Lammerton and Dave Faulkner. They were good shipmates, and there were worse places to be in with them than La Spezia in the springtime. It is a great natural harbour with a sizable town at the head of it. There are steep hills covered with vineyards and olive groves all

472

round, and away to the northward, a glimpse of snow mountains high above the clouds. The town itself is white and clean with shade trees in the streets and comical little tram-cars that run in pairs and make a crazy clatter which nobody seems to hear; and there are lots of cafés with little round tables and chairs arranged on the wide pavement outside them.

They were sitting there—Dave, Jonty and Corny—on the terrace of their favourite café at the end of the last afternoon ashore and Corny was binding bitterly.

"My first complaint," he said when invited to lay off his grievances, "is that we're spent up and can't have another round of drinks; the second is that we've got no car-fare and that means a three-mile walk back to the ship; and the third, I've got the anchor watch from eight o'clock till midnight which, as we are sailing at daybreak, means I get a lousy four and a half hours sleep."

"So what!" demanded Jonty. "I'm on at midnight and I'll get less than that."

"It's my troubles we're discussing, not yours," retorted Corny coldly. "And the fourth one is my supper, if you can call it that. The second steward—"

"I thought he was a pal of yours," interrupted Dave.

"Be your age, Davey boy!" Corny tried hard to look insulted. It wasn't easy with his kind of face. "Morgan the Mouch is nobody's pal. He'd beat your brains out for half a crown and I'll lay six to four he leaves me only half a pint of wobbly cocoa and one cheese sandwich. It'll be curling up all round the edges and smell like a wad of mouldy hay."

"There's worse smells than that." Jonty drained his glass and stood up. He was only of average height but broad across the shoulders—like a middle-weight boxer with a deep chest and big hands. In a beauty competition Corny would just about beat him for the wooden spoon. Nobody had ever heard him laugh, but he had a grin that split his face from ear to ear like a gash in an old boot. He was the senior of the three and whenever orders were necessary, he gave them. "Time we got going," he said now and set off towards the wide road that ran like a white ribbon right round the bay. Dave and Corny drank up and followed, hurrying to catch up with him.

Corny's estimate of the distance was fairly accurate and they had covered about a third of it when the careers of all three of them were almost cut short by a truck coming up from behind. It was a big thing with a high body and a tattered canvas hood and, hearing it rattling like a bag of hammers from about a quarter of a mile away, they got into single file to give it room to pass. But the scar-faced man with a walrus moustache who was driving it wanted all the road and the *Kariba's* apprentices survived its passage only by a last-minute dive into the ditch.

"Of all the crazy, cock-eyed nincompoops!" growled Dave, picking his long legs out of the coarse grass and nettles and brushing himself down. "He ought to be locked up!"

"Maybe he couldn't help it," said Jonty. "That truck's a proper old load of junk. You okay, Corny?"

"Yeah, I think so." Corny was sitting where he had landed staring after the truck with his mouth open. He

They had to jump for it as the truck roared past.

watched it bumping and swaying and anybody with half
an eye could see he was hoping it would fold up and
collapse in a heap. Instead it ran on for a couple of hundred yards and, still going flat out, suddenly hauled right
across the road and disappeared up a side-turning on the
left. Corny spat in the dust and glared at his room-mates.
"Did you see what I saw?" he demanded.

"You mean the bunch of thugs in the back?"

"I mean one of them. It was Morgan the Mouch!"

"Who are you kidding!" Jonty's voice was completely
disbelieving. "What would Morgan be doing with a bunch
of hoodlums like that?"

"Your guess is as good as mine," snorted Corny. "But
he was there in that truck. I saw him and I'll swear to it."

"So what!" demanded Dave and sorting themselves out,
they pushed on towards the ship. She was moored alongside the quay right on the far side of the harbour from the

town and when they got there, Corny was still brooding morosely about the second steward.

"I know!" he said, as they climbed the gangway. "They're going to murder him. Morgan the Mouch, I mean. They're taking him up into the hills and we'll never see him again. They'll slit his throat right across from port to starboard and dump him down a dark ravine."

"You've got a hope!" said Jonty.

"And a vindictive nature with it," added Dave; then the supper bell put an end to the back-chat and when Corny took over the watch from the stand-by man at eight o'clock, he had forgotten all about Morgan the Mouch.

Corny never fooled around on the job. He took responsibility seriously and never tried to pass the buck. From eight o'clock the ship was in his charge and, taking nothing for granted, he began by making sure she was okay. First, he checked the lights and lashings on the gangway; then he tested the moorings fore and aft; and finally, he saw the decks were clear and safe to move about on in the dark. This kept him going until about nine o'clock and from then till half-past ten he was busy checking the crew back on board.

With the ship sailing at five in the morning nobody was very late and by ten-forty-five all hands were ticked off and safely stowed. Morgan, to Corny's secret sorrow, was among the early birds and arrived just after eight.

At eleven o'clock, every berth in the ship was dark and she was as quiet as a mortuary at midnight. The pot of cocoa and the mouldy sandwich occupied Corny till seven bells—twenty minutes past the hour—and then with his watch almost finished he set off on the rounds for the last time.

The moon was still down and the night dark and soft as black velvet but he knew the ship so well he didn't even bother to take the torch out of his hip pocket; and, starting amidships on the port side, he ambled across the foredeck then climbed lazily up on to the fo'c'sle head. For a moment or two he stood there watching the lights of the town, dwindled by distance, across the bay; then he checked the moorings and, crossing to the starboard side, slid down the ladder and headed aft again.

He was unconcerned, unsuspecting and, whistling softly through his teeth, had his mind pleasantly divided between thoughts of his bunk and speculation about breakfast next morning; he saw nothing and heard nothing but before he had taken three steps from the foot of the ladder, he was grabbed from behind, a knee jammed into the small of his back and an arm flung round his throat. Helpless and realizing instantly the futility of any struggle, he took a deep breath and prepared to yell; but his attackers were waiting for that too and the moment he opened his mouth one of them stuffed a wad of cotton waste halfway down his gullet. That left him gagged and half-choked into the bargain and he was dragged backwards into one of the compartments under the fo'c'sle head.

Everybody lived aft in the *Kariba* and this part of the ship, right up in the bows, was divided into lamp-locker, bosun's store, carpenter's shop and paint-locker. The smell of turps and patent dryers was enough to tell Corny he was in the latter, then as the door clicked shut, somebody snapped on the light and that confirmed it.

The light also wised him up about his assailants. Apart from the thug with the head-lock on him, there were three of them. Number one was a great, moon-faced lummox in jeans and a dirty T-shirt. He had a big slobbery mouth and from the goofy look in his eyes, Corny guessed he was a punchy—a once promising heavy-weight who had fought too many bouts too quickly and gone over the hill before his time. Number two was a dapper little man in a silk suit, a panama hat and a beautiful pair of black and white buckskin shoes. His eyes were small and close-set, and had neither brows nor lashes to them; his mouth was practically lipless and his two top front teeth stuck out like those of a rat. In fact all in all he bore a strong resemblance to the whole family of rodents, and the sight of an open flick knife in his hand sent cold shivers down Corny's

He was dragged into the paint-locker, gagged and half-choked.

spine. He swung his head to look at number three who proved to be no other than the second steward, otherwise known as Morgan the Mouch.

Corny needed no diagram now to tell him what was cooking. The stuff stowed on the shelves and in the racks around the paint-locker was worth a pile of money in any sort of currency and these beauties were out to loot it.

Twisting his head round at considerable risk of breaking his neck, Corny now got a gander at the fourth man. It was the fellow with the walrus moustache and the fancy scar who had driven the senile truck. He had over-developed forearms like Pop-eye-the-sailor and reeked of stale sweat and garlic.

Corny had all he wanted to know now. It was plain that Morgan had planned the job; none of the others would know the lay-out of the ship and her exact routine; but he wasn't the leader. He didn't have that kind of drive or ruthlessness. Ratface was running the show, and while they were waiting for him to tell them what to do next, Corny decided the time had come to put in a counter-attack. He had gone all limp in preparation for it the moment he was grabbed. Consequently, the Walrus had no idea what he had hold of, and when the slack body in his arms suddenly stiffened and cut loose, the shock almost unmanned him. Corny's first move was to hack back at his captor's shins. He landed first time, and if he had been wearing sea-boots instead of plimsols the fellow would have needed a wooden leg to see him out the rest of his life. As it was, he let out a yell, dropped his prisoner like a hot brick and started hopping about the paint locker on one leg. It was his unlucky day and his third skip kicked over a small paint-pot someone had been too tired to empty. It was half-full of black paint which slopped over Ratface's fancy shoes and spouted twelve inches or more up the legs of his beautifully pressed silk pants.

Meanwhile Corny, free for the moment, stepped back to give himself room and socked most foully the spotty-faced Welshman. "Oouch!" said Morgan, or words to that effect and folded like a wet straw.

Head down, Corny now plunged for the door but before he could get it open, the Goofy one pulled him off it with a hand like a ham. The poor sap was as strong as an ox; for a moment he held Corny dangling at arm's length then dropped him on the deck and pinned him down with a foot the size of an elephant's. Deciding that for the moment the odds were against him, Corny stopped struggling and resumed the waiting game.

"Tie him up! Hands and feet!" snapped Ratface. His accent came straight from the New York water-front, and he had obviously mis-spent a considerable part of his life in the land of the free. He watched Walrus lash up Corny, then turned on Morgan, now painfully unwinding himself, and the pair of them went into a huddle.

Lying there, bound and gagged, just inside the door, Corny listened carefully. He gathered that Morgan, going on the apprentice's reputation for dodging the column, had expected him to be keeping his watch stretched out on a bench in the galley; and his sudden appearance on the foredeck had taken the gang completely by surprise. It had also presented them with a problem they could have done without. What to do with the prisoner?

Morgan, half-way to panic, was for tying a heavy weight round his ankles and sliding him overboard into the harbour, but Ratface would have none of it. That would be murder, and he wasn't putting his neck in a noose for a few lousy drums of paint.

"Well, you can't leave him here. He'll give me away as soon as he's found," snarled Morgan, chewing at his finger-tips. "And besides, he saw us turn off the coast road this afternoon and he'll have half the police in Italy round your necks by daybreak."

"Okay then, we'll take him with us and hold him till we've cashed in, then turn him loose way back in the hills. Now go and get your traps, quick."

"Me?" Morgan's eyes popped. "What for? I'm sailing at day-break. You pay me my cut and I stay."

"The ship's sailing, but not you, pal." Ratface tapped the Mouch on the breastbone with the point of his flick-knife. "You . . . you're coming with us. I'm taking no chances of you turning chicken and spilling the beans."

This shook Morgan rigid and he tried all ways to make Ratface change his mind; but the little hoodlum had his number, and in the end he went aft, white-faced, to pick up his dunnage.

Meanwhile Corny's brain was working overtime on the possibilities. One thing was certain; the gang would clean out the paint-locker and get clear of the ship with its contents before midnight. Nothing was going to stop them doing that or taking him with them when they went. This meant that with nobody to call him, Jonty, who had the middle watch, would go on sleeping his foolish head off until daybreak; then there would be a great big whale of a row, Corny, the paint and Morgan the Mouch would be found missing, the police would be informed and the *Kariba* would sail. She might be held up for half an hour or so, but she would sail that morning and he, Corny, would be left, lost and forlorn, in the Apennine Hills.

This was the moment when the fear about missing his passage first entered his life to stay with him for ever after.

He turned his attention now to the hoodlums, weighing them up in turn. Morgan, he decided, didn't count. He was a sucker and needed his brains examined for getting involved in a racket like this; but he wasn't bad; just a blow-hard, a big-head. Walrus too was a hard-boiled egg with a soft centre and in spite of his apparent toughness, like the Welshman, he would be a push-over in the crunch. But Goofy was dynamite. He was too far gone round the bend to know his own strength and he wouldn't scare; there was nothing left in him up topside to be scared with —no sensitivity, no coherent memory and no reasoning power. He would tear a man limb from tree and never know he was doing anything wrong. There was only one thing to do with Goofy and that was to keep out of his way. This left Ratface and his flick-knife—a dangerous combination but capable of being handled. The unknown factor was the nature and scope of the dapper little man's power over the Goof, and if ever it came to a show-down, the first thing to do would be to separate these two and keep them apart.

But there was no chance of starting anything now; and so far as he could see Corny reckoned his only hope was that Jonty would wake by instinct around about eight bells or soon enough after to work out what had happened, organize a pursuit, catch up with the thugs, release him and get back to the ship before she sailed. His part would be to lay a trail that couldn't be missed, and he concentrated now on the problem of how to do it.

While all this was going on, Walrus and the Goof were working like stoats clearing the racks and shelves. In their toing and froing both of them had trod in the spilled black paint and thereafter every step they took left a foot-print. The deck was covered with them and Corny stared at it unable to believe that such a small quantity of paint could make such a mess. It seemed to him there was a message in this for him somewhere, but he was still groping for it when the Goof, with the last drum of white lead gone, picked him up like a child and carted him out into the

Lying limp, he felt himself slid down a ladder.

night.

If there had been half a chance, Corny would have put up some kind of a fight then. He thought about it, but with his hands and feet tied and that wad of waste in his mouth, it wasn't on, so he rode it and continued his thinking about paint.

Lying limp, he felt himself slid down a ladder the gang had rigged off the foredeck on to the quay and then flung like a bundle of dirty washing into the back of what he guessed to be the same old jalopy that had crowded him into the ditch that afternoon.

"Here," he told himself morosely, "the trail of footprints will end and the way hereafter will be unknown. If only one of them with paint on his shoes couldn't find room and had to run behind. . . ."

There wasn't a hope, of course, and he was on the point of turning his mind on to a different line of thought when Ratface and Morgan the Mouch climbed aboard, one of them switching on a torch to show the way. Nobody in the business had sharper eyes or nimbler wits than Corny and that brief light revealed to him three things that clicked together in his mind like pieces of well-oiled machinery. They were first, that the floor of the truck was rotten and full of holes; second that his feet had come to rest against a ten-gallon drum of bright yellow funnel paint; and third that the three metal clips set round the rim of the drum to hold the lid secure were either broken off or out of place. This meant that if the drum fell over on its side the sheer weight of its contents would force off the lid, the paint would gush out and begin to drip through the rotten floorboards, leaving a trail wherever the truck went and nobody aboard would know a thing about it.

By the time Ratface was settled on top of the loot and the truck was under way, Corny had it all worked out. There were other drums standing behind the one that mattered, so it was no use tipping it over by pushing away from him. What he had to do was to pull the thing towards him and wasting no time worrying about what all that paint was going to do to himself, he got his heels hooked on to the rim of the drum and started rocking it to and fro in the darkness. It took all his strength to get it going but he managed it and when the truck turned sharp left off the quay on to the coast road, the lurch did the rest. The teetering drum toppled over on to Corny's legs, off came the unsecured lid and a great flood of cold, slimy, smelly paint gushed out.

Sitting up to his waist in it, Corny leaned back with a little sigh of relief. He had done *his* piece; the rest was up to his room-mates; and now the only fly in the ointment was this nagging anxiety about the ship sailing. They had five hours, he reckoned, and as the truck rattled and banged its way round the bay, he started doing mental arithmetic, changing the hours into 300 minutes which didn't look too good; then into 18,000 seconds which sounded a lot more but didn't last. . . .

As it turned out Jonty's instincts were right off form and two of the five hours had gone before he even woke. It took him another fifteen minutes to discover that Corny was adrift and the paint-locker looted; then he had to work out what had happened and rouse out Dave. The long fellow didn't like it a bit.

"Okay, Corny's mislaid himself, so what!" he said. "Go and tell the Mate or the Old Man; go and get lost with him yourself but include me out. I'm not on till four o'clock and I need my sleep."

Jonty got him awake at last and when he had wised him up they faced the big decision together. If they called the Mate and reported what had happened, he would immediately inform the police who would set their thief-catching machinery in motion. But they would hardly get started looking before daybreak and though they might in the end locate Corny and recover the loot, long before they did so the ship would have sailed and poor old Corny would be left on the beach. Apart from his feelings, this would set him back six months in his career and that could not be allowed.

"We've got to find him somehow ourselves," said Jonty.

"Yeah!" agreed Dave, "and it's got to be before the ship sails. Now tell me how? We've got less than three hours and Italy's a sizable dump. I mean where do we start looking?"

Jonty was racking his brain and suddenly he stiffened like a pointer. "You get rigged and wait here," he said. "I've got a hunch."

He slipped away soundlessly in his plimsols and in two minutes flat he was back with his mind made up and a gleam in his eye.

"Morgan the Mouch has jumped the ship!" he announced. "He's gone, bag and baggage. Suppose he did it; the paint-locker I mean; him and that bunch of spivs he was with this afternoon. . . . Remember that old jalopy

they were in? It turned off the coast road and headed for
the hills, but it can't have gone far because he was back
aboard just after eight. I saw him."

"You mean they might have a hide-out somewhere
down that cart-track? Thing is could we find it again?"

"If we can't and get wandered we'll be up the same
creek as Corny but it's worth trying. Come on! Grab a
torch and get going, brother."

"What about the ship?" protested Dave. "There'll be an
unholy row about leaving her."

"We'll have to wear that," answered Jonty. "I've wakened the bosun but told him nothing. He'll find out what's
happened after we're clear of her."

The moon had not quite topped the hills when they
started but there was already a lot of light from it and,
after Jonty had pointed out the footprints in black paint
and the wheel-tracks in the dust, they set off along the
quay at a brisk trot. Then, turning into the coast road,
they struck the beginning of Corny's trail. There it was,
about a bucketful of the stuff, right in their path, bright
yellow and gleaming in the light of their torches.

"Funnel paint!" grunted Dave. "Trust old Corny!"

After that there was no need to speculate or work things
out. There were several turns off towards the hills but the
moon lifted clear as they went and the trail, thick, shining
and unmistakable, led them unerringly and as fast as they
could go into the right one.

It was a rutted cart-track, running first through an area
of rough scrub and then, after forking a couple of times,
climbing steeply into the mouth of a narrow ravine. It was
really a blind canyon, terraced for vines. Full in the moonlight it lay and there in the bottom of it was the jalopy
backed into a dilapidated open-sided shed. The loot was
still in it and the truck was fairly plastered with yellow
funnel paint; so was the shed, the grass underfoot and the
undergrowth all around it; but they found the trail again
zig-zagging up the terracing behind.

"Lavish with it! That's Corny all over," panted Jonty

"Funnel paint!" grunted Dave. "Trust old Corny!"

without stopping. "What's the time?"

"Quarter to four," answered Dave. "Even if we started back now we'd have to go faster than we came to make it. We've got to fetch somewhere soon!"

They drove themselves on and then, at last, swinging round what must have been the tenth hairpin bend in that crazy three-foot wide path, they came on a little plateau. It wasn't as big as a cricket pitch, and right on the edge of it, built so that it projected into thin air over the ravine, was a tumble-down topsy-turvy house. It was piled up all ways but they wasted no time admiring it, for there, in the bottom of it, was a sun-bleached double door on great rusty hinges and the trail ran right underneath it. The place was some kind of cellar or store and Jonty approached it cautiously.

"Corny!" he hissed through the overlap. "Are you there, Corny? It's us; Dave and Jonty!"

"You've taken your time about it, haven't you!" came back Corny's grumbling voice. He had got rid of the gag and was working on the line around his ankles. "For Pete's sake, where've you been?"

"It's him all right and still no gratitude," said Jonty over his shoulder. He examined the door. It was fastened with an iron bar and a padlock as big as his fist. "There's more spring in that than in a yo-yo and anything lighter than a three-ton truck would just bounce back from it."

"Try this!" said Dave, who had been nosing around on his own account and now thrust into his room-mate's hands a sapling about ten feet long and six inches diameter.

It was wedge-shaped at the butt from the axe that had felled it and Jonty worked it in between the two halves of the door about waist high. He took his time and did it so well that it held right away and when he and Dave threw their weight on it, the rusty screws holding the locking bar began to give immediately under the strain. They drew like the stalks out of rotten pears but the noise they made coming out would have wakened even Corny on his watch below, and as the door swung open, somebody started banging about in the house above them, obviously investigating the disturbance.

"Quick!" snapped Jonty, dashing into the cellar; then the light of his torch picked up Corny and he stopped and stared. The prisoner was plastered with yellow paint from head to foot; it was on his hands, up his arms, over his face, in his hair and fairly oozing out of his clothes. Jonty gulped and swallowed. "Holy Cow!" he gasped. "Who did that to you?"

"I did it myself, you nit. It was the only way I could lay a trail for you," answered Corny.

Dave was already cutting the lashings on Corny's hands and feet and as soon as he was free, Jonty grabbed a gunnysack and pulled him on to his feet. "Here!" he said, throwing him the sack. "Wipe off the thickest of it as we go."

Acutely aware now of time running out on them and the

mounting danger of interception, they slipped out into the moonlight; and there, sure enough, right at the beginning of the narrow path hacked out of the wall of the ravine, stood the huge figure of the punchy whom Corny had labelled the Goof.

"Keep away from him, fellows! He's dynamite!" Corny yelled and at the same time he noticed that the great lummox, instead of standing square in the middle of the path, was hugging the wall on the inside. He seemed to be straining away from the edge and suddenly Corny understood. This was the Goof's weak spot, his *Achilles heel*; he was scared of heights!

That was enough. With Corny there was never much perceptible interval between thought and action and now there was none at all. Even as the fact about the Goof registered in his mind, he flung the paint-smeared gunnysack into the slobbering face and leapt for the edge of the terrace. "Follow me!" he bawled as he went over, and for once Jonty and Dave obeyed him without question.

Braking here and there wherever an outcropping ledge, a tuft of coarse grass or the roots of a stunted bush offered a momentary hand or foothold, they half fell, half slithered down the almost sheer side of the ravine into its floor.

That must have been the quickest unroped descent of a two-hundred foot rockwall on record and the craziest; the odds were heavy on all three of them collecting a broken leg or a fractured skull apiece; but, though they lost several square feet of skin between them and got enough bruises to keep them black and blue for a month, they landed mobile and roaring to go.

Jonty cocked his ear as he came erect. High up on the terracing behind them he could hear the pounding of the Goof's big feet as he raced down the zig-zag path. He was shouting animal cries of rage and the high-pitched singsong voice of Morgan the Mouch was cheering him on.

"Head for the truck!" Jonty grunted. "Luckily I learned to drive last time home. I reckon we've got just on five minutes start on that big ape and that will do us nicely."

He flung the paint-smeared gunny sack into the slobbering face.

Their other dead-line—daybreak—was less than half an hour away when they reached the open shed and climbed into the cab of the truck; then it seemed to take Jonty for ever to find his way about among the controls. The pursuit was already crashing through the undergrowth towards them before he got the engine running but he took no chances of stalling her. Revving her up to a real old roar, he eased in the clutch and she started to roll. If there was ever an old heap she was it but he nursed her all in one piece across the rough ground, then when she hit the cart track and settled into the ruts, he put his foot down and kept it there. Rocking and rolling alarmingly, but by some miracle holding the road even on the tightest of the many curves, she headed for the bay, gathering speed as she went.

"You're doing fine, brother," said Corny, still leaving smears of yellow paint on everything he touched. "Keep her going and we'll make it!"

490

And make it they did; but only just.

The sky beyond the lift of the hills at their backs was already growing light with the dawn when they passed the first fork and as they swung crazily into the coast road, they heard the *Kariba's* syren bleating like a sheep calling her lost lambs to come home. By this time, the old jalopy was coughing like a crocodile with the croup and threatening to disintegrate at any moment; but somehow Jonty held her together and, oozing funnel paint on to the cobblestones from every crack and corner, she rattled up alongside as the bosun whistled the hands to stations.

Their welcome was a bit mixed. Jonty and Dave were due a rocket each for leaving the ship and tackling the thing on their own instead of calling the Mate; but they were also entitled to some sort of medal for recovering Corny and the paint. In the end the Old Man decided one wiped out the other and called the record square. Morgan the Mouch, written off the Articles as a deserter, was left along with the Goof and his pals to the tender mercies of the Italian police, and the ship sailed on time. But it had been a near thing for Corny and ever after, he had this phobia about getting stuck in a pool of paint and missing his passage.

The Long Night

JOSEPH E. CHIPPERFIELD

1

THE EVENTS leading up to the long night of peril Johnnie
Dale was to experience began the instant the Steam Yacht,
Isfennel, registered in Cork City, passed Knockadoon
Head in the small hours of the morning, and took the deep
water channel to Whiting Bay. She carried no navigation
lights and a seaman stood in the bows, peering anxiously
into the opaque mist that had come up with the night tide.

In a matter of minutes after passing Knockadoon Head,
the constantly flashing light near the Barrel Rocks disclosed that the yacht was well set in the channel and moving
more to the swing of the tide than under the power of her
own engines.

A voice called: "Two points to starboard", and there
was a muffled answer from the darkened bridge.

Half an hour later, the *Isfennel* dropped anchor in a
gloomy stretch of water below the towering cliffs of Ardo-

ginna. The vessel had scarcely swung a little to port when a small boat came heading towards it. There was no light shown; no voice to guide the small craft. It was a pre-arranged rendezvous, carried out on time.

As the boat tied up alongside, somebody called softly: "All well?"

There was just the slightest trace of anxiety in the tones; the pause that followed seemed very significant. In the silence could be heard the quiet lip-lapping of the sea against the sides of the vessel, and the almost inaudible creaking of oars held inactive in the rowlocks of the boat alongside.

Then, preceded by a cigarette-end flung glowing into the sea, came the reply, terse and very much to the point: "Aye . . . all is well."

It was as though those words, uttered so impersonally, was the signal for which somebody on the yacht was waiting. Soon afterwards, the task of unloading cases of small arms and ammunition began. Nobody spoke as the cases were brought up from the yacht's holds and then lowered carefully into the boat that, all too often during the process, swung away with the slow turn of the tide. It was a race against time, for in less than a couple of hours the dawn would break and the yacht was expected to be standing at anchor in Youghal Harbour, ready for Customs' clearance by seven o'clock.

When the first streaks of daylight moved slowly over the eastern horizon and brought into relief the mist-shrouded heights of mountains inland, the yacht *Isfennel* was again not far from the Barrel Rocks light, but this time her navigation lamps glimmered and her bows were turned in the direction of the East Point of the harbour.

The first move had been made. Nightfall would see a further move put into effect—and Johnnie Dale brought into contact with forces that were to greatly disturb the even tenor of his lonely existence up in the Knockmealdown Mountains of County Waterford.

2

At twenty-one years of age, Johnnie Dale was considered by his friends in England to be a most fortunate young man. Not long down from University where he had failed to get a degree, he had suddenly surprised everybody by having published a novel that soon became a best seller. On the strength of this, he announced without warning that he was buying a cottage in Ireland and was going there to live for a year or so until he had completed another book.

Thus, with sufficient money for his immediate needs, and an Alsatian dog for company, Johnnie, now sporting a short beard that gave an austere look to his lean face, took up residence in the small, two-roomed cottage. It was situated two miles from Doon, and on an exposed ridge of the mountain, Knockshanahullion.

They said of him in the village of Araglin that he would stay but a month or two. Nobody, they argued, would stay more than that in the lonely cottage set in the very grip of the hills.

That was in the spring; by summer he was well settled in, and very friendly, so it was rumoured, with Kathleen Moore, the nineteen-year-old daughter of Mary Moore of Ballysaggart House down in Lismore. Maybe that was why he was able to withstand the loneliness . . . he and that dog of his that would have you by the throat if you as much as looked at his master.

It was just as the fires of autumn brought a blaze of riotous colour to the hills that the yacht, *Isfennel,* unloaded her illicit cargo. Twenty-four hours later, the first of the consignment of small arms was on its way to a secret hiding place in the mountains not far from Dale's cottage.

Perhaps it was a low growl from his dog, Wolf, that alerted Dale and brought him out of bed in a hurry; perhaps it was the sharp cry of pain from a man whose foot had got caught in a root of heather, bringing him face down on to the case he had been helping to carry. Whatever it was, Johnnie, after bidding Wolf to be silent, stood at his cottage window looking out on to the darkened mountain side, seeing the dim passage of men, all seeming to be labouring with difficulty over ground that was broken and split into ravines.

Johnnie's curiosity was aroused. He had heard rumours —who hadn't?— of men meeting secretly up in the hills. As far as Ireland was concerned, this was an old, old story. There was also some talk in Cappoquin and Lismore of men being trained as mercenaries for fighting in Africa. There was certainly good money to be earned by those willing to bear arms in the trouble spots of the newly liberated African States, and even larger amounts for those who were adventurous enough to take risks and smuggle guns and ammunition into such countries.

"Nonsense, of course," he thought, and was soon asleep.

Next morning, he let Wolf out of the cottage in quest of a rabbit, and the day being warm and bright, he was soon ready to set out in search of adventure himself. Whistling for Wolf, he went striding up into the mountains to see if he could find out what had brought men into the hills on an autumn night when they should have been at home in their beds. . . .

3

Wolf was soon busily engaged in sniffing the trail the men of the night had followed, and loped along with the easy manner of his kind. It was Wolf's enthusiasm that urged Johnnie on when the way became difficult. The dog certainly had a nose for following a scent, but his master was not at all sure if it was the scent of men or just that of rabbits.

Johnnie plodded on, sometimes pausing to look back over the downward sweep of moorland to where the tower of Mount Melleray Abbey rose above the trees that sheltered it.

The heather grew sparse and thin the higher Johnnie

and the dog went. Soon it had almost disappeared and all that was left was coarse mountain grass and thyme and lichen-faced boulders. The silence was such that the fluting call of a curlew brought a quicker beat to the heart. It was the silence of a world as old as time.

Then, quite abruptly, the search was at an end. Wolf gave a deep bark and stood looking up at the gaunt ruins of a mountain cabin, almost roofless and altogether windowless. In its isolation, it was forbidding and eerie. All around were boulders, scattered over the years from the heights above, and in the soft earth about the ruins were the footprints of the men who had laboured the night before.

Johnnie hesitated before entering the shattered doorway. The instant he did so he saw the cases neatly stacked under what remained of the roof. He raised the end of one, and the weight alone suggested what it contained.

The young man felt he had stumbled on something that might well bring trouble to himself. The calling of a buzzard roused him with a start and he wished himself a thousand miles away from the spot. If they saw him here, they might consider him a spy or an informer.

He called his dog to heel, and departed as quickly as he could, taking a path that struck away to the north. He must have been walking for about ten minutes before he turned a break in the mountainside and came upon the lough—a dark, awesome lough above which the cliffs rose menacing and sheer; and sitting on a boulder before the stretch of water was a man about his own age who regarded him sullenly and quite clearly with the utmost suspicion.

Johnnie gave him a nod while Wolf stood tense at his side, a low growl in his throat.

"Is he cross?" the fellow asked quietly.

"Not usually," Johnnie replied, knowing full well that Wolf was putting up the best show he could to disprove his master's words.

"Isn't the creature growlin' right now the way he'd like

496

"A man can be after dying here without anybody knowing."

to tear the throat out of me?"

Johnnie forced a laugh.

"He doesn't mean anything by that. . . . He's just pro-
tecting me."

The man nodded almost indifferently.

"Sure, it's just as well he doesn't or I might be takin' me
gun an' puttin' a bullet through his head."

Ignoring Johnnie's look of surprise at such a statement,
the man turned his gaze to the cliff, staring at it with
narrowing eyes.

"It's a bad place to be walkin' in, so it is," he said
slowly, clipping each word with marked significance. "Sure,
a man can be after fallin' an' breakin' a leg . . . an' mebbe
die without anybody knowin'. . . ."

"I suppose that could happen," Johnnie admitted.

The man then faced Johnnie, his eyes cold and calculat-
ing.

"Best be keepin' to the lower moors then," was the next
astonishing remark, "an' then it couldn't be happenin' to
you."

"What do you mean by that?" Johnnie asked sharply, stung by the underlying sneer that accompanied the last few words.

The other stood up, smiling.

"I think you know exactly what I mean. We don't like foreigners pryin' into our affairs. . . . Just remember that an' keep to the foothills."

And without another word, the man turned abruptly and walked sharply away after the manner of a trained soldier, leaving Johnnie Dale and his dog alone by the lough. The stretch of water darkened as the sun went behind a bank of cloud, and a chill wind moved down from off the mountain. But the wind was no more than the breath of a sigh that was spent as soon as it moved over the lough which was as expressionless as a mirror turned to the dark.

4

Johnnie did not lack courage when once he had grasped that he had been threatened and told to keep away from the mountain.

Even as he strolled back to his cottage, he planned immediate action. He was more than familiar with the many rumours circulating in the district, but did not know just to what extent they were justified. He now made up his mind to consult somebody about them. There was only one person to whom he could go—Mrs Moore of Ballysaggart House. She seemed to know almost everything that went on in the whole of County Waterford itself.

As soon as he had a meal, he set out with Wolf for Lismore, unaware that his progress was watched by the same fellow he had seen at the lough.

The man now held him with his field-glasses, and when Johnnie took the road slipping over the lower moors to Ballyduff, the man guessed his destination.

He shook his head angrily, Mary Moore being no friend of his or his companions who haunted the hills in the silence of the night.

Mrs Mary Moore, still very much alert despite her fifty-odd years, certainly knew most of the answers to the questions Johnnie put to her while her daughter, Kathleen, waited impatiently to have her own private conversation with the young man.

It seemed to Johnnie that Mrs Moore knew everything that made up the general gossip of the district. What was more important, she knew exactly what was going on up in the hills, and told Johnnie that he would be well advised to leave well alone.

Kathleen at this juncture emphatically agreed with her.

Johnnie, however, was a determined young man when once he had set his mind on a thing, and pressing further the points he wanted to know about, learnt that gun-running was being done on a big scale. The arms came from an American source and were off-loaded somewhere along the coast so that they could be brought up into the hills for safe keeping until such times they could be shipped to some of the African States by air freight.

"It's all done secretly, of course," Mrs Moore said, "but the right type of scoundrel prepared to kill people he knows nothing about can get a good price in fighting the private wars of the would-be dictators in Africa."

"And the training, I presume, is carried out in the Knockmealdowns?" Johnnie enquired eagerly.

"Most of it, I believe, and certainly the bulk of the arms supplies are hidden up in the hills. . . . Not all of it, you can be sure, in that cottage you found. I have heard that the Mitchelstown caves are a sort of arsenal, but that. . . ." She shrugged her shoulders.

"You doubt it?" Johnnie probed.

Mrs Moore gave him a shrewd look.

"I don't doubt it at all," she answered, "but I feel you had better forget that I mentioned it. It could be the headquarters of the group."

Johnnie was more than satisfied with what he had learnt, but pressed home one final point.

"What are the police doing about it all?" he asked.

Mrs Moore gave him another look, this time less penetrating as if she doubted the wisdom of discussing the matter further.

"There have been occasional raids," she admitted at last. "But nothing else. No arrests. You must know how things are in this country. . . ."

Johnnie nodded. He knew only too well, and felt that he would have to act, for the moment at least, entirely on his own.

But he said nothing of what was in his mind to either Mrs Moore or her daughter, and when later that evening he set off for home, Kathleen accompanied him as far as the bridge at Araglin, promising to call on him at the cottage the following day.

After they had parted, Johnnie half-wished that he had put off Kathleen's visit for a few days. He was anxious to make more investigations in the hills near the lough.

Still, he could do a lot in the morning, and in a few hours he might discover much.

5

The young man whistled a tune as he strode on in the gloom. By the time he came to the track leading to the cottage, the stars were bright in the sky, and the upthrust of the mountain was etched clearly on the horizon.

Suddenly he was aware that Wolf was close against him and walking stiff-legged, his ears pricked and his nostrils widely flared.

"What is it, boy?" Johnnie whispered.

He instinctively put out one hand and grasped the dog by the collar. Ahead, the cottage rose up like a smudge against the rising slope of the mountain. A star fell like a beacon light down the sky. The wind moved amongst the bracken and fern.

Johnnie felt disturbed. Wolf was growling as if he scented danger.

"Too late, mister—the dog is inside—you're coming with us."

The young man felt a need to gain the security of the cottage, and hastened his steps. He was still holding Wolf firmly as he inserted the key into the lock of the door, ignoring the fact that the animal was bristling and obviously wanted to be free. Perhaps he had scented a marauding fox.

When the door swung open, Johnnie pushed the dog inside and made to follow. But the door was brought to a slam in his very face, with Wolf now securely shut inside. At the same moment he was gripped on either arm.

"Too late, mister," said a voice. "The dog is inside, and you come with us."

A burst of savage barking broke the silence that till then had been so profound. Wolf's heavy weight crashed upon the door in fury, the forepaws scratching in vain for freedom.

"IIc's a killer surely, that feller," said the voice again. "March!" another voice commanded tersely.

The next instant he was propelled forward. He tried to demand an explanation for such an assault.

Neither of the two men replied, and Johnnie could do nothing but submit.

Back at the cottage, Wolf continued to bark with increasing violence, the sound echoing over the whole mountainside. But the two men beside him appeared not to worry, and continued to push him on, the track now climbing steeply.

His captors began to breathe more heavily, but neither attempted to speak. Johnnie also walked in complete silence, and being the younger man, felt the strain less. Once he glimpsed the twisted shape of a thorn tree black against the stars, and then the wrinkled stretch of water he knew to be the lough he had visited earlier in the day. There was such a feeling of loneliness about the place that he could not repress a shiver of foreboding that suddenly encompassed him. A stone rolled beneath his feet, and the grip on his arm tightened so that he cried out in pain.

Some minutes later he knew he was standing on the road that wound up from the Waterford side of the mountains, and then, at what was known as The Gap that divided the County of Waterford from that of Tipperary, he beheld the black shape of a motor van.

He was hustled towards it, still without a word being uttered, and as silently thrust into it. He then heard the motor start up and guessed it was travelling in the direction of Clogheen in County Tipperary.

It was almost daybreak before the van reached its destination, another mountain slope, this time of limestone. Still in silence, Johnnie was hurried from the van and pushed towards the yawning entrance of a cave.

He suddenly remembered what Mrs Moore had so recently said, and sensed that he had been brought to what were the headquarters of the movement—the Mitchelstown Caves.

Almost at once, however, he found himself being guided along a narrow passage, rich in stalactites, which soon gave way to a large circular chamber, and a voice remarked ironically "Here is the House of Commons, and here you will meet the Prime Minister!"

A laugh accompanied the remark, and then Johnnie saw that there was another man at the far end of the chamber, and he knew him to be the leader of the gang!

6

The sun was a glowing amber as Kathleen Moore took the winding track across the moors to Knockshanhullion. She was pleased—even excited—at the thought of Johnnie waiting for her up in that cottage of his. Would he come down the slopes of the hills to meet her, she wondered. Would he?

It was after Foildarrig that she had her first inkling that something might be wrong. An old peasant woman came by with a hen in her arms and hailed her as she passed.

"Is ut to himself yeer after goin'?" she asked.

"It is," Kathleen answered.

"Ye'd best hurry then. That dog of his hasn't stopped barkin' all night. There he goes again . . . the creature!"

She inclined her head to listen and Kathleen did the same. Wolf's bark came rasping down the mountain slopes, and it was clearly a call of distress.

Kathleen said goodbye and hurried on her way, this time striking up over the open mountain in order to reach the cottage a little sooner. She hoped events had not taken an unexpected turn with Johnnie in serious trouble as a result.

Wolf must have grown weary of barking for no sound reached the young woman as she toiled breathlessly up the track leading to the dwelling. Then as if aware that help was at last coming, the dog let out a burst of barking that made her quicken her steps.

The moment she opened the unlocked door the Alsatian

"That dog of his hasn't stopped barking all night."

greeted her frantically, and then she saw that what she had
been dreading had actually happened: Johnnie's bed had
not been slept in!

An idea came to her. She let Wolf out and followed
close behind him.

"Seek!" she said.

Wolf, however, needed no telling. He went loping over
the moor, his nose to the ground and his tail plumed. So
rapidly did he move that Kathleen had the utmost difficulty in keeping up with him.

When the dog approached the lough she felt dismay.
She was sure that Johnnie had not set off unaccompanied,
and she dreaded what now seemed a possibility—that he
had been slain and his body thrown into the lough.

But Wolf skirted the shore, swinging around the narrow
goat track that thrust up steeply to the Cappoquin–Clogheen road. It was when he came to the point where the van
had been parked that he came to a halt. He whined as he

504

cast about in an effort to pick up some further trace of his master. As the dog ran backwards and forwards over the crown of the road, always returning distressfully to the one spot, she looked hard at the road herself as if trying to wrest from it the secret it held.

Then she saw it—a patch of motor oil, and knew at once that the trail had not really ended here, but had taken a more difficult course.

Then like Johnnie, Kathleen recalled her mother's remarks about the Mitchelstown Caves.

She wasted no further time in useless conjecture. She set off for home, bidding Wolf to follow, which he did reluctantly.

There was only one person who could help her now— her mother!

7

Mrs Moore's reactions were prompt, surprising even her own daughter. She telephoned immediately the local inspector of the Guarda Siochana, the police force of the Republic. The inspector, a close friend of Mrs Moore, came himself to Ballysaggart House within ten minutes of the call, and listened intently to what both the elder woman and her daughter had to say.

"I have long expected something like this to happen," he said at last.

"What is being done then?" Mary Moore enquired suspiciously.

"We are not always without resources when it comes to taking action," came the reply. "That gang of arms experts has been under surveillance for some weeks now, and we had a shrewd suspicion that the young Englishman would sooner or later get involved. He lives too near the centre of their activities."

"Then why weren't the men stopped before this? It can be the Englishman is in danger of being killed."

"I already have men out on the hills, and the police at

Mitchelstown are on the move. We have held back because we wanted to catch the brains behind the enterprise, the man with the contacts in the United States."

"Is he in Ireland now?"

"He is indeed . . . arrived this week with the last supply of arms. We just had to be sure before taking action. The Englishman set things in motion a little earlier than we anticipated . . . that's all."

The inspector rose to his feet. "I'm away now to the hills," he said.

"I'm coming too," Kathleen said quickly.

The man looked at her speculatively.

"Can you handle that dog?" he asked, indicating Wolf who had remained at her feet during the entire discussion.

"Yes, why?"

"We might need him to scent out his master's exact whereabouts."

"Oh, he'll do that all right," Kathleen replied at once.

"But Kathleen. . . ." her mother protested.

"It's no good, mother, trying to stop me. I've got to help find Johnnie before it's too late. Wolf will certainly take care of me and help to find Johnnie, too."

In less than an hour, the girl, together with Wolf, were in a police car travelling up over the mountain road to The Gap.

8

Johnnie Dale shivered in the damp darkness of the cave. His legs were numb, the rope binding them cutting his flesh. His arms, secured to his sides, had almost ceased to feel pain. Complete darkness engulfed him and he could hear only the dripping of water through the limestone.

Nobody had come to him; he might have been completely alone in the caves under the mountains . . . maybe left there to die. . . . Only the final words of the leader of the gang sustained him. The fellow had said menacingly: "When we have done what we have to do, you will be our next consideration."

The man had laughed when he finished speaking. His accent had marked him as one of the Irish-Americans, one with a chip on his shoulder, and all the more dangerous because of it.

But the conversation had taken place hours ago. . . . This, Johnnie felt, was the longest night he had ever known. . . . In between fear and dozing from cold and exhaustion, he had tried to think. But the darkness appalled him, pressed down on him, threatened to stifle him. There was not one point of light anywhere . . . nothing but impenetrable darkness, and that slow drip-dripping from the stalactites above his head.

The hours passed slowly, drawn out and never ending. . . .

Then Johnnie Dale was jerked out of his semi-conscious sleep. A blinding light shone in his eyes and the long night was ended.

He was gripped by the collar of his coat and forced to his feet while another man bent down and released the rope about his legs. He would have collapsed but for the grip still on his collar and the wall supporting his back.

He was half-carried through the main cave and gasped for air when he was eventually brought into the open. It was dark and he could just glimpse the moon, lying on its back and sinking westwards. Once more he was thrown into a motor van. He tried to hear what the two men in the driving seat were saying, but only a couple of sentences came to him clearly, uttered with a marked deliberation as if it were intended he should hear them.

"The Commandant says we have to get rid of the fella behind. Sure, it's an informer that one is and there's only one way to settle him for good."

After that, there was a mere mumble of voices, punctuated by the sudden quickening of the car engine as if the vehicle was approaching a steep mountain grade.

Johnnie had no idea of the time, but now a grey light began to filter through the back windows of the van, and he guessed that it was nearing daybreak.

He was jerked out of his semi-conscious sleep.

At last the car topped what had been a steep gradient, glided down a slope and stopped. The rear doors were opened and Johnnie was hauled out. He gazed about him stupidly. He had no difficulty whatever in recognizing the mountain on his right. It was Knockshanahullion! They were alongside a stretch of water, dark as ebony even though the day was breaking in violent colours.

"March!" commanded a voice, and Johnnie was prodded over the road verge to where a few feet away the rock beneath the turf fell sharply into deep water.

There was the scent of moist earth in his nostrils, and on his face the cool touch of wind coming in from the west. But the thoughts in his mind were all of the lough: "It's bottomless," somebody had once told him. "It's never been known to give up its dead," another had said.

508

Beside him, revolver in hand, stood the man in charge of the operation: "This is journey's end for you," he said briefly.

But it was not what the fellow said that stirred Johnnie into life. It was the sight of his companion who was casting around for a huge stone and was even then on his knees tying a rope to it. This, he thought savagely, they would tie to his corpse and sink it. The barbarous implication stung him into madness.

9

The police inspector had calculated well, but he had not reckoned on the burst tyre that lost them many precious minutes in pursuit. Kathleen was frantic with anxiety as they changed a wheel; then back they all crowded into the car.

Almost the very moment they topped The Gap, the police driver sighted their quarry. At a word from his inspector, he shut off his engine, dowsed his lights and coasted downhill in a surprise approach.

Wolf, his ears erect, recognized his master long before the car halted. Without warning he reared up and scrambled through the open window, and bounded swiftly and silently towards the trio by the lough. His approach came at the precise moment Johnnie decided to die gamely. Although his arms were bound, his legs were still free. He would throw himself sideways into the water, risking a shot, and kick out and dive.

Johnnie acted quickly and jumped, and the black waters broke with a resounding splash.

The fellow on his knees got up in alarm, but the other merely took careful aim with his revolver at the struggling figure in the lough.

"If he wants it this way he can have it," he said harshly.

It was the last utterance he was to make for several days, for at that very moment Wolf leapt at his throat and the gun spun from his hand. The police running from the car were only just in time to save him. . . .

The task of hauling Johnnie from the lough was more difficult than had been expected, his bound arms giving them no help and the rock face being at this point six feet high. A policeman, however, took to the water, and towed Johnnie along the lake till they reached the rocky shoreline. There the others helped to pull out both.

10

That afternoon, with the autumn sun going down behind the mountains in a glowing splendour of colour, he heard how the guards at Mitchelstown had surprised both the gang and the leader only a few minutes after he had been taken away in the van.

Information had been flashed to the inspector who guessed that the vehicle was heading for the Knockmealdowns, and when it had been seen passing through Clogheen, its progress was carefully plotted and final arrangements for its intervention made accordingly.

Thus when Johnnie was brought down to Baylough, the inspector and some of his men, anticipating the move, were ready, waiting.

"So you see," Kathleen said, "you were in no real danger."

Johnnie shook his head, thinking of the leader of the gang and the long hours he had spent in the darkness of the cave under the Kilworth Mountains.

"I'm not so sure," he answered slowly. "If it weren't for you coming up to the cottage when you did, nobody would have suspected what had happened."

"Wolf did most of the work," Kathleen replied. "He led me to The Gap where they put you in the van, and from there on, it was mostly guess-work, based on certain knowledge already in the possession of the police."

They both smiled, and Wolf looking at them wondered at the strange ways of folk who seemed to talk far too much instead of taking him out.